THE SUMMER OF LOST AND FOUND

OTHER TITLES BY TONI BLAKE

THE BOX BOOKS

The Wedding Box

The Christmas Box

The Valentine Box

CORAL COVE

All I Want Is You

Love Me If You Dare

Take Me All the Way

THE ROSE BROTHERS

Brushstrokes

Mistletoe

Heartstrings

SUMMER ISLAND

The One Who Stays

The Giving Heart

The Love We Keep

A Summer to Remember (prequel novella)

DESTINY

One Reckless Summer

Sugar Creek

Whisper Falls

Holly Lane

Willow Springs

Half Moon Hill

Christmas in Destiny

Return to Destiny

STAND-ALONE NOVELS

The Red Diary

Wildest Dreams

Swept Away

Tempt Me Tonight

Letters to a Secret Lover

The Mandy Project

The Perfect Mistake

The Weekend Wife

The Bewitching Hour

The Guy Next Door

The Cinderella Scheme

THE SUMMER OF LOST AND FOUND

toni blake

Published by Montlake, Seattle

www.apub.com

EU product safety contact:
Amazon Media EU S. à r.l.
38, avenue John F. Kennedy, L-1855 Luxembourg
amazonpublishing-gpsr@amazon.com

ISBN-13: 9781662536052 (paperback)
ISBN-13: 9781662536045 (digital)

Cover design by Eileen Carey
Cover image: © Studio Firma / Stocksy; © Innocenti / Getty; © sebra, © Sunny studio / Shutterstock

Printed in the United States of America

To Lindsey, for the inspiration

I've found that there is always some beauty left—in nature, sunshine, freedom, in yourself; these can all help you. Look at these things, then you find yourself again, and God, and then you regain your balance.

—Anne Frank

part 1

lost

CHAPTER 1

I've never been a big hat person.

And yet tonight, at one a.m. to be exact, as I pull into the WRTB parking lot, I'm wearing a rather jaunty straw fedora circled by a hot-pink hatband. No one will see me besides Kevin, so I could have skipped the hat, but maybe I need it. A little hot-pink confidence.

I'm not nervous, exactly, as I slam the car door and walk toward the employee entrance while hiking a tote bag up onto my shoulder, but perhaps skulking around like a thief in the middle of the night makes me think I *should* be.

As a flash of my station badge unlocks the door and I step inside, I'm a little mad at Kev for insisting I do this. After all, I'm ready to make my grand return, emerging from the fog that has consumed me for the better part of a year, and I'm tired of people feeling sorry for me. I'm ready to be me again: Jessica Fox, WRTB 11. It should be a celebratory announcement I'm shouting from the rooftops. Instead, I'm literally sneaking into the studio in the middle of the night so no one will see me. The irony runs thick.

I pad silently past darkened offices up a carpeted hallway hung with generic framed photos of the Cincinnati skyline, thankful it's a quiet news night as we hoped. No freak weather events or political scandals or twenty-car pileups in the Lytle Tunnel to keep people buzzing around the newsroom in the wee hours—we can execute Kevin's grand plan in private, just the two of us.

Proceeding onto the set, I find it already fully lit, with just one large camera in place before the news desk where I've delivered so many stories over the years. It feels surprisingly odd to be back, but maybe that's due to the darkness and the skulking.

"Jess."

I turn to see Kevin walking toward me, wearing a tired sort of smile.

"Hey," I say, trying to summon a smile of my own.

"Look at you! Love the hat!"

Ah, sweet hat success—I can always count on Kevin to appreciate a good accessory. "Thanks—I thought it seemed fun." I turn my head this way and that, modeling it.

"It suits you. And check out your hair! Those curls are peeking out even more now."

I shrug. "It's growing." My eyes get bigger as I speak—I'm trying to look happy about it. And I am. I just wish it were growing *faster*. Right now it's a super thin, curly little helmet. Enough that I'm starting to feel more normal when I go out; not enough that I feel even remotely like myself. Hence the middle-of-the-night hat. But I don't plan to let that stand in my way. It's just hair, right? Or that's what people keep telling me.

"You look fabulous, honey—seriously."

Before eight months ago, Kevin had never called me "honey" in our lives. He reserved "honey" for small children and his partner, Patrick. I kind of want to interrogate him about the change, but now's not the time.

"Ready to do this thing?" he asks.

"Couldn't be readier," I reply, perhaps a tad dryly, eager to get this show on the road.

When his phone trills, he hauls it from his pocket and answers, not appearing the least bit surprised to be getting a call at one a.m., and I begin to wonder if his tired look is about more than just the hour.

We became friends almost twenty years ago when I was a field reporter and he was my camera guy, driving us both around Cincinnati to whatever flood or fire or traffic accident was considered newsworthy on that particular day. We were so young and ambitious back then. And that ambition paid off for us both—he's long since risen through the ranks to become news director, and I've been the evening anchor for more than ten years.

These days his eyebrows are a bit bushy and his salt-and-pepper beard needs a trim. Lines bracket his eyes and cross his forehead. All through the winter and spring, he was my rock, and it hits me for the first time that maybe I've worn him out.

I use the opportunity to lower my tote to the news desk, then reach inside to extract the Styrofoam head currently sporting a wig. *My* wig. It's long and blond, and it looks at least a little like the hair I used to have—but I seldom wear it. It's ridiculously hot—the makes-you-miserable kind of hot, not the sexy kind of hot—and I've found I simply feel inauthentic in it. Like I'm trying to fool people or be someone else, which is an odd emotion to suffer when you're actually just trying to hold on to *yourself*. And thus I've mostly become a hat person.

To return to my job, however, the wig is a must. It's true for me—for my confidence and comfort level—and it's also true for the WRTB muckety-mucks. No one's ever said that, but it's a universal truth I instinctively know. And the reason I'm pulling it on over my helmet of curls in a silent news studio in the middle of the night is because last week, when I told Kevin I was ready to resume anchoring the six-o'clock news after eight months away, he thought it was too soon.

He actually looked surprised as I sat across the desk from him in his office. "You only finished radiation last week," he informed me as if I didn't know. "Are you sure you're up to it? You're not tired?"

Radiation was personally much easier for me than chemo, of which he was already well aware, but I reminded him from beneath the bedazzled bucket hat I'd chosen for that particular meeting, "I took walks every day. I walked twice as much as they told me to in order to fend off fatigue. And it worked—I really feel fine."

"I'm so glad to hear that, honey," he said, but hesitation still floated in his gaze. "Even so, I think you should take some more time away, time for yourself. You've been through a lot."

"I don't want that," I told him firmly. This job is my life. That's what I *didn't* tell him. Because it's one more thing he already knows. I don't have—or even particularly want—a Patrick of my own. I have no family and only a few good friends. My job is how I connect with the world, how I feel relevant.

Yet he continued to argue the point. "We don't need to rush this, Jess. This job can mean long hours, stress at a moment's notice, unpredictability."

Upon hearing still more arguments that aren't news to me, I started getting annoyed, and answered simply, "I can handle it."

"I understand you're ready to get your life back," he said, "but honey, if I'm being honest . . ."

"Yeah?" I prodded.

"You do look tired."

I did? Because I'm really not. Or . . . was he telling me I looked some *other* way? Maybe I looked like a person who shouldn't be on the evening news, showing up on thousands of TV screens, because I have hardly any hair and am noticeably thin at the moment.

When I didn't reply, he gave his head a thoughtful tilt to add, "Listen, why don't you take a little more time off? Say . . . the summer. Tiffany can keep anchoring for a few more months."

That's when I decided there was an elephant in the room, and it was the curly one under my sparkly hat. "Kevin, is this about my hair?"

His eyes went wide. "Are you crazy? Of course not."

"Because I'll wear the wig, you know."

And even as he said, "I can't believe you think this is about that," sounding ultra-offended, I still knew it *was* about that.

I sat there, mulling things over. I'm a good anchor, and people like and respect me for more than my hair—but the truth is, before this, I *was* my hair. People talked about my hair, openly admiring it. My long, thick, flowing blond locks were a big part of my identity, both professionally and personally, and losing it was hard. All the things people said about it not mattering didn't fix the feeling of loss for me. I was brave about it, though, handling it with courage and grace. I even posted pictures—albeit carefully curated ones—on my social media, where tens of thousands of people in the tristate area follow me.

Yet despite people's support, and despite living in a post-#metoo world where women are supposed to be just as respected as men for who they are and not what they look like, it became glaringly clear to me that for a woman, at least in some professions, looks still matter. I should have known it all along, and maybe I actually did but simply wanted to believe something else.

And when I said nothing for a long while, I realized that I'd said . . . everything. That Kevin, by virtue of how well we know each other, or merely because it's the harsh reality neither of us wanted to acknowledge, understood exactly what I was thinking.

And in a low timbre, he finally leveled with me. "Jess, the truth is, management thinks Tiffany should stay in your spot a little longer. She tested well."

The words plunged a dagger into my heart. Tiffany is fifteen years younger—fifteen years newer, fifteen years prettier. And even though she does a decent job delivering the news, she isn't as good as me. She isn't as quick on her feet, or as smooth in her delivery, and she doesn't have the same chemistry with Rob, my coanchor. If she tested well, it's because she's "the new girl," not because she's better at the job than I am.

Our eyes stayed locked. I could have said so much more, like what a demeaning disappointment this was, in so many ways, but I didn't have to. And he could've told me he was sorry, and embarrassed it was like this, but *he* didn't have to do that, either.

I sat there seething inside as he went on, "Just so you know, though, as your friend and boss, it's about more than just that. I really *do* think you might still need some time."

"I disagree," I said, indignant.

After which he met my gaze with a long, speculative look. "Tell you what, Jess," he finally replied. "I'll make you a deal."

My just-starting-to-regrow eyebrows shot up in a mix of interest and suspicion. "A deal?"

"I'll intercede with management on your behalf about you coming back *now*, on one condition."

"What's the condition?"

"Let's have a run-through. A dress rehearsal of sorts. See how you feel back behind the desk. Wearing the wig."

I found it a ridiculous request and said so. But it was also a no-brainer, a thing I could certainly indulge him on if it moved this process along and got me what I wanted. Easy-peasy.

And that's how we've ended up the only two people here in the still of the night, me looking into the mirror near the news desk, my features surrounded by hair that isn't my own, using the pointy end of a wig comb to try to make every synthetic strand lie just right while I wonder what Kevin and Patrick have to talk about at this hour. They live together, after all.

When I realize it doesn't actually matter what the wig looks like right now, I retreat from the mirror, ditch the comb, and take my old seat behind the desk. Already I hate how I feel in the wig, both mentally and physically, but I ignore that as the beams of spotlights Kevin turned on before I arrived blast over me. I fire up the computer tablet mounted on the desk, then study the words displayed on the teleprompter near the camera—random copy from a recent newscast.

"I know, I know," Kevin is saying to Patrick now, making me worry something's wrong. But rather than eavesdrop, I refocus on where I am and how it feels to be sitting here again. The wig is hot that fast. The lights are making it hotter. But I belong here. I belong here and I'm eager for Kev to hang up so we can get going.

The conversation stretches on, though. Long enough that I'm starting to sweat. I'm sporting a sleeveless dress I sometimes wear on the news, and I'm hoping I don't have to send it to the cleaners after what I thought would be just a few minutes of "getting back on the horse."

"Seriously, honey, go home and get some rest, okay?" Kev says into the phone. "I won't be long."

When he hangs up, rather than insist we go plowing ahead, possibly tipping my hand, I ask, "How *is* your better half anyway?" For a while I was seeing them both a lot, but recovery has brought more distance. Which is actually a good thing—being needy is not my strong suit.

Kevin's sigh tells me what I already suspected, that something is amiss in Patrickland. "He's . . . well, he's amazing, that's what he is," Kev says, sounding bizarrely disheartened.

I blink, confused. "And you're upset about that why?"

He blows out a big breath. "Because sometimes I think he's too good for me."

"What?" I practically screech. "What are you talking about?" Whatever's going on here is entirely new, and so jarring that I'm pretty sure it's making me hotter than I already am.

"Have you seen him, Jess?" he asks matter-of-factly.

I lower my chin. "Yes, he's incredibly handsome, I know, but . . ." I stop and shake my head, needing more to go on and desperately trying to ignore my growing discomfort.

"Oh, it was all good and fine to date a younger guy when I was a fairly fit thirty-eight and he was twenty-nine," Kev says. "But look at me now."

It's true he's put on some weight and, as I just noticed, has developed a few wrinkles, but so what? "Okay, so you don't look like a youngster anymore." I sigh. "None of us do. At least you still have your hair." I point at my wig ironically as I raise still-thin eyebrows. "You're being ridiculous. You know that, right?"

But he balks. "Am I? Because not only is the man I want to marry wildly attractive and almost ten years my junior, he's also the most loving person I've ever met. You know how caring and compassionate he is. He should have been a nurse. I tell him that all the time." That's all a hundred percent true. Yet Kevin is edging toward full-on ranting now, and my head is starting to feel like it's on fire.

"Okay, what on earth does that have to do with anything?" I ask, still attempting to get to the bottom of this and also unwilling to admit I'm roasting alive. I intend to appear cool as a cucumber, no matter what. "He loves you just as much as you love him, so what's brought this on?"

He looks down at himself. "The last five pounds, I suppose." He blows out one more sigh. "And I guess some days I have to wonder . . . what I bring to the table for him, you know?"

I've never heard Kevin sound this way, and it bothers me. "No, actually, I don't." I try to ignore the sweat beginning to run down my temples under my fake locks. I'm perspiring under my breasts, too, and on my stomach.

"Okay, example," he says. "Right now Patrick's Nana's health is in decline, and no one in his family is lifting a finger to help besides him. He's spending every spare moment at Nana's house trying to take care of her, making sure things are where she can get to them when he leaves, making sure her bills are paid—not to mention getting her groceries and mowing the lawn. The situation is running him ragged. He's just now heading home at this hour, if that's any indication. And I'm doing almost nothing to help. I mean, I try to pitch in a little here and there, but you know how busy this place keeps me."

I can't deny that. And it's hitting me for the first time that, despite his heavy workload, Kevin insisted on taking me to my chemo treatments, and staying with me after, and holding my hair while I vomited—until it fell out—and that he and my BFF, Sydney, and sometimes Patrick, took turns watching over me each time until I regained my strength. I want, in this moment, to acknowledge that. I mean, I thanked them all profusely when it was happening, but I was pretty caught up in my own problems at the time, and it never occurred to me how challenging it must have been for him to do all that in addition to running the newsroom.

Though Kevin isn't one to seek a bunch of thanks, and it's only in rare moments that he and I indulge in talking about how much we mean to each other—so I hold back and instead give him what I think he *really* needs right now. "Listen to me," I say. "You and Patrick are great together. I guarantee you're the only person he wants to come home to at night. Especially when he's going through a difficult time. He loves you."

Kev looks at least slightly comforted, or maybe he's just feeling for me what I'm feeling for him right now: silent appreciation. "Thanks, Jess." And indeed, when our eyes meet, I see our longstanding friendship resting in his gaze—until he silently affirms our mutual aversion to mushiness by moving on. "You ready?"

"More than," I say. More than because the spotlights now officially feel like the white-hot light of a thousand suns. More than because I'm pretty sure my face is melting off. But I'll still be damned if I let Kevin see it.

He steps up to a small stand near the camera to operate the teleprompter, then points a finger my way, directing me to begin.

It's all I can do not to wipe the sweat from my forehead as I say, "Good evening, and let's start with a traffic update. If your commute involves Columbia Parkway, you'll want to consider an alternate route home this evening. Today's heavy rain caused a mudslide near Torrence, blocking both east- and westbound lanes. Crews are working in the area, but there's no indication as to when they expect the road to reopen." The words come out of me, but all I can think is: *Rain sounds nice, cool.* I would *love* some rain dumped on me right now. My whole body is slimy with sweat.

"Seventy-one southbound is at a crawl all the way from Pfeiffer to downtown due to an accident near Ridge Road and another near Gilbert, and the cut in the hill in Covington is slow in both directions."

How red are my cheeks at this point? How wet from sweat is the artificial hair around my face? I just began the fake newscast seconds ago, but already I'm struggling. My voice isn't normal; it sounds labored, like I've been on a long run.

But I can do this. I can get into a groove. "Breaking news out of Newport, where this afternoon, just before two o'clock, a bank robbery suspect led police on a high-speed chase up Monmouth Street before finally speeding onto Interstate 471 in Southgate. Police caught up with the suspect when he apparently ran out of gas on the Daniel Carter Beard Bridge leading into downtown, and you better believe *that* created a traffic snarl."

Okay, my whole *brain* is beginning to feel snarled. I'm forcing out the words, but they sound pained, tortured. Though I'm determined to persist. "Now let's go to Monique for a quick check on the weather. Now that the rain is ending, Monique, I hear things are going to start heating up out there?"

And that's suddenly it—all I can stand. My brain has left the station, shooting out words nowhere on the teleprompter. "Because they're definitely heating up in here! Oh my God, what the hell is happening?" With that, I rip off my wig and fling it across the desk to land in a blond heap at Kevin's feet. It looks like a dead animal.

We both stay quiet and go still, the fresh silence deafening. In that moment, even with just Kev, I feel naked, exposed, in more ways than one, and wish my fedora were within reach.

Finally, he speaks, using the same gentle tone as he did with Patrick. "Jess. Honey."

"It's the lights," I say, exasperated, embarrassed. "I never realized how hot they were before."

He nods. "I know. They *are* hot." He casts a compassionate gaze as he takes a step toward me around the equipment and the dead wig. "But I think . . . you're not quite ready for this yet."

Even now, though, I can't accept it. I try not to grit my teeth as I reply in open desperation, "Kev, I *need* this. I need something more than . . . what my life has been for the last eight months."

"Jess, what if we'd been live?"

"But we weren't."

"And that's why I wanted a dress rehearsal to see how things went. Now we've both seen. If this had happened on the air, you'd be mortified."

That's true, but I don't want to agree with him, so I just start shaking my head in denial and despair. This was supposed to be easy, supposed to work, supposed to get me back where I belong. I can barely think straight now, feeling sorry for myself as I whine, "I'm so tired of illness and sympathy and doctors. I'm tired of working through it and being patient, tired of *being* a patient. And I'm so tired of my house right now. I need a change of scenery. I need a change of pace."

I immediately regret that last bit of randomness, though, when he latches on to it to say, "Hey, that gives me a great idea!"

Whatever it is, I already hate it. I say nothing.

Which he takes as his cue to keep talking. "Go to my grandma's cottage down in Kentucky. After she died, we decided to keep it in the family as a place for quiet R and R weekends. It's a cute little house, next to a lake. A perfect place for getting away from it all."

I'm flabbergasted by this out-of-the-blue suggestion. I remember when his grandma passed away a couple of years ago, but he never mentioned the house. I don't think he went there much, even when she was alive. "But I'm wanting to get *back* to it all," I remind him. "Not get away."

"Trust me," he insists. "You'll love it there. And no one has plans to use it this summer. And you keep saying you want to do that big kitchen remodel, but you can't stand the idea of coming home to workmen and dust for two or three months. Schedule that while you're gone. Sydney or I can drop by to check in once a week, make sure it's going okay. By the end of the summer, you'll be fully revived and so will your kitchen."

When I don't answer, running out of mental energy at this point, he stoops down, right across the desk from me, putting us at eye level as he promises, "It won't be this way forever. And I'll be here looking out for your best interests. You know that. Just give it a little time."

I swallow the lump that's somehow snuck into my throat. "Are you sure?" My voice suddenly sounds small. Not at all like Jessica Fox, WRTB 11. "Sure it's just a time thing?"

It's at least slightly reassuring when his nod comes without hesitation. "If you're worried about Tiffany, her lack of experience shows. And you're loved by the viewers. Management understands that."

I take that in and try to let it bolster me, but it doesn't. My chest has gone tight, and my heart has sunk. I don't want to get on board with this giving-it-time plan, at all—I just want my life back. But what choice do I have?

So I attempt to play devil's advocate with myself.

The truth is . . . sometimes I *am* a little tired. And the job *can* be demanding.

I've been watching the news, and I know that Tiffany—who I trained—probably appreciates the airtime, a chance to get some footing behind the desk and something on her résumé that might be a springboard for her elsewhere.

And I *can* do the kitchen remodel if I actually go away for a while. I already have everything picked out, and I'd only have to make a few calls to get it organized. I've been putting it off for literally years.

"So what do you think? Free vacation in the mountains? A little more recharge time? Am I getting anywhere here?" His eyes look as sad as I feel right now.

And I'm trying my damnedest to regroup. A big part of me wants to just collapse into a heap, but I don't do that because it's not who I am. I'm Jessica Fox, strong but relatable female news anchor with a killer wardrobe. Nothing fazes me. Not even cancer. That's how the world sees me—and how I see myself. One tough cookie.

So even in this moment, I don't want to be any less than that. I won't let myself.

The regrouping efforts pay off. "Well," I begin slowly, feeling like the most admirable team player ever born, "you say that this cute little cottage is next to a lake?"

For the first time since I literally flipped my wig, Kevin's eyes brighten, and he appears to relax as he rises back up and sits on the edge of the desk sideways, looking down at me. "The lake is gorgeous," he promises me. "There's a big back porch with an awning and rocking chairs, perfect for reading or just watching the sunset. You can see the stars in a way you can't from the city, the shade trees dotting the yard keep it cool when it's hot out, and there's even a winery across the lake."

I raise my eyebrows and tell him simply, "You should have led with the winery, Kev. Do you not know me at all?"

We both laugh—something that hasn't happened since my arrival tonight—and he concludes, "Seriously, it's the perfect getaway spot for soaking up nature, not far from a cute little country town tucked into the mountains."

Okay, I have to admit, he's making it sound pretty idyllic and appealing. I mean, if you don't count the fact that I actually grew up in a small town and moved to the city because I wanted to be around people and excitement. But maybe it won't be terrible to go back to that kind of existence—for just a little while.

"What's the name of the town?" I ask.

And he tells me, "It's called Lost and Found."

CHAPTER 2

I live in a pre–Civil War mansion facing the Ohio River, just across from downtown Cincinnati and long ago divided into a duplex, which I'm now standing in front of, staring at the place as if I've never seen it before. Or maybe it's more like I'm afraid I'll never see it again. Like I think the mountains are going to swallow me up and never let me come back.

My neighbors, Bob and Nancy, are late-middle-aged former yuppies, very tidy and tailored even if a bit out of style. Bob still turns up the collars of his golf shirts before climbing behind the wheel of his shiny red Corvette, as I'm sure he did back in the eighties, when I believe the cool guys called them polo shirts. Nancy wears flowy, gauzy garments, large rings, and enormous sun hats.

They're good neighbors who sent flowers and a casserole when they found out about my diagnosis, so I knocked on their door the other night and told them I'd be away for a while and made a point of apologizing in advance for the remodeling noise. Nancy responded the following day by gifting me with a big straw sun hat to take on my trip. As if I'd told her I was going to the beach. But I'm grateful just the same because I'm supposed to shade my radiation area—which is pretty much my whole chest—from the sun for a while, so the ridiculously large brim will help. And given that my scalp can be seen through my immeasurably short, currently brown hair, I suppose I should keep my head protected from sunburn, too. Even more than the fedora, the floppy hat isn't my usual style, but who's gonna see me?

Right now I'm wearing a ball cap Sydney gave me, which looks far cuter on her than on me. Maybe because she has long, dark, spiraling locks that hang from the sides of the hat, making her look sporty and fun—and I don't.

The home I share halves of with Bob and Nancy is pretty extravagant, mainly because of the location on historic Riverside Drive—classy digs for a news chick. After moving to Cincinnati from rural Wisconsin after college, I decided to invest most of my parents' life insurance money in the place, plus the proceeds from their hardware store. The store was the kind of old-fashioned Main Street business that went the way of the dinosaur decades ago, and I'm pretty sure my father's secret dream was for me to take it over. But my parents both knew I was cut out for other things, and their early deaths only motivated me to leave my hometown a little sooner than I might have otherwise. I like to think they'd be happy to know I have an extremely cool and desirable home—and it's always increasing in value, too. I love my place—the history, the view, the fact that I'm right in the middle of an urban area but have a lovely yard. And Bob likes to mow, so that's another Bob-and-Nancy perk.

It turns out I'm finding it a bit difficult to leave. For many reasons.

Like trusting the remodelers to do a good job when I can't see how things are progressing, even if Kevin and Sydney *are* checking in.

Plus I *love* summer in the city! Free outdoor plays, concerts in parks, festivals, food trucks—these are all things I firmly expect *not* to find in the quirkily named town of Lost and Found, Kentucky.

And standing next to my car—which I've jammed with suitcases, my favorite pillow, and a few other personal items to keep me company—I'm struck all over again by how much I adore my house. I know I told Kevin I needed a change of scenery, but do I really?

Or maybe I just don't want to go where I'm going. I took Kev up on the offer without really thinking it through, trying to be agreeable, trying to get on board—and admittedly liking the idea of finally getting the kitchen done—but what was I thinking?

When I hear a car door slam, I look up to find Sydney walking toward me on the brick-paved sidewalk. She came to see me off and get a key. "Sorry I'm late." She offers up a small smile. "Jayden." Her new beau.

"No worries," I reply. Even if I'm a little bummed—I'd hoped we might sit on one of the park benches that face the city skyline and just chat awhile since I won't see her for a couple of months. But it's all right—she tends to get pretty swoony when there's a new man in her life.

"You look sad," she says, coming to stand next to me.

"I guess I am." Then I confess more truth. "I feel a little . . . banished or something. Sent away until it's convenient for me to come back."

"I don't think Kevin meant to banish you." She shrugs. "He just offered you a place to go—you didn't have to take it. You make it sound very Dickensian."

I'm starting to feel a little silly until she grabs my attention with, "You don't *have* to leave—I wouldn't blame you if you changed your mind."

I exchange looks with her and realize two things: I already feel too committed to the trip to back out now. And I'm going to miss my fun friend. She's the person I see the free plays and seek out the food trucks with. We have a Friday-night ice cream tradition in the summer.

Or . . . well, we do when she doesn't have a boyfriend. She's not the kind of woman who ditches her friends for a guy, but *I'm* a reasonable enough person to know you shouldn't hold someone to a Friday-night commitment no matter what's going on in their lives and that Friday is a prime date night, so we have an understanding that we go with the ebb and flow on that. She'd do the same for me if I ever found anyone I wanted to date more than just casually. With Jayden on the scene, maybe she'll be doing plays and food trucks with *him* this summer and I'd just be the third wheel with the big hat trying to keep the sun off my chest.

So I simply say, "No, the wheels are already set in motion." I hear it now, though—I do sound dark and despairing, like I have no choice. I know I can opt out, but it just doesn't feel that way. Maybe I'm more fragile right now than I want to admit—maybe I'm like a flimsy willow tree allowing myself to be blown this way and that, without the will to stop it.

Okay, she's right. Comparing myself to a willow tree—I've gone pure Dickens. *Snap out of it, Jess. Pull yourself together.*

This is Jessica Fox, WRTB 11. In my mind, I hear myself saying the words that always remind me who I am—a calm, dignified voice of reason who guides people through all the ups and downs of the world. Not the despairing whiner I resemble at the moment.

I attempt to come off as more decisive and in control as I tell her, "The workers are coming tomorrow and I really don't want to be here for that. Kev's right about that part anyway—it's a great reason to go away for a while."

"You could always switch things up and head to the beach instead," she suggests cheerfully. "Ain't nothin' wrong with doing your 'me time' with your toes in the sand and an umbrella drink in your hand."

"Nothing except the fact that Kevin's cottage is free, and my remodel is expensive," I point out. "I could afford a middle-of-the-road beach rental *or* a new kitchen, but not both—and the kitchen guys already have my down payment. Besides"—I stop, sigh—"given my new need for floppy hats, this probably isn't really the summer for lounging seaside all day."

"Oh . . ." She wrinkles her nose, clearly having forgotten that part but feeling my pain.

"I mean, sure, I could finagle a way with the right bathing suit and heavy-duty sunscreen and a beach umbrella, but I don't want to spend all summer having to *think* about it constantly, you know?"

She nods. "I get it." Something in her eyes makes me think that, for the first time, she's realizing she'll miss me, too. Or maybe that's just what I *hope* I'm seeing. She came into my life at a time when I'd accepted the fact that I wasn't a woman who had girlfriends—we hit it off when she did some PR work for the station about ten years ago. But same as with Kevin, we don't talk about our affection for each other—it's a thing that simply *is*. "So what are you planning to do with yourself down there? How will you pass the days?"

I've given this some thought. "Well, I'll take walks—that's a good habit I intend to continue. And Kevin says there's a winery nearby, so that might be a pleasant destination. And he mentioned that the back porch was a great reading spot. But to be honest, on hot summer days, I'm thinking more . . . Netflix. And every other streaming service I can get my hands on." During chemo, I didn't have the mental acuity to even watch a simple sitcom, and now I've decided it's an activity I took for granted. "I'm going to catch up on every show and movie I've missed in the last year."

"Sounds like a good plan," she tells me with a smile.

I look up at my pretty house once more, then back to Syd. "Not how I'd *hoped* to spend the coming months," I say, shifting slightly back to Dickensian me, "but I simply have to face facts. This is just going to be the great lost summer. I'll get back to real life, real living, in the fall, but for now I'll do my time in the country until the big bosses either realize they miss me or decide my hair's gotten long enough—whichever comes first—and then I can *finally* put all this behind me."

After which I press my house key into her palm and say goodbye. To my friend, to my home, to my city.

As you travel south through Kentucky on I-75, the rolling hills and split-rail fences of horse country eventually give way to mountains—the

Appalachians, to be exact. The interstate gets curvier, twisting like a snake through valleys where the mountains intersect. I'm beginning to feel farther and farther from home, even though I've been on the road less than three hours.

As I take in a landscape of green, tree-covered inclines rising up from foothill towns that cater to travelers with fast food and gas, I keep thinking about—trying to dissect—why I'm really traversing this winding road.

First I return to the willow theory, overdramatic metaphor or not. When you get a diagnosis like breast cancer, you *become* that willow. See this doctor, have that test. Go to this hospital, get that operation. Read this article, do that exercise, have that treatment, put on this cream, take that pill. No matter what strong, independent person you started out as, you find yourself constantly bending, swaying, letting yourself get whipped about by the process. So maybe this is simply a continuation of that. I haven't had a chance to change the pattern yet, so when Kevin says, "Go to my grandma's house," I just do it, because I'm a willow.

And . . . maybe if I'm still a willow, it means I *do* need more time to heal. Not my body, but inside. Maybe a quiet resting spot *is* what I need, and even though my brain is rebelling against it, perhaps something deeper within me knows it's right.

Or . . . maybe I can't stand the idea of sitting around waiting to be invited back to my job. Watching Tiffany deliver the news from behind my desk was one thing when I was physically unable to do it myself. But now it would make me seethe inside. *Note to self: Don't watch broadcasts on your phone, no matter how tempting.* Maybe I think I'll hold on to more dignity if it appears I'm *choosing* to take more time away, and getting out of the city for a while makes that look or feel a little more real.

Or maybe it's merely . . . retreat. Running away from what I don't want to see. The equivalent of going to the garden to eat worms, as the old children's song says.

And maybe it's *all* of that. Maybe I don't know what else to do and can't find my way right now, so I'm letting forces beyond myself choose my path. I glance briefly from the road up into a hot blue sky, already pale from an early-June blast of summer humidity.

One last possibility hits me then. That I'm tired of being a burden. Kevin and Sydney both had to take care of me when I was sick. They did it lovingly, generously, and I didn't have to ask—they volunteered. When you don't have any family, your friends *become* your family, and they're who you turn to when you need something—whether that's a lift when your car's in the shop, a place to spend the holidays, or someone to help you with the aftermath of having heavy-duty chemicals pumped into your veins.

But deep down, I felt like a burden. I mean, it's not fun work they were given. It was so freeing each time I regained enough strength to stay by myself and let them get on with their lives. So if it makes Kevin feel better about the Tiffany situation for me to just get out of town—if it's easier for him if I'm out of sight, out of mind—then perhaps I'm only trying to . . . be the opposite of a burden for a little while.

Everything around me simply feels . . . wrong. I was so sure things would start feeling right again when I finished treatment, and that expectation was the thing that got me through. Where's the rightness, though?

When my cell phone rings, I glance to the passenger seat thinking it must be Sydney, that maybe she already has a question about the house—only to see Tiffany's name and picture on my screen.

This is unexpected. I don't really want to answer.

But that's childish, so I reach for the phone. "Tiffany, hi."

"Hey, Jessica." We go through the "how are you?" niceties, and I mention I'm driving, until finally she says, "So I was just talking to Kevin."

"Oh?" *Get to the point please.*

"I was asking when you were coming back to work, and at first he was pretty elusive, but he finally explained what's going on."

"Going on?" What exactly does she know?

"Yeah, he told me you were ready to come back, but that since management wants to keep me at anchor for now, you decided to take an extended vacation. And I wanted to let you know I feel awful about it."

I sigh. *Thanks, Kev. You couldn't have said I'd be back in a few months and left it at that?* Try as he might, discretion has never been the man's strong suit. But I guess I should just be thankful he didn't fill her in on the failed dress rehearsal. And I know Tiffany's attempting to do the right thing, but I feel awkward and embarrassed, two emotions I'm not good with. So I try to play it off lightly. "Well, I appreciate that, but it's fine."

"I've learned so much from you," she says, which is nice. "And I hope you know this wasn't my idea." Which is less nice, because it's about covering her ass. And it also implies she *has* the power to make such things happen, which isn't true and annoys me. "I miss my morning spot with the Cockadoodle Crew, and I'm ready to get back there as soon as . . . well, as soon as that can happen."

I truly don't know what to make of any of this now—what she really wants, where she really stands, whether this gesture is sincere or, again, just covering her butt to keep me from having it in for her. Call me crazy, but I'm finding it hard to believe a pretty, ambitious twenty-five-year-old misses getting up at three a.m. to come to work.

Though I take the high road, even as my car dips so deep into a valley that I need to apply the brakes. "It's truly fine, Tiffany, I promise. All is well."

When she answers, it's garbled, just bits and pieces of her voice coming through. "Understand . . . Knowing . . . Try . . ."

"Tiffany?" I say a bit more loudly than before, as if that makes a dead zone clearer.

"Are you there?" she asks.

I can hear her clearly again, but I still say, "Tiffany, you're breaking up. I'm driving through some mountains. We should probably disconnect, but thank you for calling."

"All right. I hope you have a good summer, Jessica."

I push the button to hang up without even saying goodbye. None of this is her fault, and I know she probably meant well and I'm only being paranoid right now, but the call still makes me feel worse instead of better.

Just then, my GPS tells me to exit in two miles—and I suffer a slight sense of doom, like I'm about to pass through some kind of dark gateway. I was so ready to emerge from the fog when I went to the station last week, but now I'm about to sink even deeper into it.

At first, when I turn off the ramp, the road stays wide—four lanes dotted with an old auto-repair place, a little white church, and a few clapboard houses, one with a barn out back. But soon the asphalt narrows to two lanes, sloping gradually upward as I pass a few farms—after which I find myself navigating dark, shaded hairpin curves, my car hugging a rugged mountainside and carving a path I can't quite believe someone once carefully determined was the most efficient way to get wherever it is I'm going.

At some point my GPS quits directing me. Usually, even in a dead zone, the GPS gets me to the place I keyed in and *then* I find out I have no internet after I arrive. But when I see my screen telling me the connection is lost, I understand why Kevin insisted on writing out directions "just in case." I pluck them from the outer pocket of my purse, trying to keep my eyes on the curvy road before me.

Just when I'm beginning to wonder if I've missed a turn—because how can a town exist anywhere around here?—I find myself winding my way back into the sunlight and down into an open valley cradled between mountains on all sides. And that's when I pass an aging wooden sign that says WELCOME TO LOST AND FOUND.

The town is even tinier than I expected. I'm suddenly on a mostly deserted Main Street and can see only a few houses and buildings dotting the area beyond the main drag. The name of the town suddenly makes sense—you start feeling pretty sure you're lost just before you find it.

It's clearly one of those forgotten places, the kind the expressway bypassed a long time ago and left for dead. Probably a Walmart showed up somewhere an hour or two away in the eighties or nineties to deliver the final blow. Although the buildings and storefronts are old and mostly empty, I can easily imagine Bonnie and Clyde or Pretty Boy Floyd racing up the thoroughfare, guns ablaze. No new buildings have been erected here since the Great Depression.

Before I reach the end of the two-block-long strip, I spot an antique store and barbershop still open for business, and then a café—so the place isn't *completely* abandoned.

And that quickly, I'm through the town, back onto country roads, my written directions instructing still more turns over another few twisty miles.

I'm getting tired of driving and wondering just how much more deeply into the Kentucky mountains I can go—when I at last reach my destination, Lost Valley Lane. Another aptly named place.

As I turn onto the narrow, wooded lane, a tiny part of me is suddenly almost excited to see this idyllic cottage Kevin promised—maybe it'll sweep me away with its charm. After passing two or three small, average, well-kept ranch houses, all spaced far apart and separated by lengthy clumps of trees, I reach a classic white farmhouse. And just beyond that—no tree clumps in between—I see "the last house on the right," as Kevin's directions read. I know it's the last because of the unceremonious dead end, the road stopped by a tall stand of pines. Across the dead end from Kevin's grandma's house rests a small older home painted an interesting combination of peach with lavender trim—but the place barely garners my attention because of the house where *I'll* be staying.

Sporting faded yellow clapboard trimmed in chipped cottage green, it possesses a cracked concrete porch edged with 1970s twisted iron railing and a detached garage. A flower bed in front is overrun with weeds. It's . . . not charming.

It's so not charming that I'm confused and find myself questioning if I'm even in the right place.

I look at Kev's directions again, but they still say "Lost Valley Lane," same as the street sign. I sit in my parked car blinking at the house, as if that's somehow going to change the view. As if I'm going to open my eyes and suddenly see the fresh coat of paint it needs, or the updated porch, or something that's not just . . . a little depressing. This isn't what I hoped for. Nor is it the bill of goods my dear friend sold me to get me here. I was promised charm, and instead I'm three and a half hours away from home, stuck in Drabsville.

I don't really want to get out of my car. I actually want to drive right back to where I came from, kitchen remodel be damned.

But I do what I always do—I take a minute and regroup. Then I get out, walk around the car, lean against the fender, and just look at the place.

I'm still standing there, trying to wrap my head around this, when a deep country drawl comes from my right. "You must be my new neighbor."

I nearly leap out of my skin I'm so surprised, and I look over to see a guy in his early forties, average build, T-shirt and jeans, with dark hair peeking from beneath a beat-up straw cowboy hat. He's wearing dirt-covered work boots.

Stopping about five yards away, he offers up a slight grin. "Sorry. Didn't mean to startle ya." He has such an easy way about him that I can't tell if he's laughing *at* me or *with* me. Especially since I'm not doing any laughing.

"No worries," I reply. "Just wasn't sure I was in the right place."

"Lotta people say that when they reach Lost Valley," he tells me. "And most of 'em really *are* lost." His expression makes him appear generally amused, though I'm not sure about what. "But if you're lookin' for Mabel Callahan's house, you've found it."

Kevin's last name is indeed Callahan, so this seals it. "In fact I am. Thank you for letting me know I'm in the right place," I say. Dismissing him. Sending him on his way. Since I have no idea who he is and I'm a woman alone here and all that.

But he doesn't go. "I live right there." He points to the white farmhouse in the adjoining yard. "And I take care of Mabel's place for the family."

"I see." I'm still trying to dismiss him. And feeling glad the yards are at least expansive, far more than most in the city or suburbs, since I'm just wanting to do my time here and hadn't given a thought to the possibility of neighbors.

"Kevin asked me to get in some groceries for ya—just a few staples. I picked up milk, bread, eggs, and some chocolate chip break-and-bake cookies."

Although I should perhaps focus on the fact that his mention of Kevin does something to confirm he's on the level, I feel my eyebrows—what's left of them after chemo—shoot up in doubt for an entirely different reason. "Cookies are a staple?"

"They are for me." He winks.

What is he doing? Flirting? Or feeling sorry for the lady with no hair? Since it seems likely big-mouth Kevin explained why I'm here. Or . . . is this guy just Mr. Neighborly? I really can't get a bead on him.

"Of course, my belly might argue that." Still smiling, he pats it through a maroon T-shirt advertising Ruby Falls, though it looks fine to me. He has a slow, relaxed, country way of talking. "But we all got our weaknesses, right?"

I have no intention of discussing weaknesses with this guy, so I say, "Well, thanks for the food."

But he still shows no signs of leaving. "There's a market in town where ya can pick up the basics," he informs me. "Or there's a Walmart about an hour away in Hazard."

Aha. I knew it.

"Can I help ya get your stuff inside?"

So now he's a bellhop, too. I mean, I know he's just being polite, but . . . "No thank you. I appreciate the offer, but I'm good."

He eyes my packed-to-the-gills car dubiously. "You sure?"

I nod succinctly and decide that changing the subject might be the most useful tactic I can employ. "Mostly what I'll need is the Wi-Fi password." I glance at my phone to see that I still have no signal, phone or internet, so I'll need that password even worse than I expected.

"Oh," he says, losing the welcoming look for the first time. "No Wi-Fi out here."

My eyes open wider, and I begin to blink. "I'm sorry—what?"

"No Wi-Fi," he repeats, loudly, like maybe I'm just hard of hearing.

I narrow my gaze. "How can that be?" Since this makes no sense to me. Isn't there Wi-Fi . . . everywhere now? This isn't the dark ages of 1999, after all.

"Well," he says, looking confused now, too, but perhaps more by my reaction than the question, "there just isn't."

Though surely he's mistaken. Because Kevin would *not* have sent me to a place with no internet connection. Then again, he promised me a charming cottage and I'm not getting that, either. But I still refuse to believe this. "Are you sure?"

At this point the neighbor's eyes have gone wide, and he gives an exaggerated nod, like I might not be the sharpest tool in the shed.

I'm still trying to puzzle this through, though, certain we're simply not communicating well. "Okay, I understand it's a dead zone—I lost my GPS a while back—but if Kevin's grandma never had Wi-Fi installed in the house, I gladly will. I need it." For my TV and movie streaming. For my social media. For my texting and phone calls. For

. . . pretty much everything I plan to do here to kill time. "Just tell me who to contact—who's the provider in this area?"

"No provider," he says, simple as that.

But I'm still perplexed, squinting at him now. "What does that mean? Every city has a provider. Or even a lot more than one."

"Afraid you're not in the city anymore, darlin'." Oh boy, did this man just call me "darlin'"? Does he think it's 1955? Of course, if he's telling me there's truly no way to connect to the internet, it might as well *be* 1955.

"Yes, except . . ." I don't even know what I'm planning to dispute here, so I trail off.

And he goes on. "A provider has to put the lines in the ground, or towers in the sky, and we don't have that luxury here yet, and maybe never will. Don't think we're real high on Verizon's list of places urgent to get connected to the rest of the world."

I'm pretty sure I'm looking at him like he's got horns growing out of his head. "But how . . . ? But what . . . ? I mean, how do I call out?"

His laughter irritates me. "Well, we do have telephones," he assures me. "We might not have the latest technology, but we're not *that* far behind."

I find that debatable. "So there's a working landline in there," I ask to confirm, pointing to the yellow house.

"Yes ma'am."

"And that's . . . it," I say, to make sure I'm really understanding this correctly. "That's the only way to communicate with the outside world here."

"Unless you wanna send up some smoke signals," he says, "yep, pretty much." I'm fairly certain he's making fun of me now. But then he points in the general direction of Lost and Found. "Mind you, some folks claim if you stand in just the right spot in the old Piggly Wiggly parking lot outside town you can get a decent signal. Apparently it sneaks through the gap between the mountains there."

"Some folks?" I inquire.

He holds up his hands in a "search me?" kind of way. "Can't confirm it myself—don't have a cell phone."

"Because you . . . can't get a signal anywhere around here," I say, thinking out loud. Sadly, I'm starting to catch on to the reality of this situation.

"And you can always go to the library over in Brandywine if it's that important to ya."

"How far is *that*? And *they* have internet? Why do *they* get so lucky?"

"About half an hour thataway." He points in a northeasterly direction. I think. Given the loss of my connection, I'm not sure of anything right now. "Guess a public library rates high enough for that sorta thing—even here." Another wink from him. I'm getting pretty tired of his winking and making light of my personal nightmare. Now he looks back toward my car. "Sure I can't help with the bags?"

Surer than ever. "Yes. Thanks," I remember to add. Though I'm so disgruntled now that I don't really mean it. His hospitality, and all that winking, is wearing on me.

He finally turns to go. Thank goodness. But not before casting yet one more grin over his shoulder to say, "It's not so bad here. You'll get used to it. Might even come to like it."

As if he would have any notion what it's like to be me, what it's like to have people far away to stay connected with, what it's like to have had your body ravaged by cancer treatments, what it's like to have come here just wanting to watch some Netflix or Hulu, for God's sake. I can scarcely imagine anyone I could have less in common with than this fortysomething country bumpkin home in the middle of the day, whose only job is probably taking care of his deceased neighbor's house.

When I don't reply—I've got enough on my mind right now without having to keep summoning answers for this guy—he says, "Well, key's under the mat. And if ya need anything, I'm right next door."

"I won't," I assure him, "but I appreciate it." I'm seething inside, for many reasons, but remind myself that most of it's not actually his fault and manage at least that measure of politeness.

"You're Jessica, right?" he asks. "I think that's what Kevin told me."

I nod. Leave it at that. *Would you please go already?*

At which point he tips his frayed hat and says, "Lost and Found Police Chief Matthew Cordray, at your service." Then turns and walks away.

CHAPTER 3

As I watch the worn-out hat and equally worn blue jeans saunter back across the yard, I barely know what to process first. My head feels like it's about to explode.

He's the police chief? That guy? And there's truly no conceivable way to connect to the internet here? And Kevin knew this and sent me anyway? I'm supposed to exist here with a landline and nothing else. Is there even regular network TV? Or do the mountains keep that out, too? *This* is the perfect little getaway spot? No wonder it came for free. Kevin must have really wanted me out of his hair to send me *here* for the whole summer.

In this moment, I scarcely know what to do. Part of me wants to march into this little yellow house and call Kevin and give him a piece of my mind. Another part of me wants to just get back in my car and go home.

The second option, though, has some serious drawbacks, like the workers showing up tomorrow at seven a.m. to rip my house apart inside. And without a job to go to, I wouldn't even have a place to escape the remodeling. I suspect that becoming some sad, wandering person searching for places to go every day would not help my current state of mind.

Of course, Kevin and Patrick have a guest suite at their house. Me showing up with a suitcase is pretty much exactly what Kevin deserves, in my estimation.

But Patrick doesn't. And he probably doesn't need an uninvited houseguest at the moment, given all that he has going on.

Sydney *doesn't* have a spare bedroom at her condo, but she does have a couch. And . . . a boyfriend who's probably sleeping over sometimes, and none of us would feel comfortable with me being there for *that.*

What it boils down to in my heart is . . . I just don't want to be a nuisance anymore, a person who's in the way. I don't want to be somewhere I'm not wanted. And right now I don't feel especially wanted . . . anywhere.

Standing there in the middle of nowhere, wearing an ugly hat to cover my ugly hair, with no place to go but this shabby little abandoned house, remembering all the people back in Cincinnati who think I'm strong and resilient and happy, I feel like I'm . . . none of those things. I feel alone.

Almost as alone as when my parents died while I was in college. It's different certainly, in so many ways. But it's a familiar feeling. One I never wanted to feel again.

I suffer the urge to just get back in my car and cry. At least it's a familiar, private place to lick my wounds.

But what good would *that* do? Besides, I hardly *ever* cry, so I'm not gonna start now. This situation is pathetic enough without a total breakdown.

Thus, once again, I regroup. I take a deep breath, walk up onto the old concrete porch, reach under the black rubber welcome mat that looks right out of 1975, and pluck up the promised key.

Inside, it's pretty much what I expected at this point. I see hints of bygone charm in arched doorways, a redbrick fireplace with a dark wooden mantel, nooks and cubbies tucked in here and there. But like the exterior, it's all in pretty serious need of a makeover.

A glance out the sliding glass doors in back brings the lake into distant view, but I'm too miffed right now to even step outside and investigate. After all, I've envisioned a cozy couch, a big-screen TV, and hours and hours of losing myself in other people's drama—real or made up,

I didn't even care. What I've got instead is a just so-so couch, a not-especially-big screen, and probably very little to watch on it. Shallow as it may seem, I'm still trying to get over that particular disappointment.

On a fridge that was state of the art twenty years ago, I see a slip of paper that says "Matt," with a phone number, beneath a Kentucky-shaped magnet. I already dislike that this man Kevin never even mentioned seems to be my lifeline for all things Lost and Found. Is he really the chief of police? More like some Old West lawman wannabe with that silly hat of his.

Then, just when I think I have late Grandma Mabel pegged—typical sweet older grandmother who wore sweatshirts with cows or sheep or teddy bears on them, went to church every Sunday, didn't get enough visits from her grandchildren, and cooked up a storm of meat and potatoes in this small galley kitchen—she throws me a curveball when I open her bedroom door.

I'm gobsmacked to find a room covered from top to bottom in blue skies and clouds. All four walls and the ceiling, too. Only the floor is spared, but it's sporting sky-blue carpet, so maybe it really wasn't.

I've seen rooms with accent walls like this, but I've never seen one where every surface is meant to make you think you're up in the sky. At first I think the overwhelming look is a very detailed mural, but a closer look reveals that it's wallpaper. As a decor choice, it hovers somewhere between garish and a step too far into whimsical.

The furniture is painted white—white bed, white dresser, white nightstands, and a small white wooden chair in one corner. The bedding and curtains are white, too—a creative conglomeration of white lace, white eyelet, and white cotton with white ruffled frills. Although the rest of the home is graced with old family photos or random chain store art, there are no pictures on the walls in this room—the clouds *are* the art.

I don't like it at all, and in fact, I wonder how I'm going to stand sleeping in this room, until I remember that at least it'll be dark. But even as I'm mentally maligning Mabel's extremely bold choices, a part of me is intrigued. *Mabel, there was more to you than I was giving you credit for.* I vaguely wonder what else I might find to tell me who Mabel was.

I begin to unpack my car. Which I guess means I'm planning to stay. At least until my renovations are done. Unless I make the bad financial move to just spring for a hotel or rental someplace else entirely, it seems like the only real option I have. This is no longer about being committed to a plan so much as it's about having few other choices. Hell, I can't even google other destinations without venturing to the library the cowboy wannabe next door mentioned or getting some good luck at the Piggly Wiggly.

Upon realizing I brought way too many clothes for the middle of nowhere, I unpack only one of three suitcases into Mabel's closet, stowing the rest in a corner. I put Nancy's gift sun hat on the pegboard by the front door, where it'll be easy to reach. I place a keepsake teddy bear from my past, Edgar J. Growlington III, on the bedside table, feeling bizarrely glad I brought him for reasons I don't even understand, and I pull out framed photos of my parents, Kevin and Patrick, and Sydney, placing them in the living room. In the one of Kevin and Patrick, they're standing in front of a Mayan pyramid, both wearing wide-brimmed hats with drawstrings that make them look more like explorers than city-slicker vacationers. I sneer at Kevin in his travel hat as I arrange the pictures on a table near the window.

As I tote my toiletry bag into the bathroom—a pink-tiled affair from days gone by that makes me roll my eyes—I begin carving out a plan in my head for tomorrow. Plans, activities—that seems key to surviving this without going stir-crazy.

I'll call the remodelers and ask them to put a rush on the kitchen redo as much as possible. I didn't bother with that originally, telling them I'd be away all summer.

I'll try to find a picturesque locale to take a photo, which I'll post on my social media if I can find the sweet spot at the Piggly Wiggly, to let my followers know I'm going off the grid for some "me time." And if the Piggly Wiggly fails me, I'll sojourn to the library. I don't like not being able to connect with people who actually valued me delivering their news, given that they might be the *only* people who really miss me, but I can't see any way around that for now.

And then . . . well . . . I guess I'll have to figure out what "me time" truly means. If it can't be movies and internet and texting, I'll have to think through what it would have been for me in a pre-internet world. I guess I don't honestly know myself anymore without that level of connection.

Again, I need plans, activities, no matter how simple—ways to pass the days, and the nights. Doing my time here already seems like it's going to be much harder than it did this morning when I left. But I'll figure it out. I have to. I slept away too many days waiting for the chemo exhaustion to wear off—if there's one thing I won't do, it's sleep the summer away.

When the avocado-green table phone rings, I jump. My first thought: Police Chief Matthew Cordray. Lord, I hope it's not him. And I instantly miss being able to decide whether to take a call based on knowing who it is.

Reluctantly, I pick up. "Hello."

"Oh good, you're there. I was starting to get worried when I didn't hear from you." Kevin. Glancing at a wall clock, I see that day has somehow already turned to evening.

"Serves you right," I snap.

"What? What do you mean? Is something wrong there?"

My jaw drops. "Is something wrong here? Are you serious?"

"Yes. What's wrong? What's going on?" He sounds alarmed, like he's worried the house fell down or something.

"Okay, for starters, no internet connection, Kev? What were you thinking?"

He stays silent a moment. Then finally replies, ever so casually, "Oh yeah. I guess I didn't think to mention it."

"How could you *not* mention that?"

"I guess because . . . it's always just been that way. And when I'm there, I just . . . deal with it. There's actually a spot at the—"

"At the old Piggly Wiggly," I cut him off. "Yeah, I heard."

"So you met Matt then."

"Yes, I met Matt then. That's another thing you might have mentioned."

"What's to mention? He lives next door and takes care of the place."

Okay, that throws me a little. Because he's right—Matt wasn't earth-shattering news. The lack of internet is far more important. "Well, okay, but it just would have been nice to know a strange guy was going to approach me the second I got out of my car. Stranger danger, you know?"

At this, he actually laughs a little. "Matt's a good guy. Friend of the family my whole life."

"Is he really the chief of police?"

"Yeah. Why?"

"I don't know. He just didn't seem very police-like."

"I'm not even sure what that means," Kev replies. Then asks, "Why do you sound so mad about everything?"

The question hits me like a brick to the head. I want to scream at him: *Why wouldn't I sound mad about everything? My life has turned to shit!* But I keep my cool. Because only *some* parts of that are Kevin's fault at the moment. "Kev," I say, "this place, um, isn't exactly what you described."

"It's not? How so?"

Okay, so my friend did not purposefully and willfully send me to this unpleasant living environment—he's just delusional. "The house," I say. "It's, um, well . . . you made it out to be some uber charming cottage, but it's kind of run-down. I don't think much has been changed in fifty years."

When he stays quiet at this, I feel bad and go on. "I'm sorry. I know it was your grandma's house, and I'm sure it was nice back in the day."

Finally he admits, "I guess I haven't paid attention. And I've only been there a few times as an adult."

Well, that explains a lot. He was describing it the way he remembered from his childhood, not as it actually is. "Has . . . anyone in your family been here recently?"

"My parents stayed there for a few days after Grandma died to clean out her clothes and the food from the kitchen. A cleaning person comes every few months, but I guess our grand plan to use it for getaways hasn't really materialized the way we thought it would." He adds, "Is it . . . that bad, Jess?"

"No," I say quickly. "It's fine. It's clean. It's just not . . . the quaint cabin-in-the-woods vacation rental I envisioned from your description. Add in the lack of the internet, and, well . . . there might have been a short period of time when I wanted to rip you limb from limb."

"And now?" he asks cautiously.

"I'm over it. The harming-you part, I mean. I'm still trying to wrap my head around the rest." I sigh. "Though speaking of wanting to kill you, Tiffany called on my drive down. To tell me none of this was her fault. Did you have to be so honest with her, Kev?"

"I know, I know. I'm sorry about that, too. I was trying not to answer her questions, but she started out as an investigative reporter, you know. She's not afraid to keep asking the tough questions until you crack."

"You make it sound like she had you in a dark room shining bright lights in your eyes."

"I feel like a cruddy friend right now. And not even a great boss."

Crap, now I feel bad. He took me to chemo, after all. And even that aside, I cherish him. "It's okay," I promise. "This too shall pass." I don't bother to tell him my plan to come home as soon as I have a put-together home to come back to—that can wait for another day. "How's Patrick's grandma?"

"About the same," he answers on a sigh. "Is it wrong that I'm kind of jealous Nana gets to spend so much time with him lately? I barely see him."

"Yes," I confirm. "That's *very* wrong. Insanely wrong."

"I know. I'm a terrible person. I just miss him. I miss our normal . . . us—the way we usually are, the way we've been up to now. I miss normalcy."

I hear ya, buddy.

"I'm going on a diet, though," he says.

"When?"

"Tomorrow."

I can't help it—I laugh.

He does, too. "Hey," he says then, "what about the lake? Surely the lake's still nice. What do you think of the view from the back porch?"

"I haven't gone out back yet," I confess. "I've been unpacking all afternoon."

I can almost feel him shaking his head. "You have to check out the lake, Jess. It's beautiful. You'll love it."

"I've heard *that* before." I snicker.

"I mean it. The house might have gone out of style when I wasn't looking, but a lake doesn't really change."

"I'll check it out tomorrow," I promise, though I can't help feeling skeptical at this point.

"Tomorrow? It's right outside the door, Jess."

"I know. I'm just . . . tired, I guess."

I hang up a few minutes later thinking about that old adage: The only constant in life is change. I feel like it's got me surrounded lately and won't let me escape. And the things I want to get back just seem farther and farther away, no matter how hard I chase them.

I dig into the staples delivered by the cowboy wannabe and make breakfast for dinner—eggs and toast. I don't make very good eggs—I like them over easy, and they're always either too hard or too runny. Tonight it's too hard. But it's fine. A mediocre meal pretty much matches the rest of my day. Tomorrow I'll check out the market near town, and if I have to, I'll make the trek to Walmart. I'm pretty tired of being in my car after such a long drive today, but what better do I have to do?

After cleaning up the dinner dishes—there's no dishwasher, big surprise—I plop back down in the easy chair by the window, pick up the phone, and call Sydney.

I get her voicemail, though. *Of course* she's busy—beautiful summer night in the city, long days where it doesn't get dark until after nine, new man in her life. It's Friday. She's probably having ice cream.

"Hey," I say, trying not to sound sad, "just wanted to let you know I made it to Lost and Found. It lives up to the name—it's in the middle of nowhere. And the house is . . . a letdown. And get this—there's no internet. And I have zero bars. Seriously. So you'll need to call me back on this number and hope I just happen to be here. I'm going to venture out tomorrow to . . . you know, keep busy. But it's fine. Everything's fine. I hope you're doing something fun."

I could go outside myself, check out the lake, enjoy the cooldown that comes at the end of a hot June day before darkness falls. But my heart just isn't in it. It's that simple. Seeking out a pretty view and a bit of fresh air just sounds like too much trouble to me right now. Besides, my new neighbor might be out there.

Instead, I reach for the TV remote. By flipping around, I do find a station, and it's showing a rerun of a sitcom I've already seen. I watch it anyway, trying to get pulled into that world—anything to get pulled out of mine for a little while. It doesn't work, and I lament the loss of my streaming capabilities anew. Sometimes escape feels so . . . vital.

When the show ends, I turn off the TV and walk to the built-in bookcases across the room. A quick perusal tells me that Mabel was big into doing jigsaw puzzles and reading mysteries, with a little romance mixed in. I see a John Grisham novel I haven't read and pull it down, returning to my chair. But the light isn't good enough for reading—I'm instantly squinting. I could go around to other lamps and other sitting spots, but that quickly I feel defeated.

When a shock of orange neon light draws my gaze out the back window, I realize a spectacular sunset is happening outside and that apparently the back porch faces west. But even this is not enough to lure me out.

I wish I hadn't come. But the truth I face just now is that if I'd stayed home and not scheduled the remodel, I'd still feel empty. Alone. Forgotten. Irrelevant. Being stuck on an isolated mountain in a cottage at the end of Lost Valley Lane just shines a brighter light on it.

As darkness finally swallows the little house, I decide to call it a day. I resolved not to sleep my life away, but right now, it feels like the only thing to do.

It feels strange to undress in the middle of Mabel's clouds, but I change into a tank top and pajama shorts, then walk into the bathroom. I look in the mirror to apply scar-minimizing cream to my lumpectomy and chemo port scars. I wash my face and moisturize. I see myself.

I really . . . see myself.

The truth is, I try to avoid that these days. And I usually do pretty well. But for some reason, tonight, I'm seeing . . . me.

I see my head covered with this painfully thin, brown, curly cap of hair. I see my eyes looking larger for the lack of hair, and a little sunken, from the general trauma, I guess. I see my cheekbones more prominently for having lost some weight, and again, no longer having a mane of hair to balance it all out. I see dark circles beneath my eyes, and a complexion that for some reason looks ruddier to me lately for no particular reason. I see wrinkles and lines like the ones I observed on Kevin last week and can't deny that my cancer journey has aged me.

I feel like me on the inside, but I don't look like me on the outside. It's a strange feeling. I am, of course, still me. But aren't we also what we see in the mirror? When that changes, suddenly, it can be hard to recognize yourself.

I think of those women who carry this all so well, the ones who walk around so cool and confident without their hair, some even by choice. I envy them. I view myself as a confident person, but it dawns on me now that maybe there's a fine line between confidence and arrogance. Maybe true confidence comes from a place where you really don't care how you're seen or if you fit society's standards of beauty and normalcy—and maybe arrogance needs . . . hair.

I'm mad at myself for caring. Mad at the world for caring. Mad at the station managers for caring. My eyes get glassy and feel strained until I'm forced to reach up and wipe away a tear. *Do not cry. You're tougher than that.*

I cried a lot back when my parents died, and after that, I just . . . stopped. I quit giving in to that level of despair. I refuse to give in now, when all the hard times are over. Or they're supposed to be anyway.

A moment later, I turn back the fluffy white covers on Mabel's bed and ease into it. It's . . . incredibly soft and cozy. I feel cradled. I feel like I'm floating. I look up at the clouds and suddenly see the appeal.

Did Mabel want to float away from her own life, too? Float away from everything to a place where none of it matters? Where it's all just about the floating? I understand Mabel a lot more in that moment.

I take in the floating sensation and let it own me for a few minutes. It's honestly the best I've felt all day. Floating in Mabel's clouds, it doesn't matter what I look like, who cares about me or who doesn't, what my plans are, what my life is. It's just floating.

When I reach over to turn out the lights, I expect full darkness to descend, but enough moonlight seeps through the windows to softly illuminate the whiteness in the clouds that I can still see them a little in the dark.

So I still feel like I'm floating on a cloud. And when I least expect it, I drift sweetly and swiftly off into a more peaceful sleep than I've had in a while.

CHAPTER 4

Waking up the next morning to find myself surrounded by clouds is jarring for a second. Have I died and gone to heaven? But whether or not I now like Mabel's sky bedroom more than I'm willing to admit to myself, I quickly remember that my current situation feels a little closer to the opposite end of that spectrum.

I feel surprisingly well rested, and the morning sun is cheerful. Not that *I'm* actually cheered by it in my current state of mind, but it motivates me to get out of bed anyway.

I discover that in addition to chocolate chip cookies, the cowboy next door also considers Cheerios a staple, and a bowl of cereal and a slice of toast work fine as breakfast.

I dress in a summery top and capris, slapping on my fedora—which I also tossed in the car with my other key hats—and waste no time setting off for the Piggly Wiggly. Not that I know where it is exactly, but I would rather figure it out myself than go knocking on my neighbor's door.

I feel pretty accomplished upon locating it by heading back to Lost and Found, then turning down a road that intersects with Main. The sight of the abandoned grocery store a short distance later makes me both happy and sad—or at least I'll *be* happy if I get my promised connection to the outside world.

It takes some time and a lot of walking around while I hope no one's watching, and I'm wishing I'd asked more about where this special spot is—because it's a pretty big parking lot for a town this small—when my phone suddenly connects! Halfway to the end of the lot and directly in front of the unlit neon pig in the sign. Both internet and two whole phone bars! I'm so excited that I want to call someone—only there's no one to call. Sydney has a standing Saturday-morning hair appointment, and if Kevin isn't at the station, he and Patrick are at their favorite farmers market, which they take very seriously, and are not to be interrupted.

Though a text from Sydney comes in with the connection. You probably won't see this, but I got your message. I'll call tonight. I'm sorry the place is so disappointing. ☹

I return the text just to explain why I can text now but not later, and tell her I'll look forward to her call.

Upon realizing I forgot to take my picturesque shot to post on social media, I look around and realize the green mountain that hovers over the town across the road from the old store will do fine. I consider making it a selfie but decide against it. Though I've posted pictures of myself since hair loss, I don't have the patience for taking the perfect, acceptable photo right now. And if I'm being honest with myself, maybe I felt braver then. That makes no sense, but I'm just tired and a little depleted at this point.

I do the post, happy to connect, sad to know I won't be able to see the responses easily.

Then, while I've got this nifty connection, I pull up the remodeler's number, call and talk to the receptionist, and put in my plea for fast work. She tells me she'll let the guys know, but that it will take as long as it takes, probably a month minimum. I swallow back my disappointment and thank her.

It could be worse. If it's a month, maybe I could be home by the Fourth of July. Maybe I can find a hat or a top with some stylishly patriotic design and tag along with Sydney and Jayden to some neighborhood fireworks. A little thing, certainly, but it feels like a goal to work toward.

Next up, the market. The truth is, it's hard to get back in my car and leave my blessed signal behind. It occurs to me that I could bring a camp chair and pretty much just hang out here all day if I really wanted to, but something about that seems sad and desperate, and too hot as there's no shade. Still, I'll keep the idea in my back pocket for a sad and desperate day.

Before I go, though, I google "market near me," and get only the Walmart in Hazard, an hour away. Now I wish I'd asked my neighbor more about the place in town he mentioned, too.

Making the short drive back to the main drag, I pull into one of the many vacant spots that line both sides of the street. The town *could* be cute, in a way, but mostly it's just sad. It feels as forgotten as I do lately. Of the few open businesses, I decide to step into the Last Chance Café, a name I find too romantic and enigmatic for its location.

Other than an old man drinking coffee at the counter, the place is empty. I had only planned to ask directions, but it's close enough to lunchtime that I decide to slide into one of the old, cracked-vinyl booths and support the place. As I grab a laminated menu from behind the metal napkin box, I realize 1950s music is echoing from a neon-lit jukebox and begin to wonder if I've stumbled into an episode of *The Twilight Zone*.

I study the menu until a too-skinny waitress in a denim mini-skirt and a pair of well-worn platform wedge sandals slowly approaches my table, eyeing me suspiciously. Because I'm a stranger? Because I have very little hair? Because this probably isn't a fedora-wearing town? The possibilities are endless. She finally gets close enough for me to take in her messy ponytail and a name tag that says JOY LYNN.

"Can I help you?"

I wish you could. Rather than make that confession, I place an order. "I'll have the hot ham and cheese, with a Coke."

"Chips okay?"

I nod. Then add as she starts to walk away, "Could you tell me where the nearest market is?"

"Freeman's?" she asks as if I know the name of it when clearly I don't. Then she points. "Turn right past the barbershop, then go a ways and you'll see it."

Not exactly Google Maps, but it steers me in the right direction. "Thanks," I tell her.

As I'm waiting for my food, I see her whispering with an older, heavyset woman with silver hair behind the counter and suspect I'm the topic. It's confirmed when my plate is delivered along with the question, "You're not from around here, are ya?"

"No," I say. "I'm visiting. For the summer."

"The *summer*?"

This seems like bad news to Joy Lynn, who I can tell has taken an instant dislike to me. It's probably the fedora. Or that she thinks my hairstyle is a choice, which makes me unrelatable to her. I've recently discovered that some people fear women without hair and don't have the simple skill of hiding their shock.

"Yes," I confirm.

"Who ya visitin'?"

"I meant I was visiting Lost and Found, not someone who lives here," I try to explain. "I'm staying in Mabel Callahan's house."

"Oh." Her eyes change, and I can tell she knows where that is.

And I wonder why I'm giving her information about me she doesn't need. I guess it's partly my inclination to put people at ease, and partly because I dislike her dislike of me. It would be nice to feel more welcomed while I'm here.

"How come?" she asks.

Well, aren't you a nosy one, Joy Lynn? I keep it simple. "My house is being remodeled, and her family offered me the place."

She nods slowly, and I can still see her analyzing me. I kind of regret my decision to support the Last Chance Café.

The food is good, though—diner casual but just right for right now. I used to be something of a foodie, always seeking out the latest trendy restaurant in the city, then recommending it—or not—to my online followers. Since treatment, though, my taste has taken a turn toward the simpler. Maybe because I'm not much of a cook, I'm not currently up for fancy restaurants, and I'm by myself a lot these days. But whatever the case, the ham and cheese sammie hits the spot.

I say goodbye as I exit, and Joy Lynn lifts her hand in a wave, but I can tell she's glad to see me go. Me and my highfalutin fedora.

Following her vague directions to the store, I realize that vague is actually all it takes in some places. Freeman's Market is the only building other than a few houses on the street just past the barber and resembles a small, weathered barn. The remains of what was once clearly a larger selection of hanging potted petunias catches my eye as I walk in, highlighted by the weathered gray wood behind them. Other flowerpots hang from the awning as decorations for the store, but the ones for sale down below look kind of sad.

A tall, stout older man with a caterpillar mustache and black hair turning to silver greets me from behind the counter. He appears less offended by me than Joy Lynn did, though the clear fact that I don't belong here prods him to ask, "Anything particular I can help ya find?"

"Just getting a few groceries," I say. "I'm staying here for the summer in a house outside town."

The raise of his bushy eyebrows makes him look as surprised as Joy Lynn, but less suspicious. "Welcome to Lost and Found. We don't get a lotta outsiders."

"Thanks," I answer. "And I kind of gathered that." I add a smile, and he smiles back, and I like him already. "Are you Freeman?" It's an assumption I wouldn't make in a more populated area, where business names don't always mean much, but already I get the impression this is a personally owned establishment.

"One and the same," he tells me. "My daddy started this place when I was knee-high to a grasshopper, and I carried it on when he passed."

"Well, it's nice to meet you, Mr. Freeman. I'm Jessica."

He returns the sentiment, and I start perusing the shelves. Pretty quickly I know my afternoon will be spent on a trip to the Hazard

Walmart. This is the place to pick up your bread and milk, but as a woman who likes to buy her salad in a resealable bag and her chicken boneless and frozen, there's not much here for me that I don't already have at Mabel's. Even so, I place a few cans of soup into the little plastic basket I picked up upon coming inside, then add some chips and a jar of peanut butter, happy to support the nice man.

As I step up to the counter, he points to a tidy row of tomatoes lining a wooden windowsill. "Grew these myself and they're just about ripe," he says. They're shiny and pretty and red, and I like the image in my head of Mr. Freeman tending his tomato plants.

"They look yummy," I reply. "I'll take two."

As I'm paying, the hanging flowers again catch my eye out the window, and I think of the few still left for sale. I'm not a big flower person, but maybe it's because I don't need to be—Nancy takes care of that for me. When I moved in, she offered to plant and care for the beds on my side of the yard as well as hers and has done so ever since. She even puts a few potted flowers on my side of the divided terrace in back each summer, too, and keeps them watered. No muss, no fuss.

Mr. Freeman sees me looking and says, "Give ya everything out there—five pots, I think is what's left—for fifteen bucks."

Even though I don't buy a lot of flowers, I know that's dirt-cheap. "That seems like a good deal."

"They don't start gettin' some love soon, they won't make it. Already on their last legs. Or stems, I should maybe say," he adds with a chuckle, and I smile, liking him all the more.

I step over to the store's open door and peek out at the petunias. Two pots of hot pink, two lavender, and one white. Five seems like a lot. Like five more than I was considering two seconds ago.

"If you don't have a place to hang 'em, you can just unclip the hangers from the pot," he volunteers.

"What would I need to do to give them their best shot at survival?" I hear myself ask. I'm not sure why I'm going down this path except that Mabel's place looks pretty bland, and it's not like I have anything better to do this summer than tend flowers.

"Mostly just water 'em," he says. "Ever' day, unless it rains. Mornin' or evenin' is best, just to avoid the heat of the day. They need at least six hours of sunlight, but if you got a spot where they won't get much more than that, might help 'em bounce back."

Okay—for fifteen dollars, what the heck? And if they make it, I can always pack them up and take them home with me next month. I can only imagine the surprise on Nancy's face when I have baskets of petunias to offer her.

Late that afternoon, I return to Mabel's with enough food to last awhile, all the frozen stuff piled on the passenger seat floor with an AC vent blasting down on them, given the length of the drive and the fact that it's a hot day.

While I was in Hazard, I took advantage of the internet there to check my social media again, but I resisted posting anything new since I'd just said I was off the grid. It was heartening, however, to see all the likes and comments already on my earlier post, nice to feel cared about. Even if it's by people who don't really know me. I like to think on some level they do, that those connections count, because some days they really matter—days like this one, when I don't feel too terribly valued by anyone else. People also raved about the beauty of the mountain picture I posted, but I think they're just being nice—it was just a bunch of green.

Now that I'm back in what feels like no-man's-land, I put away my groceries, then change from my fedora to my sun hat before going back outside, remembering I need to be careful about sun protection.

A glance in the mirror above the pegboard tells me the sun hat looks . . . ridiculous. I'm a tiny face holding up a big disk of straw—I look like a human mushroom. But as through this whole cancer journey, you do a lot of things just looking forward to the time when you won't have to do them anymore, and this silly floppy hat is the least of them.

Toting my flowerpots from the back of my SUV, I decide the two lavender ones will sit on the front porch, one on each side of the concrete steps leading up to it. As I detach the plastic hanger parts, my eyes are drawn once again to the weed-filled flower bed, but hopefully the petunias will divert my attention from that.

Next, I carry the other pots around to the back, where I finally see the fabled lake. I stop, take it in. It's down the hill of Mabel's expansive backyard and feels kind of far away, but it's nice, about the length of a city block, the border rimmed with cattails and the occasional tree. A breeze ripples the surface. On the other side, I spot the promised winery—a rustic old barn to which someone has added an arched stone facade. Rows of grapevines stripe the hillsides around it.

All in all, it's a pretty view. Kevin was right that the back porch will be a nice place to sit. And I should probably be more enthralled by the lake—it's definitely the best part of Mabel's place—yet something in me that's grown stiff and wooden refuses to be wowed. I guess I'm just a bit depressed. I was doing okay with that, with *not* being depressed, until I was banished. It's like I've become a human game of Jenga—I was holding up okay until someone pulled out the wrong little block of wood, and then everything came tumbling down.

Turning back to the matter at hand—my petunias—I inspect the covered porch. Same cracked concrete as out front, sporting two white wooden rockers at one end, a small round table with two chairs at the other.

I'm unduly excited to find a little metal plant hanger jutting down from the porch ceiling at the rocking chair end. (Life's gotten strange if I'm bored with a pretty view but excited about a plant hanger.) After hanging one of the bright-pink petunia pots, I situate the other on the table, even though it takes up most of the surface, and place the white one on the concrete next to a green-painted porch post, then remove the hangers.

"Well, look at you, sprucin' things up."

I jump at the sound of Matthew Cordray's voice—damn, the man's good at sneaking up on me. I probably seem like a nervous wreck to him. I say nothing in reply, too busy catching my breath.

"Sorry. Didn't mean to scare ya there." Again with that lazy grin that leaves me not quite knowing if the country mouse finds me an amusing city mouse. I notice dark stubble on his jaw, and dark hair beneath that same silly cowboy hat. And today there's a Yorkie standing next to him, ankle-high. It's adorable, but I refuse to acknowledge it.

"No worries," I say. "But shouldn't you be off protecting the people of Lost and Found?"

"Already did that today." He's still flashing that little smile as he taps the watch at his wrist. "Workday's done."

Oh, I guess my excursion *did* take all afternoon.

This guy still doesn't look like a cop to me. Today he's in gray shorts and a Kenny Chesney concert tee, suggesting that even the country bumpkin occasionally ventures beyond the surrounding mountains. And the Yorkie is . . . well, it's not the dog I would have expected him to own.

He motions to the hanging pot of flowers. "Does this mean you're feelin' more at home than you were yesterday?"

"Can't say that I am," I reply, not returning the smile.

"I can get you a garden hose from Mabel's shed for waterin'." He motions to a small building painted in the same fading color scheme as the house, situated halfway down the hill and near the woods that meet that side of the yard.

"Thanks, but I can do it," I tell him.

"You sure?"

Just what I need—some guy who thinks women are incapable of performing simple tasks. And given the fatigue I've successfully fought off, I feel particularly eager to *not* need anyone's help.

"I'm sure."

"Okay," he says, starting back toward his own yard. "Just watch out for the snakes."

Oh crap. "Snakes?"

He stops, looks over his shoulder, nods. "Sometimes. Generally the good kind, though."

I raise my eyebrows doubtfully. "There are good kinds of snakes?"

He chuckles, and this time I'm pretty sure I'm being laughed *at.* "They keep down the rodents."

I blink. *"Rodents?"*

He tilts his head. "You really *are* a city girl, aren't ya?"

"I wasn't always," I confess. "But guess I've become one."

When I sense him considering asking for more information on that, I head him off at the pass. "If, uh, that offer still stands, I'll take it." *Just please don't ask for anything in return, even a conversation.*

He gives a short nod. "I'll get it hooked up for ya right now."

"Thanks," I say. Then quickly add, "I'm gonna head inside, get out of the sun."

Of course, mostly I'm getting away from *him.* I don't mean to be rude exactly—I'm just not looking to make a buddy here, and my impression is that he'd be perfectly happy to hang out. I would have maybe even liked to pet his dog, but again, I don't want to encourage interaction.

Back inside, I rummage in my newly packed fridge to decide what's for dinner—but from the corner of my eye, I'm glancing out the window to see my neighbor carrying a dark-green coil of hose toward where I noticed the spigot a little while ago, his trusty sidekick Yorkie trotting along behind.

Snakes. Great. Now I can never go near that shed. Hopefully I won't have a reason to now that the hose is out.

After putting a small chicken breast under the broiler, I locate a flowered plate in one of Mabel's overhead cabinets, then break into the bag of salad I bought today, creating a masterpiece that involves one of Mr. Freeman's tomatoes. The thought occurs to me to Instagram my work of fresh garden art—before I remember I no longer have that capability. I'm off the grid.

By the time I've eaten and cleaned up, the sun is sinking lower over the winery and I'm hopeful Chief Cordray has gone in for the evening. Plopping my sun hat back on, I head out and get acquainted with Mabel's garden hose, grateful it has a spray nozzle attached, and I drag it around to give my new flowers a healthy drink to start reviving them. My mother was great with flowers, and I think she'd be pleased to see me trying to care for some.

It's when I stop spraying that I hear the phone ringing inside. I drop the hose and run to answer like a woman on fire. How did people ever survive without caller ID?

Inside, I snatch up the avocado-green receiver. "Hello?"

"You sound out of breath," Sydney says.

"And you sound like a breath of fresh air," I reply, since hearing her voice makes me happier than I've been all day.

"Is it as bad as you made out, Jess?"

I plop down in the easy chair next to the phone and spill every truth in my head. "No, it's not horrible—it's just . . . not what I expected. And it's so secluded. And there's not much to do without the internet I reasonably anticipated. And I had to drive an hour to get a bag of salad and some boneless chicken breasts. And I guess it's all just making me feel . . . even more alone than I am."

"I'm sorry you feel so lonely. Is there no one you could socialize with at all?"

Okay, I instantly see the irony. "Well, there's this neighbor guy who seems friendly, but I don't want anything to do with him. I practically ran away from him an hour ago, even though he was doing me a favor."

"Is he creepy?" she asks. "Ugh."

We've both dealt with our fair share of creepy men, so I have to be honest and tell her, "No, I don't get that vibe from him. And he's the chief of police, which I know doesn't automatically absolve someone from being creepy, but he seems like . . . a normal enough guy who means well."

"Thennnn . . . why are you running away from him?"

It's a great question, I admit. I think through it carefully. And I get somewhere. I don't like the place I come to, but I tell her anyway. She's the woman in my life I can do that with, say all the things in my head, good or bad, smart or stupid. "Maybe I'm just embarrassed. About not liking the way I look right now."

"You're attracted to him then," she says, like she's just catching on to something I already know.

But I quickly correct her. "Not even remotely. He's your classic country bumpkin. He wears a stupid, tattered cowboy hat that looks like it's been nibbled on by mice. Not my type at all."

"Then why does it matter what you look like with him?" She sounds truly puzzled.

Which I understand. But I have an answer. "I think it's because he's . . . a man in my age range who seems to be single—at least I *think* he lives alone. And even though I'm not attracted to him—it's just that I . . . wouldn't want him to think I *was*. I wouldn't want him to think the poor cancer patient is into him. I wouldn't want him to be nice to me because he feels sorry for me. Which is . . . maybe why he *is* being so nice to me."

"How do you know he knows you had cancer? He's never met you before, so he doesn't know anything about you, including what you usually look like."

I take that in, let out a sigh. "Maybe he doesn't. But Kevin probably mentioned it. And even if he didn't . . . my hair. No matter who you are, this isn't normal hair."

"Um, I disagree. Many strong women choose to wear their hair super short or not there at all."

"They're prettier than me." It just comes out, quick and honest.

"No," she says knowingly. "They just know they're beautiful, with or without hair. You need to know that, too."

Sydney, Sydney, Sydney. I love her for saying that, but the truth is, she loves her hair as much as I loved mine. She's never been where I am.

We talk a long while, catching up: Jayden is amazing and she might have sex with him soon even though the non-horny side of her intended to wait longer, the kitchen crew ripped up my old flooring today but seem tidy about it, she's having lunch with Kevin on Tuesday, and she's excited about a new shampoo she's trying. Though she adds to that last part, "Oh my God, I'm so sorry. I'm an insensitive lout."

I let her off the hook because we've been talking about shampoo for years, and I'm actually pretty excited to be washing my hair again these days. Funny the things you don't think you'd miss. Anyway, I tell her about Mabel's clouds, and the lake, and the five pots of flowers I bought, and about nice Mr. Freeman and mean Joy Lynn. We go on and on for two heavenly hours, and I love her for giving me that much time when I'm sure she's tired and has stuff to do.

"It'll get better," she tells me. Because of course it's the right thing to say, and Sydney is good at that.

"And if it doesn't?" I ask.

"Then we'll get good and drunk together on the Fourth of July."

I hang up feeling . . . loved again. Which is nice. Helpful in my current position. The sun has set, darkness falling around the little house in the mountains, and just like last night, I don't see that I have anything better to do than go to bed early.

After a quick shower in a pink-glazed tub with a matching shower curtain, I put on pj's and load my toiletries into Mabel's old-fashioned medicine cabinet above the pink sink.

Moving out into the clouds, I unpack a little more, unzipping a tiny fabric bag containing one simple pendant necklace and a few pairs of earrings. Usually, in my real life, I'm a jewelry aficionado, a queen of attention-grabbing statement necklaces and bold earrings, but in Lost and Found, I'll be surprised if I even bother with the simplest pair of earrings. Still, I spill out the bag's contents and open the lid of a white jewelry box on the dresser, hoping it will be empty so I can use it.

It's not empty, though. Sadly, no one thought to clear out Mabel's jewelry, and I instantly find myself thinking she might have a few interesting treasures—but the main thing that catches my eye is the folded sheet of paper lying flat across the top of the little jewelry dividers.

It says, in blue ink: *To my son, my grandchildren, or whoever may find this and care to act on it when I'm dead and gone.*

CHAPTER 5

Oh boy. Should I save this for Kevin? Yes, I probably should.

In fact, it's not late, so I could call him right now—see if he wants me to read it to him over the phone or just mail it.

And yet . . . he's been here only a few times in his adult life? I love the guy, but I can't help thinking he might have taken the luxury of having parents and grandparents for granted.

And Mabel has, this quickly, begun to feel like a friend to me, or as Anne of Green Gables would put it, a kindred spirit. Which is to say, I'm not sure Mabel and I have much in common, but she seems like an enigma in certain ways, and who doesn't love an enigma? I confess to feeling a little mad at Kevin, fearing that he neglected his enigmatic grandmother.

And if his family hasn't found this note two long years after she died . . .

And if I'm the one to find it, and if the way she addressed it makes me feel at least a little bit acknowledged . . .

Though it may be unfair and I'm clearly making a lot of assumptions, I get the sense I'm more interested in Mabel at the moment than anyone in her family, so I pick up the piece of paper and unfold it.

At the top is a common brass key, taped securely to the page with several pieces of Scotch tape. And below that, in jagged handwriting:

This key leads to things once beloved and always sacred.
Do not use the key unless you intend to care for these things.
People so often say "they're just things," but things sometimes do matter, and there is no shame in that. Things represent people's lives, people's loves, people's dreams. I am a reluctant keeper of these precious things, caring for each of them for at least a moment, an hour, a day. If you take up this key, my hope and prayer is that you will do the same—for at least a moment, love these things as they were once loved by another.
To reach them, a treasure hunt. That will make the finding sweeter, I think.
Here we go.

1. *Begin at the trunk of the big mimosa.*
2. *Walk twenty paces to the east.*
3. *Turn to the left until the one-eyed chicken comes into view.*
4. *Walk to the one-eyed chicken, and standing directly before it, look southeast to find the faded rainbow.*
5. *When you reach the rainbow's end, face to the right and locate the tallest tree.*
6. *At the base of the trunk, follow the fern path to the great stone frog.*
7. *Look to the north for the green gateway, behind which rests forgotten treasures.*

Okay, a lot to unpack there. I think I *need* a mimosa, but I'm pretty sure that's not the kind of mimosa she means.

What on earth is Mabel talking about? Would Kevin know if I asked him? I have the distinct feeling he wouldn't. Which means this is just between Mabel and me.

My observation that Mabel liked puzzles has just exceeded my expectations in a big way. These "forgotten things" are clearly hidden somewhere nearby—but why? They sound like a nuisance and a treasure at the very same time, which makes no sense. Why does her family not know about these things if they were of value to her?

All questions without answers, but in this moment, it feels important to me to *see* Mabel, find a photo of her. I have no idea what she even looked like.

With the list of instructions still in hand, I head to the living room, to a wall of hanging pictures I noticed without really studying them. Pay dirt: a black-and-white wedding photo from probably the early fifties. This has to be Mabel in a simple, white, below-the-knee dress and lacy veil, a handsome young groom holding her hand. She was beautiful with dark, tidy, shoulder-length hair and precise lipstick that was probably red.

But what I really want to see is Mabel as she was toward the end of her life, the Mabel I find myself wishing I'd met while she was still here.

Other pictures on the wall get me nowhere in this regard—though I learn that Kevin was a cute kid and an awkward teenager—so I locate photo albums on the built-ins and go digging.

I start from the left end of the vertically stacked albums and get lucky pretty fast: I quickly find a shot of Mabel, probably in her seventies at the time, next to her Christmas tree. She's wearing a collared sweatshirt with a reindeer embroidered on it—I just knew it! But I don't linger on the sweatshirt—instead I focus on her face, her eyes. She's smiling, and her eyes hold . . . love, and hope, and kindness, and her own personal history. Even though she's just looking at the camera, I feel as if she's staring right at me. Kindred spirits.

"Tomorrow, Mabel," I say out loud to the picture—because I guess that's the point I've reached now, talking to pictures of dead people. "Tomorrow I'm going hunting."

I wanted an activity, after all. I think I just found one.

If I knew what a mimosa tree looked like, this would be easier. The next morning finds me standing in the backyard in my sun hat, as lost as I felt upon my arrival, albeit for different reasons now. I start back toward the house, thinking to google it, only to remember I can't and that's why my phone isn't with me—it's become a fairly useless thing. But I head inside anyway and pick up the landline. Of course, I then have to use my phone to find Kevin's number, because who on earth actually has to dial a number these days—except for me.

"Hey there, what's up?" he answers cheerfully.

I cut to the chase. "What's a mimosa tree look like?" I have just resolved to bother him with every single question I want to google but can't, until I get tired of it or quit feeling the need to have information at my fingertips.

"Um, why?" Understandably, he's thrown.

"Just wondering." Like I said, it's between me and Mabel at this point.

"Okay. Well, it's got . . . fronds, you might say, sort of in a . . . ferny way. And it gets these puffy pink blooms that are very pretty. They might be starting to bloom down there right now actually, and if not, probably soon."

"Okay," I reply, taking all that in. "Big or small?"

"Um, all sizes. From very little to mega huge. So . . . are you becoming a nature buff?" he asks hopefully, clearly pleased I'm calling for some reason other than to berate him or complain about my surroundings.

"No," I say. "Was just interested in that particular tree. Thanks. Gotta run."

"You do?" It's a super reasonable question, all things considered.

But I keep it simple. "Yep. Talk soon—bye." Then I hang up. I'm on a mission. A mission from Mabel.

Armed with this new information, I step back out onto the rear porch and peruse the yard.

It takes me a minute to zero in on them because the pink blooms he mentioned are just starting, and they kind of blend in until you look closely. But over the course of a few minutes I begin to realize . . . there are mimosa trees *every-damn-where.*

Tall and gangly ones, small and wispy ones. There are other types of trees in the yard, too, but mimosas dot the expanse more commonly than any other. The pink, fluffy blossoms make me certain.

Shoring up my determination, I venture down into the yard and refer back to Mabel's instructions. *The big mimosa tree.* Such a description suggests one that stands out from the rest. And . . . I'm not sure any of these really fit the bill. Most of the larger ones are similar in size.

Even so, I do my due diligence and approach every tree that's even remotely on the large side and walk the twenty paces east—grateful to know the sun sets directly over the lake, showing me which way is west—then try to find anything that could in any way whatsoever represent a "one-eyed chicken." Now, on the one hand, I have no idea what that might be, and thus it could be frighteningly easy to miss. But on the other, no matter which tree I walk from, a look to the right leads into Cowboy Matt's backyard, which has a few big billowy trees and a small shed to the far side, but nothing resembling or even shaped like a chicken that I can find.

At some point it occurs to me to hope the police chief is off police-chiefing this morning and not watching me out a window and deciding I'm even weirder than I've already seemed. Not that I care what he thinks of me. I don't.

I turn back toward the lake, scanning the yard once more with a sigh—when I spot what appears to be an absolutely *massive* tree with boughs practically aglow with pink in the morning sun . . . across the lake at the winery.

That has to be it! After all, Mabel didn't say the mimosa was in her yard—that's just an assumption I made. Maybe if I asked anyone around here about "the big mimosa," they'd say, "Oh, that's at the winery!" And I really do need to reinstate my daily walks after a couple of days not getting them in, so this gives me a destination I intended to check out anyway. It might be too early in the day for wine, but it's a good idea to go before it gets hot out. I head inside only long enough to grab a water bottle and exchange my flip-flops for walking shoes.

As I depart, I immediately miss the comfort and security of something as simple as a sidewalk, since of course Lost Valley Lane doesn't rate such luxuries. I keep an eye out since any approaching car could mow me down—it's a fairly narrow lane. Most of the walk is shaded, which is, so far, the only real perk the route holds as the sun rises higher.

At the end of the lane, I turn left, again praying for no cars, but reminding myself they do seem rare here and that it's not called Lost Valley for nothin'. I cross a bridge located beyond one end of the lake over a runoff stream and soon come upon a big wood-and-stone sign that welcomes me to Lost Valley Vineyards. In smaller print, it informs me that the tasting room is open Wednesday through Sunday from one to five, but hopefully that means no one is here to mind me investigating their "big mimosa."

The barnlike building I saw from Mabel's backyard is located up a long gravel drive, more challenging for walking than the road was. And now I'm back out in the bright sun, getting hot despite the early hour. But I'm on a mission, so it's okay, and the place indeed seems quiet and empty as I approach.

I make my way straight to the tree, situated on the hillside below the winery and grapevines, to find it's truly enormous. This has *got* to be Mabel's special tree.

After walking to the large twisty trunk, I take twenty steps in the right direction. Then I look to my left, hoping against hope to see something besides the wide-open meadow all around it. And . . . nothing. Nothing at all. Just field. Recently mown, no chickens, one-eyed or otherwise. I stand and look for a long time anyway, though, just to make sure. Because if this isn't the right tree, I'm at a dead end as absolute as the one outside Mabel's house.

"Excuse me—can I help you?"

Oh crap. I turn to see a woman with striking silver hair hanging long and wavy nearly to her waist. She's wearing hippie sunglasses, Birkenstocks, and a long, flowered sleeveless dress. A black-and-white collie mix trots along behind her.

"I'm so sorry," I say. "I don't mean to trespass. I'm staying at the house across the lake this summer and wanted a closer look at your mimosa tree." I point toward the cottage.

"Mabel's place?" she asks, her countenance lightening.

I nod. "I'm a friend of the family," I explain. "I thought no one was here—I apologize for coming onto the property anyway—I like to take walks and was lured by the tree."

"Don't worry about it," she says easily, and I can already tell we're friends. "If we ever want to keep people out that badly, we'll put up a gate. And we're almost always here—we live up above the tasting room." Now it's *her* pointing, to the second floor of the barn, and I'm instantly intrigued. I'm not sure who I expected to be running the place, but it wasn't her. "Feel free to take your walks here—we don't mind."

"Are you sure?" I ask from beneath the wide brim of my hat.

"Absolutely. I'm Joanna, by the way. But call me Jo. My husband, Conrad, is working in the vines on the other side of the barn. And this is Socks." She motions down to the happy-looking dog at her side.

"Nice to meet you. I'm Jessica. Jessica Fox." *WRTB 11.* That last part of the introduction, however, echoing in my brain from pure habit, feels less like who I am in this moment than ever before.

"Come up to the barn with me," she says with a welcoming smile, and we start toward it.

When we arrive, she motions to one of several round wrought-iron tables with chairs dotting a shaded area near the front door and asks, "Wine? Water? Soda?"

"I'd love to try the wine another time," I tell her, "but I'm good for now, thanks." I hold up my water bottle.

"Well, I'm going to grab a soda for myself, so I'll be right back." The dog shadows her movements, step for step, and after she returns with a drink, joining me at a table, she asks, "So what brings you to Lost and Found, Jessica Fox?"

I actually enjoy how direct she is—I can tell she already likes me and wants to know my story. And whereas I would perhaps skirt the facts with most strangers, something about this one draws out blunt, to-the-point honesty. "I just finished treatment for breast cancer," I tell her. "Hence my lack of hair. I'm cancer-free now, which is, of course, a huge relief. But I'm a news anchor in Cincinnati, and I've kind of been . . . sent away for the summer while someone younger and prettier delivers the news. Someone who has hair. She's who I used to be."

"Wow," she says. At first, I think it means I misread her vibe and dropped too much on her too fast, but I know it's okay when she adds, "That's reprehensible. I'm so sorry."

"Thanks," I reply. And that quickly, I understand why I shared. Because I can tell she's strong like I am. Stronger, in fact. She won't baby me—she'll treat me with reverence and respect. It's like I felt discovering Mabel, like we might be kindred spirits. I'm not sure being kindred spirits means you have everything in common—only that you get each other.

I even confide a little more then, explaining the wig-flipping dress rehearsal, which I maintain was much more about a physical reaction than a mental one, but that regardless, the whole situation makes me feel old and unattractive and unworthy. Like I suddenly don't matter. I tell her how I expected to be welcomed back with open arms, the triumphant cancer survivor, and instead was told to take the summer off because Tiffany tested well with focus groups.

"You know you're more than your job," she says.

And I answer, "Of course." But do I? I mean, without it, who would I be? I've never even thought about having to figure that out.

Kevin said it's just for the summer, though, so hopefully there's nothing *to* figure out. "My boss tells me it'll be fine," I explain, "but even so, this is . . . an eye-opening experience, to say the least." Ageism.

Beautyism. Things you don't think you'll ever have to deal with—until suddenly you do.

"Well, I'm sorry you're here under such lousy circumstances, but I hope you can enjoy your time in our little hamlet."

Little hamlet? Who is she trying to convince, me or herself? I reply with, "I get the feeling you're not from around here, either."

She lets out a laugh. "The mountains of Kentucky would go right at the top of the list of places I never thought I'd end up. But here I am."

I tilt my head slightly, sun hat and all. "I'm waiting for the why and the how."

When a small smile turns up the corners of her mouth, my eyes are drawn to the fine lines there, to the messy waves in her long hair. I wish I could see her eyes behind the sunglasses. She points in the general direction of where she told me her husband is working. "It's all for that man." Though she says it lovingly.

I wait for more.

"I grew up in California, near San Fran, and Conrad is from Seattle. We lived in LA for a while, and then Vegas. He was in the corporate world—of windowpanes. That's what he devoted his life to—windows. He started in IT, ended up in management, and he was well rewarded for his work. I managed a kennel in LA, and ran a funky little flower shop in Las Vegas. And then one day he told me he wanted to retire and build a winery in the country somewhere. Just wanted to start the whole thing up from scratch."

"Was he a wine expert?" I ask.

"Not then, no. Now he's becoming one. He just felt this passion to pursue a quiet life among the mountains and vines, to do something entirely different and get away from it all."

"Well, if he wanted to get away from it all, he came to the right place."

She laughs once more. "And I was happy to follow. Happy to let *him* follow his bliss."

"Are *you* happy here?" It's too personal—I regret it the second I ask.

But she seems not to notice. "What's not to be happy about?" she asks in an easy-come-easy-go way. "Fresh air, beautiful scenery, and all the wine I can drink." She adds a wink with that last bit.

"You don't mind the, uh, isolation? The lack of . . ."

"Everything?" she asks with a knowing smile. "Sure, I did at first. But I just replaced one thing with another. Streaming TV and movies with reading books. Social media with getting to know people when they come in, and running the tasting room. Restaurants with cooking. Running around town with tending to grapevines. It's just a matter of retraining your brain, letting it get back to basics."

"You're a stronger woman than me," I confess, my earlier thought officially verified. "But I admire your attitude." Even if I don't quite understand it. I guess it's a testament to her love for her man.

She confirms that, saying, "Conrad worked hard for so many years. And, well, he still works hard now, but in a very different way. It feeds his soul. It took a while to get used to Lost and Found, but there's so much peace here. I've come to value that more than I ever expected when this little adventure started."

"Can I ask you something else that's none of my business?"

"I'm an open book," she says, and I admire that about her, too.

"Do you, um, get enough customers out here to make it worth your while?"

Another small smile graces her face. "Well, people don't just stumble across us—it's named Lost Valley for a reason. You have to be even more lost to get *here* than you do to reach Lost and Found. But we do have a website—that we maintain from the Brandywine Library—and we're in winery guides for people who seek out vineyards for day trips and travel, and we're fortunate to have placement in wine shops in Knoxville, Lexington, and Louisville. It's enough to keep us afloat."

Before I leave, I insist on buying a bottle of wine—then realize I have no form of payment on me because while my phone is with me in order to count my steps, it no longer works to pay for things, either. Jo makes me take the bottle anyway, telling me it's a welcome-to-the-neighborhood gift. I argue, "I'm definitely paying for it on my next visit," and we bicker good-naturedly about it until I finally set off back to Mabel's. So in my attempt to support the business, I instead abscond with a free bottle of wine.

Still, as I make the return journey, I feel better than when I arrived. I liked Jo and felt welcomed by her. I think about the kind of love that's truly happy to put the other person first. And I remain inexplicably taken by her appearance—she makes aging look good. She's clearly a woman of her own, a woman who grows where she's planted, a woman who probably wouldn't give a damn if she lost her hair—even though it's as long and striking as mine once was. I think I might want to be her when I grow up.

CHAPTER 6

I make myself a sandwich for lunch, feeling discouraged. I mean, sure, I thought maybe the one-eyed chicken would stump me or that the faded rainbow would throw me off, but I never imagined I wouldn't even make it to the mimosa. What am I missing?

After eating, I grab up the same Grisham novel I pulled off Mabel's shelves the other night, park myself in a rocking chair on the back porch, and read all afternoon, grateful the story pulls me in. I occasionally suffer internet withdrawal: the repeated urge to check social media, or the weather forecast, or the Lost Valley Vineyards site. It's hard to remember I can't do any of those things after years of having the world at my fingertips. I take a picture of the winery across the lake, thinking that when I next make it to the Piggly Wiggly I'll post about it and try to drum up a little business for Jo and Conrad—but I also feel annoyed that I can't just do it now.

Of course I *could*. I could drive to the abandoned grocery store and stand around the pockmarked parking lot like a junkie getting my fix. Frankly, that sounds more satisfying than the empty, pointless evening stretching before me. But again, I told my followers I was going off the grid, so it's going to seem silly if I post every day or two. Thus I'll hold on to the winery picture for the next time I sincerely need to go into town. And I tell myself that if Jo can adjust to the nothingness here, so can I. Somehow.

I try to think of things to do. Kevin and Syd are both still working at this hour—it's not quite five. I could clean something, but the place really *is* pretty clean. I could pull out one of Mabel's cookbooks, which I discovered in a kitchen drawer, and throw myself into making something creative for dinner—but I'm still gravitating toward the simple-meal lifestyle and don't feel like devoting an hour to something it'll only take me ten minutes to eat, no matter how bored I am. I could water my petunias, but it's still too hot out.

Out of the sheer need to do *something*, I shove Mabel's folded directions into my back pocket and recommence looking for any mimosa trees I possibly could have missed. It's surely a fool's errand, but I already feel fairly foolish the last couple of days, so what does it matter?

It's clear that this simple life doesn't suit me—I'm not enjoying the peace and quiet, I don't like being unplugged and disconnected, and nothing about this forced vacation is working for me. It's turning me from someone I've always pretty much liked into someone I'm not sure I even recognize. I managed to keep my spirits up through cancer, but living in Lost and Found is seriously depressing me.

Despite all this, or because of it, I retrace my steps, going from mimosa to mimosa. I make sure there aren't any I somehow overlooked in the front yard. I even search Police Chief Cordray's lawn, but nary a mimosa in sight.

After which I find myself standing in the side yard, between the two houses, looking this way and that, so frustrated I think I would pull my hair out if I had any long enough to pull—and I consider just ripping Mabel's treasure map to shreds and pretending the damn thing never existed.

"You look confused."

As usual, I nearly leap out of my skin—then spin to see my neighbor heading my way, today wearing a dark-gray policeman's uniform.

It changes everything about his appearance, transforming him from random country guy to respectable officer of the law. The dumb, worn-out hat is gone, revealing thick, dark hair that doesn't look as unkempt as usual. The only thing the same about him is the Yorkie frolicking around his feet.

"You have a way of sneaking up on me," I say, not trying to hide my annoyance. "Did they teach you that in cop school?"

"Yep." He nods, grins. "Sneakin' 101, and I got an A."

I refuse to acknowledge the clever comeback and instead tell him, "You actually look like a cop for a change."

"Did you think I was pullin' your leg?" He arches one brow.

"You just haven't seemed much like a cop to me. You don't even have a cop car."

He shrugs, looking amused. "Not sure what we're supposed to seem like. And the cruiser stays at the city buildin' when I'm not on duty."

"Are you going to introduce me to your dog?" I have no idea why I ask.

"Sure. This is Goldie. Official name: Little Miss Golden Paws, but Goldie for short. *And her's a good girl, isn't her?*" He's bending over, nuzzling her, using baby talk. I'm thrown, as much by that as the Golden Paws thing.

It's adorably cute, but I refuse to say so. Instead I tell him, "I wouldn't have pegged you as a Yorkie man."

"Neither would I," he replies, "but sometimes life throws you curveballs."

Our eyes meet. Is he wanting me to ask about his curveballs? Or is he acknowledging mine? That I've obviously been thrown one or two. He can't even imagine how many. I choose not to respond.

Which leads him to, "Was I right? You confused about somethin'?"

"I'm . . . looking for a mimosa tree," I confess, deciding to come clean.

At which he laughs, motioning with his arm, Vanna White–style. "Got a whole yard full of 'em, darlin'."

"No, not those," I say, then try to explain. "I found something Mabel wrote, where she referred to 'the big mimosa.'" I don't tell him more, though, because I still feel secretive about the instructions. It would be just like him to want to help me and take over the hunt. "And I don't think any of those are the right one."

"Oh, I know what she's talkin' about," he immediately replies. "The one ya can't see."

Okay, now he's starting to sound as cryptic as Mabel. "That's as clear as mud."

"It's right over here," he claims, taking just a few steps from where we stand and then studying the ground. He stamps his foot on something that sounds harder than grass, and I come closer to see what looks like the remains of a tree trunk sawed off at ground level. "Had to take it out last year when half of it came down in a storm and just missed the house. But it was definitely the biggest one. Only one she ever actually planted—thank God."

"Thank God?"

"Mimosa trees are a menace."

I raise my eyebrows. "They are?"

"Oh sure—they look all pretty and nice with their pink, puffy blooms, but see all the other mimosas in this yard?" He motions again. "Know where *they* came from?"

I shake my head.

"From the ugly seed pods that grew on this one every damn fall." He stamps his shoe on the sawed-off trunk again. "They blow everywhere and multiply like rabbits. I have to pull up a dozen that get started in my own yard every summer. If ya ask me, the only good mimosa is a dead mimosa."

"You seem to feel strongly about this."

"You would, too, if you had to constantly police your yard for runaway mimosa trees lest they take over the place." Then he gets back to the topic at hand. "Why'd you wanna find the tree anyway?"

Good question. *But you're still not getting in on my treasure hunt, Chief Cordray.* "Just . . . something to do." It's a terrible answer, but it's all I come up with.

"Might wanna get ya some better hobbies, Jessie," he tells me.

"I used to have some," I reply. "They were called 'the internet.' And it's Jessica."

He nods. "My bad. Jessica." Then he points toward his house. "Well, Goldie and me are gonna go make us some dinner. Just holler if you need help findin' any more missin' trees." And with that, he's gone.

And I'm back on the case, more quietly excited about this mimosa revelation than I can easily contain. As he walks away, I peer down at what remains of the tree. This is it! This is the big mimosa! Sweet success is mine!

Once I'm sure he's *really* gone, tucked safely inside his big farmhouse for a while, I start at the site of the chopped-down tree and take twenty careful and calculated steps away from the direction of the lake, which leads me into the front yard.

At which point I turn to the left, a little terrified. Because I'm pretty sure there's not going to magically be a one-eyed chicken and all my joy will be short-lived.

Only . . . there it is! Much to my surprise, an old white iron decoration of some kind, in the shape of a chicken's head, protrudes from the front of Matt Cordray's front porch post!

Needless to say, I start toward it. But then I stop. He's right inside. This man I want to avoid. What if he glances out and sees me? The jig will be up. So I just resolve to be casual about it—and hopefully quick. With any luck, he's already busy whipping up dinner and I can come and go undetected. Who's the sneaking expert now?

Approaching the chicken, I see it's an old-fashioned thermometer, which I'm guessing has been screwed into this post for decades. It possesses a certain country charm, and indeed one eye if you only look at it from the side.

Pulling out my instructions, I stand in front of the thermometer and stare in a southeasterly direction, hoping like hell for a rainbow. But none appears. Instead, I'm studying a sizable old outbuilding in the yard across the street from Mabel's, the one with the peach-and-lavender house. The building is a shed or a garage, way less colorful than the home, with an old tin roof and aging advertising signs covering the entire broad side of it. It's like Matt's one-eyed chicken—full of yesteryear character—and I'm wondering how I've been here for over two days without having noticed it.

I stand there a minute longer, scrutinizing the shed—searching above it, below it, to both sides—hoping to find something shaped like a rainbow, or a series of rainbow colors. But I come up empty.

And I want to keep looking, finding that elusive thing that just hasn't yet quite come into focus for me—but when I think I hear movement inside the farmhouse directly behind me, I scurry away like a bunny without looking back. And I scurry to the southeast, of course, because I'm not giving up; I'm just hoping I don't have to stand exactly where the directions indicate to find the rainbow.

It's as I'm rushing toward the old plank-sided building, the wood grayed with time and most of the signs rusted, that I spot that which I seek. Within one of those rusted, fading signs, behind an old 7UP logo and the words "the uncola," is a groovy hippie-vibe sunshine, and above that sunshine is a thin, little, three-striped rainbow in pink, white, and blue—though I'm guessing the pink was once red. Rainbow found!

"Yes!" I whisper triumphantly under my breath, and I can't stop myself from doing a tiny victory dance right there in the middle of Lost Valley Lane. I guess there *is* something to be said for isolation, occasionally anyway, like knowing you can dance in the road without anyone seeing you.

"You there! What are you doing? Can I help you with something?"

So much for not being seen. I look up toward where the screechy voice came from to spot an old woman peeking around the back corner of the pastel house.

"Hello!" I call, instinctively putting on my best Jessica Fox, WRTB 11 voice as I begin to walk toward her. "I'm staying at Mabel's for a while. My name's Jessica, and I'm a friend of the family." I hike a thumb over my shoulder toward the cottage.

As usual, the mention of Mabel's name seems to smooth things over and put her at ease. She speaks more quietly to say, "Mabel was a good friend to me. Miss her, I do."

"I never got to meet her," I explain, still approaching the woman, "but I feel like I'm getting to know her just from being in her home."

"Why don't you come back here and sit with me a minute, honey," the old lady says. "Won't keep ya long—got a pot of cottage ham and green beans on the stove just about done."

Her house sits up on a rise, so I make my way to a set of concrete steps in front that have seen better days, then circle around to the back. As I turn the corner, though, I'm overwhelmed and flabbergasted by what I see.

Metal, iron, steel, tin—filling the backyard, and all of it crafted into a strange mishmash of . . . art? Some of it has been pieced together to make likenesses of animals or buildings, but much of it is just randomly welded together as if to create a perpetual jungle gym. It's painted a variety of colors, every bright or pastel shade on the color wheel.

The old woman, in an outdated flowered housedress and sturdy Easy Spirit gym shoes, sits on a bench of welded-together metals, one of many I instantly spot here and there in the mad, messy beauty of it all.

"Somethin', ain't it?" she asks proudly, apparently seeing the reaction on my face.

"Indeed." I'm kind of speechless.

"Ever' bit of it made by my Walter, God rest his soul. Been gone nearly ten years now, but he's still with me ever' day when I come out to the backyard."

"It's incredibly unique," I remark.

She pats the metal seat beside her. "Come sit. I'm Grace Whitcomb."

I join her, reintroducing myself. "Jessica Fox."

"Matt told me we'd have us a new neighbor for a spell, but I plumb forgot. He's a sweet boy, Matt. Looks in on me to make sure I'm gettin' along okay. My son lives out in Saint Louis with his family. Cain't get home as much as I'd like him to because he's got him an important bank job."

Feeling her pride in him, I say, "I'm sure you miss him."

"Sure do. And my grandgirls, too. Got two of 'em—twenty-four and twenty-two." She stops, shakes her head. "Grew up too dang fast for me. Just all went by in a blip. The girls used to come and stay for a while ever' summer, but ya know how it gets—they outgrew it. Got busy lives of their own now."

I'm not sure what to say because her words add up to a similar loneliness I sense in Mabel, even though Mabel's not here anymore to share it. Given my own recent bouts with loneliness, I instantly want to make her feel better, though I'm not sure how. "Change is hard," I hear myself say. Totally weak response. Totally true response.

"That's why I miss my Mabel," she says. "Our husbands died within a year of each other. Was neighbors most of our lives and was always friendly and all, but it was after we both ended up alone that we really got to be friends."

Oh man, she's killing me. My own loneliness suddenly feels superficial compared to what I imagine hers to be. "I'm glad you both found each other."

"We raised a little garden together over yonder." She points to a flat patch of ground near the sign-covered garage. "We cooked dinner together many a night, and we'd play board games of an evenin'. Was a right nice way to pass the time." She seems to come back from her reverie and pats my knee with her hand, like we're already friends. "But now tell me about you, honey. What brings ya to these parts?"

Apparently today is the day of explaining my situation to strangers. And just like with Jo, I could sugarcoat it—but for some reason, I don't. "Long story short? I'm a newscaster who lost my hair from chemo, and they don't want me back until I look better."

Her eyes go wide, and whoa—even *I'm* a bit taken aback by the short, harsh way I've broken it down in this particular telling. The truth I suddenly see: I've actually been sugarcoating it *in my own mind*, making it even less heinous than it is because it's so ugly and hurtful, and I simply didn't want to believe that of the people I work for. The toughness in me just didn't want to let any weaker parts truly accept that.

"That's a damn cryin' shame, honey," she says, patting my knee more fully now.

"Thanks," I softly reply, still a little thrown by my own brutal honesty.

"No fun to be judged by how ya look, is it?" Grace is African American, and though white chick me has no idea what she has experienced, I suddenly feel like she gets me—in a way I couldn't have been gotten a year ago.

So I've found three new kindred spirits—two living and one dead—all in tiny, not-even-a-town Lost Valley. I'm going to chalk that up to something like a miracle I could have in no way expected when I set out looking for Mabel's mimosa tree.

"Just gotta know you're beautiful anyway, that's all," she goes on more gently, her voice full of conviction. "I didn't always know that about myself, ya see. It took my Walter to make me see it. You got somebody who makes ya see it, honey?"

"No," I whisper, still taken aback by this whole unexpected conversation. Sure, there's Kevin and Sydney. But I don't think that's what she means. She's talking more about someone who makes you feel beautiful effortlessly—a lover, a life mate. And beautiful is something I haven't felt in quite a while now. Maybe it's a thing that shouldn't matter, to any of us—but the WRTB managers and Tiffany have shown me, undeniably, that it does.

"Well, I promise you are, my dear," my new friend tells me. "I promise you are."

"Thank you," I gently reply. Mostly out of words. Because I'm not at all sure how this happened—one second I'm looking at an old 7UP sign and the next I'm bonding over unseen beauty with an old woman I've never met.

"Goodness me," she says. "How on earth did we get so serious here so quick?"

My thoughts exactly, Grace. This is not who I am, nor the level of intimacy I'm cut out for.

Then she smiles. "Can I ask why you were doin' a little dance down on the lane?"

Okay, to my utter surprise, that's a better subject. And as much as I intended to keep my search between Mabel and me, I feel different about it with Grace. She might value knowing I'm on a hunt for Mabel's secrets.

So I reach into my pocket and pull out the list of instructions. "I found this in Mabel's jewelry box." I give her a minute to read over it before I say, "I was dancing because I'd just found the faded rainbow. In your 7UP sign."

This makes her grin at me. Then she looks back to the sheet of paper, now kind of crumpled. "Will you do me a favor?" she asks. "Will ya come back sometime and sit with me a spell? Maybe let me know whatever it is ya find of Mabel's? I could make us up a pot of brown beans and some cornbread one night."

I have no idea what "brown beans" are and no idea what Grace and I might have to talk about once we exhaust Mabel and unfair judgment. But maybe those things are enough, especially given our kindred-spirit moment. Plus I don't exactly have a lot on my day planner right now. So I say, "Yes, absolutely I will."

"That'll be right nice," she replies with a smile. "Now reckon I'll let ya get back to your rainbow, and I'll get on to my cottage ham. Nothin' like fresh green beans—got me a mess of 'em down to Mert Dwyer's roadside stand last week since my knees don't let me do my own garden no more."

We end the conversation then—I tell her to enjoy her dinner, and she tells me to enjoy my hunting. And I feel gladder than I might have guessed to have been caught dancing in the road.

CHAPTER 7

When you reach the rainbow's end, face to the right and locate the tallest tree.

Standing back in front of the 7UP sign, I do as the directions say. Tallest tree located—the top of it billows out from the edge of the woods near the dead end, noticeably above the rest—and I only hope no one chopped down an even taller tree, leaving me to falsely identify this one.

Of course, as I make my way past the dead end and into the woods, I realize Mabel has had some fun with this because there are much shorter and simpler paths to where I now stand.

But it's the journey.

I have no idea where those words come from—it's almost as if someone whispered them in my ear. I even stop in place and turn to look, but I'm still alone.

Well, today has been a journey indeed. The last *few* days have been a journey. The last eight months have been a journey. And here I am, still looking for whatever it is I'm supposed to find at the end of a faded 1970s rainbow. I'm pretty sure it won't be a pot of gold.

It's not entirely easy to keep track of which tree is the tall one as I step under the boughs and foliage—it's a jungle in here. But I follow the logic that the tallest tree should have one of the bigger trunks, and before I know it, I'm standing at the base of an enormous tree I'm pretty sure is the right one, mainly because of the wild ferns scattered on the ground around it.

Of course, I need a "fern path," and this is more of a sprinkling of them. But when I study them for a moment in the dark, shady coolness of the forest, I see that they sort of create a twisty line, if you look at it in the right way—so I follow it.

I seem to be heading back to the edge of the woods, just in a different direction, and then, lo and behold, at my feet I find a lichen-covered concrete frog wearing a crown. I breathe a sigh of relief, because the stone frog is really just a stone frog, nothing cryptic or mysterious to decipher, and also because a stone frog would have been so, so easy for someone to pick up and carry away at some point, and I'm grateful no one did.

Up ahead, past the frog, the sunlight creates an opening in the trees, and beyond it—voilà, a green wooden door. The green gateway, surely.

"What on earth are you doin' in the woods?"

I jump nearly a mile because—oh my God, *of course* the cowboy next door has followed me into the forest. Though when I spin to face him, he no longer looks like a responsible police officer and is back to being a random country dude, now in worn-out cowboy boots, a Buffalo Trace bourbon T-shirt, and that stupid hat.

"If you're not careful, you'll get lost," he warns.

I'm already lost. I don't say it, but it's what comes to mind. The truth has a way of sneaking in through little cracks and crevices when you least expect it. I feel more lost than I have in a very long time, and now I'm following some crazy treasure map hoping to find . . . something. Something that matters.

"Don't worry, I know where I'm going," I claim anyway.

He gives his head a doubtful tilt. "How is that possible?"

I hold up Mabel's directions. "I have a map." Okay, so much for not letting him intrude on my private hunt. And since I can't call back the words, I quickly try to change the subject. "Are you following me?"

"Yep," he admits, like that's an okay answer.

I'm moderately outraged. "Why?"

"Because when I step out the front door to see you barrelin' off into the woods like you know where you're goin' when you don't, I consider it my civic duty as an officer who's been sworn to serve and protect to keep you from breakin' an ankle, fallin' off the edge of a mountain, or gettin' bit by a snake."

Hmm. Okay, those are pretty good reasons. But what he doesn't know is . . . "No need to fear—I'm not going far."

"What's this map you're wavin' around?"

So much for diversion. And I'm hardly waving it—it's just in my hand. But I guess the jig is up. So I hold it out and show him.

He snatches it away and starts to read. "What the hell *is* this?"

"I found it in Mabel's things."

After a moment, he eyes me suspiciously, and something about his look runs through my body. "Why didn't you just show me this half an hour ago when we were talkin' about the big mimosa? Why so mysterious?"

I shrug. "I don't know." And as much as I dislike being so honest with him, I feel like he's forcing my hand. "For some reason, I wanted to keep this just between me and Mabel. I wanted a . . . private project. Something to do quietly on my own."

"Well," he says, looking as if he feels a little guilty, "sorry I messed that up. But on the bright side . . ."

I glance up at him from beneath the brim of my hat. "Yeah?"

"You found the garage key. I've been lookin' for that for two years."

I blink. Twice. That's the garage I'm seeing through the trees? I haven't found a magical door to a magical hobbit house in the woods? I mean, it makes sense, logically, now that he's saying it's the garage, but it's a serious letdown. *Mabel, Mabel, Mabel—you really had me going. All this and you could have just written "Go to the garage."*

I take a deep breath and cast my neighbor a sideways glance. "You've been trying to find this key since Mabel died? Couldn't you have just broken in?"

He shrugs, considering it. "I suppose. But there's nothin' in there I particularly need. Just seemed like a good idea to be able to get inside." He grins. "Now we can."

As we walk toward the light, he tells me, "My grandpa put that chicken thermometer on the house. Mabel always did like it."

"I can't believe she sent me—well, me being the person who found this—on such a wild-goose chase just to get to the garage," I mutter, still wrapping my head around that.

"Well, Mabel had some time on her hands the last few years of her life. Reckon she thought it'd be her family to go on this hunt. And at the same time, she probably wondered if they'd bother. Kevin's dad was raised here, but once he left, the family didn't come back a lot, and even less after Kevin and his sisters grew up."

"So you're saying . . . what? That she was screwing with them a little?"

He raises his eyebrows, flashing an amused expression. "Could be. Nobody likes feelin' forgotten."

You're tellin' me, pal.

"And besides," he says, working to separate the key from the note, "it's not a wild-goose chase unless there's nothin' good inside." He gives a little wink that makes my chest ripple.

I jerk my gaze away just as we emerge back out into the early-evening sunlight and find ourselves behind Mabel's garage, facing its back—green—door.

Getting the key free, he looks closely at it—then lets out a hardy laugh.

"What?" I ask.

He holds it out to show me: The side that was taped down is labeled with the word Garage. If I'd just removed the key to begin with, the answer was right there.

"Oh my God," I say, laughing, too.

And so we're suddenly laughing *together*. Which comes with a funny sensation in my solar plexus—until I remember that I really have no intention of hanging out with the police chief, for many reasons, so I stop and say, "Well, let's see what's inside."

I pluck the key from his fingertips before he can stop me, because I earned the right to unlock this door. The sun is starting to dip toward the horizon in the distance, softening the light, and my heart beats too hard with anticipation. I don't know why.

Part of me is a little mad that I have to share this discovery with Cowboy Matt—but in all honesty, another part of me is glad he's here, just in case there's something wild or crazy or confusing inside. Or if there's snakes.

Grabbing the old enamel doorknob with one hand, I use the other to slide the key into an antique lock that I hope still works. When I turn it and hear a slight click, I automatically lift my eyes to my companion and our gazes meet—until I immediately pull mine away. Then I turn the knob and ease the door open.

Inside, it looks like a normal old garage: a well-aged, built-in worktable, tools on a pegboard, two rakes and a shovel, a grease stain on the cracked concrete floor. The only things that come with question marks are the cardboard boxes and plastic storage containers. Stacks of them line the back wall.

Police Chief Matt must be thinking along the same lines since he walks up to the nearest cardboard box, rips off a strip of thick masking tape, and pulls back the flaps. Then, peeking inside, he says, "Uh-oh."

I stand up a little straighter. "Uh-oh? What is it?"

"You found the Lost and Found lost and found."

part 2

beauty

CHAPTER 8

"I found the what?" I blink my confusion.

"This," he says, motioning around him and looking surprisingly exasperated, "is the Lost and Found lost and found." He shakes his head. "I wondered what the hell happened to it all. One day about a year and a half ago, we realized the whole damn thing had just disappeared from the post office. Nobody knew when because it had been in a back room, just gatherin' dust. And nobody looked for it because havin' it gone was kind of a blessing in a way." Another headshake. "I shoulda known Mabel had somethin' to do with it. She had a soft spot for it."

"Um, I need more to go on here, Chief Cordray," I inform him. Since so far, I've got nothing.

He unleashes a sigh and looks tired out by the whole thing. "Well, when you live in a town named Lost and Found, every now and then, somebody sends ya somethin' they think somebody else lost, hopin' for some crazy reason that you know who it belongs to."

I squint. "Huh?"

"The reason you look confused by this," he tells me, "is because it makes no damn sense whatsoever. But it would seem there are people out there who, after findin' somethin' that seems lost, and then discoverin' there's a town called Lost and Found, Kentucky, just randomly mail that item *here*. Guess it makes 'em feel better than throwin' it away.

"Mabel worked at the post office up until she retired, and she took to puttin' it all in a storage area—since nobody here knew what to do with any of it, either. And it mostly stopped once social media came along. Reckon people started tryin' to find homes for lost things *that* way. Thank God."

"Ah," I say, thinking this is the end of the weird story—but alas, no.

"The post office was still storin' all this old stuff, though, and sometimes the town council talked about gettin' rid of it, just puttin' it out for the trash collector. And when Junior Barnett became postmaster and wanted himself an office, the storage room was the prime location, so he lobbied for emptyin' it out. But other folks didn't think that seemed right, and at some point it just fell off people's radar screens.

"Until one day Jeannie at the post office went into the storage room and it was all gone. Every bit of it. MIA. Of course, folks blamed Junior. But he seemed as shocked as anybody and said he'd long since given up his dreams of privacy. Even so, people were sure Junior had destroyed all this stuff. Only looks like instead, Mabel saved it by hidin' it away."

"Wow." That's all I can summon after such a tale. I don't know what I was expecting to find by following the treasure map, but it wasn't this.

"I can't believe it," he murmurs, taking in the pile of stuff. Then he chuckles softly. "Mabel never cared for Junior much. Probably laughin' down from heaven about him takin' the blame. Maybe once he hears it's all been found, he'll finally get brave enough to claim that office—he didn't dare once folks accused him of throwin' away the lost and found."

I blow out a breath, thinking through all this new information. "Well, at least now it's not taking up space someone else needs. I guess it can sit here and rot for eternity."

At this, however, Police Chief Cordray casts a pointed sideways glance in my direction. "Well, now, Miss Jessica Fox, it seems to me that by openin' that door, you agreed to do somethin' about all this stuff."

I let my eyes go wide in disbelief. "I most certainly did not. And besides, what could I possibly do?"

He shrugs. "I don't know. But you read the note. You shouldn't have gone on the hunt if you weren't gonna honor Mabel's wishes. She took such things seriously, seriously enough to squirrel this stuff away—apparently by the dead of night, since no one ever saw her take it. She'd long since retired, so she must've kept her keys and gone sneakin' around after hours. Think how hard it musta been for a lady her age to lug all this crap back here."

"I guess she *also* took Sneaking 101," I say, mainly to divert his attention from pressuring me to somehow "do something" with all this stuff.

He grins in reply. "Guess she did. Know what other class I did pretty good in?"

"What's that?"

"Advanced Changin' the Subject."

I tilt my head to inform him, "I'm sorry, but this stuff is not my problem."

"Guess the *actual* problem," he says in a pondering way, "is that it's *nobody's* problem. But Mabel would be heartbroken to know somebody followed her little map to all this stuff and then did nothin'."

"Well, maybe Kevin or his sisters or parents or nieces and nephews can do something with it all."

The cowboy next door just casts me a knowing look. "Jessie. They didn't even find the note. How much you think they're gonna care about a bunch of stuff that didn't belong to her when they don't care much about the stuff that did?"

After slanting him an annoyed look the whole time he was speaking, I now begin, "It's—"

"Jessica, I know," he cuts me off. "Sorry. Jessie just rolls off the tongue easy."

"You know, it's not that I don't want to be helpful. It's—"

"You've made out," he cuts me off a second time to say, "like you got nothin' to fill your time here without your precious internet."

"Well, if you'd stop interrupting me, I was going to say that even if I did want to do something with this stuff, I have no idea what it would be. For the same reason no one else has ever known what to do with it, either."

He stays quiet a minute, but then uncrumples Mabel's instructions, the paper now torn from having removed the key. He smooths out what's left, pressing it up against the pegboard in between a hammer and a saw, then stabs his index finger at the first part. Where it says: *Do not use the key unless you intend to care for these things.*

After which he then stabs the same finger at a slightly lower part of the note:

> *Things represent people's lives, people's loves, people's dreams. I am a reluctant keeper of these precious things, caring for each of them for at least a moment, an hour, a day. If you take up this key, my hope and prayer is that you will do the same—for at least a moment, love these things as they were once loved by another.*

"You're suggesting what?" I ask, needing clarification about all this pointing.

"That even if you can't find where they belong, you could honor Mabel's wishes by . . . just lookin' through the boxes, seein' what's there. Who knows? Maybe you'll come across somethin' that . . . I don't know, gives some clue as to where it came from. I mean, if even one thing found its way home, that'd be pretty great, don't ya think? And worst-case scenario, you see some things that once mattered to somebody and grant a dead woman's final wish."

"We don't know that it was her *final* wish," I can't help but point out.

"Well, we don't know that it wasn't, either," he quickly retorts. And with that, he presses the piece of paper back into my hand. "Give it some thought. And if you decide ya wanna look through it all, or even some of it, I'll gladly move it into the house, into the spare bedroom."

"I can move it myself," I tell him. Because old habits die hard and I'm a capable woman and all that.

"Suit yourself," he says.

"Thank you, I will," I reply smartly, then approach the cardboard box he already opened, gripping it on each side, ready to pick it up.

"But there are probably snakes in here."

Returning my hands to my sides, I say, "Well then, thank you in advance for moving the stuff," after which I exit the garage. I guess I'm starting to accept that, like it or not, even a strong woman can have certain limitations.

The spare bedroom in Mabel's cottage, done in shabby-not-quite-chic country blue—shabby mostly because it still sports the hearts-and-geese trend of the nineties—is packed to the gills with boxes and bins.

Now, whereas yesterday I was dying for something to do, today I'm avoiding my something-to-do with all the nothing I can possibly think of.

I take another morning walk to the winery, which brings another visit with Jo, and today I meet Conrad, too. With tidy gray hair and glasses, he looks more like a college professor than a winemaker, but I can already see that he balances Jo and is the yin to her yang.

I water my flowers very thoroughly, even though it looks like it might rain.

I read some of Mabel's cookbooks. I don't know that I'll actually cook, but you never know.

And I read some more of my John Grisham novel on the back porch—but then it does begin to rain, driving me back indoors, where there's no light good enough for reading, even during the day.

Fortunately, it's almost lunchtime, so I whip up a grilled cheese and heat a can of soup—the perfect rainy-day lunch—and sit at Mabel's old kitchen table watching trails of rain trickle down the windowpane, blurring the yard and lake beyond.

But after that, I'm fresh out of time killers, especially since it looks like the kind of rain that might last all afternoon. Glancing from the kitchen in the general direction of the spare bedroom, I guess I know what I'm about to do. I don't know why I'm so averse to the idea, but I'm falling prey to some sort of obligation wrapped in utter boredom. Arming myself with a can of soda to keep me awake during this dreary task, I gird myself and venture into the room, opening the first cardboard box I come to.

The first thing I pull out is a photo album. It's a brown vinyl one that resembles my own family albums from childhood. Opening it reveals it indeed belonged to a family and holds everyday pictures of life on a farm somewhere. Mom decorated a nice Christmas tree and was fond of those thick ribbons that flow all the way down from the top to the bottom, taking the place of garland. Daughter and Son seemed to enjoy riding on the tractor with Dad, who wore a green John Deere hat and T-shirts with no sleeves. He looks like a hardworking man. They drove a Ford Taurus and a Dodge pickup. Daughter won the middle school science fair that year and Mom got a ribbon at the county fair for a quilt she made.

As I close the album, already I understand why Mabel didn't want these things thrown away. It's someone's memories. And in this particular case, these kids are probably still very much living, and quite possibly the parents, too.

Then I find a note stuck between two pages, clinging to the plastic page coverings. It's dated fifteen years ago and says:

> *Found this in our library drop box in Moville, Iowa. Seemed like something that wasn't meant to be put there, but no one around here seems to know this family. Not sure what to do with it, so sending it to you.*

It occurs to me that if I really went digging, and maybe broke out a magnifying glass, I might be able to find some clues about these people hidden within the pictures, maybe the name of the county in which Mom won her quilting ribbon, that sort of thing. But right now I'm suddenly curious to see what other kinds of stuff random people have gone to the trouble of mailing to Lost and Found, Kentucky, so I set the album aside.

Next I pull out a padded manila envelope. Inside is a silver pendant on a chain. The note with it tells me it was found on the street in Depot Bay, Oregon, which it refers to as "a seaside spot that draws a lot of tourists, so it could have come from anywhere." Ugh. Helpful but not helpful. I examine the engraved pendant. On one side in very small script: *To our beloved daughter, Jasmine.* On the other: *We are so blessed that God made you ours.*

My heart clenches a little at that. Maybe it doesn't matter; maybe Jasmine was just a little girl and her parents replaced the necklace when it was lost. But maybe Jasmine treasured it; maybe her parents are no longer with her and it meant the world to have that gift reminding her of their love. And sure, okay, maybe I'm injecting my own baggage here, having lost both my mom and dad before my twenty-first birthday. But no matter how you slice it, I hate that this token of love for a daughter is . . . here, in *my* hands, in Nowheresville, USA, and not wherever it belongs.

Taking a deep, sad breath, I return the pendant to the envelope with its note and set it atop the photo album with a heavy heart.

The next thing I pull from the box is a very small, worn leather envelope of sorts. But then, no, I discover that when you open the envelope, it's actually a tiny book with an interlocking cover. It's black, though much of the black has worn away over time, and I look inside to discover it is, in fact, a Bible.

I'm instantly fascinated, and even more so when I carefully investigate it to find it was published in 1834! Just inside the front cover, the name Sarah J. Hawkins is written in ink in the fancy script common in historical documents. The pages are thin, delicate, so I carefully turn the first, which is blank, to find on the second a faded inscription: *Died on the 18th of May, Charles Samuel Hawkins, son of Isham K. Hawkins and Sarah, his wife. Aged 4 years and 2 months and 18 days.*

My heart seizes. Was this a gift to Sarah from her husband on the death of their little boy? Or did the couple simply choose to record their son's death in Sarah's pocket Bible? Either way, the gesture reminds me that loss is loss, and that it hurt someone just as much to lose a child in 1834 as it does now. I feel the heartbreak within the jagged handwriting.

This one comes with no note or anything else to tell me where it turned up or who sent it to the Lost and Found post office, but the act of holding the miniature Bible presses down on my heart in a way I can't escape. I set it on the floor next to me and cry a little. Which is ridiculous. I mean, a woman who hardly ever cries breaks down over a little boy who died almost two hundred years ago? Even Sarah and Isham are long gone, so many generations ago that their descendants wouldn't know them beyond just a name in their family tree at best. Yet still this seems like a treasure—a heartrending slice of someone's history—and certainly something that should never, ever go into the garbage. And the truth is, here in Lost Valley, without all the usual connections of the modern world, time seems . . . different, and for a brief moment it's not all that difficult to feel myself within Sarah's skin, suffering her pain, back in 1834.

As I wipe away tears, thinking what I really should have armed myself with was a box of tissues, now I know why I was so turned off by the idea of looking at this stuff. Maybe I've had enough loss of my own without having to carry other people's, too.

I get up, grab my can of pop, exit the room, find a box of Kleenex in the living room, and blow my nose. It's still raining.

As I stare out into the soggy gray day, Mabel's yard looking especially green and lush in contrast, it hits me that . . . without quite realizing it, I'm doing exactly what Mabel asked. She didn't ask me to find out where these things came from or to whom they belong—she asked me to care about them, to care about them as they were once cared for by the people who loved them.

Maybe not such a hard request after all.

Especially on a rainy day.

Even if it comes with a few tears.

Taking back up my soda and adding the tissue box, I return to the room I now officially think of as the lost and found. I could think of it as merely "the lost," but no—just like Mabel, I'm finding them. One by one, they're being found, at least by me.

CHAPTER 9

Those next June days are filled with rain and the finding of lost things. With not much better to do, I become consumed by the task. Turns out I'm still on a mission from Mabel.

Some of the items fall into categories—lost photo albums or framed pictures that seem meaningful, family Bibles, and jewelry (including more than one wedding ring). Whereas other things are more unique: the occasional trophy (one from 1957 for car racing and another from 1988 for some kind of international shooting match), a painting of a family home, another of a young woman in the 1950s, and an antique clock with personalization on the back.

Just as when I started this project, I don't want to care about these things, but I'm moved by them anyway. I'm moved by their journey as much as anything else—how they were once loved, and then someone cared enough to send them here, and Mabel cared enough to . . . turn them over to me. Even if unwittingly.

I'm not sure what to do about them or with them, more than anyone else whose hands they've passed through, but I still feel I'm doing my duty to Mabel by spending time with all the things, just digging and looking and thinking about the people who lost them.

Somehow, with each box or container I open, I see Mabel more clearly, too. There have been instances, surely, when I've wondered if she was a little dotty—finding her clouds, and at certain frustrating moments, like discovering I've been following a treasure map to the garage sitting right outside the door—but more and more, I can't deny a distinctive, quirky beauty in her, and oddly, I find myself missing her without ever having met her.

Probably a sign of spending too much time alone, but that's where I am.

Whereas upon my recent arrival here, a week of rain would have sounded like the seventh level of hell, instead those days take on a certain rhythm for me, the first sense of rhythm or balance I've experienced since I left Riverside Drive.

In between scouring the lost-and-found items, I keep an eye toward the sky, looking for breaks in the clouds. When they come, I grab up my ball cap and a raincoat—I didn't bring one but find a nice blue Lands' End jacket in Mabel's closet—and get in my daily walk. I recommit myself to them. They were easy to skip the first couple of days when I was so out of sorts, but no more.

I start checking the mail since I'm having mine forwarded, and given the weather, I take to checking Grace's, too, and just leaving it tucked inside her screen door. As it's starting to pour one day and I'm scurrying back across the road, I glance back to see her open the door and give me a wave as she yells through the screen, "Thank ya, hon!"

Sometimes it's dry enough on the back porch to sit outside with a cup of coffee and look out over the lake. I finish my Grisham book, but rather than start another right away, I find myself taking in the view instead. Suddenly everything seems greener, lusher. During those dry periods, I grow more aware of the bright-pink tufts on the mimosa trees, and I see some Queen Anne's lace and purple clover starting to bloom down near the water's edge. Sometimes when it's not raining, I hear frogs ribbiting all around the lake's perimeter.

One night I take the time to make a simple but tasty chicken casserole from one of Mabel's handwritten recipe cards, and since it's way too big, even with leftovers, I deliver some to Grace. She seems delighted, then holds up one finger. "Wait right here." She returns with a covered bowl of the "brown beans" she mentioned before and some cornbread in Tupperware. "Good rainy-day food," she informs me.

Turns out she's right. For something that looks so simple and bland, the beans provide several delicious meals, and when I run out of cornbread—which Grace instructed me to "sop up the juice with"—I discover plain white bread tastes delicious as a sopping tool as well.

I haven't seen the cowboy next door since the rain began. I confess to glancing toward his house at moments when I'm out, but his pickup truck is always gone. I even consider leaving some casserole on *his* porch, and have suffered the mild urge to tell him how deeply I've gotten into studying the lost and found—but I still don't want him to think I'm . . . attracted to him in any way. Since I'm not.

One night toward the end of the week, I sit down in Mabel's easy chair and pick up her phone to call Kevin.

"I'm so sorry I haven't kept in closer touch, honey," he tells me when he hears my voice. Though, honestly, that hasn't even occurred to me. I mean, maybe when I first arrived I was desperate for communication, and sure, I had that grand plan to harass him with every thought or question I was unable to google, but I guess exploring all the lost items has kept me busy enough that I've quit fretting over things like that. Yes, I still hunger for an internet connection, but by the same token, I seem to be getting by okay without one.

"The phone works both ways and I haven't called you, either," I absolve him. "And I know you're busy."

"Still, I meant to check in more. How are you?"

"I'm . . . okay." I say it with more contentment than despair. "And believe it or not, *I've* actually been busy, too."

"With what, pray tell?"

"Did your grandma ever tell you about the Lost and Found lost and found?"

"I have no idea what you're talking about."

Just as I suspected. So I tell him. About the instructions, about how it led me to meet Jo and Grace, about what I finally found and what Matt told me about it all.

"You're kidding," he says when I'm done. "That's wild."

I *don't* tell him I think his grandmother felt neglected by her family. That would be cruel. I just hope she knew she was loved.

"What are you going to do with it all?" he asks.

Again, as if there's something *to* do. Clearly every person who's mailed stuff here—some of the postmarks dating back to the 1970s, for heaven's sake—thought there was something to do with it, but I breezily reply, "Nothing. Just look through it and appreciate it a little."

Part of me is surprised by my new breeziness—but maybe these days of wading through the lost and found have brought me to the realization that we *all* lose things. Big things, small things. Jasmine lost her necklace. Sarah and Isham lost their son. For me, it's hair and my parents. Oh, and my respect for the WRTB station managers—since even if I *wasn't* quite ready, that's not why they want Tiffany at my desk right now. It's not that this notion makes me feel *better* about my own losses, but perhaps . . . less alone.

"How's life in Cincy?" I ask.

"Well, I've been spending more time with Patrick's grandma. She's a spunky lady. We've been having movie night twice a week—the three of us take turns picking. I even make popcorn. And okay, I confess I started this just trying to sort of . . . do my part, make sure Patrick knows I care—but turns out it's a nice way to spend time. With him *and* with Nana. And by the way, when you come back, we need a fourth for euchre. Nana loves to play euchre. So I'm enlisting you."

"I'm terrible at euchre," I remind him of my least-favorite card game.

"I know. We'll draw straws to see who's stuck with you on their team. And maybe with some regular play, you'll get better."

I laugh. Even if I don't enjoy euchre, it's nice to feel valued. "All right, I'll play. And that's so nice about Nana, Kev—I'm glad to hear it."

Then I ask, "How's work?" It's the topic we're probably both avoiding, so I make the split decision not to.

"Fine. Busy," he says. "If you're wondering about Tiffany . . ."

"I am. There, I said it. And I can handle the answer, whatever it is."

He hesitates before replying, "Nothing much has changed. I still see her as someone who's doing fine but not as good as you, and no one is saying much about the situation."

So maybe they really *are* just waiting for my hair to grow? Not ousting me altogether, as I sometimes begin to fear? Maybe it really is just about letting the summer pass?

"Buuuuut . . ." he goes on, his tone planting an additional seed of hope in my heart.

"But what?"

"She mispronounced 'goetta' on the air the other night," he tells me, giddy as a little kid.

I sit up straighter in my chair. "Really?"

Pronounced "getta"—the *o* is silent—it's an only-in-Cincinnati German concoction of meats, spices, oats, and a few other things boiled together. Sometimes it's a breakfast food; other times it's served in a sandwich or as a burger topping. I wasn't sure how to say it, either, when I was new to the area, but I made it a point to find out before I had to report on the city's annual Goettafest.

"Yeah, and it wasn't a surprise to her," he says. "Not a filler piece stuffed in at the last minute. It was in her script, which apparently she didn't bother looking over before airtime. Rob even corrected her with live cameras rolling."

"Wow," I say. Rob, like me, has been in the business for twenty years and, also like me, doesn't like his newscast to come off as incompetent. And it's not that he or I have never made a mistake, but fortunately it's been pretty rare. "What happened then?"

"Well, she tried to laugh it off—they both did—and she was like, 'The secret's out—I'm new here,' but it was awkward, and she looked uncomfortable, both about the flub and being corrected on-air. Afterward—"

I'm so enthralled, I cut him off to say, "There was an afterward?"

"Yeah, Rob confronted her during the break. Told her, 'The script isn't just a backup for the teleprompter. It's so you know what you'll be reading and make sure you get it right.'"

"Yikes," I say, ever so glad not to be involved in that kind of high-level drama.

"To her credit, Tiffany fell on her sword and apologized, saying it wouldn't happen again. But she was rough for the rest of the show and even a little dicey the following night, too."

Thinking through that, I almost feel bad for her, but . . . "It's not that I wish Tiffany ill, so . . . is it wrong that I'm kind of happy she messed up?"

"Under all the circumstances, nah."

And indeed, my job feels a little safer than it did just an hour ago. Tiffany really *is* just a fill-in. Who happens to look prettier than me right now, which apparently counts for a lot. But my hair will get longer and life will get back to normal *then*.

"You sound . . . better," he says. "Happier than when we last talked. Even before I told you about Tiffany."

"Hold up there now, speedy. 'Happier' might be taking things too far. But . . . I guess I am. Better. At least a little. I don't know why." Then I venture cautiously, "Um, by the way, how's the diet?"

He laughs and says, "I'm starting tomorrow."

When the rain finally ends nearly a week after it started, the sun comes out, white fluffy clouds recommence floating across a blue sky, and it feels a little like Lost Valley has just emerged from a dark cave back out into the light. People come outside.

I see Jo playing with a happy-looking Socks in the distance across the lake, and I spot Conrad heading out into the vines in rubber rain boots, which I suspect in this case are mud boots. Grace is sitting on her front porch when I take her the mail, so I compliment the brown beans, and she again offers to make me some for dinner at her place. I even see one of the neighbors from farther up the lane, a young mom out pulling a toddler in a wagon, and we introduce ourselves.

Me, I'm inspecting the petunias and just generally soaking up the sun. Well, under my sun hat, that is. Safety first for us radiation patients. But it's still nice to be outside. I even find an old broom in the garage, now that it's unlocked, and sweep the front porch to remove twigs and debris left behind by the wind. The weeds in the flower bed have gotten bigger, and while this is no showplace, they don't help. Shouldn't the cowboy next door be taking care of stuff like that along with the rest of the upkeep?

"Haven't seen you out and about much lately."

Think of the devil. For once, however, I don't flinch at the sound of Matthew Cordray's voice. I just look up to find him crossing the yard toward me, his trusty Yorkie trotting along at his heels. Today he's in shorts and a maroon Eastern Kentucky University tee. He needs to shave. And he's got the dumb hat on, too, but I try not to hold that against him.

"It's been raining. And I've been busy," I tell him, halting my broom.

"With lost-and-found things?"

"No, just lost ones," I say, feeling clever.

"Nah, somebody found 'em—now you're findin' 'em, too."

This leads me to confess, "You're right. I've had the same thought myself."

"Anything interesting?"

As recently as a week ago, I would probably be glib and sarcastic, critical toward people who can't manage to hold on to their photo albums and family Bibles—but I again let go of my tendency to act above-it-all with him, answering, "Yes, actually. It's turned out to be a . . . rather amazing collection of what matters to people."

He slants me a soft smile that reaches his eyes, which I would be able to see better if he'd lose the stupid hat. "Mabel would be pleased."

I find myself laughing good-naturedly as it hits me for the first time: "I like how you shove all the responsibility of caring about this junk onto me, guilting me into it, when you could just as easily be the one to go through it all."

He shrugs. "I have a job, responsibilities, a town to protect, a dog to parent."

I give a playfully dismissive shake of my head, even if I think he's kind of funny, and whereas I once wondered if he was laughing at me or with me, I now realize he's okay with laughing at himself, too.

"Well, I wouldn't want to deprive your dog of quality time with you," I tell him, "so I'll just be over here in the lost-and-found salt mines, working away to make Mabel happy."

Now he laughs, too—before saying, "I wouldn't mind seein' some of it. I mean, anything you think is worth showin' me."

I roll my eyes, but only teasingly. "So what you're telling me is I can keep doing the grunt work, and you can reap the rewards of seeing the good stuff."

"Somethin' like that," he admits.

"So how did Junior and the post office gang react to the news that the lost and found had been found?"

He holds up one finger. "Wait right here and I'll show ya."

I resume my sweeping as he and his dog return to the farmhouse. A minute later he comes back with what appears to be a newspaper and steps up onto the porch, handing it to me.

I glance down to see a header for the *Lost and Found Chronicle*. "You still read newspapers here?" I ask. I know they're still around, but I can't remember the last time I actually saw one.

"How else would we get the local news?" he replies in all seriousness.

"Oh yeah, I keep forgetting. It's still the Dark Ages in this town."

He reaches over to point at the top headline: Postmaster Barnett Vindicated in Disappearance of Lost Items. I skim the article, which gives a history and timeline of the lost-and-found collection, including the accusation after it went missing. My eyes quickly reach the last paragraph.

> *The missing items have been found on the premises of the late Mabel Callahan, though no explanation has been forthcoming as to how they got there. Mr. Barnett says he plans to let bygones be bygones and proceed with his plans for an office now that this unfortunate incident has been settled and his name cleared. "I bear no ill will to my accusers," Barnett said on Thursday.*

"That last part's a lie," Matt informs me with one arched brow.

Meeting his gaze, I remark, "I haven't seen you out and about, either." Ugh, why did I do that? It implies I was paying attention, maybe even looking, when I wasn't.

"One of my deputies was on vacation for a few days. Had me pullin' doubles."

"Wow, that must be hard, eating twice the doughnuts." Okay, apparently my sarcasm was only taking a short break.

He replies with, "Hey now—that's uncalled for. We don't eat doughnuts on the job in my department. Because we'd have to drive all the way to Hazard to get one."

There he goes, laughing at himself again. It strikes me maybe I should try to do that myself more often. Though I'm not sure I even know how. I find myself asking him, "What do cops snack on here then?"

"You can get a pretty decent soft serve at the Last Chance Café. They'll even dip it in chocolate if ya ask nice."

"I probably won't get that lucky," I tell him. "I don't think the waitress there likes me."

"Joy Lynn?" he asks with a small grin. "Don't take it personally. She doesn't like much of anybody."

"Then how do you get *your* cone dipped in chocolate?"

He shrugs. "Me she likes." Then he winks and walks away, Goldie the Yorkie following.

And my head's kind of swirling. I'm still holding his newspaper. And did I just use a dipped cone as an unintentional metaphor for his penis? Did he hear it that way, too? Please God, no. And is he telling me he has a thing with Joy Lynn? And why do I care? I mean, I don't. In fact, I should be glad if that's true because it indicates I've been misreading all his grins and winks and he's not flirting with me at all. Which is what I want, right?

Absolutely right. Because I have no hair and I feel ugly and any sort of flirtation still seems to me like it's just awkward and perhaps accompanied by pity. Plus he wears that stupid hat. Even with shorts, for heaven's sake. What kind of cowboy wears shorts?

CHAPTER 10

To my surprise, I'm actually grateful for all that rain. Oddly enough, it seemed to help me find myself here, figure out how to spend my time. Okay, yes, all the lost stuff did that, too, but without the rain, I might have just kept avoiding the lost and found.

And now that the rain is done, my days take on an even better rhythm. For the first time in my adulthood, I discover that I'm okay without a schedule. I mean, a newsperson lives and dies by schedules. I can't remember a time when I didn't have my planner constantly in motion, when there wasn't always someplace to be. Some of those places were fun, by choice—but there was always the next broadcast, and the next event, and other aspects of life were just squeezed in around the obligations. Now my days are filled with activities based largely on the weather or my mood.

I take my walk every day. I usually read awhile. I tend to my flowers. And sometimes I take pictures with my phone. I've found a use for it here at last!

I'm not sure why I'm taking them, but perhaps I'm seeing things here I didn't at first—things I think other people might find interesting. Maybe it makes me look harder, too. I've taken photos of Grace's wall of signs and Matt's one-eyed chicken. I've captured sunsets and grapevines. The other day I spotted a praying mantis on a daylily in Matt's side yard, and what would normally have me saying "Eek!" instead had me reaching for my camera. Turns out that when you start *looking* for interesting things, you often find them.

I spend at least a couple of hours a day with the lost and found, usually in the late afternoon, when it's hottest outside. Some evenings, I make phone calls to Sydney or Kevin, or I go over to the winery and have a glass or two with Jo and Conrad. Other nights I just keep to myself, sitting outside watching squirrels play—there are several of them running around Mabel's yard—or taking in the sunset.

Sydney says I've suddenly gotten very Zen when I give her the deets on any average day. Whereas Kevin just sounds happily surprised. I don't blame him—it's his fault I'm here, so naturally he feels less guilty if I seem marginally content.

I'm as shocked as anyone that I'm coming to appreciate this level of alone time and adjusting to such an unstructured existence. Thing being, I couldn't do this forever. This is me accepting my situation a little more gracefully. This is me waiting. This is me doing what Kevin wanted me to do: go away for the summer and heal. I'm beginning to accept that maybe there *was* more healing I needed to do. And I wouldn't say I'm suddenly *enjoying* my time here—only that I'm learning how to make peace with it until it's over.

I'm thinking through all this as I drive into Lost and Found for the first time in a while. I've changed out my usual ball cap or sun hat for the fedora and my usual tank top for a flowy summery top that protects my scars and chest from the sun. Yeah, some days I'm all Zen and praying mantis pictures and others I'm still concentrating on which hat to wear.

This hat-wearing me, this scar-covering me, this barely-there-hair me—she's still different than the me I've always been. I know I'm still the same person, of course, but it's the mirror that continues to trip me up in that way. This me isn't a monster or anything, but she's also not Jessica Fox, WRTB 11. Some moments, I'm not sure *who* she is, or what she's about. And just like everything else about this summer, even while I'm getting okay with this version of me for the time being, I'm also waiting for the old me to come back.

Still, as I twist and turn my way into town, I consider the story in the newspaper Matt showed me, recognizing that there was a time when I would have wanted to see my *name* as part of that—if not my face as well, back when I had hair. There was a time I would have thought it mattered that WRTB anchor Jessica Fox was the one who discovered the lost items at Mabel Callahan's house. And yet, right now, I'm actually pleased that all this transpired without any mention of me, or even of some stranger staying at Mabel's house. I'm okay without getting that attention.

In fact, the thought reminds me that I've practically forgotten all about my social media. Those acknowledgments—that I matter, that I'm entertaining, that people care about the things I do—used to feed me. And suddenly, they don't. Changing one's activities can change the way one's mind works, I suppose.

Off the grid or not, though, I should make my way to the Piggly Wiggly while I'm out and let people know I'm still alive. But my first stop in Lost and Found: Freeman's Market.

"Well, hello there!" Mr. Freeman greets me in a deep baritone. "How's our summer resident today?"

"Doing just fine, thanks," I say with a smile. I'm pleased he instantly remembers me—but then again, the fedora is probably pretty memorable in this otherwise fedora-free town.

I pick up bread, eggs, and soft drinks, as well as a small head of lettuce—deciding one can't *always* buy their salad in a bag, unless they're willing to drive an hour for it, and I'm not right now. As I check out, I also take a couple more of his tomatoes, again proudly displayed in a row on his windowsill. I inform him, "I think I've saved the petunias—they're all looking healthier."

"That's good to hear," he says with an approving nod.

When he offers to help carry my stuff to the car, I almost decline—because I'm perfectly capable—but the twenty-four pack of pop is heavy, and I don't want to crush my bread or tomatoes trying to lug it all. So after a slight hesitation, I gratefully accept.

As we're closing the back hatch of the SUV, I notice some of the same yellow daylilies by the store's front porch as are planted alongside Mabel's back one. Spur of the moment, I say, "Mabel has some of those, but they seem like they're not doing well. I've been watering them—and of course there was all that rain—but they have hardly any flowers."

"Those are Stella d'Oros," he tells me. "They'll blossom all summer long, but ya gotta get rid of the spent blooms. Come here and I'll show ya."

He leads me to a clump of the bright-yellow flowers and explains how to distinguish between an old bloom and a new one—and they do look similar until you know the difference. "You snap it off right here, below this little green part—see?" He breaks off a dead bloom while I watch, nod. "And the blooms only last a day, so it takes some stayin' on top of it, but each one you remove makes it more likely new ones'll take its place. Oh, and ya gotta get rid of them seed pods, too." He points out a light-green blob at the top of a stem where you'd normally see a bud. "That's the whole thing we're tryin' to avoid—lettin' 'em go to seed. Keep 'em from goin' to seed, ya get flowers right up into fall."

I thank him for the lesson and hope it's not already too late.

My next stop was going to be the Piggly Wiggly, but first I decide to step into the Last Chance Café for lunch. For someone who used to eat out almost daily, the least I can do is treat myself to lunch in the only restaurant in town.

Today, two of the six booths are taken, and three counter stools—it's the lunch rush in Lost and Found, and I'm happy to see there *is* one, small though it may be. My fedora and I draw the usual brief stares as I take a booth near the back. As before, music from a bygone era fills the air—I think it might be Johnny Mathis.

As Joy Lynn approaches, I remember my conversation with Matt. He knew exactly who I meant when I mentioned the waitress, so I'm guessing Joy Lynn is here a lot—maybe she's the sole waitress the Last

Chance requires. "Know what ya want?" she asks without bothering to look at me.

Menu in hand, I order the chicken salad and a sweet tea.

"Be right out," she says, voice wooden, just before calling to another customer in an entirely different, much nicer tone, "Marv, sweetie, I'll get ya a refill in a jiff, all righty?"

Okay, I'm not imagining it—she really dislikes me.

Fortunately, the chicken salad is quite good, which helps make up—a little—for the rude service.

By the time I'm done, only two old men remain, drinking coffee at the counter. When Joy Lynn slaps my bill down on the table and starts to walk away, I say, "Wait."

She turns back with a glare that suggests I'm extremely demanding.

"Could I get an ice cream cone?" I'm not sure why I suddenly do this—my lack of ice cream Fridays with Sydney? Or am I seeking a way to bring up Matt to her? Perish the thought. But then I hear myself add, "Matt told me you had good soft serve here." Okay, apparently he is indeed the reason. Though why I care what his relationship is with this unpleasant woman, I have no idea.

"*Matt* told you that, did he?" She sounds like a mean girl in high school who just found out I've been talking to her boyfriend.

"Yes," I say, still trying to sound pleasant. "He lives next door to me." By which I mean: *Not trying to steal your man, lady—just having neighborly conversation and now trying to get a cone.*

"I know that," she snips.

"Oh?"

"Well, you said you're stayin' at Mabel's house, and I certainly know where Matt lives."

"Ah." She's a little scary. Thoughts flit through my mind. Like I hope they don't have sleepovers at his house—I don't need her scaring me at my own place, too. And that he can do better. I mean, yes, stupid hat, but this one's a piece of work. And she dresses badly. And has scraggly hair that doesn't seem well cared for. And maybe I shouldn't judge anyone's hairstyle right now, but Joy Lynn just really rubs me the wrong way.

A minute later she delivers my cone. I'm slightly afraid to eat it—in case she spit on it or sprinkled arsenic on top or something. "Tell Saint Matthew I said hello," she snidely demands.

I pull back slightly from the sheer venom in her voice. I didn't see this coming. "Saint Matthew?"

"Thinks he's the savior of Lost and Found," she informs me.

I don't reply, utterly thrown. Matthew Cordray thinks he's the town savior? I mean, I know I'm very critical of his hat—and have been annoyed by the way he just pops up when I least expect him—but laid-back Matt is the last man I would expect to have a savior complex.

Nonetheless, it doesn't sound like she likes him as much as he thinks. Maybe they *had* a thing and it ended.

Lot to take in here, but the main thing I experience is . . . a little relief. That they're not a couple. I'm not sure why. But I chalk it up to the fact that she's not a very nice person and, despite my criticisms, Matt seems like an okay guy. Maybe even a nice one. And I also feel less apt to get beat up by her for talking to him. Maybe.

I cautiously eat my cone after she walks away, relieved when I don't suddenly keel over. The Last Chance Café seems like a horrible—and ironic—place to bite the dust. Soon enough, the two men at the counter finish their coffee, pay their bill, and leave—and then I hear Joy Lynn on the phone, saying quietly, but not quietly enough, "I know it's past due, Charlie. Toby's tryin' to get a summer job and help out, but he ain't found one so far . . . Yeah, I know a boy his age shouldn't have to help pay the bills, but what am I supposed to do? . . . You know Bobby left us with nothin'."

Hearing even just one side of the conversation steals my breath. I have no idea what her life is like, but if I were her, maybe I'd be mean, too. Five minutes after being angry at her, it dissolves into feeling sorry for her. I find myself leaving her a big tip, nearly as big as the bill itself. Just call me Saint Jessica.

Before leaving, I walk to the jukebox and peek at some of the songs. They're *all* from the fifties—which explains a lot. And then I realize this jukebox might indeed be that old itself, crazy as it seems, and that maybe no one has changed out the songs since they were new. Maybe they're afraid if they bother it too much, it won't work anymore.

I've pulled a coin from my purse and had thought I might play a song I like, but I don't know fifties music well and don't care to scour the whole song list. So, on a lark, I call, "Hey, Joy Lynn—do you have a favorite song on this thing?"

As soon as the words leave me, I fear I'm about to be verbally attacked, so I brace myself—until she tilts her head from behind the counter, looking surprised to be asked what she likes, and quietly says, "L7."

I drop in my coin, press in L7. Elvis Presley begins singing "Loving You" as I walk out the door.

At the Piggly Wiggly lot, I sit in my car preparing a social media post with several pictures—of my thriving petunias, of Mr. Freeman holding up a tomato, of Grace's signs, of a beautiful pink sunset over the winery. The caption: *Having a quiet summer in a place where life moves a little slower. By the way, if you ever stumble across a little town called Lost and Found, Kentucky, find your way to the Lost Valley Vineyards for some fabulous vino.*

Getting out of the car, I hold up my phone, locate the signal, and hit the button to post it. Once you know where the signal is, connecting isn't hard.

As I start to get back in and head home, something stops me. It's warm but not hot today—the air feels more fresh than summer humid. I don't know how long ago the Piggly Wiggly closed, but a look around reveals signs of nature trying to reclaim the land: low trees billowing around each end of the building with boughs easing their way up under the store's awning, bigger trees in parking lot islands looking too large for their space, bits of grass and weeds poking up through the many cracks in the asphalt.

But then a monarch butterfly flutters past, making its way across the lot, and I hear the sounds of nature all around me—noises I can't identify, maybe insects in trees? Whatever it is, it's loud and sort of jungly. On all sides of the store rest steep, mountainous slopes covered with thick foliage and, up above, blue sky dotted with white clouds reminiscent of Mabel's bedroom. Much to my surprise, suddenly even the abandoned Piggly Wiggly doesn't seem like such a bad place.

I must be losing my mind.

A little while later at home, after putting my few groceries away, I change out my fedora for my sun hat and use the pleasant temps to work on Mabel's daylilies. Turns out that looking for the old blooms and quietly snapping them off is weirdly relaxing. After that, I try to clean up around them in general, pulling away dead undergrowth and weeds. Maybe I'll get a couple of bags of mulch the next time I'm in Hazard to tidy it up completely.

When I'm done, standing back to look at my handiwork, I suddenly flinch, blink. What is happening here? Am I becoming . . . a gardener?

My mother enjoyed flower gardening, but I never developed an interest, and frankly, it always seemed fairly boring to me. I mean, I like pretty flowers, but not the work it takes to make them happen. Hence my appreciation of neighbor Nancy. Now, standing here in a flowy garment and a sun hat, holding a gardening trowel, I realize I've *become* neighbor Nancy.

It's a strange observation, considering I've already spent part of the day not knowing who I am anymore. And—oh my God. I didn't even look at my social media earlier when I had the chance! I just posted, then turned off the phone and started staring at trees! I'd actually been looking forward to taking the time to catch up on comments on my last post, but it totally slipped my mind. This thing that used to be an integral part of my day, something I valued, totally disappeared from my thoughts.

"Who *are* you?" I whisper to myself.

"Talkin' to yourself, darlin'?"

I gasp, jump a little. Then turn to see my usual source of alarm. He's in his police uniform and I'm guessing he just got off work.

He doesn't wait for me to answer, instead asking, "You doin' anything later?"

My first instinct is to say yes, but what on earth could I possibly be doing? "Um, not really." Crap. I could have said I was going to have wine with Jo and Conrad—the one actual evening activity I have enjoyed since arriving here—but too late now.

"I was thinkin' you could show me some of the lost stuff. If ya want."

I've been wondering when that would come back up, but since it hadn't, I'd decided maybe it wouldn't. I guess it's no big deal to show him some of it, though. Mabel would like that, I'm sure. I feel like every person who sees any of it would go a little further to fulfilling Mabel's wishes. "All right," I say. "After dinner? Seven? Eight?"

"Or I could cook us *both* up some dinner on Mabel's grill."

I've been vaguely aware that a gas grill sits tucked away beneath an old plastic cover near the back porch. And again, I can't think of a good reason to say no. "What would you grill?" I ask instead.

He pulls back slightly, clearly surprised I'm even considering the offer. "Burgers? Corn on the cob? I just picked up a few ears from Mert Dwyer's stand the other day."

"Corn on the cob can be grilled?" I ask, surprised.

He shakes his head in mock derision. "City girl."

"Still guilty as charged," I confess.

"Grill 'em right in the shucks. Best you've ever tasted."

"We'll see," I challenge him. But then I add, "I got some fresh tomatoes from Mr. Freeman today. I'll slice one for the burgers, and maybe make a small salad."

"Sounds good," he says. "I'll be back over in an hour to get the grill goin'." Then he turns to walk away.

I have no idea why I stop him with, "I got soft serve today at the Last Chance."

He stops, looks back. "Chocolate dipped?"

I shake my head. "I was afraid that would be one request too many. Speaking of which, I don't think Joy Lynn likes you as much as you think she does."

He shrugs easily. "It comes and goes with her moods," he tells me, then saunters away, leaving me to think: *Typical man. Doesn't even care about Joy Lynn's reactions or feelings.*

Maybe whatever the two of them have is something that, like he just said, comes and goes. Maybe that's what he likes: a convenient, casual sex partner. I'm not personally opposed to that, yet the thought instantly makes me feel kind of yucky for reasons I don't understand, so I don't examine it too closely. I don't want to dislike him anymore. And I don't want to feel any sorrier for *her*. And I *certainly* don't want to become embroiled in either of their sex lives. It's none of my business—he's just my neighbor, and maybe getting a little closer to being something like a friend.

Who's suddenly coming over for dinner. How did *that* happen?

CHAPTER 11

I've moved the petunias off the little table on the back porch and set it with coral-colored place mats I found in a hutch and two of Mabel's flowered plates, along with condiments, burger toppings, and a small salad with tongs from Mabel's drawer. When Matt squeezes the platter of grilled food in between it all and takes a seat across from me, the table feels even tinier and I find myself turning to the side to make sure our knees don't bump underneath.

"This is . . . cozy," he says, also clearly aware of the table's smallness. I can't really see his eyes for the worn cowboy hat, but something in his tone makes me think that even he finds it a little too close for comfort, and for the first time with him, I feel less alone in my awkwardness.

As I assemble my burger, I'm seeking a source of conversation, and my eyes fall to an electronic device on his belt. "What's that for?" I point with my fork.

"Pager," he says. "In case of a police emergency."

"Wow," I reply, shocked anew by the lack of up-to-date technology here.

"I know, I know—Dark Ages. But it works well in mountainous areas. And fortunately, it doesn't go off much."

"Not a lot of high crime in Lost and Found?"

He peeks up at me from beneath the brim of his hat as I start shucking my corn—which I must admit looks and smells delicious. "Nope, it's a pretty low-pressure job. Won't make out like it's not."

"So what kind of hoops does one have to jump through to rise to that position in a bustling metropolis like Lost and Found?" I ask as I butter my corn.

He tilts his head to say, "The biggest hoop of all around here—agreein' to take the job. In my case, that hoop was kinda on fire, so guess I jumped through to put out the flames."

"On fire how?" I'm surprisingly intrigued.

He casts a small smile across the table as he piles some salad onto his plate and reaches for the dressing. "Well, you might've noticed that our little town isn't exactly . . . thrivin'."

"Um, you can say that again."

"The more stuff that shuts down, the more folks move away. Can't blame 'em—gotta have jobs, gotta have food. But the more things that close up, the closer we get to losin' other things, too. When Big Willie Kane retired as police chief about eight years ago, they couldn't get anybody to take the job. And if you can't support a police force, it gets absorbed by the nearest town that can. For some little towns, it's one of the final death knells. You lose your police, then you lose your post office, then you lose your town government altogether, then your town completely disappears and gets swallowed up by the mountains.

"And I don't know—maybe to an outsider it doesn't seem like there's much worth savin', but I grew up here, right in that house." He uses his butter knife to point at the white farmhouse where he still resides. "So guess it's different for me—felt worth holdin' on to. I came home and took the job."

At this, my eyebrows shoot up. "Came home from where? You haven't always lived here?"

He chuckles as he answers, "Hell no, I haven't always lived here. I was rarin' to leave when I was growin' up. Got my degree in police studies with a minor in criminal justice at Eastern, then got a job on the force in Lexington. And truth is—I'd have gladly moved *farther* away, but the opportunity there came and I took it."

I'm agog as I bite into my corn on the cob. He's college educated.

But the corn totally steals his attention when I least expect it, spurring him to say, "Now you tell me that's not the best, sweetest corn you ever sank your teeth into."

My mind is on other things besides corn, yet . . . "Okay, I can't. It's delicious."

He nods with as much pride as if he grew it himself.

"And then what happened?" I ask, wanting to get back to the subject of . . . him. "In Lexington."

"Well, about five years into the job, I met a girl, got married, had a baby, all that stuff." He's chomping away on his burger now and tossing this out between bites like it's just your common everyday run-of-the-mill information.

"Oh," I say, taken aback. In ever so many ways. Is it really possible he has a wife? Where does she fit into this picture with Joy Lynn? And there's a child, too? My head might explode.

"And we were happy," he says. "Things were great."

Okay, "were." Past tense. But this still sounds like a much more complex life than I anticipated Matthew Cordray having. "Until . . . ?" I venture cautiously.

"Until my mom got sick. My dad had already passed away, not long after we had Samantha—she's fourteen now. He died of black lung from workin' in the coal mines. Hell, that alone was reason enough to get outta here—uncles, cousins, both my grandpas, all ended up in the mines and most didn't live to be very old, much as big coal still doesn't wanna talk about that. But as I say, my mom got sick—she was diagnosed with a brain tumor about five years after Dad passed. So I took a leave of absence from work and came home to care for her while she was dying."

I'm suddenly finding it hard to breathe normally. The part about his dad is awful—I've always heard of black lung, but didn't know it was a thing that still existed—yet the part about his mom is even worse. And he's just . . . saying it, telling me this like he really knows me, like we're more than just casual acquaintances, like it's easy to talk about. When I can't even tell Kevin and Sydney how much they mean to me.

"I'm so sorry," I manage to get out.

He looks up from his food and says, "Whoops—didn't mean to ruin the meal. It sucked, but it was a long time ago, and it's how life goes sometimes."

"Still, I know that kind of thing is hard." Understatement of the century.

"Yep. But no need to dwell on it. It's just how I came to be at home when Willie announced he was hangin' up his holster and they couldn't find anybody to take his place. What timing, huh? Hadn't been back much other than holidays in fifteen years until then, and suddenly Lost and Found needs a police chief or the whole place is gonna crumble."

"So you stayed. Gave up your life in Lexington? That easy?"

He looks up from under that dirty brim. "Easy? Nope. Hardest damn thing I've gone through, even harder than Mom dyin' the way she did."

"What happened?" I almost don't want to know because this has all gotten so heavy and I'm wondering what else is as hard as nursing a parent to their death. But I'm still waiting to hear about the wife.

"I thought it over long and hard, about the job," he says. "Didn't make the decision lightly. I have other family here, too—people who, frankly, need some lookin' after sometimes. And I didn't exactly want that to be my responsibility, but once Mom and Dad were gone, I felt like . . . it was what they'd want me to do. So I talked to Kristin, my wife, and told her I wanted to accept the job offer, move our family here, and build a quieter life in the country. She agreed, and I took the job. And shortly after that is when I found out . . ."

"What?" I admit I'm on the edge of my seat here, barely able to eat.

"That she had a boyfriend."

My jaw drops. I nearly drop my burger along with it but manage to keep it in my grip.

"Apparently the three months it took my mother to die was three months too long to leave my wife alone."

"Wow." Is that the wrong response? I'm not sure, so I move on with, "I'm so sorry, Matt."

"I won't lie—it sucked the life outta me. I mean, if she'd said she didn't want me to take the job, I wouldn't have. But since she didn't . . . well, Lost and Found seemed like a good enough place to lick my wounds, so I kept the job, just not my marriage."

"What about your daughter?" I ask.

And this is the first time I've ever seen Matthew Cordray look truly sad. "That was the roughest part. We share custody, with the plan that Sam would come down on weekends and for the summer. For all her faults, Kristin's never been unreasonable or tried to keep me from bein' part of Samantha's life. She got remarried, and her husband, Vince, is a good stepdad. So it's been as amiable as such a situation can be. But it's just not the same, ya know?"

I nod, as if I know, even though I don't. But I can imagine.

"You have a kid and you think—assume—you're gonna be in that kid's life every day, and them in yours, until they grow up, that you're gonna get to do all the normal dad stuff and have a normal dad life. And then—kaboom—that's gone."

"But she comes on the weekends and in summer?" I ask. I tilt my head, the whole sun hat tilting with it. "Because I haven't, um, seen . . ."

"Yeah, that's the other sucky part," he tells me. "She's gettin' older. So when there's stuff at home—*her* home in Lexington—that she wants to do on weekends, am I gonna keep her from it? No. She's always sweet as hell about it, sayin', 'I was invited to a swim party this weekend, but I'd rather come see you.' And I know that's not true, because it's hard for a dad to compete with an in-ground pool and a party with boys, so I tell her she should skip this weekend and go. And it's fine. But the older she gets, the more weekends we skip.

"And then in May she was offered a trip to Florida all summer with her best friend, stayin' at the friend's grandma's, and was I gonna say no?

I mean, hell, it's a teenager's dream—*I'd* like to go stay on the beach all summer, too." He's grinning softly now.

But I still say, "You miss her, though."

"Of course. Summer's our time. We grill out. We get ice cream. We go to baseball games in Hazard. We take day trips to Gatlinburg or Mammoth Cave—we usually go to Myrtle Beach for a week every July. Just not this year." He pauses, trying to look like it doesn't matter. "But she calls me every few days and promises she's takin' tons of pictures to show me come fall. And she's a great kid. Couldn't ask for better."

"It's nice that you've stayed close with her despite the obstacles."

We go quiet for a moment then, eating, and I'm suddenly bitten with the awareness that despite that hat and his country drawl, Matt Cordray isn't quite the bumpkin I originally thought.

"Can I ask you somethin'?"

I look up from taking the very last bite from my corn on the cob—which *is* truly amazing.

"Why are you here?" he asks. "At Mabel's. For the whole summer."

"You mean you don't know? Kevin didn't tell you?"

He shakes his head.

And I bite my lip, suddenly sheepish. I think I forgot to feel that way with him for a while, but without warning, here it is, back again. "Well, I'd guess it's obvious—I'm recovering from cancer."

He casts me a thoughtful look. "I suppose maybe I thought that, just because you always wear hats. Are you . . . okay? In remission?"

I swipe a napkin across my mouth as I nod. "Yes, I was lucky. Stage one breast cancer and it was caught early. I'm cancer-free."

"That's great," he says. "Really great. Though . . . I'm sure it was a tough thing to go through."

"It was," I answer simply, then drop my eyes. I don't care to talk about it. Not because of how hard it was, but because this is exactly what I don't want—to be thought of as a cancer patient, to have that be the main thing someone thinks about when they see me. Even though I know it's hard not to—I've been guilty of that with others myself, until I was suddenly the one wearing the hats, suddenly the one looking gaunt. The hard part is over—I just want it to *feel* truly over.

And the truth is, now I want to run away. I want to pull the plug, announce that dinner's over and we'll look at lost things some other time. I want to retreat into the house and be alone. Because from the very moment I met this man, something about him I can't pin down has made me . . . not want his pity, not want any kindness that stems from that, not want him to think I'm attracted to him at this moment when I feel so unattractive myself. And the further truth is that he's never made me feel *any* of those things; it's all been in my head, an irrational fear. But right now, I feel like we're getting too close to it, too close to pity, too close to how I look.

Yet, at the very same time, pride compels me to . . . stay. See this through. Not embarrass myself any further with him by making some excuse to cut things short.

I just need to change the subject, get back to a dynamic I find more workable. Apparently I find it much more acceptable for him to open up and spill his guts to me than for me to return the favor.

So I push back my chair and say, "I'm going to clean up a little, take some stuff inside."

He's still eating, but is quick to ask, "Need help?"

"No—keep eating, no rush. Finish your burger." I grab up my own plate and a couple of condiments, then head in before he can argue.

As I put dirty dishes in the sink, I think about what's next. I decide I could use a drink, so I pull out a chilled bottle of Lost Valley Summer Blush, a light, fruity blend I've been wanting to try. I was saving it for some pleasant evening when I felt like watching the sunset with a little wine, but I don't mind sharing, so I grab two stemmed glasses from Mabel's cabinet.

Only . . . wine with Matt. Is that a good idea? I know I just ate, but I should make sure it doesn't go to my head. So I start rummaging around the kitchen, peeking in the food cabinets and the fridge—until I spy the break-and-bake cookies he bought as a "staple" before I arrived.

Chocolate chip cookies and white wine? No idea how that works as a pairing in the fancy wine world, but it's good enough for me, and I'm betting the police chief won't complain, either. I turn on the oven.

"You don't seem to dislike me so much anymore."

Matt Cordray and I are sitting in the white wooden rockers, watching the sinking sun paint purple neon streaks across the sky while we drink wine and eat cookies—indeed, he got right on board with my on-the-fly dessert—when he tosses that out with a knowing grin.

"I never disliked you," I claim.

"Coulda fooled me."

"Okay, I disliked things *about* you," I confess. It would be silly to pretend I haven't been pretty rude and dismissive to him until just recently.

He's still casting me a sideways grin when he asks, "Where'd I go wrong, pray tell?"

I think it over. "You called me darlin'."

"Well now, that's just how I talk . . . darlin'. May not be very PC, but if it makes ya feel any better, I call my daughter darlin', too, and sometimes the dog—if she's lookin' especially cute." He ends with his usual wink. Which I ignore, trying not to think *he's* cute.

Best to continue with his offenses. "You also called me Jessie," I say.

He looks more perplexed by that one. "No one ever has? I mean, that just seemed like a normal thing to me."

"No," I lie. I don't know *why* I bother to lie about it, but I do.

"So that's it?" he asks. "Those are my big sins?"

I realize they're weak arguments, so I go on. "They're enough to rub a person the wrong way. And then there's that hat." I gesture toward it with the cookie currently in my hand.

He appears surprised, mildly offended. "What's wrong with it?"

I just blink. This should not be a question that needs asking. "It's horrible," I tell him. "It's dirty. It's tattered and worn. It ought to be in the garbage."

"I've been wearin' it since high school," he announces.

"That explains a lot," I say. "And kind of makes my point for me."

"I won it at the county fair."

"That also explains a lot. I'm not sure county fair prizes are known for their high quality."

He shrugs in a way that almost makes me think he sees my logic before adding, "It's kinda part of who I am."

I don't hesitate to suggest, "Well, maybe it should be part of who you *were*. Maybe it can . . . hang on a coatrack or something where you can just remember it fondly. I can't even see your eyes half the time when you're wearing it. And you look much better without it."

"Hmm." He pushes out his lower lip as he takes this in, then turns to me with another classic Matt Cordray grin. "So you notice how I look, huh?"

Oh boy. I sigh. *Head this off at the pass.* "I'm simply saying I like to see the person I'm talking to, and when you wear that thing, I feel like I'm talking to a big, ugly hat. That's all."

He only laughs, takes a healthy sip of his wine, and says, "You're one to talk there, darlin'. Jessie. Jessica." It seems like he can't remember exactly *what* he's supposed to call me and hopes to figure it out by trying them all on for size.

But I'm much more stuck on the first part of what he said. "What do you mean, I'm one to talk?"

"You don't need that hat, girl."

Okay, the honest truth is that I totally forgot I've been wearing my sun hat this whole time. Maybe I would've been less openly critical of *his* headwear if I'd remembered, and maybe I should be addressing what he's really saying, which I'm pretty sure is about my lack of hair. But be all that as it may, I simply reply, "I do, actually. I have to protect my head and chest from the sun right now."

"Darlin'," he says softly, pointedly, leaning a little closer, "it's dark out."

I blow out a breath. The sun is indeed gone for the day and has left behind a deep-purple dusk that seems to have snuck up quickly.

A bolder woman would perhaps just take off the hat. It seems sillier to wear a big floppy sun hat in the dark than any other headwear I can think of. I may as well be sporting a Mexican sombrero for all the sense it makes. So the fact that I am in no way willing to remove my hat forces me to be more honest than I'd like. I choose my words with care . . . but also with utter honesty.

"I used to have a lot of hair," I tell him. "And I'm not yet comfortable with the way I look without it." My stomach plummets unexpectedly at the last part. It was a big thing to admit to a man with whom I like to feel in control. Maybe the wine has made my lips a bit looser than they would have been an hour ago.

"You should be," he says without missing a beat. "You're a beautiful woman. Trust me—you don't need the hat."

I take that in, feeling the words settle in my solar plexus. I suffer the same fast little barrage of questions that commonly come over a woman when she's told she's beautiful by a man she doesn't know well. Is it real? Sincere? Or manipulation? Does he want something? Or is it both?

There's one last question flitting about my mind, and I let this one leak out. "Are you flirting with me, Police Chief Cordray?"

A slight head tilt, a familiar hint of a grin. "What if I was?"

"Then I'd say you were barking up the wrong tree," I inform him, my voice pleasant but firm.

He goes quiet for a few seconds before replying, "Well then, guess it's lucky for me I wasn't. I was just tellin' it like it is since I figured you should know."

I feel kind of put in my place. Though maybe he's lying about the not flirting. Wine can make it so hard to tell. So can not knowing a person very well. I don't quite know what to make of him in this moment.

So I stay quiet and instead absorb the heart of the message—him saying I should feel comfortable about my hair, that he doesn't think I need the hat. It's a nice thing to say. But . . . wouldn't anyone say that? To make me feel better about what I've lost?

I respond by doing what I did after dinner—deflecting. "More wine?" His glass is almost empty.

"Sure." He points through the window. "Inside? On the counter?"

It's hard not to like that he doesn't expect me to go get it, even though it's my house and I offered. "Yeah." I smile softly.

He comes back a minute later carrying the bottle and refills both our glasses without asking. I don't mind.

We don't speak, and I hear crickets and tree frogs making the summer night loud with life. But I feel the need to fill the space with words, perhaps not any more comfortable with him, at night, alone, than I am with my lack of hair. "I was thinking about blackberries," I tell him.

"It's the season for 'em," he replies easily.

"Mabel has a recipe for a blackberry cobbler I thought I might try, if I can find anyone selling them."

"Might be some around. Let me look into it and get back to ya."

"Thanks," I say.

We stay quiet a moment longer before he asks, "Would you let me see you without your hat?"

CHAPTER 12

I don't answer, shocked by the question, and also trying to feel my way through it.

I am a vain woman—I would never deny that. And yet, recent circumstances have forced me to let go of that vanity and just be . . . who I am, with or without hair.

And maybe I thought the one good thing about planting myself out in the middle of nowhere for the summer would be the fact that no one here knows me, and that somehow it would make me feel less "different" without my hair—because they don't have my old hair to compare to. When I walk into the Last Chance Café or the market, they just see a woman with very short hair in a too-trendy hat—they don't see Jessica Fox without her gorgeous mane. Being an unknown quantity has made it easier for me here.

And, of course, as Sydney is fond of reminding me, many women choose to have very short hair or no hair. They're not looking in the mirror feeling they've lost something or wishing they had it. I envy them because they're . . . free. So much freer than *I* feel right now.

But regardless of my internal thoughts, it's too personal of a thing for Matt Cordray to ask of me in this moment. Too personal by far. What the hell is he even thinking to make such a request?

It's likely the wine. It's potent. We've each had less than two glasses and quite a bit to eat, yet I feel pretty loopy. *Note to self: Scold*

Conrad for making such intoxicating wine and scold Jo for not warning me.

I guess it's also the wine that makes my long-in-coming reply: "Why?"

"I like you and just wanna see you, that's all."

It sounds very honest—and makes me be honest in return. "I don't really ever let *anyone* see me without a hat these days." And it's true. Not Sydney. Not Kevin—except for when I'm flinging a wig at him. No one. I don't want anyone feeling sorry for me anymore. Yes, there were carefully curated pictures online in early treatment days, but that was . . . a public service of sorts. A bravery I faked.

"It must be hard," he says, "feelin' that way."

My stomach hollows at his words. He feels sorry for me not because of my lack of hair—but because I can't bear to show it. Damned if you do, damned if you don't. And I instantly hate that pity, worse than I would hate having him think I look awful.

"I'll make a deal with you," I say before really weighing it.

"Let's hear it."

"I'll take my hat off right now . . . if you retire yours. For good."

He leans back in his rocking chair, lowering his chin, clearly caught off guard by the enormity of the ask. "Retire, you say."

"Retire, I say."

He grins. "So what you're tellin' me is—if I show you mine, you'll show me yours."

He's obviously very amused with himself, but I just answer, "Pretty much."

"You're leavin' at the end of the summer," he reminds me. "What's to keep me from puttin' it back on after you're gone?"

I shrug. Fair point. "Okay, just retire it for the summer. And I'll live in the hope that by then you'll realize it's disgusting and should be burned. How's that?"

He thinks it over for a minute. Then reaches up, plucks the worn cowboy hat from his head, and sends it sailing into the backyard like it's a Frisbee. "Consider it retired for the summer."

We face each other. Add a nearly full moon to the light shining through the back windows of the house, and I can see he's sporting some serious hat head. But he doesn't appear to care, and he still looks more handsome without it, even with his hair smashed down in weird directions.

All of which means it's *my* turn.

I take a deep breath, followed by a bolstering sip of my wine.

Then I do what he did—fling my hat into the yard.

I feel naked. And ugly. More so than if I were with Sydney or Kevin. It goes back to my need not to let this man think I'm attracted to him when I look my worst.

But I try to face him bravely. If I see even an ounce of anything in his reaction that hurts me, I can just go back to not liking him. Which was maybe easier than having to do all this analysis anyway.

He tilts his head as he looks me over, then says, "It's like I told ya, darlin'. You don't need the hat. You're beautiful just the way you are."

I generally find Matt more laid-back than charming—but his words sound sincere, and not like he's trying to put the moves on me, and charming it is. So rather than argue the point, I meet his gaze and simply say, "Thank you." I still feel sheepish, but it's a better sheepish than I've ever felt without my hat up to now.

"Truth is," he tells me, "I can't even imagine you with . . . ya know, a lotta hair, like you said."

My hair has always been such a big part of me that this concept is hard to wrap my brain around. So since my cell phone rests on the small table between our rocking chairs, I say, "Would you like to see? What I usually look like?"

He shrugs. "Sure." Though this seems way less important to him than seeing me without the hat.

I open the photos and scroll to an album of professional headshots I had taken last summer. I'm wearing a hot pink but very tailored dress and full makeup, and my long blond locks fall in soft, wavy tendrils over my shoulders. It's almost startling to be reminded how different, how vibrant, how pretty I looked—like a knife to my heart.

"Whoa—that's you?" he asks, leaning closer.

"Yep," I say staunchly. Point proven. There's no denying that I'm almost unrecognizable as the woman in the pictures.

Without even asking, he lifts the phone from my hand and starts swiping through photos, studying them closely. Clearly he's starting to understand how radical the change is and how much I've lost. I wait patiently, taking some solace in the fact that he's seeing how attractive I used to be, even if it's surely making him realize that, by comparison, I'm not as beautiful as he thought a minute ago.

Finally, he hands the phone back to me. I turn it off, set it down.

He looks over and says, "Your hair was real pretty, darlin'."

It's the most awkward compliment I can imagine getting, yet I manage a quiet "Thanks."

"But . . . your face kinda got lost in it."

"Huh?" I murmur.

"And your face is . . . you. I like you better this way. I can really see you—I can see your eyes, I can see your smile. You have a nice smile."

I'm slightly stunned and back to wondering if he's just trying to make me feel good, even if out of kindness. Which, in this case, is perhaps just a nicer, more palatable word than "pity." I respond with brutal, unmeasured honesty. "I can't see it that way. I loved my hair. I think I looked a thousand times better with it."

Clearly thinking it over, he scrunches up his nose a little, and says, "Maybe that's just habit? What you're used to? But hey, if not, it'll grow back, right? Over time."

I nod. "Right." Some women have told me their hair was never the same after chemo, so that's a worry I carry, but I don't bother sharing since, somehow, I already feel shallow enough here.

"I'm just sayin'," he tells me, "that you got nothin' to feel uncomfortable about if you don't wanna plop a hat on your head every second of the day. I get the sun-protection part. But otherwise, you look pretty great without it."

"Well," I answer softly, "I appreciate that. And maybe I'll . . . try seeing it that way the next time I look in the mirror." I know myself well enough to realize that's a lie, but it's the only gracious reply I can think of at the moment.

That's when he glances at his watch and says, "It's after ten."

I'm surprised. "Wow, really?"

"I should take off—early shift tomorrow."

"I guess we forgot to look at the lost-and-found stuff," I muse.

"Maybe talkin' was nicer. Another time soon, though?"

"Okay," I agree.

Matt swallows the last of his wine as we both get to our feet, then he ventures into the yard to retrieve both our hats. When he returns to the porch to hand me mine and our eyes connect, I see mischief in his gaze and something more I can't identify. "I'd offer to walk you home, but we're already here," he says. Then he gives his head a speculative tilt. "Do I get a goodnight kiss?"

Where on earth did *that* come from? That potent wine, I suppose. I simply flash a wide-eyed look of contempt.

"I'll take that as a no," he tells me on a soft chuckle.

"You take it correctly," I confirm.

After which he leaves the porch again, this time starting across the yard. Looking over his shoulder, he calls, "By the way, *that* was flirtin'."

◆ ◆ ◆

I leave the dishes in the sink, a little tired from . . . everything. The wine. The intense conversation. Matthew Cordray's compliments.

It's hard not to think he's just sweet-talking me. But on the other hand, if he doesn't find me attractive, why would he be flirting? I know for some men the nearest available vagina will do, but if he's that kind of guy, there's always Joy Lynn. I scrunch my nose as I head to the bedroom—the idea of them together bugs me worse now. Though maybe them having some kind of relationship is just a figment of my imagination.

Wine is jumbling all my thoughts together nonsensically. And after I change into pj's, I walk into the bathroom to wash up and I peer into the medicine cabinet mirror hoping I see . . . what *he* sees. What he said he sees. That my eyes and smile are all I need to feel good about myself.

I try to see it, I really do.

Despite those aspirations, however . . . despite the soft, optimistic touch of hope that warmed my heart when he called me beautiful . . . all I can see looking back at me is a hollow, damaged version of the woman I used to be.

I can't help it—I'm the woman who loves her hair and makeup and jewelry and wants to be pretty, *my* version of pretty, not some settled-upon version that people tell me is okay.

I fall into Mabel's fluffy white bed not wanting to think anymore, feel anymore. I even find myself reaching over to the nightstand for my old teddy bear, Edgar. It's silly, I know. I'm a grown woman. But he reminds me of my mom and dad, and there are moments in life when hugging him feels like the closest I can come to hugging *them*.

I don't want to think about my hair, or my scars; I don't want to think about Matt's losses or his kindness or his flirtation or what on earth he thinks is going to happen between him and a woman who is obviously not in a good place in her life. I don't want to think about all the lost things in the spare bedroom that no one cares about anymore.

I'm ready to float away in those clouds—they're comforting, and they kind of hold me up, keep me afloat.

A man I accidentally found myself thinking of as handsome tonight told me I am beautiful without my hair. But if I can't see it that way myself, maybe it doesn't count for much. Sleep feels like a welcome escape from a confusion I didn't expect to feel even an hour ago. Maybe whatever was making me hold Matt Cordray at arm's length up until tonight was an instinct I should have kept following.

CHAPTER 13

The next couple of days are hot, the oppressive kind of hot that smacks you in the face when you walk out the door. So I mostly stay in, other than tending my flowers and morning walks to the winery with only a quick wave to Conrad in the grapevines. I'm grateful to have the lost and found to continue digging through.

It's the usual fare, with some added treats: a couple of specially inscribed books, a set of engraved silver candlesticks to Eddie and Lorraine for their wedding in 1975, and an embroidered baby quilt made for Justin in 1992. Each item holds a little magic for me now, if I'm being honest. What started as boxes of old junk has become a treasure hunt of its own, each piece a treasure in one way or another.

I find myself creating little displays of some of the items around the bedroom. Partially to organize them into categories—for what purpose, I have no idea. And partially because it seems silly to stuff them back into the boxes where they've been sitting for years. Plus some of them need airing out, like the letterman jacket that once belonged to a guy named Hopper in '81, according to the sleeve. I've taken a bottle of Febreze to the baby blanket and a hand-knitted sweater with the words *For Pam* on the sewn-in label as well.

As I handle each piece, I marvel over the fact that I'm holding part of someone's history in my hands. They were givers of gifts and people who received them; they were makers of crafts and people who used them. They were thinkers who spent the time to write poetry inside book covers; they were people who loved their families and recorded their births and their deaths in Bibles. Each item feels . . . loved to me.

And sure, I get it—maybe some of these things aren't lost. Maybe they were thrown away by someone who no longer cared about them or never did. And yet I can't believe that. My late Aunt Lana was a New Age gal who once told me things were filled with energy, the energy of the people and experiences they came into contact with. I had no idea what on earth she was talking about when I was twelve and she imparted this wisdom to me one day over milkshakes at Burger King. But now I do. Because I can suddenly *feel* that energy—in all these things. And as woo-woo as it sounds, I have to believe that if so many strangers went to the trouble of packing these things up and mailing them in desperation to a random Kentucky town, they had to be giving off an energy of *being* lost, and being *loved*.

Or perhaps I've just spent too much time alone with boxes of old things.

Or . . . maybe the spirit of Mabel is getting inside me, making me see them the way *she* did. But that's pretty woo-woo, too.

I begin to snap pictures of a few items, thinking I'll text them to Sydney and Kevin from the Piggly Wiggly, only the ones I think they might each find interesting. Another way of honoring Mabel's wishes.

And on a day when the humidity seems a little less intense, I decide to venture to town.

It's wise, I realize immediately as I begin the drive. As bad as I was at being isolated when I first got here, now I'm so good at it that maybe I forget what it's like to be outside. Or . . . maybe I'm just noticing things I haven't in a long time.

An almost periwinkle-blue sky is sprinkled with watercolor-white clouds, softer than the ones on Mabel's ceiling and walls, but like a bucolic painting I want to step inside. Sunbeams turn thick, billowy trees a hundred vibrant shades of green. Has it always been this way? Or is it only here in Lost Valley? Or are these things I couldn't see for the fog of cancer? Or for the fog of loss, and life, and busyness, and stress?

As I continue toward Lost and Found, I take in all the scenery more than usual. You'd think I've been quarantined inside a bunker for a month rather than willfully staying in at Mabel's cottage for a couple of days, but maybe the close scrutiny I've been giving the lost items has me somehow . . . more aware.

I pass a picturesque, weatherworn barn with a stone foundation and an antique tractor sitting out front. I notice orange lilies growing wild in clumps alongside the road. A glance to the right as I cross a bridge I've crossed many times before suddenly reveals a small waterfall emptying over a rocky embankment into a stream below. Once in town, I stop at Mr. Freeman's for bread and soft drinks—and of course one of his beautiful tomatoes—and before I drive away, I look around at the sloping mountainsides above me and feel pleasantly cradled there.

Turning back onto Main, I find that, today, through these new eyes of mine, the town actually looks more rustic and old-fashioned than run-down and forgotten. Instead of heading straight to the Piggly Wiggly, I pull over into a parking spot in front of the long-abandoned storefronts.

The peeling paint around plate glass windows and doors comes in a variety of colors: gray, teal, dark red, harvest gold. I get out and peer inside some of them to see old countertops, worn hardwood, and pressed tin ceilings from a hundred years ago. And just like when I'm examining the lost items, I find myself wondering about the people who once cared about these places, who worked and shopped here, made their lives here. Who wore the grooves into the hardwood floor? Who stood behind the counter handing out whatever was sold here? I'm suddenly sad I didn't get to see the town in its heyday, when every shop was filled, and I wish I had a time machine to go back and look.

Reaching the Piggly Wiggly a few minutes later, I locate my signal and text my friends.

I send Kevin a shot of a hand-hewn wooden box, the inside of the lid inscribed with a line from Shakespeare: *To thine own self be true.* Kevin admires wooden pieces and would probably dabble in woodworking if he had the time—plus he's a fan of the bard.

Sydney gets a picture of what I believe to be an antique music box with some hand-painted details. It has a German vibe and is inscribed *To Anna, from Dad* on the bottom. Syd has a thing for music boxes, so she'll appreciate it.

Though they're both probably going to wonder who kidnapped their friend and replaced her with this sentimental softy.

Next, a social media update. I carefully select a few pictures: the mountain view behind the market, the mimosa tree at the winery in full puffy, pink bloom, another sunset over the lake. I type a caption, waxing poetic about the quiet beauty here.

But as I'm going on about it, I realize . . . I'm not being entirely honest.

In the couple of posts I've done since my arrival, I've made it appear I'm here by choice, on some idyllic getaway. It hits me now that I was lying, even if just by omission. And maybe it doesn't matter—maybe my followers would be happy believing that even on the heels of cancer, I'm living the beautiful life. But something makes me want to hit the backspace key and attempt to be more . . . real.

> *The truth is . . . I didn't like it here at first. It's very isolated with none of the conveniences of the city, and no internet but for a small signal on the edge of town between two mountains. I felt like I'd been cut off from the world at a time when I least wanted that. My body has recovered from my treatments, but I'm just now accepting that maybe my mind is still healing, and as much as I rebelled against it a few weeks ago, I'm suddenly understanding that some peace and quiet isn't so bad, after all. When I first arrived, someone told me the place would grow on me. And to my surprise, I'm starting to think he was right.*

I tap the button to post it.

It's the first time I've let myself think about Matt Cordray today. It comes with an odd little warmth I'd rather not feel, since indeed he suddenly seems like a complication in this simpler existence I thought I'd finally started to figure out. I push it away.

As for the post, I feel . . . if nothing else, authentic. It's not that I've ever been fake, but I've also never been one to post my woes. People like happy better than sad. And even when I shared my cancer journey, I was always upbeat—and there were days that *having* to be upbeat helped me hold my head a little higher than I would have otherwise. But maybe now I'm just . . . tired. Of the Jessica Fox show.

Maybe, right now, in this moment, I simply wish I were Jessie again. Jessie, a name I told Matt Cordray I'd never been called. Because it was easier than explaining the truth.

Next up, I decide to again treat myself to lunch at the Last Chance, though "treat" feels like an inaccurate word when it comes to having to order my food from Joy Lynn. But I try the egg salad, and despite her usual brash demeanor, I decide it's deliciously worth what I have to put up with to get it.

As she slaps my bill face down on the table, she says, "Thanks for playing that song I like the last time you were here."

Whoa. What just happened?

It's hard for her to thank me—I feel that. But she did it anyway.

And such a small thing. Playing a song for someone on a jukebox.

Maybe no one ever does nice things for Joy Lynn. Maybe she doesn't make them want to.

"You're welcome," I tell her.

After paying, I go to the jukebox again and peer down at it in all its old-time glory. "Hey, Joy Lynn," I call to where she's refilling ketchup bottles behind the counter, "any other requests?"

She almost smiles at me, but not quite. She thinks a second, then says, "J23." I type it in. "Only You" by the Platters. She likes soulful ballads, the kinds of songs that dig into your heart a little. It's the best thing I know about Joy Lynn so far. I walk out thinking: *Please don't have romantic ties to Matt, please don't have romantic ties to Matt.*

And then I catch myself, having the thought. Which means apparently I care about that.

Ugh.

Well, I'm sure it only matters to me because my world has gotten very small here, so what else do I have to focus on? If I *am* a little attracted to him, so what—I'll be leaving soon enough.

In the meantime, I won't go back to being rude to him—that's just silly. But no more backyard dinners that almost felt like a date, and no more deep, intimate conversations. Only madness that way lies.

As I'm getting out of the car at home, I hear a voice call, "Jessica dear! Jessica!"

I look over to see Grace waving a cane at me from her front porch, so I leave my things and walk to the bottom of her front steps, smiling up at her. "Hi, Grace."

"Well, ain't that cute." She's motioning to my fedora. I guess I'm usually wearing my sun hat or ball cap when I see her, but the fedora has become my "goin' to town" chapeau. "My Walter had one just like it. Well, minus the pink hatband. His band was black. It was his summer church hat."

I respond with a simple "Thanks," though it's not lost on me that she's the only person who's had anything nice to say about the fedora since I got here.

"Ya wanna have supper tomorrow night?" she asks. "I know ya liked my brown beans, so I got some soakin'. They can cook all day tomorrow and be ready come evenin' time."

I feel my eyes widen. "Those beans take multiple days to prepare?"

She just shrugs. "Do I got somethin' better to be doin'?"

I would never cook something that takes days, no matter how tasty, but I'm wildly impressed that Grace will. "I would *love* to come have brown beans with you," I tell her.

Having leaned her cane against a porch post, she clasps both hands together in joy. "Well, that's right nice," she answers, and I can see how much my acceptance delights her. "I'll make us up some cornbread in the skillet, too, and I'll fix us a cheesecake for dessert."

"Oh wow," I say, truly taken aback. Given my lack of cooking, this sounds like a feast, and I confess I haven't had anything particularly exciting since Matt's corn on the cob. "That sounds amazing."

"It ain't really the season for beans—they're more a winter food that sticks to your ribs when it's cold out—but since I know we both like 'em, I'm happy to make 'em. And the cheesecake'll be a nice cool dessert for us."

"I can't wait," I tell her. And as I walk away, I'm aware that I actually mean it.

Note to self: *Socialize with Grace more often. Like she said, do I got something better to be doing?* I've liked Grace from the word go, but now I realize I want to spend time with her.

The groceries take a couple of trips because the case of pop is awkward and the tomato is too delicate to take that kind of chance with. I'm toting my sack with the tomato and loaf of bread when I see a flash of tan and black fur bounding toward me across the yard.

I free up one hand to bend down and nuzzle Goldie as she darts around my feet in wild enthusiasm. *"Hewwo dere,"* I hear myself say. "Oh my goodness, you is so coot." Unlike Matt, I don't do doggy baby talk—except suddenly . . . I do.

Of course, where Goldie gallops, Police Chief Cordray is sure to follow—and there he is, sidling over in a Garth Live! T-shirt, blue jeans, and cowboy boots. He's also sporting at least a day's worth of stubble on his jaw. I like a clean-shaven man, but I suppose I've grown used to his more laid-back facial hair when it's present.

"Afternoon," he says with his usual easygoing smile. His eyes twinkle in the sun. When did *that* start? And how have I never noticed how blue they are?

"Hi," I say casually, still petting the dog and wondering if he heard my baby talk. It's nothing to be embarrassed about since he does it, too—yet the Jessica Fox, WRTB 11 in me hopes he didn't.

I imagine he's going to suggest getting together, for the purpose of looking at lost things or eating something, and I'm going to decline. Because, as I decided, it just seems easier.

Then I notice: "Hey, you're not wearing that stupid hat." It's the first time I've seen him out of uniform without it. I can't help giving him a small smile.

"A deal's a deal," he says pleasantly. "And I see you *are* wearin' yours."

I shrug. "I kept my part of the arrangement," I point out. Even if I don't especially want to dwell on "the big reveal" of me with baby curls for hair.

"Fair enough," he replies. And I'm still waiting for him to invite himself over when he says, "Come here, Goldie girl. Time for the groomer. Need to get you a summer cut."

"You actually have a dog groomer around here?" I ask.

"Nope—gotta drive to Hazard. But has to be done. I'm a lotta things, but a dog groomer ain't one of 'em." He's still flashing that lazy grin, and I'm realizing it's far too early for dinner and he's obviously busy right now, but he's probably about to suggest stopping by later.

"Well, you take care and have a nice afternoon . . . *Jessica*." He's smiling, proud at having gotten it right without even a slip-up—then turns to go. Not having suggested anything at all.

Which is fine, of course. It's what I wanted. It's totally what I wanted.

"You too," I say, standing there feeling surprisingly, confusingly forlorn.

CHAPTER 14

If Grace's little house is a cacophony of color on the outside, the interior is a more muted, old-fashioned collection of plums, beiges, and warm greens. The furniture is old but has aged well, and seems to have been chosen by pulling different shades from the wallpapers that cover each room. None of it is my personal taste—and in fact Mabel's place comes a lot closer to appealing to me in a country-cottage way, even if one sorely in need of updating. But Grace's home has a certain comfort about it, a yesteryear warmth that cocoons you when you walk in the door. I can feel that it's been her home for a very long time—she belongs here. And if her colorful metal backyard is Grace's happy side, the inside of the house is the more serene her.

The fluffy black-and-white cat curled up on the dark sofa seems completely undisturbed by my arrival—still as a knickknack. "Oh, who's this?" I ask. Though I've always been too busy for a pet, my family had a cat when I was growing up.

"That there's Ophelia. Came to me as a stray about five years back."

"She's gorgeous," I say. "Will she let me pet her?"

Grace nods. "She's a good lap cat, likes that kinda attention."

I sit down next to Ophelia and stroke her fur, and her quick, easy purring makes me feel appreciated. Until, that is, she suddenly lets out a very loud meow for no particular reason.

"Loudmouth, though," Grace adds. "But I still like her."

I continue petting the cat. I guess I do, too.

"I don't get a lotta comp'ny these days, so thought we'd use the good dishes," Grace tells me cheerfully, and I follow her gaze to a small oval dining table in the next room, covered with a lace cloth and set with white bowls and plates rimmed in gold.

I tell her they're lovely just as a timer goes off and sends her moving slowly back to the kitchen.

Leaving the cat, I head into the cozy dining room, where old wallpaper peels in spots but is mostly covered with lots of family photos as well as a ticking cuckoo clock.

"Bring our bowls in, honey," Grace calls, so I grab them both up and join her near the stove. The kitchen is a sunnier place with old wooden cabinets painted pale yellow, an old enamel sink like my grandma had back in Wisconsin when I was little, and what appear to be original Formica countertops that any retro-style hipster would die for. Brown pinto beans and chunks of ham float in a creamy brown broth in a big pot on the stove, and next to it rests a black cast iron skillet of cornbread just taken from the oven judging by the warm, sweet aroma and steam wafting from it.

I didn't know I liked country food so much, but my mouth is practically watering as Grace uses a large ladle to carefully scoop beans and ham and juice into the two bowls I'm holding. She follows me back to the dining room toting the skillet, the handle covered by a special potholder-type thing clearly made specially to fit a frying pan, and an old metal spatula for cutting and scooping, I presume.

The meal is scrumptious, and I can't stop raving about it as I butter my second piece of cornbread. As I sit there soaking up the mood of her home and taking in the pictures on the walls, I want to know more about her. "How old were you there?" I ask, using my butter knife to gesture to a photo of a much-younger Grace and her husband, their apparel rocking a '70s vibe.

She glances up at it and smiles softly. "Thirty-somethin', I reckon. Me and Walter both."

"You look beautiful," I tell her. In the photo, her eyes shine bright, and the vibrant blue of her dress contrasts beautifully with her dark, smooth skin. She looks happy.

"Well, that's sweet of ya," she says. "That was back afore age got ahold o' Walter and me."

"You made a handsome couple." If I'm really analyzing it, Walter is not an overly handsome man, but they look good together somehow—right—and I can tell he treasures her just from the expression on his face. "Were you and Walter raised here?"

Grace spoons a few beans into her mouth and swallows before answering. "No, honey. We moved up from Mississippi." She says it easily, but then gets a faraway look in her eyes.

"What brought you to Kentucky?" I ask. "A job? Family?"

"Guess there's a little o' both in why we come to this particular spot on the map." She takes a sip of sweet tea from a tall glass, then swipes a napkin across her mouth. "We was both raised poor—both our families was sharecroppers. We didn't know each other until one day Daddy brought home one Walter Whitcomb. Not the most good-lookin' fella, not the most confident or slick. But Daddy was schemin' to make sure I got a good husband, and I've always been grateful for that. And like I say, he wasn't the most excitin' man . . ." She stops to chuckle. "But there was a sweetness to him, and he seemed to want nothin' more than to please me, and that made me fall in love with him. He also wanted to head someplace new, where he could build a better life than he could in Mississippi in them days, and afore I knew it, we was married and headed for Kentucky. Walter had cousins over to Pikeville. In fact, got most of my good recipes, like my beans, from his Aunt Philomena.

"Walter got a job in the mines, but he was so smart he eventually got put in management, which kept him aboveground and probably gave him a lot more years than he mighta had otherwise. We found this little ol' house here in the valley and had us a good life. We raised us a son here." She points to a faded photo on the wall of a young man in a high school football uniform. "That's our Daniel. And we found us a nice little community to be a part of. Back then the town was . . . more of a town. Ya wouldn't know it now, but Lost and Found was once a busy little place."

I can't help thinking about how much courage it must have taken to leave the only life she'd ever known at such a young age, and yet she tells the story as if it were easy. Having heard the pride in her voice when she mentioned her son, I say, "Tell me about Daniel."

The question sends a big smile unfurling across her face. "He's the best thing Walter and me ever done—we always said that. Good, smart boy. Nearly sixty now, which tells you I'm almost as old as these hills round about us." She stops, laughs. "He's done real well for him and his family."

Grace goes on to tell me about her grown granddaughters, and her one great-grandchild so far. "They use to come for Christmas and a week every summer, and some of 'em still make it for Christmas, bless their hearts, but they're all awantin' to move me to Saint Louis, into Daniel's finished basement. And don't get me wrong, it's real nice there—but I like my little house. I like my life. I like my backyard with Walter's art. So I ain't aleavin' until I cain't take care of myself no more. And with any luck, I'll be like Mabel and just pass on quick-like some night in my sleep, without bein' no trouble to nobody."

Then she grins over at me, dropping her glance to my empty bowl. "Want more?"

I feel sheepish when I reply, "Yes—but I'm afraid I won't have room for cheesecake."

Yet another broad smile tells me how much pride she takes in her cooking. "Tell ya what. I'll grab ya just a dab more, and then after we have our cheesecake, we'll fix up some for ya to take home."

The sun has sunk low and the air grown cool enough that Grace suggests we eat our dessert in the backyard. I'm stuffed, but the cheesecake is worth cramming a little more in.

I inquire further about Walter and his metal menagerie, and when I finish my pie, she encourages me to walk around the yard to study it from all angles. It's like strolling through a Willy Wonka world of metal and paint. "What a playground this was for my granddaughters when they was youngins," she says.

I find myself a little envious of such a place to play as I examine pieces of metal that form a large yellow-and-orange sun, then make my way between zigzagging pastel pipes that create a path to a hand-crafted fountain. Walter was an artist. I wonder if Grace was his muse.

"We've talked and talked about me," she says then, "when I'm just a boring old lady. Tell me what you been doin' with your time over to Mabel's."

And that's when it hits me. "Oh my gosh, Grace. I can't believe I never told you what I found at the end of the treasure map!"

Her eyes light up. "Did it lead to somethin' good?"

I nod, then fill her in about the lost and found. She laughs upon hearing how Mabel secretly moved everything into her garage, remarking with wonder, "And she never told anybody, not even me."

I feel bad for not remembering to fill her in before now, but I end up spending the whole evening with her, regaling her first by dusk and then moonlight about the countless treasures hidden away in Mabel's garage.

And the longer I look at Grace, the more I realize she wasn't just beautiful as a woman in her thirties, but that she retains beauty still. I notice the joy in her eyes, the freckles that cross her nose. I take in the way the wrinkles in her face show me how much she's lived. I bask in the richness of her laugh. And I think again of how brave she must have been as a young girl, the struggles she's likely come through that I know nothing about, and how she's ended up mostly alone now but still finds reason after reason to smile. Every time she does, it lights up my soul.

The following afternoon leads me to the Lost Valley Vineyards. Mild, cloudy weather has me taking my walk later than usual, and Jo invites me for a wine-and-cheese-and-grapes-and-crackers kind of lunch on the stone patio outside the tasting room. Though as I sit enjoying her company and the impromptu lunch, a part of me is already looking forward to leftover brown beans and cornbread for dinner tonight. And then I laugh out loud, partly from the wine and partly because I don't recognize this person having these thoughts.

"What's so funny?" Jo asks from across the table.

I smile, shaking my head. "Only that I guess I'm really starting to appreciate the little things in life." Then I tell her about Grace's beans.

"Beans are that exciting?" she asks. Clearly they don't have them in California, either. "I may have to snag myself an invitation to Grace's for dinner." Today Jo is wearing a much more attractive straw cowboy hat than Matt's, along with a loose sundress and her usual John Lennon sunglasses.

Conrad is in his usual place, somewhere among the grapes. "What does he do in there all the time?" I ask.

And now she's the one laughing. "Pruning, pruning, pruning. It's all about making sure the grapes don't get too much shade from the leaves, but also not too little. For a one-man operation, it's kind of a full-time job. Though I think it's also his personal form of meditation."

She invites me to come and look, so we venture into the vines. The grapes are lush and translucent and pleasingly smooth as I run the tip of my index finger over them. Tiny curlicues of vine curve around them, almost protective and decorative at once. She tells me they'll be harvested come late summer.

When I start the walk home, after I'm probably twenty yards away, I look back for some reason. She lifts a hand to wave, still as striking to me as when I first met her weeks ago. And suddenly I understand why.

I don't know why I haven't put it together before. She's talked about growing up a California hippie and told me specific years that she and Conrad lived different places—but now I *see* it. For the first time. She's over seventy years old.

I never noticed before because she's so simply beautiful. Even with wrinkles and sags. It's her confidence, her choices, the ease with which she navigates life. She makes growing older look effortless. Way more effortless than I've treated my early forties.

I think more about her, and also about Grace, as I walk beneath the clouds—two strong, brave, beautiful women who probably wouldn't have complained a bit if they'd ever lost their hair to chemo.

On both sides of the road, the fields are awash in Queen Anne's lace and tall purple clover. Now that I notice such things, I have to wonder what else I've been missing—what other simple, beautiful things in life I just haven't seen. From wildflowers to the charm in an old woman's face. I resolve to *keep* seeing them. It suddenly seems, well . . . like a crime not to notice beautiful things. Surely God put wildflowers in this field for that purpose, because I can't think of any other.

I'm walking up Lost Valley Lane, aware of a dragonfly making a swirly path around me, when a pickup truck I happen to recognize as Police Chief Matthew Cordray's approaches. I haven't seen him in a couple of days, which I still think is best, even if it surprises me that he hasn't been around.

I suspect anew that he's probably going to stop and chat with me, or suggest we grill out again, and I'm still going to be cordial but decline any such invitations.

So of course I'm not surprised when the truck eases to a halt and the window goes down. His police uniform tells me he's off to serve and protect. "Hey there, neighbor," he says with the usual grin.

"Hey." I smile back, just a little. Noticing again that he definitely looks better without the hat. And that maybe the unshaven look he sports gives him a slightly rugged vibe. Maybe I picked a bad time to start noticing things. Even so, I brace myself for being pleasant yet not encouraging to whatever he's about to say.

"I was gonna mow your yard today before my shift, but Grace asked me to move some stuff and then it got too late. Get to it tomorrow."

"Oh. Okay." I'm nodding, once again thrown by his . . . lack of wanting to get together.

"See ya," he says.

"See ya," I return.

And off he goes.

Maybe he was completely lying and thinks I look hideous without the hat and that's why he's suddenly keeping his distance.

Or maybe Joy Lynn came back around.

Oh my God, stop. You don't even want him to pursue you, remember? If he doesn't find you attractive, that's probably a good *thing.*

Only . . . if I'm honest with myself, it was nice, so very nice, to think he truly liked my face better without my hair. Nice to think it was possible for someone—anyone—to think that. Even if I don't.

I turn and watch his truck amble on down the lane, wondering when on earth I started caring if the cowboy next door wants to spend time with me.

CHAPTER 15

The truth is, I'm getting a little tired of going through boxes of lost things. I think because I'm feeling the fruitlessness of it. Yes, Mabel wanted them seen and appreciated, and I'm honoring that, but it's not lost on me—no pun intended—that in the end, most of them will just go back into the same box they came out of, so I'm not sure what I'm doing is changing anything.

With each item I examine, I really *feel* its lostness—I feel how it's just floating around in the world not where it belongs, serving no purpose. Feeling things is not my strong suit and something I often try to avoid. As a newsperson, it's a good trait, not getting emotionally sucked into every story—and I find it helpful in other ways, too. I don't get too emotional over romantic entanglements that don't work out, which is *always* for me. I also tend to suffer other general losses well—if a friend moves away or someone dies, I can handle it. And when the dreaded cancer came calling, who was courageous about it? This girl. I have emotions of steel.

Except lately, it seems. Getting banished to Nowheresville, Kentucky, wounded me far more than Kevin ever intended it to, because it made me feel . . . dismissible. And losing my hair has obviously bothered me a great deal despite the brave face I tried to show the public. Now . . . all this lost stuff. It evokes emotions in me that I didn't even know I had.

Though maybe that seems healthy. Sydney always says she thinks I'm a little *too* tough. Kevin, conversely, is more like me, and we joke through our pain—it's just how we deal.

Regardless of which way is the right way, though—if there *is* a right way—I've decided to take the day off from the lost and found. Instead of digging into another box of someone's lost history, I'm going to finally dig into the weeds in the flower bed out front. I need an unemotional activity, and this fits the bill. The weeds have bugged me since I arrived, and the property caretaker doesn't seem to be doing anything about them, so I will.

Plopping my sun hat on and applying sunscreen, I step out into a bright sunny day, the summer country air humming with the sound of a lawn mower that means Matt is probably nearby. I head to the garage and locate a wheelbarrow, a trowel, a pair of gardening gloves, and one of those little foam kneepad things gardeners use. I feel very industrious as I push the wheelbarrow, filled with my other tools, to the flower bed. If Nancy could only see me now.

I'm down on my kneepad thing, trowel in hand, when the mower gets much louder, closer, rounding the front corner of the house—and when it suddenly goes silent, I glance up to see a look of alarm on Matt's face as he comes rushing toward me. "Whoa, whoa, whoa! What on earth are you doin'?"

I flinch, blink—he's gaping at me like I just pulled the pin on a hand grenade. "I'm digging up these weeds," I inform him smartly. "They're an eyesore, and I can't take it anymore."

I'm anticipating either praise for my help or remorse that he's neglected the task—not the utter confusion I feel when he says, "Those aren't weeds, girl. They're snapdragons."

"Huh?"

"Take a closer look at what you're about to dig up there. They've all got buds on 'em, gettin' ready to bloom."

When I do as he instructs, I feel like an idiot. "Oh. I just thought . . ."

"They reseed themselves and start growin' in the spring, so it takes a while for blooms."

I don't know enough about flowers to really compute what he's saying, so I reply with, "My mom always planted snapdragons when I was growing up, but she got them at a nursery every year."

He nods and says, "They're tender perennials."

He might as well be speaking Greek. I look up helplessly from my kneepad. "Which means?"

"Mostly they're treated as annuals in climates like ours, but in good soil, they can reseed themselves, and that's what Mabel's have done since she passed. Takes longer for 'em to blossom, but you get free flowers the rest of the summer." He ends with one of his little winks.

"Hmm," I say, still slightly embarrassed. To the contrary of my earlier smug thought, Nancy would be cringing in horror if she could witness what I almost did. "Well, I'm glad you stopped me."

"You'll be *extra* glad in a week or two," he says. Then he retreats and fires back up the riding mower, soon traversing the space between our two houses in straight lines and around the trees that grow in between as I sheepishly lug all my gardening equipment back to the garage.

Heading into the house, I rehang my hat on a peg near the front door, eat an early lunch, then contemplate the long afternoon looming before me. I still can't believe what I saw as weeds are actually going to be flowers. Some things take time, I guess.

I eventually return to the spare bedroom, resigned to looking at lost stuff, like it or not. It's starting to seem like . . . my mission here. So maybe I shouldn't be trying to avoid it. Though the first box I open contains a lost teddy bear that says *To Liza from Mommy 2011* on its paw and nearly sends me bursting into tears.

That last part throws me. Oh my God, I *am* getting too wrapped up in the loss of it all. Even if I know this particular item is affecting me because of Edgar, my own teddy bear. Mabel is right—things really *can* be important, really can be the nearest path to lost loved ones or lost love period or just the past in general, and that's okay.

But for heaven's sake—2011. We have the internet now, people! Why didn't whoever found this use the internet to seek out its home rather than mailing it off to Timbuktu?

I'm still fretting over the bear—like Edgar, he's a quality, jointed bear, and was clearly meant as a keepsake for Liza—when I hear a banging on the back door and realize the mower has at last gone silent again. It sounds so urgent that I drop the bear on the spare bed and rush to answer.

I open it to find Matthew Cordray, hot and sweaty in a Dollywood T-shirt and old, gray "work pants," as my dad would have called them. I didn't notice his apparel earlier, too caught up in shock and embarrassment, and he looks surprisingly good given this combo. Still I say, "Dollywood?" with raised eyebrows.

He tilts his head and flashes a don't-start-with-me look. "My girl likes the rides and it's a nice place."

I shrug. "Fair enough. Did you want something?"

He turns around, facing away from me, then cranes his head at a funny angle. "Is the back of my neck sunburned?"

"Yes," I reply. "Most definitely." It's lobster red, in fact.

He spins back my way and says, "Thought so. Know why?"

"Lack of sunscreen?"

"Well, ya see, I got this hat I usually wear when I mow—straw cowboy hat, you mighta seen it before—but I made this deal not to wear it the rest of the summer, and it usually shades my neck, which I never thought about until I realized it was on fire."

I purse my lips, feeling bad for him, but only slightly guilty. "Well, one has to think ahead and be careful about that sort of thing. Take it from the radiation queen. Do you *have* any sunscreen?"

"Somewhere," he answers. "Guess my arms and legs get enough sun that I don't usually burn." Indeed, his arms look fairly tanned and just fine.

"Lucky for you," I tell him, taking pity, "I have a ton right now. Wait here."

Knowing *I* had to think ahead this summer, I packed several bottles of the highest SPF I could find, so I grab one from a bench in the foyer below the pegboard and return to the back porch.

When he sees the spray bottle, he says, "Help a guy out?" and turns again.

The request makes sense—I can see where it needs to go and get it there—but . . . something feels weirdly intimate about suddenly being that close to him as I study his neck and spray on the sunscreen. I can smell his perspiration, but rather than offending me, it reminds me of the way my father used to smell coming in the house after tilling the garden or repairing a car, and it strikes me as masculine, the scent of a man who works hard and fixes things.

"Hey, you busy right now?" he asks as he turns back toward me.

I'm a little taken aback, for multiple reasons, and instantly feel that a yes would sound silly, since how busy am I *ever* really? "Not . . . especially." It comes out with clear hesitation. "Why?"

"I think I know where we can get some blackberries."

Huh? I'd already forgotten my brief urge to find some. "Where?"

He points in a vague southwesterly direction that tells me little to nothing. Not that a specific answer would have been a great deal more helpful to me. "I'll grab a couple buckets from Mabel's shed while you put on some long pants and walkin' shoes."

I balk slightly. According to the little thermometer on Mabel's back porch, it's ninety degrees out. "Why do I need long pants?"

"So your legs don't get scratched up."

I flinch. "This is sounding . . . unpleasant."

He just laughs and says, "Only if you don't put on a pair of pants. And . . ."

When he stops, I ask suspiciously, "And what?"

"Much as I hate to mention it, you should probably grab your giant hat, too, for the sun."

Crap. The whole time we've been talking, my head has been bare—no hat. I didn't even think about it, but now I'm embarrassed because that's just where I'm still at right now. In a rush to change that, I choose the path of least resistance. "Okay, back in five," I tell him, then slam the door in his face.

I tend to dress for the weather in summertime, so I packed only one pair of long pants—a fairly cute pair of sporty hiking pants with lots of pockets and loopy things I bought two years ago for a fall hiking and biking trip to the Smoky Mountains with Sydney. But instead of hiking, we mostly drank wine on the deck of our chalet, and instead of biking, we mostly sat in the hot tub and talked about fashion and hair. So part of me is happy to finally give these pants a whirl, but another is thinking: *Argh, so much for not spending time with him.*

Oh well, a few blackberries—no biggie. And when I slap my sun hat on and glance in a mirror, I realize that what's happening up top pretty much cancels out any cuteness of the pants, and that he was surely just being kind when he called me beautiful and it was the wine talking when he got all flirty.

All of which is best, actually. My noticing things about the police chief is not the same as wanting anything to happen with him, and possibly having developed a slight attraction to him is not synonymous with wishing for it to be mutual. This is the weirdest summer of my life, and the weirdest I've ever felt about myself, so my firm commitment to keeping things super platonic with Chief Cordray stands.

When I join him in the backyard, he's gotten us a couple of small pails, and I suddenly have the sense of setting off on an adventure—a good one or a bad one, I don't yet know. As he leads me deep into Mabel's backyard, toward the edge of the lake, he says, "Just hit me while I was mowin' that I know where some berries used to grow wild—lots of 'em. My mom brought me and my sister down here every June to pick 'em when I was a kid. Bettin' they'll still be there and probably good and ripe—if the wildlife ain't already got to 'em."

When the yard Matt just mowed ends and turns to wilder, more untamed land, he leads me onto the remains of a thin dirt path that cuts through tall-growing grass, and I understand why I needed the pants.

We're suddenly surrounded by more of the white Queen Anne's lace that's drawn my eye lately, along with tall, spiked, lavender-blue flowers. The summer sounds of insects and frogs echo from down by the water's edge, where velvety cattails jut up at the shoreline. I feel immersed in it all and am struck with the thought: This is here all the time, all these flowers, all this nature, and no one even knows it.

"What are these blue flowers?" I ask from where I follow Matt on the trail.

When he glances over, I realize he didn't even notice them, that they're so much a part of his world he doesn't see them anymore. "Those? Those are weeds, darlin'." He laughs, then catches himself. "Jessica." After which he looks back at the flowers dotting the meadow. "Or a coffee substitute, dependin' on how you look at it."

"Really?" I ask, surprised.

"We called 'em blue daisies growin' up, but they're actually chicory. Mountain people used to grind up the roots to make a bitter kinda coffee, and I think a few of the older ones still do. My grandma used to claim it was good for her gout and worked as a laxative, but can't say as I've tried it for either." He tosses a quick wink over his shoulder.

"Well, I think the flowers are pretty," I tell him.

"Then you're in luck," he says. "They bloom all summer."

I look around, taking it all in. A heavily treed area sits just above the incline where we're walking, the lake below. Though the lake is getting narrower, like maybe we're near its end, the end I've never seen.

"Was all this Mabel's?" I ask. "Or is it yours?" Maybe his property somehow curves around Mabel's yard.

"Nope and nope," he says. "Mabel's property ends where I quit mowin'. My own goes in the other direction a little ways."

"Then I'm confused. Who does *this* belong to?"

He does another vague finger point. "Neighbor on the other side of the mountain."

I pull up short. "So we're, like, trespassing right now? And we're going to pick someone else's blackberries? Like, steal them?"

He glances back at me and laughs. "Those are harsh words you're usin' there, Jessica."

"Well, aren't you an officer of the law? And isn't trespassing and stealing illegal?"

He shrugs. "Only if anybody cared. You wanted blackberries. Jeb doesn't pick 'em—they just go to waste."

He resumes walking, so I follow, but this still feels dicey to me. "You don't even ask if it's okay?"

Now he stops, turns, and flashes me the same look you'd give a child who just doesn't possess the intellect to understand what you're saying. "Things work a little different here than in the city. And if it'll make you feel better, we can take some to Jeb's place after we pick 'em." He resumes walking. "But it's a good half hour's drive from here to there, and I promise you he'd be happier to know they're goin' to use rather than just feedin' the deer and the bears."

"Bears?" I come to a quick halt. He couldn't have just said "bears." Could he?

At this, he just looks over his shoulder and shrugs. "We occasionally get us a black bear or two roamin' around. Tend to see 'em more over by Pine Mountain than here, but happens every now and then."

"Um, this sounds dangerous. Why has no one mentioned to me, given all the walking I do, that there are *bears*? And by no one, I mainly mean you."

He's giving me the same look as when we discuss snakes, like I'm such a girl but he's going to humor me. "Look, I probably haven't seen one in five years, so likely you're safe."

Yet I'm not reassured. "Probably?"

"And if you *were* ever to see one, just make some noise to let it know you're there—just talk loud—and back calmly away from it."

I must still look terrified since he adds, "Know when the last bear attack here was?"

My eyes go wide. "No. When?"

"Never," he says. "Doesn't happen. You respect their space and they'll respect yours. *If* you were ever to see one." He walks on, shaking his head and murmuring, "City girl," like I'm exhausting him.

Of course, now I'm darting my gaze in every direction on the lookout for bears, my heart beating a little faster, and even though I don't see any, I have to ask myself: What happened to just coming here and keeping to myself? Resting, reading, taking it easy? How did I end up following a man I barely know down a secluded path in bear country to contraband blackberries?

That's when Matt says, "Here we are. And just look at that. Blackberry heaven."

I don't see them at first—but then I do. I would have walked right by them, but once you catch sight, they are indeed plentiful, and as promised, look plump and ripe, beautiful little bits of nature hidden where it would be easy for no one to ever find them.

"They run up along this old fallen-down fence row," Matt tells me, pointing again, "and they're growin' up around these trees." When he hands me a bucket and leans a little closer than usual, I feel his nearness in my kicked-up heartbeat. "Now, Miss Jessica, don't freak out when I tell you to just mind where you step and keep an eye out for snakes, okay?"

I'm pretty sure my eyes go as wide as the two pails we're holding.

In response, he says, "If you want, just stay here and watch, and I'll do the pickin'."

But this particular indulgence drives home for me what a baby I'm being and reminds me who I really am. Jessica Fox, WRTB 11. That woman isn't afraid to pick blackberries. That woman has the sense and patience to watch where she steps. Coming into this rural setting where so many things are different has turned me soft in ways I couldn't have anticipated, but it's time for that to stop. "No," I reply. "I want to pick some. I'll be careful."

"Good." He adds a short nod. "Now you only want to pick the ripe ones, the ones that are dark, like this." He cups a berry in his palm, and as I step up to look, I realize how close we've gotten again.

"Got it," I say, then move back.

And then a funny thing happens. I feel surrounded by . . . wildness. The beauty of the wild berries. The wild growth of the tall trees up above, the sun casting dramatic rays down through thick green boughs. And suddenly something seems a little wild to me about Matt Cordray, too. His messy hair, the way his T-shirt hugs his shoulders and forearms, the bits of dirt clinging to his skin from his earlier yard work, and that he doesn't even care. He's a different sort of man than the ones I've known. There's something slightly gritty and very real about him.

Okay, it's a good time to pick berries in an entirely different area than where he is. And that's all the analysis I'll do about that—no more.

"Damn, lotta berries here," he comments as we work. "More than when I was a kid for sure."

"Should we pick them all?" I ask. I have no idea how many berries either of us can actually make use of. "I think my cobbler recipe only calls for two or three cups."

"You're gonna want more than *that*," he says, like this should be very obvious.

"I am? Why?"

"Well, they make a nice breakfast with a little sugar and milk poured over 'em in a dish."

"They do?"

"And you can mix 'em into some pancake or waffle batter."

"Oh, well . . ."

"And there's nothin' better on a biscuit than some blackberry jam."

I hold up my free hand. "Now, whoa there. You're just getting farther and farther out of my wheelhouse. Even the cobbler is flirting on the edge for me."

He shrugs, grins. "Well, I'll keep some, and we'll give some to Grace, and take some over to Jo and Conrad. I'm sure my cousins would take some. And Melva at the Last Chance would probably be happy to whip up some blackberry pie." Melva, I've learned, is the older lady I've seen there—she owns the café and does all the cooking. "If we end up with extra beyond that, I'll drive 'em to Jeb or drop 'em off to Mr. Freeman. Point bein', folks are never gonna turn down fresh blackberries."

"That's really . . . nice," I say. "I mean, where I live, you maybe give your extras of something to your friend or your neighbor, but I wouldn't think of . . . *getting* extra just to give to everybody I know."

He shrugs. "That's just how people do down here. You think to help out your neighbor with extra blackberries, they'll think of you when they end up with more corn or green beans than they can use. That's just how it is."

And so it's decided that we'll fill our buckets or pick until we get tired, whichever comes first.

As we work, I ask if he's heard from his daughter lately, and he tells me about a phone call last night. "She's off to Disney World for a couple days tomorrow. And she met a boy at the beach, which makes me nervous as hell, but guess I just have to hope that the grandma's a decent chaperone. And Sam's a smart girl—I need to remember that."

Then he tells me he's been working more overtime this week to cover for yet someone else's vacation, which I guess might explain why I haven't heard from him much. Not that I care, mind you, or am keeping track of such things. "How many deputies do you have?" I ask.

He hesitates only slightly before replying, "Two."

He knows, of course, that I'm going to make fun of that a little. "So you're head of a big police department of three," I say, both to clarify and to tease.

"Yes ma'am," he answers, still plucking berries nearby. "But three's better than none."

"True," I agree, recalling what he explained about keeping the town from disappearing completely. And I get it. I guess I'm starting to understand that there's plenty worth saving around here, things I wouldn't have been able to see just a few short weeks ago.

"I never asked what *you* do for a living," he says when I least expect it.

And it's strange to me—I tend to forget that people here don't know. At home, people know me—*strangers* know me. It's not a question I have to answer often. But here I've already told Grace and Jo, and now I tell Matt, too. "I'm a TV news anchor. I deliver the evening news on Cincinnati's Channel 11."

"Wow." He's clearly impressed. "I had no idea. I mean, maybe I should have—I know about Kevin's job. But he called you a friend, so I didn't realize you worked together, too."

I explain about my past with Kevin, our twenty years together in the biz. And I share that Kevin suggested I come here for the summer to finish recovering, "even though I thought I already had and wanted to go back to work."

I didn't exactly mean to say that last part, however, and it makes him reply with, "Why didn't you just tell him that?"

I weigh my options. Fluff it off with a lie about deciding to take more time away or . . . tell him the truth? I told Grace and Jo with ease—I knew other women would understand. And I didn't bother to feel embarrassed about it because every woman has been treated like "less than" at some point in her life. We all have times when we're not the prettiest girl in the room, and it matters in a way it wouldn't for a man. And we all know there are ways in which women are pitted against one another—to be the prettiest or the sexiest, to get chosen by pageant judges, or the male boss, or the hot guy who can have his pick of girls. But telling Matt would be different.

And yet . . . I do it anyway. I don't know why. Maybe I want him to know I'm not as weak as I seem here, that I'm simply out of my element, but that if it were up to me, I'd be totally back behind the news desk. I even go so far as to give him a slightly watered-down version of the wig incident, explaining about the heat and the lights, and that wearing it just wasn't feasible. Then I add, "I didn't even suggest doing it without the wig because I knew it wouldn't fly with management. And thus my summer fate was sealed—Tiffany's in my chair and I'm out in the country waiting for my hair to grow."

"That's tough," he says when I'm done. "Guess I can understand a little better now why you seemed so . . . unhappy when you first got here." Then he stops picking berries and looks over at me. "Can I ask you somethin', though?"

"Sure."

"If you don't even like bein' around me, or Grace, or anyone else without a hat on your head, how would you have felt about bein' on the news that way?"

The question smashes down on me like a sledgehammer. Oh God. He's right. I've been so, so smug about the unfairness of not being accepted as I am right now. I've felt so horribly slighted and angry. I was so bold marching into Kevin's office, ready to do whatever, be whatever, to get my life back.

And if he'd said okay and that I didn't need the wig, I guess I would have figured that out, come to grips with it. Or . . . maybe I wouldn't have. Maybe I wouldn't have been able to deliver the news *without* my wig any more than I was able to do it *with* my wig. I thought having a little bit of hair back would instantly make me feel normal again—and it hasn't. And maybe I've been a little in denial about the moment I flung my wig and Kev said I wasn't quite ready. I accepted that I wasn't going to get my way, and that the wig was too hot—but maybe until right now I haven't truly accepted that it was true: I *wasn't* quite ready.

"It's . . . definitely a thing I'm still working on," I tell Matt, though he already knows that. So I step deeper into honesty. "I thought it would be easier to get used to how different I look. So I confess that . . . maybe it's not all bad that they didn't want me back yet. By fall, it will have grown some, and I'll feel better about it. I mean, I took my hat off with you, so that's a step in the right direction, right?"

When he smiles over at me, I'm actually glad I told him—I feel braver for having done it, and less weak than I did just five minutes ago.

"Hat or no hat," he says, "that other newswoman's got nothin' on you."

"Well, she's got *hair*," I point out.

"Hair today, gone tomorrow," he quips on a laugh, clearly amused with himself. "Things'll work out, I'm sure."

I nod. "Kevin said to just give it time, and I can see now that he's right. But it's still really horrible to devote yourself to a job for years only to find out you're not valued for the quality of your work as much as what you look like."

At this, his smile fades, and I notice again from a few feet away how blue his eyes are as he says, "Seriously, Jessie—Jessica, sorry—it sounds like a cruddy situation to know you're bein' judged that way. But if they don't think you're pretty enough to deliver the news, then they're not really lookin'."

CHAPTER 16

Our eyes are locked, and I struggle not to look away because his gaze burns intensely on mine. A lump rises to my throat. It's from gratitude. It's from the connection I don't want to have with him but feel right now anyway.

I'm relieved he's standing too far away to do anything crazy like kiss me or I fear he might. We stay quiet a moment, and I again feel the wildness of the world all around me. Until finally he glances down into his bucket to say, "Think we probably got enough now."

I nod. Then force a smile to lighten things. "Blackberries for days."

He steps closer to glance in my pail as well. "You did good, young blackberry apprentice."

I can't stop the small laugh that sneaks out. "If the broadcasting thing ever falls through, maybe I can fall back on my new blackberry-picking skills."

Despite having decided we're done, I grab another berry hanging right in front of me—I guess the picking is a little addictive and I feel almost like I'm leaving behind tiny ripe treasures—and he follows suit, picking another himself.

We're standing side by side, still picking those last few berries—when suddenly his hand closes over mine and he whispers, "Shhh," near my ear. "Be still."

I feel his breath on my skin. And I'm hyperaware of his hand holding mine. Freezing in place, I'm a little afraid, my heart beating too fast, but also aware that various body parts are tingling.

"Don't move," he instructs me in the same whisper, "but look to your right."

Slowly, I turn my head. When I find a deer standing less than ten feet away, I softly gasp. It's so big close up. But I sense how gentle it is, too.

"Wants some berries, I'm guessin'," Matt says, low. And with that, he smoothly sets his bucket down and scoops into it with one hand, still holding *my* hand with the other, then reaches out an open palm full of berries beyond me, to our visitor.

We both stay motionless—I'm trying not to exhale lest even that scare the beautiful white-spotted deer away. As I look at it, I could swear it's looking back, that we're having a moment as it tries to decide if it can trust what's being offered. I instinctively send a mental message: *It's safe. I promise. You don't have to be afraid.*

I know it's crazy, but as if the deer can grasp my thoughts, it cautiously comes forward—one step, then two. It pauses, and I'm holding my breath as Matt squeezes my hand tight, and then it moves closer until it's eating the berries from Matt's outstretched palm.

The three of us stand there that way, all just trying not to frighten each other, until finally the deer turns to bound gracefully away through the brush. We watch it go, listening to the shushing sounds it creates as it disappears out of sight.

I look toward Matt and our eyes meet. I fear my heart might erupt through my chest.

He leans forward, his face coming closer to mine—and I can smell him, feel his nearness—until his forehead bumps the brim of my big hat.

He seems to almost bounce backward off it, clearly surprised by the obstacle even though I'm not sure why. I pull my hand away, take a step back as well.

I decide to address the deer and only the deer. "That was amazing," I say, and I mean it—I'm still as stunned by that as by suspecting Matt just tried to kiss me. And by not knowing if I was going to stop him.

"Yeah," he replies, sounding a little taken aback—maybe by the deer, maybe by the hat bump. "I've never had that happen before."

"Really?" I mean, he grew up here, so maybe I thought he was a deer whisperer, but apparently this was as rare for him as for me.

He nods. "Once-in-a-lifetime occurrence probably."

I nod, too, and make more conversation about the deer as we pick up our buckets and start for home. But as we walk, I notice the top of my hand is purple where he touched it with fingers he'd been picking berries with. It's like left-behind fingerprints, proof, a reminder that touching occurred. It makes me keep *feeling* the touch even though it's over now.

I can't help thinking that this stupid, silly hat of mine protected me from more than just the sun today.

That night, as I get ready for bed, standing in front of the mirror and putting on my scar cream, I'm still feeling it all somehow—the sensation of his hand on mine, the moment the deer looked me in the eye, the blackberries sitting in my kitchen still making me sense the wild, beautiful bits of nature all around me.

I study my hair, the flat little curls that have taken shape on my head, a darker brown than I remember my natural color being. I take in my cheekbones, the prominence of my eyes. I try to see what Matt says he sees in me.

I still miss how I used to look—I just do.

But I don't rush to look away this time. Usually, I do hurry, making a point not to look too long. Tonight, though, I stand there, take my time, and really see myself. I try to make friends with my reflection again.

◆ ◆ ◆

The next morning, I scoop some blackberries into a shallow bowl, pour milk over them, sprinkle a little sugar on top, and dive in with a spoon. Matt was right—a simple, tasty, natural breakfast.

After that, I dress, skip my walk, get in the car, and start the drive to Brandywine. Of course, I soon realize I have no idea where it is and can't consult a map app for help. So I stop at the Last Chance and get directions from Joy Lynn of all people. I'm wearing my fedora, but I really do think I'm starting to grow on her anyway.

Later I'll make the cobbler and put some berries in containers for Grace and the winery—Matt agreed to find good homes for the rest. But I woke up with an idea—and, all things considered, it seems like a good day to get away from the house for a while.

I mean, yes, I'll be immersed right back into my Lost Valley life in a few hours, but a change of scenery sounds good. Because I don't want to get too mired in thoughts of Matthew Cordray trying to kiss me. He never alluded to it afterward, and I'm hoping he realized that, as I told him once before, he's barking up the wrong tree.

It doesn't matter if I'm getting more accustomed to how I look—nothing good could come of having some sort of affair with the guy next door. My stay here is temporary, he and I have nothing in common, and sex was not on the agenda for my summer of healing. As I've known all along, I'm getting used to my scars, and used to my new hair—so it's not a great time to get naked with some guy I just met. Healing is a process—it doesn't happen overnight. And it's all right if it takes a while to get okay with looking in the mirror again.

Brandywine is another little town tucked into the mountains, but it's slightly more lively than Lost and Found. On an idyllic twisting, turning Main Street, I spot a bank, a lawyer's office, a flower shop, a Subway sandwich shop, and then, lo and behold, the library—a blessedly somewhat modern building with its own parking lot and even a flashing digital sign in front showing me that it's eighty-one degrees at 10:11 in the morning.

It was a long, winding drive to get here, but it already feels worth it as I park. I instantly know I'm treating myself to Subway for lunch! I'm not even a big Subway fan, but the familiarity of it feels so . . . comfortable.

Still in my car, I pull out my phone to find that I already have a connection—phone bars and internet! Not a *great* connection, but it's enough to make me wonder if maybe that's why this little town is thriving more than one without it.

Inside the library, things are relatively quiet—two librarians work behind a large counter, a teenager taps on a laptop at a long table, a few kids and moms meander around tall bookshelves. When I hesitate slightly, standing just inside the door, a thirtysomething librarian asks, "Hi, can I help you with something?"

"I'm here for the Wi-Fi," I respond.

Her smile tells me I'm probably not the first person to come to her library for this hot commodity. "Of course," she says, then points to a sign with the password.

I went so far as to bring my laptop for this task, so I take a seat in an easy chair near a window and get signed on. Just like at the Piggly Wiggly, it feels like a triumph.

I dive right into what I've come here to do. I pull out the pocket Bible once belonging to Sarah Hawkins, which I wrapped in a soft dish towel to protect it in my purse, and I carefully open it up to relocate the key pieces of information inside. I type the name Isham Hawkins into a search bar. I want to know more about Sarah and Isham, who lost their young son two centuries ago, and I also want to see if I can find someone—alive today—to whom this Bible might have belonged before it showed up in Lost and Found.

It doesn't take long to turn up some info about the family on a genealogy website. I learn that they had many other children—not surprising given the times, despite that somehow I'd seen them as a little family of three who'd ended up a mere two. While I can't imagine the pain of losing a child, I'm heartened to know they had others to comfort them. I also learn that Sarah's maiden name was Hall, she was Isham's second wife, they were farmers from Woodford County, and they're buried side by side in the Kentucky state capital of Frankfort.

But I don't learn much more. I add the word "bible" to my search, knowing it's a long shot that I would find anyone saying, *Hey, I lost my great-great-great-great-great-grandparents' teeny-tiny Bible*, but you never know. This search turns up a few more mentions of Sarah and Isham, but the only new info it reveals is that Isham died at the age of sixty-five in 1870.

I'm simultaneously happy to have learned what I did about Sarah and Isham, especially that they lived only a few hours' drive away, and sad to still have a million questions about them that can never be answered, and that I'm no closer to having any idea what to do with this Bible.

One school of thought would be: Sarah and Isham probably have thousands of descendants by now. Family trees start multiplying at astronomical rates once you get a few generations down the line. So maybe it's fair to say no *one* descendant owns this Bible more than another. And yet—it had to come from *somewhere*. Someone had to have kept it and passed it down, and passed it down, and passed it down.

That's when I get another idea. I have, of course, planned to take full advantage of this bountiful Wi-Fi and do a social media check while I'm here. I intended to create a post with pictures of grapes and blackberries and Queen Anne's lace, wanting to share more of the beautiful bits of nature I keep noticing around me—but it occurs to me now that can wait.

Instead . . . I take a few pictures of the Bible, closed up with its worn leather tab that makes it look like a miniature pouch, and also held open to show the intricate handwriting explaining why Isham is giving it to Sarah. Along with the photos, I fashion a post explaining that while "away for the summer," I've come across many lost items people have seen fit to mail to the little town of Lost and Found, and that this is one of them. I ask my followers to share it in case any descendants of the family have somehow lost this historic family treasure.

Then I read it over, asking myself if I really want to do this. I could end up having to decide this Bible's fate should more than one person come forward, or I could be at risk of giving it to someone who won't care for it as they should. And yet, I think Mabel would approve, so I hit the button to post it.

And that's when my brain nearly explodes with a fresh new thought. Here I was, criticizing whoever found Liza's teddy bear for not searching for Liza online—and *I* can do that! Even here, I have the technology to search for whoever lost the lost items!

I bite my lip at the mind-blowing revelation, though, as my chest goes tight. It suddenly sounds like an enormous undertaking.

Okay, keep a cool head here.

And just . . . work on a few key items. See how it goes.

Don't let it get overwhelming—you have the power to control it.

Like Matt once said, if even one item gets returned to someone who lost it, it'll be worth it. It would make Mabel's dreams for the lost and found come true.

I glance back at my post, and already it's getting a ton of likes and comments about how cool and unique and historic the Bible is. One comment says how nice it is of me to look for the owner while I'm on vacation. *Vacation. If you only knew.* And already it has a few shares—which tells me a lot more are coming. Maybe I'll really find the Bible's owner. I resolve to take pictures of the teddy bear and a couple of other items to post as well.

All this and a Subway sandwich coming my way, too? It feels like a banner day in my mountain exile.

On the way back, I stop at Mr. Freeman's with a list of ingredients I need for the blackberry cobbler. When I arrive home a little later, I glance over to see Matt sitting on his front porch in a T-shirt and blue jeans, bare feet crossed at the ankles and propped on the white wooden railing near the one-eyed chicken. He tosses me a lazy wave as I pass by.

Despite myself, I'm reluctantly pleased to see him get up and start walking my way as I exit the car. Noticing his bare feet in the grass sends a million thoughts flitting through my head: The insulting regional joke I learned when I moved to Cincinnati about people from Kentucky not wearing shoes. That I haven't gone barefoot in the grass since I was a kid. That maybe just now I . . . miss it. There's something carefree about it, and something that *looks* carefree about *him* right now.

"Thought you'd be busy makin' a cobbler today," he says, "but you must be gettin' into somethin' else good since you look like the cat who ate the canary."

His old-fashioned phrasing amuses me, especially since I'm in a good mood and want to tell him what I've done with the Bible. So I explain it all, adding that I plan to try it with other items, too, to see if it leads anywhere.

He lowers his chin, giving me a look. "Damn, that's a good idea." Then he smiles. "Mabel would be happy."

"I think so, too."

"First pair of feet you've ever seen, Jessie—Jessica?"

Oh crap. My eyes do keep dropping there—I just didn't realize I was being obvious about it. So I'm honest. Well, partly anyway. "I'm sure you know that in the city they make fun of that, saying people in Kentucky don't wear shoes."

He chuckles lightly. "Yep, I'm aware. We're all backward hillbilly folk down here."

I squint a little, pondering aloud, "Why does that equate to not wearing shoes, though? I never thought it through before."

He tilts his head. "Well, my grandma was one of thirteen kids raised a little north of here. They lived on a farm back before most folks had cars, and they only went into town once or twice a year. Each kid got a pair of shoes with the fall harvest money, for school, and that one pair had to last 'em until the next September. So I guess there were a lotta bare feet, whether to save the shoes for when they really needed 'em or because they wore out. So . . . maybe the real joke is that we were all poor." He says it with an ironic grin, and it hits me how cold such ridicule is.

"That's awful," I remark.

He shrugs. "Sometimes people *are* awful. It's the world we live in."

I say nothing for a moment because it's true, and sad. "This is ruining my good mood," I finally tell him.

"Guess I shoulda worn shoes over," he says with a wink. Those winks of his—sometimes I feel them in my belly, or my chest. It's getting a little unnerving.

"Well, what's on your agenda now?" he asks.

Are you trying to spend more time with me, Matthew Cordray? Well, nope. No way, José. Yesterday brought us too close for comfort. So I gesture toward the house. "As you pointed out, I've got a cobbler to make. Blackberries, here I come."

"Good luck." Then he asks, "Hey, did you have some for breakfast like I told you?"

"Indeed I did."

"And? Was I right? Tell me they weren't delicious."

"They were. Delicious." Though I don't like the way I feel as I say that particular word while looking into Matt's eyes. So I add, "See ya," and go inside.

CHAPTER 17

I find Mabel's mixing bowl, baking pans, and measuring cups and spoons. I set the oven for 350 as the recipe instructs, then put on a ruffly blue-gingham apron I found hanging on a hook in the broom closet. I'm just about to start mixing together ingredients when the phone rings, nearly making me leap out of my skin—the sound of a landline is alarming compared to the gentle trill of my cell phone. I drop the tin measuring cup in my hand and go answer.

"Hey, it's me." Sydney. Funny how people have to identify themselves when they call now—a habit long since dropped when we all started seeing each other's names and faces pop up on our screens. "What's up?" she asks.

"I was about to bake a cobbler," I tell her.

"You were about to what a what?"

"Bake. A cobbler," I say a bit proudly. "With wild blackberries I picked myself."

"Who are you? And what have you done with my friend?" It's an understandable reaction. "Though the music box pictures were pretty cool," she confesses.

"I know, right? I guess I'm . . . just starting to explore some different ways of spending my time."

"Well, you sound in a good mood, so it must be agreeing with you."

Hmm. Intriguing thought.

"I wanted to give you a remodeling update," she goes on. "Even though you never ask."

Huh. Funny how that's dropped out of my mind. I should care. I *need* to care. I'm spending a lot of money on it. "I guess having to carve out an existence for myself here has kept me preoccupied. But yes, I'd love an update. How's it going?"

"I went over last night and it's looking gorgeous! The new flooring is fabulous, and the cabinets are beautiful."

I'm trying to envision it all—it feels like a long time ago that I finalized my choices. I ask Sydney a few specific questions and learn that the new granite countertops have arrived but aren't installed yet, and the backsplash will happen after that.

"Sounds great," I say, even though I feel very disconnected from the project.

"The guys were just leaving when I showed up last night, and the only bad news is . . ."

Ugh. "There's bad news?"

"Well, just that it won't be quite done by the Fourth of July like we were hoping. He says a week or two after, though. I hope you aren't upset."

Okay, the truth is, I'm aware that it is now late June—but I haven't been paying close attention to the calendar, even which days are weekends and which ones aren't, because that doesn't seem to matter right now. And despite knowing it's almost July, I'd kind of forgotten my desperation to be home by then. "I'm not," I tell her quickly, "so no worries."

I can almost hear her confusion in the silence before she says, "Again, who are you? A couple of weeks ago, you were climbing the walls wanting to come home."

"I know," I answer. "I guess I've . . . relaxed a lot since then."

"And you pick blackberries now and make cobblers? So you just, like, stumbled upon these blackberries or what? And you just felt safe picking them?" These are all fair questions as we are both city women who do not pick things.

"Well, I found this cobbler recipe and mentioned it to Matt."

"Matt. The neighbor."

"Right," I say. "And he knew about these wild blackberries we could walk to, so we took buckets and picked them yesterday afternoon. And we saw a deer! Like right next to us! And it actually ate berries right out of Matt's hand. It was pretty amazing."

She stays quiet when I finish, until she asks, "Was it wearing a wreath of flowers on its head and talking? Have woodland animals started helping you clean your house and decorate it with daisy chains?"

I let out a laugh. "Okay, I suppose that's fair. But the deer was cool."

"I'm sure it was," she appeases me. "It's just that the last thing I expected was for your life in Lost and Found to start sounding like a fairy tale. And so, next question—is your neighbor Prince Charming?"

I instinctively blow out a sharp "Ha!" sound and tell her, "Only if Prince Charming wears a dirty cowboy hat and goes barefoot."

"Hmm," she says. "Is it just me or does that sound kind of sexy?"

I push out another disbelieving breath. "It's just you. This guy is many things, but Prince Charming he's not. Besides which, just . . . no."

"No to what?"

"That's . . . the last thing I need right now."

"*What's* the last thing you need right now? Exactly."

I take a deep breath. Here I was, minding my own business and trying to make a cobbler, and now I'm suddenly defending my life choices. "As you know, I've pretty much dismissed the idea of a man ever making me happy." And I'm content with that. Romance has never gone well for me. My relationships end quickly for the most part. Sydney says it's because I'm closed off emotionally. Kevin says I'm too inflexible, expecting a guy to want everything I want and like everything I like. But whatever the case, I've made my peace with it and am a perfectly strong, happy, independent single woman who doesn't need a man. "Which leaves dating for social purposes or physical needs, and right now, I don't require that kind of interaction and I don't feel physically needy—or physically attractive. I'm still getting used to my scars and very short hair. And even if none of that were true, this guy . . ."

"Yeah?"

"He's nice, but we have nothing in common. And I'll be leaving in a month or two anyway."

"Sounds like perfect affair material to me," she says. "You both know it's temporary, so that keeps it uncomplicated."

"What about the I-feel-ugly part? What about the I'm-not-into-sex-with-strangers thing?" The one actual problem with accepting that I'll probably never marry is that I do have a sex drive—when not coming off cancer treatment—but I've never felt comfortable being intimate with someone until I get to know them. It creates a conundrum. Fortunately, I do occasionally date someone long enough that it leads to sex before it all falls apart for one reason or another. "Further," I go on, having just remembered this part, "I'm not exactly . . . in the mood. Not only because I don't feel pretty, but because my body has had a lot of stuff done to it recently, you know? So sex really isn't on the menu for me right now, for many reasons."

"But blackberry cobbler is," she observes.

"Yes. I guess I'm . . . discovering new things."

"Man in a cowboy hat sounds like an interesting new thing to me," she mutters judgmentally under her breath. "But whatev." Then her voice returns to normal. "And you know how much I hate that you've decided romance isn't in the cards for you."

I let out a long sigh. Yes, we disagree about it often. But I decide to throw her a bone—a bone of diversion. "You know what?" I begin. "When I get home, who knows? It's going to be a whole new chapter in my life, kind of like starting over. My hair will be a little longer, I'll be back on the air, I'll have a new kitchen great for entertaining—so maybe I'll reopen my mind to the possibility of romance *then*. But not now. How's that?"

"That," she says, "is something I fully intend to hold you to. So I'll drop the cowboy prince thing, but you can count on me shoving romance down your throat come fall."

Oh goodie. But it does the trick for now. "Speaking of romance . . ." I begin.

I don't even have to finish my question. "He's dreamy, Jess. I'm in love."

I take that in. My dear, sweet friend is in love.

I'm so happy for her.

I'm so curious what that feels like.

I'm so . . . broken to know that if this is really love for her, it will change my life when I get home—how much I see Sydney, everything we do together. But that's so utterly selfish—I'd be ashamed to ever let her know the thought entered my head, so I share only the first one.

"I'm so happy for you, Syd. Tell me everything."

"Don't you have a cobbler to make?"

"It's the only thing on my docket this afternoon—I have the time. I want to hear all about Jayden."

And so she tells me. And I love her enthusiasm. I love the pure joy I hear in her voice. Even if I feel a little alone already as I think again about how this will affect my own life—which feels pathetic to me. It's just that . . . alone is a hard place for me. I've been alone a lot. Alone . . . with thirty thousand social media followers. Life can be ironic at times.

I truly am happy for her—love couldn't find a more deserving person than Sydney. And Jayden is a lucky man, which I will let him know at some point as I size him up more closely and make sure I think he's good enough for her.

I just have to remember who *I* am: Jessica Fox, WRTB 11—strong, independent career woman and cancer survivor, with a fabulous wardrobe and . . . well, hair that will grow back and be *just* as fabulous again, eventually.

The truth is, I'm not sure I've seen that woman in a while.

I've seen pieces of her, but not really *her.* I've become someone else—someone who digs through boxes of lost memories and bakes cobblers and oohs and aahs over nature.

I don't dislike this version of me—but I'm not sure she's as strong and tough as that woman behind the news desk. And that makes me glad this is only temporary.

But I'm still happy to return to the kitchen and make my cobbler after we hang up.

When I put the cobbler in the oven, it just looks . . . blah. Like a bunch of cake batter I've accidentally dropped berries into. But then . . . magic. Thank God someone somewhere put interior lights on ovens and small glass windows you can look through, because I can't take my eyes off my cobbler as it begins to turn golden and flaky and bubbly with tiny purple sizzles. And oh, the aroma!

I'm welling with pride as I finally remove it with two big oven mitts to cool on the counter. And while I've nearly lost the habit of photographing every little thing in my life for social media, this one feels worth capturing, so I find my phone and snap a few fun pics. I kind of miss the immediate gratification of being able to post it to the world in an instant—but not as much as I used to. It'll still be just as beautiful a piece of culinary art the next time I'm at the Piggly Wiggly.

I'm not sure how long it should cool. If I had internet, I'd google the answer. As it is, though, I get by fine the old-fashioned way: I wait about half an hour, during which the whole house smells like sweet, baked perfection, then I carefully but eagerly slice into it with a knife from Mabel's butcher block. I scoop a square onto a plate, wait a few minutes longer to make sure I don't burn my mouth, and then, practically holding my breath, I grab a fork and take a bite.

Oh. Wow. It's . . . yummy. Sweet and warm and gooey and bready.

The second bite is just as good. And the third, and the fourth. I smile, pleased with myself. I'm a baker! I wish my mother could see. And Mabel, too. Maybe they can. Who knows these things?

It's soon dinnertime, so I reheat part of a simple casserole I made last night and eat while peering out the window across the lake, where the sinking sun casts a silver ribbon over the water. The vineyard barn and grapevines become dark silhouettes against a pastel sky.

Afterward, I slice a chunk of cobbler and put it in some Tupperware for Grace, and another chunk gets packed up for Jo and Conrad. In separate containers, I divide up most of my remaining blackberries for them, keeping just enough for another couple of breakfasts. I'll deliver them tomorrow morning.

I sort of want to give some cobbler to Matt, too—since without him, there would *be* no cobbler. But at the same time, I'm still not wanting to encourage anything more there. Those moments we shared while picking berries—I felt it too much, a . . . closeness or something that I'm not comfortable with. I've been pushing it aside since then, not really letting myself think too intensely about it, but creating this amazing dessert from the very berries that those moments revolved around makes it hard to ignore. And just like with the lost items, feeling is not something I'm good at. After my parents died, I spent a long time learning not to feel so much—I don't want to backslide now.

As for what I experienced with Matt . . . I think it was something like . . . intimacy. That sounds weird to me—it was a couple of looks, his hand on mine, a shared moment with a deer. But it was also more. A thing without words. My heart beat too fast. I got tingly and kind of breathless. I'm sorry to say I've probably had sex that made me feel less than I did in the berry patch with Matthew Cordray yesterday.

Okay, so here's what I'll do. I'll pack up a slab of cobbler (thank goodness Mabel had a healthy selection of plastic storage containers) and I'll leave it on his porch. Perhaps after it gets a little darker. Like a thief in the night. Yes, that's a good plan.

Between now and then, I could wash the dishes. Or I could take a slice of cobbler outside to the rocking chairs and enjoy the rest of the sunset. I'm fairly tired, so the rocker and sunset win.

It's nice, sitting there eating something delicious I created with my own two hands, from a pretty flowered plate that makes me happy just to look at it, with a soft, warm summer breeze wafting over me as the orangey light in the sky fades to a deep purple.

That's when I notice a firefly, the first I've seen since getting here. Truthfully, the first I've seen in a much longer time, living in the city—so the sight takes me back to my childhood in Wisconsin. Soon, I realize there's more than just one—a whole little fleet of them blink across Mabel's backyard as night replaces day.

"First lightnin' bugs this year."

I flinch at the sound of Matt's voice, as is so often the case, then look over to find him walking toward my back porch, carrying a bottle of wine.

Uh-oh. Nope, this seems like a terrible idea. Once, after our little cookout, was one thing, but twice makes it a pattern, a thing we do together. Drink wine. Wine plus feelings equals a potentially reckless combination.

"We called them fireflies up in Wisconsin," I inform him. Since I can't be rude or dismissive to him anymore. And despite myself, I've come to like talking to him.

"Is that where you grew up?"

"Yes." It reminds me how very little I've shared with him about myself. "In a small town about an hour west of Green Bay."

"I brought wine," he says, lifting it so that I catch sight of the Lost Valley Vineyards label.

Thanks, but I have things to do.

Or: *It's been a long day and I'm planning to turn in early.*

Or: *I'm expecting a phone call, so I'll have to pass, but have a good night.*

Yet none of those ring true. I've managed to turn Bob and Nancy down for similar invitations a thousand times without blinking, but fibbing, at least to Matt, is suddenly becoming harder for reasons I don't understand.

Yes, it seems like a bad idea, but he's standing right there, with the wine.

Looking kind of handsome, much as I hate to acknowledge that.

And I do have cobbler to share, after all, and no reasonable excuse to send him away other than: *I'm starting to find you attractive and don't need the complication.*

So wine with Matt it is.

"I have cobbler if you'd like some." My way of saying okay to the visit without having to actually say okay to the visit. I lift my plate of half-eaten dessert to show him.

"How'd it turn out?" He pulls back teasingly, like I might be trying to poison him.

I announce smugly, "It's quite yummy, if I do say so myself."

"Well then, sign me up."

He's already uncorked the bottle, but we decide to go in together so he can grab glasses while I cut him a piece of cobbler and another for myself. "It's my third today," I confess as I step around him to grab a fork while he pours, "but having become an expert baker, it seems like the right time for such an indulgence."

He laughs, and I catch the scent of him as we maneuver around the small kitchen. He apparently uses some masculine sort of soap I like the smell of too much.

Although it's a lot to carry and we struggle and laugh and wonder out loud why we're not making two trips, we eventually get ourselves back into the rocking chairs.

"All right, here we go," he says, digging his fork into the cobbler.

He's talking about the dessert, of course, but I'm thinking about this thing I keep telling myself I'm not going to do, spending time with Police Chief Cordray, and how I seem to keep doing it. Here we go, indeed.

"This is real good, darlin'. Oh my goodness."

I hear the Southern man in his diction just then, plus the sincerity of the compliment, and I am drawn to appreciate both.

"You done Mabel proud."

I was acting arrogant before, but getting someone's praise makes me happier than I anticipated. "You really think so?"

"Absolutely." He points his fork at me between bites. "You can bet I'll be back for more of this before it's gone."

"If you can't resist," I say jokingly, unthinkingly. Like, not even trying to push away the contact now. It's as if I'm losing all my good senses, bit by bit, as if this place is just gradually washing them all away.

When I ask about his daughter, I get the latest Florida update, and he also informs me he dispersed his blackberries today and even froze some to use later. In turn, I tell him more about my library trip and some of the items I plan to post about in the coming days.

I ask if he wants to see them, and immediately regret having effectively invited him inside, at night. But to my surprise, he declines. "Think I'd prefer to just sit out here and enjoy the evenin' with you. You and the lightnin' bugs and somethin' tasty." He finishes with his classic grin, his eyes sparkling on me, effectively saying he's more interested in my company than the lost items. Which I guess I already knew. But it still makes my skin ripple.

We talk more, about random things: neighbors, fresh green beans from a garden, favorite alcoholic beverages, college experiences, his dismay that his daughter is growing up so fast. Then he looks over at me and says, "I really like seein' your face tonight, Jessie."

I don't even react to the name—it's the other part. I'm not wearing a hat—I haven't been this whole time and didn't even know it. I, of course, suffer that familiar strangeness because he's not seeing me as I've always been, and as I see myself. Yet it leaves me warm inside to realize . . . he's looking at me the same way he always does.

It takes a minute to summon a response. I finally settle on, "I forgot I didn't have a hat on." It comes out more softly than intended.

"Good." He picks up the wine bottle and tops off both our glasses—before flashing me a questioning look. "But aren't you gonna yell at me for callin' you Jessie? Which I swear was still an accident. I don't know why it just keeps comin' out that way."

I take a while to concoct a reply to this, too, and I don't know whether it's the wine talking or simply the part of me I don't recognize that keeps sneaking out lately, but I eventually reply, "No. I lied about that."

At last, I've made Matt Cordray the one who flinches. "Lied about what?"

"When I said no one ever called me Jessie."

"You did? Why?"

"It's what my mom and dad called me."

CHAPTER 18

His eyebrows shoot up. "Really?"

I nod and get even more honest. "Actually, everyone did, once upon a time."

"Then why don't you like it?"

"My mom and dad died," I explain, "when I was young." As I hear the words leave me, I'm pretty sure I've had too much wine too fast.

"Oh. Damn, I'm sorry."

"I mean, you weren't exactly old when yours passed away, but . . ." I don't want to imply that my losses are any worse than his—losing your parents sucks at *any* age.

"How old were you?" he asks.

"Nineteen when my dad died—massive heart attack at fifty-one. My mom died a year later, the winter before I graduated from the University of Wisconsin. She got an infection during an outpatient surgery and became septic before it was caught. It was too late—she passed after a week in the hospital."

"That's rough," he says reverently.

I sense him wanting to reach out and touch my hand, but that's still a bad idea, for more reasons than one. I'm not even sure why I'm spending my evening with him when I know I don't want this to go anywhere. And I'm even less sure why I'm suddenly spilling my guts here. Other than the wine.

"Do you have brothers and sisters?" he asks.

I shake my head. "Only child."

"So you went by Jessie growing up then," he seems to want to clarify.

I nod, but tell him, "I haven't been Jessie since . . . since I left Wisconsin the fall after Mom passed. As soon as I got their affairs settled, I was outta there. And I'm . . . just not that girl anymore." I sigh, remembering how quickly I was forced to grow up, how quickly I became the capable, independent go-getter I've been since arriving in Cincinnati. "I've been Jessica ever since, professionally and personally." Even Kevin and Sydney don't know I spent my entire girlhood as Jessie Fox. "I guess I left that girl behind with the rest of my life up north."

"How come? Because the name makes you think about your mom and dad?"

I sigh, weighing it. "Maybe. Maybe it reminds me of simpler days. But mostly I think it's because . . . I *couldn't* be that girl anymore, you know? Get left on your own that young and you have to toughen up, start over. You have to sort of . . . become someone new." I don't know why I sound sad as I say it—I *like* myself, I *like* who I became. My parents would be proud of me.

But if I'm being totally real, maybe sometimes I *miss* that girl who didn't feel pushed into being so strong and independent. And maybe it's not horrible to be reminded of who I once was. There are good memories there. Only . . . "Jessie was . . . softer than me, I think," I hear myself muse aloud. I'm staring off into darkness as I say it, slightly mesmerized by the fireflies.

"She sounds nice," he says. "But you're talkin' about yourself in the third person, you know? You're still her."

I glance over at him. "What makes you think so? It's not like I've been so nice to *you* since I got here."

A small smile plays about his mouth. "Sometimes you have. When you forget not to be. And more lately."

When I say nothing in reply, he adds, "I see softness in you all the time. I see it in the way you play with my dog when you think I'm not lookin'."

It's true that sometimes when Goldie's running around the yard, I scratch her head or throw things for her to fetch—which she only bothers bringing back about half the time because she's a terrible fetcher.

"And the way you care about Mabel's lost things even though you wish you didn't."

Well, yeah, okay, he's got me there.

"I see it in your eyes right now," he concludes, and I realize I'm meeting his gaze as he talks, just taking it all in, melting in the moment a little—and now I wonder what exactly it is he's witnessing there. Emotions, maybe. I knew the wine was a bad idea.

"You think you're so smart—some kind of rocking chair psychiatrist," I accuse, half teasing, half not. I'm not comfortable with this revelation of his; it feels like being unmasked, my inner self laid bare.

But he only laughs. "About time you figured out how smart I am, Jessica."

And now it suddenly sounds almost funny to me. My own name. On his lips, in his voice. Oddly, it just doesn't sound right coming from his mouth, even after all the correcting I've done. So, as much to my surprise as his, I say in a hushed tone, "You can call me Jessie if you want."

He arches one brow and flashes a skeptical look, like maybe I'm trying to trick him. "Really? 'Cause I'm truly tryin' to quit. I don't wanna be annoying. Or disrespectful."

"Well, you already failed miserably at both of those things," I inform him, laughing. "So why change now?"

He laughs, too, but then says, "Seriously. I mean, the world's changin' all the time, and I'm not sure I'm always the *best* man, or that I've got my finger on the pulse of what's politically correct, but I do try to think about . . . how I want my daughter to be treated, you know?"

I can see in this moment that he really *is* doing his best to be a good guy, even if that comes with imperfections. And I'm not sure it's reasonable to ask for more. I explain to him, "At first, when you called me Jessie, it stung. Stung some part of me deep down inside. But maybe it also reminds me of a time when life felt easier. When I didn't have to worry about anything and was just . . . me. Maybe it's actually *nice* to be reminded of my mom and dad now when I hear it. And nice to . . . feel that part of me again." I stop, aware that word vomit has spilled out of me. "Oh my God, I've clearly had too much to drink."

"So tomorrow I'm gonna be in trouble if I call you Jessie?" he ventures.

I look over, meet his gaze, and realize I honestly don't know the answer. I'm not sure I know the answers to *anything* about myself right now. So I just say, "Time will tell."

It's another night when I fall into Mabel's cloud bed grateful for the cozy comfort it provides. *Damn you, Matthew Cordray, for being so easy to talk to.*

I *never* tell people stuff like that. I never even think about it.

My life has always just been *before* my parents died and *after*, and I was one person prior to it and another person following it—a child who transformed instantly into an adult. I never feel sorry for myself about it. I never reason through it like I did with Matt, recognizing that I had to change in order to get through it.

If I hadn't, I'd have drowned in grief. Instead, I got a job and a new life and stopped the madness of all the feeling and missing. And it's not like I don't think about my mom and dad. I do. A lot. But when I sold the family store and the house I grew up in to move away, I had to pack up all my grieving to be a productive human being.

Right after that conversation, I told Matt I was sleepy and ready to say goodnight, and he offered to help me carry everything in, but

I insisted we just leave it on the back porch. He thanked me for the cobbler, and I thanked him for the wine, and I tried to laugh about the fact that I'd had too much, but I'm pretty sure he saw just how soft "Jessie" is in those moments and that I was pretty much running away. From letting him see it. From seeing it myself.

I'm drunk, and certain I'll wake up tomorrow full of regret. I fall asleep feeling . . . vulnerable. Yuck. I maybe even cry a little—I'm not sure. I can blame the wine all I want, but why on earth have I let this man I barely know see under my armor—when I don't let *anyone* see that part of me?

When the sun comes beaming in the window the next morning, I open my eyes to the clouds on the walls and ceiling, to the brightness of a new day, to the notion that I have blackberries to eat for breakfast, and more to deliver to my new friends—and then I remember. Confessions. I made unplanned confessions to Matt Cordray.

But as I get out of bed and glance in the mirror, I realize . . . I don't feel so regretful after all. Maybe I even feel a little bit . . . free. Unburdened. Unfettered.

I mean, all that and I'm pretty sure he still likes me.

And if he likes the me who's been lurking under my tougher surface all these years . . . maybe she's actually a likable person? Though he's right—I really have to knock off the third-person bit.

I stare more fully at my reflection—a thin woman in shorty pj's and a light covering of brown curls on her head. She's not so bad. In fact, nothing has changed since last night except that . . . maybe I like *myself* a little better now.

The "blackberry cereal" somehow tastes even sweeter this morning. I like the way the berries turn the milk purple. I let the milk-saturated berries linger in my mouth, tasting them fully before swallowing. I even indulge in drinking the milk from the bowl afterward.

And then this crazy, random emotion hits me.

I'm happy to be alive! I've beaten cancer!

All this time, I've been well aware of that, and relieved about it, but I've been so wrapped up in getting my normal life back that I've fretted a lot, too. Maybe I haven't celebrated enough that *I'm elated to be alive! And healthy! And getting stronger every day!*

After breakfast, I shower and dress, applying my scar medicine, then bring in the stuff from last night and notice my sink is brimming with dirty dishes. But I feel too upbeat to wash them right now. Instead, I grab up the containers to take to Grace, open the front door, step outside—and then, whoa.

Color! So much color!

My snapdragons have blossomed! Overnight! It's an amazing profusion of hues: corals and yellows and oranges that are almost neon. A yellow-orange blend that looks like a sunset climbed into a flower. Light pinks, bright pinks, whites, purples, and some magenta ones that mimic velvet.

It feels almost like waking up on Christmas morning to find this bounty of beautiful flowers in front of my house. Even though my mother always had snapdragons in the yard, I've clearly forgotten how gorgeous they are.

Merrily, I cross the road and climb the old steps to Grace's house to knock on her door. It takes her a minute to get there, but she opens it to look right past me and say, "Oh, honey—your snapdragons bloomed!" That's how vibrant they are.

"I know," I tell her with a smile. "Aren't they incredible?"

"Sure are. And my, don't you just look bright-eyed and bushy-tailed this mornin'!"

I'm stumped by this. "I look what?"

She just laughs. "Chipper," she says. "Ya look chipper." Then her gaze drops to my hands. "Whatcha got there?"

"Blackberries. And part of a cobbler I made."

"For me? Well, now, ain't that sweet! I'm gonna enjoy these, I am—you just wait and see."

"I hope so. The cobbler is from Mabel's recipe."

"Then that'll be an extra special treat. Might just make it my lunch today." She winks and adds, "When ya get old, you can do that sorta thing."

We part ways and I return to my flowers, utterly wowed by them. I sit on the front steps, next to my petunias, enjoying the way all these bright new colors seem to punctuate the morning air. When a striking blue butterfly trimmed in black alights on one of the pink snapdragons, I study its wings, thinking they look so delicate but must be strong to hold up amid all that flying. I've never ruminated on butterflies before.

Okay, maybe woodland animals *are* going to start hanging out with me soon. Sydney is right—who am I?

I mean, I'm still me. I keep acting like there's more than one me, but it's just that new—or old—aspects of me are rising to the surface. And one part that's undeniably rising is that I've simply never noticed so much *beauty* until now. Things truly appear different to me.

I look at Grace, an old woman, and see something beautiful. I look at Jo and see a truly beautiful woman there, too. They both have wrinkles and imperfect bodies. They are, by most people's standards, past their prime. Yet they're still so vibrant and unique and magnetic.

When I go inside, I'm drawn to photos I put out upon my arrival, particularly the ones of my friends. I know Syd is a beauty, but have I ever noticed how flawless her complexion is, or the kindness in her eyes? Have I ever seen the little freckles on Kevin's nose that make him look more boyish than he would without them? He and Patrick look so stoic in front of their pyramid, but I can still see the love for each other in their eyes even as they both face the camera.

I study my mom and dad then, too. My dad's smile was infectious. I hear his laugh in my mind, hear him talking with customers at the store, and my heart swells with the memory. And my mother looks so gorgeous in this picture. She didn't think she was pretty, but she was actually a stunner. Her dark eyes were almost hypnotizing. I wish she'd known that. I wish I'd seen it so clearly back then, so I could have told her. But I'm happy to be seeing it now.

I'm filled with a sense of purpose as I go about the rest of my day.

Slapping on my floppy hat for sun protection, I walk toward the winery, carrying my containers in a tote bag I found in the broom closet, all along the way enjoying the wildflowers. I spot an owl—an actual owl, for heaven's sake!—on a tree branch and try to take a photo, but it's too dark. So I just stand down below soaking in the moment, glad I happened along when I did. I can't help thinking, same as on the way to the berry patch, how many wonderful things aren't seen, but they're still there, existing, being. Heading up the vineyard lane, I spot grapes on the vines—some purple, some green, all glistening in the sun.

When I give Jo the cobbler and berries, her eyes light up, her smile brings out a sense of youth, and I find myself wishing I'd known her for much longer than I have. She offers me wine, but I decline today—too much to do.

Back at home, I take pictures of the lost teddy bear and of some photos in the first two family albums I found. There are more in the collection now, but I have to start somewhere.

Changing over to my fedora—after all, would Joy Lynn even recognize me without it?—I hop in the car and drive to town.

First stop: Piggly Wiggly. There's no news about the Hawkins Bible—no one coming forward to claim it—but it's been shared, whoa, *hundreds of times*, and the post is overrun with comments. The Bible's gone viral! People find the history fascinating and the family's loss heartbreaking even two hundred years later.

The lack of an owner for the Bible doesn't discourage me—it's early days yet—and I craft new posts about the items I just photographed. I include when and where they were found, and anything else I know about them. But I obscure the name on the bear's foot—anyone could say it was theirs, but I'm going to need someone to tell me the name Liza.

I grab lunch at the Last Chance, the café busier today than usual, yet despite that, Joy Lynn is less frosty to me. I see customers eating blackberry pie and wonder if the berries came from Matt, but I think better of asking. Instead, I study the menu for something new, try the Kentucky hot brown, and fall in love. Then I order some egg salad to go. By the time I'm departing, the place is emptier, and I make my usual trip to the jukebox, coin in hand. All I have to do now is glance over at Joy Lynn—feeling my gaze, she looks up from where she's wiping down the glass-front pie case and says softly, "B15."

I insert my coin, press the letter and numbers, and watch the old vinyl record drop into place on the turntable. "Since I Don't Have You" begins, and I look down to see who it's by—the Skyliners. I turn to go, unable to quash the notion that Joy Lynn suffers from a broken heart, and I wonder who or what did the damage. Matt? I'm not sure. This feels deep, timeworn. Like something or someone has shattered her somewhere along the way.

But even so, and even despite her tacky appearance and often unpleasant demeanor, when I glance back from the door, she lifts her hand in a small wave, and she's wearing a half smile that changes everything about her: her eyes, her cheeks, the shape of her face. And for the first time, I even see the beauty in Joy Lynn.

When I pull back in the driveway at the end of Lost Valley Lane, I'm greeted by those spectacular snapdragons again, and I spot Grace out on her front porch. As I wave, she calls to me, "Honey, them blackberries was mighty tasty!"

"I'm glad." It seems almost as if she thinks I made them myself rather than just picked them.

"Ya ever eat breakfast for dinner?" she yells.

A little out of the blue, but who doesn't? "Absolutely!" I answer across the road.

"Why don't ya come over tomorrow night around six. I was thinkin' of makin' some blackberry pancakes and it'll be way more than I can eat myself."

"I'd love to," I answer with a smile. Okay, not so out of the blue after all.

The afternoon looms before me, and I'm feeling a little too happy today to go digging into lost items—it's a worthy way to spend time, but I'm realizing I need a more balanced existence. I decide that today I'll find balance by grabbing another book from Mabel's shelves—this time a paperback by JoAnn Ross with a lovely lighthouse on the cover—and enjoying the beautiful weather from the back porch. Turns out Kevin was right—it's a pretty idyllic reading spot and the story sweeps me away.

I don't know how much time has passed before I hear a cute yapping noise. When I look up to see Goldie running around her backyard, it leads to a Matt sighting as well. We make eye contact—he smiles and starts toward me. I'm not sorry to see him—and that's even with the knowledge I'm not wearing a hat.

"How's your day, Miss Jessie?" he asks in that Southern way of his.

"Pretty great, actually," I admit.

He leans back playfully, as if stunned. "Havin' a good day *and* didn't get all bent outta shape when I called you Jessie—I musta shown up at just the right time." Then he points to the glass of iced tea on the table next to me to ask, "Got any more of that?"

"Suppose I have enough to share," I reply, aware that I'm not only hatless but returning his smile. Like . . . return flirting, I guess. I decide not to ruin my day by questioning it. Or questioning that I suddenly really don't mind him calling me Jessie. My name. My name the first twenty years of my life, so why *should* I mind? Why did I ever? I've felt so carefree today that I'm not going to overanalyze *anything*. Then I motion inside. "Help yourself—it's in the fridge."

"Reckon I will," he says, and I play with Goldie while he's gone.

A few days ago, I would have been more . . . calculating about our next encounter. I would have been trying to put distance between us, making sure he doesn't get the idea anything is going to happen. But now . . . maybe it doesn't feel as necessary. I still don't intend for anything to happen, but that doesn't mean we can't be friends. And it doesn't mean I can't enjoy his company for a simple glass of iced tea. Which is a way smarter, safer beverage to be drinking with him.

A minute later, he joins me in the neighboring rocking chair and the dog bounds up onto his denim-covered thigh.

"Did you see the snapdragons?" I ask.

"Sure did." He grins, then tosses me a wink. "Aren't you glad I stopped ya from diggin' up perfectly good flowers?"

"I never expected them to be so many different colors and shades."

"They cross-pollinate when they reseed," he explains. "Never know what you're gonna get out there. To tell ya the truth, since Mabel passed and the reseedin' took over, I kinda enjoy seein' what pops up each summer."

As he mindlessly nuzzles Goldie, I observe, "You still don't seem like a Yorkie man to me."

At this, he lets out a laugh. "I wasn't—until I was." When he drops his gaze to her cute little face and then looks back at me, I realize he's going to tell me more than the last time I brought this up. "She was my Aunt Rita's. When she passed a few years ago, I was put in charge of finding Little Miss Golden Paws here a good home. Local fella named Darnell Henry took her—his wife wanted a little lap dog—but then she killed one of his chickens."

I gasp.

"That's right—Goldie here's got a dark side."

"Oh my God, Goldie," I hear myself lecturing the adorable dog, who I can't even imagine being a murderer, "why did you do that?"

"Darnell thought she was friendly with the chickens and just liked playin' with 'em—but terriers were bred as huntin' dogs, so there ya have it. I took her back . . . and then my daughter fell in love with her and I *couldn't* get rid of her. And even though I'm the one who does all the dog parenting around here . . ." He glances down at her again. "Can't really imagine my life without the little goofball now."

As I reach across the table between us to scratch Goldie's head, Matt says, "Sometimes life has a way of forcin' things on us that turn out to be the best gifts of all."

CHAPTER 19

Grace tells me stories, her rich voice adding an extra layer of history and memory as she lingers over the words. I watch her face, sometimes study her hands. Her nails are long and strong and well groomed, a practical woman's small self-indulgence that pleases me. I've grown to enjoy sitting in the colorful playground of Walter's metal artwork. What a magical thing to have left behind. Like the owl and the deer and so many other things, I never would have seen it if I hadn't ended up on this secluded little spot on the globe.

When she asks what I've been doing besides picking blackberries, I tell her about trying to find the owners of Mabel's lost things, saying maybe it's an impossible task, but that it seems worth a try. Her eyes light up and she reaches over, squeezing my hand as she says, "Mabel's smilin' down on you from heaven, honey. I feel it sure as anything."

We're so deep into conversation that even when the sky darkens to gray, neither of us bothers to mention it. The air cools with a breeze that smells like rain, and when a heavy drizzle begins to fall, she announces with a grin, "Guess that makes it suppertime."

Inside, I ask if I can help, but she's quick to say, "Heavens no—you're a guest," and I can see that even as slow as she moves, she enjoys cooking for me.

She does allow me to set the table, after which I play with Ophelia the cat, taking up a ball of yellow yarn that clearly belongs to her, while Grace pours blackberry-laden pancake batter onto a griddle. Even as

I lure the kitty with a string, listening to loud meows I find cute and annoying at the same time, I watch Grace's movements, thinking at moments she appears unsteady, but she never mentions it, so I have faith it's okay.

She asks me to fetch a bottle of maple syrup from an overhead cabinet, and I'm carrying it to the dining room when my eyes fall on two framed photos I didn't notice the last time I was here. The one that grabs my attention the most is a wonderful picture of Grace, looking just a few years younger, standing outside her house. The pastel paint job seems fresher—or maybe the camera just made it look that way. I'm instantly in love with it, and in love with the very idea of people who love their homes enough to take such photos. I have one of my parents in front of our old house in Wisconsin, too—yet I seldom see newer pictures like this, and it feels to me a bit like a lost art.

"Grace, this picture of you with your house is amazing!" I call, leaning my head back around into the kitchen.

She glances over at me as the house fills with the sweet aroma of berry pancakes. "Had it took last time I got the place painted," she says with a smile, then goes on to tell me the house has been many different color combinations over the years, but she likes this one the best.

"I like it, too," I assure her. The photo, the home itself, is brimming with a uniqueness that makes me feel full inside. I decide that come fall, I should find the picture of Mom and Dad with our house and have it framed as well.

The pancakes are just as delicious as they smelled, and as we sit eating, I turn my eyes on the other photo I'm admiring, hanging just below the one of the house. It's old—like probably 1800s old—and is a portrait of a distinguished-looking gentleman in a suit and a big neckcloth that feels to me like something between an ascot and a tie.

"Who's this man?" I ask, thinking perhaps it's her grandfather.

"Can't say as I know," she tells me instead.

This stops my fork midair. "You don't?" Because of how much I adore Grace, I'm trying not to sound confused.

She swipes a napkin across her mouth and says, "But he looks important, don't he?"

I nod. He does.

"Found that picture a long time ago, frame and all, sittin' out next to the curb on trash day down in Jackson, Mississippi. I was only a girl then, but didn't seem right to let such an important-lookin' fella go in the garbage. In fact, ain't even sure I'd ever seen a Black man in such a fancy suit before that, so I picked him up and brought him home. My mama thought he seemed important, too, so we hung him on the wall in our house, and I brought him with me when Walter and me came north. I come to think of him like . . . a friend, I reckon. And I used him as an object lesson for Daniel back in the day. Now my boy wears a suit and tie to work, so I like to think I done good."

"You definitely did," I tell her, moved by the story, and looking again into the eyes of the mystery man on the wall. "It does seem . . . like an odd thing for someone to throw away. It must have been valuable to someone, even if it was a long time ago."

She nods and gives me a wink. "Guess I got a little bit o' Mabel in me." Then adds, "Take him with you when you go."

Again, my fork freezes in place. "Huh?"

"See if you cain't find who he belongs to. Or at least somebody that makes more sense than me."

I think this over as I pour more syrup over my plate, concluding, "Seems to me he belongs to you completely—you're the one who cared enough to rescue him, and you've kept him all these years. He's practically a member of your family."

She grins. "All that's true, but I ain't gonna be around forever, and like it or not, my boy and his girls just ain't as sentimental as me. I cain't see any of 'em holdin' on to this the way I have. If you could find out who his family is—any of 'em, or even anyone who'd appreciate his picture the way I have—it'd be a burden lifted from me."

After we each have a second plate of pancakes and I insist that she let me clean up the dishes, she walks over to the picture and takes it off the wall. It's been there so long that it leaves a dark square on the faded wallpaper.

Of course, I have no idea if I can find anyone who would have a connection to this man. It's a long shot at best. But I promise I'll try. And I walk away with it feeling pretty certain that if no one comes forward to claim Grace's distinguished gentleman, I'll end up hanging him on my own wall, out of respect for her.

The next day I'm watering my snapdragons when Matt comes out in his police uniform, headed to his truck. He calls over, "Fourth of July at my place!"

I squint over at him, sun in my eyes. "Huh? When is it?"

He chuckles silently. "Don't you have a calendar?"

I shrug, hose in hand. "Only in my phone, which I don't really look at anymore."

"Well, it's day after tomorrow," he informs me.

I'm a little surprised. That snuck up on me. "What happens at your house?"

"Burgers and dogs, fireworks and sparklers, that sorta thing. There'll be people you know there. Party starts around five."

A few days ago I probably would have declined, then sat around on the Fourth mad because the neighbors were making so much noise. Now, though, I try to think like Grace or Mabel, and what comes out is, "Can I bring anything?"

"If you want. A dessert or somethin'."

I nod shortly. "Got it."

After he drives away and I finish watering, I take pictures of some lost items, recording details about each on a notepad from Mabel's kitchen. As I'm doing it, I resolve to get more official and create a log on my laptop.

Then I photograph Grace's gentleman with the big tie. I take the time to really look at him now, too—I study his historic clothing, the distinguished way he holds himself, and the pride I see in his solemn gaze. I really want to find out who this guy was, for many reasons, but mostly because I'd love to be able to tell Grace more about this man she's carried with her through most of her life.

I also inspect the frame—it's wooden and worn—then flip it over to look on the back. And in one corner I discover faded writing! *Thomas B. Hartfell, 1882.* That's amazing info to have, to share, to google when I get to a place where I can google.

Next, I put on my fedora and head to the library in Brandywine, photos and notepad in hand. The same librarian I've seen on my previous visits sits behind the desk and seems to recognize me. She smiles and waves, and I head to what has already become my usual chair.

Once my laptop connects, the first thing I do is google Mr. Hartfell. But a search turns up nothing, not one shred of a clue. *That's okay, though. Don't be discouraged. Just move on.*

So I start checking my social media.

And to my extreme delight, I have private messages from strangers! Normally, this would not please me, but since that's how I've asked people to contact me about the lost items, I'm excited to open them.

Oh my God! The very first one is someone claiming one of the photo albums. Her name is Keri, and it's from her childhood. Her parents divorced, and amid the drama, their pictures were tossed out. Which breaks my heart. But she's so happy to discover some of them were saved. *My brother, David, and I are so grateful, and so excited to get these memories back!* She lives in Chicago and offers to pay for the postage, but no way—it's on me! I think I'm as thrilled about this as she is. I find myself glancing toward the ceiling to whisper, "We did it, Mabel! We did this!"

And if not even one other item ever finds a home, any work I put into this project is going to be a hundred percent worth it just knowing this one piece is being returned to its rightful owners.

I want to text Matt! And Grace! And even if I'm getting used to life without texting for the most part, at moments like this, when I want the insta-thrill of sharing my joy, it stinks that I can't. So I just sit there and smile. I smile at the screen and think of Mabel, and of Keri and David, and I feel so happy that I worry my heart might leap through my chest.

Then I calm down and message Keri back, telling her how much this pleases me, that I'll drop it in the mail in the coming days, and that I'd love a picture of her with the album to share online since I know people will enjoy seeing the satisfying outcome.

After my heart rate eventually settles, I open the next private message—and wow. Just wow. The other photo album has been claimed, too! By a grandchild of the people in the pictures. I stop, lean back in my chair, and suddenly feel like I'm doing something really good here. Something that matters and will make a difference in people's lives.

In only a small way, maybe, but it's true that sometimes the small things are the big things. I can feel in both of these messages just how important it is to these people to be reclaiming their lost memories.

In fact, this feels like . . . when I deliver the evening news on Channel 11. Like I'm providing a service, doing something relevant. This is the most relevant I've felt in a long time.

Part of me wants to laugh deliriously, and part of me wants to cry with pent-up emotion—but rather than give in to either urge, I put on my game face and get back to work. That's what this is to me now: a sacred sort of work, a labor of love.

I go to the original posts and edit them to include a new caption: ***Items claimed and owners found!*** I explain a bit, of course leaving out names. I also see that the posts were shared hundreds of times, which explains how they reached the right people. So I thank everyone on my page for sharing, and then I see . . . holy crap, I've gained ten thousand new followers in the past week. Just from all this sharing. People *like* helping lost things find their way home.

I dive into crafting new posts—for the music box I texted Sydney about, for a family Bible where the birth and death entries end in 1956, and for another photo album, this one appearing to have belonged to a young woman in the 1980s. Lastly, I put Thomas B. Hartfell out there, too. I explain the photo was found in Jackson, Mississippi, estimating the year. And I hope the same miracle occurs for these items as for my two claimed photo albums.

I take a look at the teddy bear post and see lots of comments that don't really go anywhere, but I'm still holding out hope that Liza will somehow magically materialize—and given that it's been shared seven hundred and fifty-six times, I have faith.

I leave the library with a kick in my step, and I'm walking toward my car when I spot a Dollar Tree down the street. On impulse, I bypass the car and go to the store instead, heading straight for the school supply section. Before I can talk myself out of it, I select a colorful binder, some loose-leaf notebook paper, a pack of colored ink pens, and some sticky notes.

Keeping a lost-and-found log in my laptop would make so much more sense and be so much easier and quicker in so many ways, but somehow I want to hold it in my hands. I want to fill it with color and flourishes and my own handwriting. The way Mabel would have done if she'd started one back when the items first arrived in Lost and Found.

I'm almost surprised there isn't one, in fact—but maybe it seemed pointless. Now, though, it's not.

The long days of summer are upon us, darkness not falling until after nine—though twilight does seem to arrive a little earlier here, tucked down between the Kentucky mountains.

After I grill a chicken breast and add it to a salad, I take an evening walk over to the winery. It's still hot out, even at this hour, but more tolerable than earlier. Jo tells me she and Conrad have been enjoying the blackberries, and Conrad passes by, announcing that I've given him an idea for blackberry wine. Then he asks me to taste test a few versions of a Chardonnay-type blend he's been working on, and I gladly oblige.

Returning home, I see Grace sitting on her front porch, so I go tell her about finding homes for the two photo albums and that Mr. Hartfell is now out there for people to see, too. She claps her hands together in joy, then invites me to sit with her for a few minutes and look at the sky.

Joining her, I follow her eyes upward. It's still an hour until sunset, but all the signs of day's end are already there, in unusual ways. Dark blue-gray wispy clouds waft fast and furious across a larger pink-cloud backdrop, moving like smoke in the wind.

Grace says, "Cain't say I've ever seen clouds like that before."

I haven't, either. "Do you think it's going to storm?"

"No." She sounds very sure, like a woman who knows the sky well.

We keep watching the clouds drifting speedily past, like they're in a hurry to get somewhere. After a few minutes in silence, I ask, "What do you think is making that happen?"

"God," she answers.

"God?"

"Everything's God, ya know. The world's a beautiful mystery."

Now Grace's face draws my attention more than the sky—I watch her looking up at those clouds with wonder and reverence. I watch her seeing God.

I wonder if Mabel saw God in the clouds on her ceiling. These are very different, of course—dark blue on a sea of neon pink, ghosts in the breeze—but I see it, too, the beautiful mystery of it all. As we watch quietly, taking in the subtle majesty, there's no place I'd rather be right now. I sit stunned by the beauty.

It's so many different things, beauty. A pretty face, a piece of art, a night sky. Maybe even a face that *isn't* pretty. Beauty goes much deeper in ways I'm only just beginning to understand.

CHAPTER 20

When I find a card in Mabel's little recipe box for something called Fourth of July poke cake, I have no idea what that means, but I know I'm making it. I get the ingredients I need from Mr. Freeman, and next thing you know, I've created an absolute work of confection art! It's a white sheet cake in which I poked little holes with the end of a wooden spoon and poured in strawberry Jell-O while it was hot, so the strawberry flavor spreads lightly through. Then I iced the top, first with vanilla pudding, then a layer of Cool Whip. And then—here's the most exciting part!—I created an American flag design using blueberries in the star area and rows of sliced strawberries for stripes.

I'm pretty pleased as I carry my incredible cake toward Matt's backyard, now bustling with people and dotted with folding camp chairs. I'm wearing a red tank top and a blue ball cap embroidered with a little American flag that I also found at the market. It's not a look I would ever have considered before this moment of my life, but . . . things are different here. *I'm* different here.

I find a dessert table, where I spy brownies and lemon bars, a plate of chocolate chip cookies, pies of strawberry, blackberry, and apple, a patriotic-looking Jell-O mold that also seems to involve berries, and . . . another American flag poke cake that makes my heart drop like a stone. Because I'm just that immature. I guess I wanted to make a nice impression on the Lost and Found crowd, and now I feel way less original than I did five minutes ago.

"Oh, you done a nice job on that, honey." I look up to see Grace's friendly face—a welcome sight. She's leaning on a walker and sporting not only a glittery flag T-shirt but a headband from which red, white, and blue sparkly stars sprout up like antlers. I've never seen her in anything other than a simple housedress, and in this moment, I love her all the more.

I love her enough that I'm comfortable saying exactly what I'm thinking. "It never occurred to me there'd be another one."

Grace just swipes her free hand down through the air and says, "Pshaw. Can't have too much strawberry poke cake." Okay, so it's not original at all—at least here. Everyone knows about strawberry poke cake. "I made the strawberry pie," she tells me. "The two should go mighty nice together on a plate."

"See you made it," comes a deep voice from my other side.

I look up to find Police Chief Matthew Cordray giving me a smile. And in that smile I suddenly see how much he holds this place together. He doesn't have to throw this party, but I suspect he does it every year and that it reminds these people they have a town, and a community.

I smile back. "I did."

He glances down at my cake, which I'm still trying to place on the table—I'm scooting a couple of desserts around with my free hand to make room. "I'm lookin' at a thing of beauty right there," he says, then raises his gaze from the cake to my face in a way that turns my cheeks hot. "You're gonna be in trouble with Joy Lynn, though." He adds a wink, but I'm not amused.

"What do you mean?"

"The flag cake's kinda her thing."

Well, *that* figures.

He leans in close enough for me to feel the heat of his body, which isn't quite touching mine but feels like it is anyway. "Yours is prettier, though."

Okay, flirtation aside, I'm strictly focused on the matter at hand. "Just when she was starting not to hate me, too."

At this, Matt shrugs. "Joy Lynn's affection is about like the weather. Never know when it's gonna blow one way or the other."

I just look at him, thinking he sounds like a man who knows her well.

"Point bein'," he goes on, "that it's best not to let it bother ya."

I offer a nod, intrigued anew about the nature of their relationship.

"I'm about to start grillin'," he announces. "You okay hangin' out with Grace?"

"Of course," I say, struck by his concern. It's nice that he recognizes he invited me to a party where, despite his claims, so far there aren't many people I know. It also strikes me that in my usual life, no one would ever worry about me at a party—because I know how to talk to people, and as a local celeb, people usually want to talk to *me*. This, now, feels more like middle school—once again, Jessie Fox is on the scene.

But the truth is, I'm not that young girl anymore, and I can *still* talk to people, even if they don't know what to make of a stranger with such short hair. I get acquainted with a farmer named Billy who tells me he and his boys "work coal," and I think of Matt's father dying from that particular profession. Neighbors from farther up Lost Valley Lane ask how I like staying at Mabel's and compliment the snapdragons they've seen on their walks—as if I had anything to do with them. When I meet a woman named Kaylie, who cuts hair at the Snip 'n' Clip near the Piggly Wiggly, she tunes in instantly to my post-chemo hair situation, saying, "Now them fine little baby curls'll grow out in a few months and need to be trimmed once you get some length. If you're still here then, come and see me." I thank her, but explain I'll be back home in Cincinnati by that time.

Soon enough Mr. Freeman arrives, and then Jo and Conrad, and I realize I'm actually enjoying myself. Conrad brought a case of wine, which of course makes him a popular guest. I notice that he and Jo are as different from most people here as I am, but that we all three fit in anyway, that everyone welcomes the outsiders more than I might have expected a month ago.

Grace, Jo, and I are sitting in camp chairs, balancing paper plates in our laps, when a man I haven't met comes walking up to say, "Are you the news lady stayin' at Mabel's place?"

I blink, surprised. No one here ever associates me with being a newscaster. "That's me."

He holds out his hand. "Junior Barnett. Pleased to make your acquaintance. I heard from Matt what you been doin' with our lost items, tryin' to find 'em homes, and I can't thank ya enough."

I think he's probably also thanking me for clearing his name in the big lost-and-found scandal, but I just smile and tell him I'm happy to meet him as well.

"That pile of stuff has long been . . . well, like an anchor weighin' down this town, and to think that even some of it might get back to wherever it belongs does my heart good."

Junior Barnett is clearly a glad-hander with a bit of used-car salesman about him, but I can tell he cares about the town, perhaps in the same way Matt does, and I like him. "I kind of stumbled into it," I tell him, "but I'm happy to help as much as I can. I've only found the owners of a couple of things so far, but it's a start. I'll keep at it while I'm here, and maybe someone else will want to take over the effort when I leave."

Junior Barnett's face falls. "Leave? Oh, you can't leave, Ms. Fox. This town needs you."

I gape at him. The very suggestion is absurd. This is a limited-time gig, no two ways about it. But I'm careful not to be rude or insulting to the town as I choose my next words. "That's kind of you, but I'll be returning to my job at WRTB in another month or two. I'll do what I can in the meantime, though."

We exchange a little more conversation, but I can tell I've really burst his bubble. I guess Matt neglected to explain how temporary my stay here is. After he departs, I say to Jo and Grace, "I feel bad now. But once the ball is rolling, it should be easy enough to get someone else to take over what I've started, right?"

Jo lowers a fork to her plate and holds up both her hands. "Don't look at me—I've got a winery to run and a dog to take care of." As if on cue, Socks, who came along to the party, trots up next to her chair.

Grace isn't any more helpful, saying, "Cain't imagine who else would have the know-how for such a thing besides you, honey."

I get it. She's older and has no internet knowledge. So I try to explain, "Well, a lot of people know how to use social media, and even if it requires a trip to Brandywine—or actually just to the Piggly Wiggly—it's a pretty easy task."

"Except for the parts you're forgetting," Jo says knowingly.

I switch my gaze to her. She's wearing pink-lensed sunglasses today, her silvery locks falling in waves around her face. I'm not liking everyone's resistance to the idea that someone else could operate the lost and found, so it comes out a bit dry when I say, "Enlighten me."

"Most people around here *don't* know how to use social media. Because they have to work too hard to access it. And even those who do . . . well, you, my dear Jessica Fox, have a platform. Many thousands of people who are interested in what you have to say. You have a built-in audience happy to spread the word about all those lost things. No one else here has that."

Oh crap. She's right. I guess it's something I've almost come to take for granted. I have the ability to reach people in a way no one else in this town can.

But that's not my fault, and there's nothing I can do to change it. So I simply say, "Those are good points, I admit. I'll just have to post as many of the lost things as I can until I leave and hope for the best."

I'm approaching the dessert table a little while later when I come face-to-face with Joy Lynn. I've seen her from a distance, and had kind of hoped to keep it that way, but nope, here she is—sporting star-spangled boobs in a tight, strappy top and another denim mini-skirt, saying snippily, "I heard you made that other flag cake."

Oh boy. I was having such a nice day. I'm tempted to tell her to get a life. But then I remember that conversation I overheard, the one where it sounded like she has a lot of problems, and I also remember suspecting her heart was once broken in a way she's never come back from, so instead I reply, "I found the recipe in Mabel's things and thought it would be a nice way to commemorate her. I didn't know it was your thing—sorry."

She seems surprised by the apology, like it completely threw her off her game. When she answers, her voice comes out a little softer, more like when she's telling me what numbers to punch on the jukebox. "That's okay. You did a nice job—just a little heavy on the strawberry stripes. That part takes a light touch."

It's a fair criticism—her strawberry stripes do look better than mine, wavier and less rigid. "Thanks," I tell her. "I've never made anything like that before and I appreciate the tip."

She nods casually. "Anytime."

Then she walks away. I feel like I've dodged a bullet.

As I peruse the dessert table, I hear Matt nearby and steal a glimpse of him talking with a lanky, awkward-looking teenage boy. "Tobe," he says, "what's up, bud? How's your summer?"

I instantly recall hearing Joy Lynn on the phone, referring to someone named Toby—who I assumed was her son—so I find myself listening closer as I cut a square of my own cake, eager to see if it's any good.

"Sucks," Toby replies. "Workin' on Chuck Pelfrey's farm every damn day, and don't even get to keep any of the money."

Ah, yes—because he has to help Joy Lynn pay the bills. So far he sounds like a punk to me, but I feel for him anyway.

"I hear ya," Matt tells him—so apparently he's aware of this situation, too? "It's a tough spot to be in. But I know your mom appreciates it, even if she might not be good at showin' it."

At this, Toby softens a little. His mood appears to shift with the breeze, like his mother's. "She shows it enough, I guess. Tells me all the time how shitty she feels about it."

"I know this sounds like a line," Matt tells him, "but things'll get better. Just gotta hang in there for now."

The boy says nothing, but I catch sight of a nod as I maneuver a slice of Grace's pie onto my plate as well.

"Fish bitin' in Chuck's pond?" Matt asks.

The boy perks up some. "Pretty much, I reckon."

"Why don't you give me a call later this week—we'll make plans to do some fishin'."

"Sounds good," Toby concludes.

I use a pair of tongs to add a lemon bar to my plate, then start back toward my little group of friends, filled with fresh questions. Matt acts like a dad to Joy Lynn's son? What's *that* about? And I assume that fishing in Chuck Pelfrey's pond is kind of like picking Jeb's blackberries—you don't have to ask, you just do it? And exactly what is the nature of Matt's relationship with Joy Lynn anyway? I haven't even seen them communicate with each other today, but he's buddying up with her boy?

Of course, what do I care?

I don't, in fact. Since he and I are just friends.

Friends who flirt some, I suppose. And earlier he was a friend whose flirtation I felt . . . well, between my thighs. In fact, I feel a little shiver just remembering it as I ease back into my chair.

"Almost time for the fireworks," Grace says.

CHAPTER 21

After the Fourth of July, life in Lost Valley takes on a pleasant, easy rhythm for me. I guess I've truly adjusted to the pace here, at last.

My days are about walks to the winery, watering my flowers, doing a little cooking and baking, trips to the market and the café, and working with the lost and found. I've become a regular at the Brandywine Library as well, enough that they know who I am and why I'm there, and they seem as pleased by my mission—Mabel's mission—as the residents of Lost and Found.

More items get claimed. The family Bible last dated 1956, the music box, and Liza's bear! That one was emotional, and heartbreaking—turns out Liza died as a toddler. But her older sister wants the bear, which their grandmother made—there was one for each of them—and I'll be shipping it out tomorrow.

And more items get posted. My three-ring binder logbook is a busy place!

As a side effect to all this, people seem curious to learn about the town of Lost and Found. So I've also shared more about the town itself online, about the few businesses still surviving, and even the remains of those that have passed—attempting to capture with my camera the charm in the chipped paint of empty storefronts and the faded lettering on plate glass windows. It's like those faces that hold beauty for me without necessarily being pretty in a traditional way—the rustic wearing down of things holds an unexpected appeal, a history I can feel when I take the time to look closely.

Much to my surprise, a TV station in Lexington caught wind of my lost-and-found exploits and did a small feature about the project on their evening news, using some of my posts, including a short video where I talk about some specific items. It's satisfying to be doing something people find worthwhile. And though I think the locals are far more excited about the fanfare part of it than I am, I love seeing them begin to take pride in their small town, which, it turns out, is not nearly the fresh hell I first thought upon my arrival.

Matt wanders over every couple of nights with a bottle of wine, though I've learned to have only one glass—no more! I've taken to keeping a dessert on hand to go with the wine, too, even if it's just break-and-bake cookies. But I also made a no-bake cheesecake that was cool and light for summer, and yesterday I got some of Melva's chocolate cream pie to go from the Last Chance. Like many things, I've simply accepted his presence in my life while I'm here. We talk about his daughter, my friends, our jobs, whatever else comes to mind.

But that's as far as it goes. Well, okay, that and some flirtation. Because that just seems to be who he is—a natural flirt. I don't flirt back. Or I try not to. I blush, though. I feel it sometimes, the heat climbing my cheeks like little licks of flame. But I try to ignore it.

Perhaps the most amazing part to me is how all these things fill up my days. Six weeks ago, I couldn't have dreamed my existence here would be anything more than wandering around looking for things to do. Now, some days, I actually wish I had more time to read.

Even so, I can't deny that life moves slower for me here—and it turns out the slowness is, in fact . . . a gift. Having the time to take the walk or bake the cake or sit in Grace's backyard with her is a gift I never saw coming and couldn't have imagined I would value. But maybe it's like Matt said. Sometimes life has to force on us the gifts we wouldn't have gotten any other way.

Over the course of about a week or so, I realize my snapdragons aren't blooming very much anymore. And since I can't just google it, I do the next best thing: I go knock on Grace's door.

She doesn't answer, which is often the case, so I walk around the house to find her out back. "Grace, I have a problem," I announce.

She looks up from her metal bench knowingly. "I know ya do, honey. And I was wonderin' if you was ever gonna talk to me about it."

Getting closer, I peer into her eyes, trying to figure out what on earth she's alluding to. "If I was going to talk to you about *what*?"

She leans forward slightly. "You and Matt."

As my eyes go wide, I sway backward a little, like something has smacked me in the face. "I'm here about snapdragons," I correct her.

She looks disappointed. "Well, that ain't nearly as interestin'." Then she lets out a sigh. "What *about* snapdragons?"

Okay, I'm still stuck on whatever her assumption was about Matt, but I try to get back to the relevant topic. "They're not blooming anymore. They look healthy, but they're not getting new blooms."

She tips back her head in a way that tells me she indeed has the answer I seek. "Part of that's the summer heat. Sometimes they don't bloom as much in the dog days until the weather cools a little. But the bigger problem is likely that they go to seed if you don't deadhead 'em."

"If I don't what 'em?"

It no longer even throws Grace when I don't know what she's talking about. "Deadhead 'em, honey. Ya gotta pinch off the Martian heads."

I shift my weight from one foot to the other. This sounds potentially similar to what Mr. Freeman taught me to do with daylilies, but no Martians were involved in that. "Okay, Grace, I'm sorry, but you've really lost me here."

When she laughs, I know that without saying it, she's echoing Matt's frequent comment about me: *city girl.* And it's true—despite my small-town upbringing, one would never know I ever lived outside the metro area.

"That's what my mama used to call the seedpods on a snapdragon," Grace says. "Martian heads. When the petal falls off, underneath it leaves behind a seedpod that looks like a little green head with one antenna stickin' up out of it. Now, if ya left it there, it'd dry out and let new seeds fall into the ground, which is how most o' them flowers got there in the first place. But to get your blooms for the rest of the summer, ya just find some of the Martian heads and pinch 'em off, simple as that. That'll get your flowers all pretty again."

"And it'll be easy to figure out what I'm supposed to pinch off?" I ask to clarify.

She gives a nod. "The antenna makes it real clear it's a Martian head and not a new bud. If in doubt, though, just squeeze it real gentle-like—new flowers are soft, but seedpods are rock hard, like a pebble."

"Look for the antenna and pinch off the Martian head," I repeat back.

"That's right, honey," she answers. "And I'll look forward to seein' them flowers burst back into bloom."

As I turn to go, against my better judgment, I peek back over my shoulder and ask, "Um, what problem did you think I was having with Matt?"

"Well, that ya like him but don't think you should start somethin' since ya won't be here long, or . . . maybe ya just don't feel quite yourself after what you been through this year." It's like she's been reading my diary—except I don't keep one.

Yet I nip this in the bud. "Matt is a great guy, but there's nothing like that between us."

"Pshaw." Grace rakes an aged hand down through the air. "You two been flittin' around each other like a couple o' June bugs all summer. And all I got to say about it is—get to my age and ya realize life is short, and that we cain't really know how many opportunities we got left, and that maybe we oughtn't pass up good things when they come a courtin'."

Rather than argue the point, I instead take all that in, nibbling on my lower lip, then ask with a tilt of my head, "Do you have regrets, Grace? Things you wish you'd done differently?"

"In romance, no," she says. "But in other ways, yep. Wish I'd seen more o' the world. But livin' in the country my whole life made me just wanna . . . stay there, in my little cocoon. Gettin' very far from home made me nervous. I wish I hadn't let fear rob me of seein' different places."

That makes me sad, but rather than let her dwell on her past, I assure her, "Don't worry. I'm not letting fear rob me of anything."

"So you say," she retorts as I turn to walk away.

"Thanks for the flower advice!" I toss over my shoulder, then head back to my own house and, perhaps, into my own cocoon.

Grabbing a little bucket from the garage, along with Mabel's kneepad, I put on my floppy hat and sunscreen, then head into the flower bed. It only takes a minute to recognize the seedpods—and to instantly understand the Martian head analogy.

There are, predictably, a lot of them. As Grace indicated, though, they're easy to pinch off. It takes a while, but somewhere along the way I realize that, just as with the daylilies, I find the task relaxing.

Afterward, my back is stiff, but I discover myself standing near the street, studying the cottage, thinking about improvements Kevin and his family should make to it. Replacing the old concrete porches with wood composite decking and adding new rails would do wonders for the exterior. A little paint on the inside would also help a ton. But then I remember no one in his family actually uses the house or seems to care much about it, so I decide it makes more sense to keep the ideas to myself than share them with Kevin.

When the phone rings inside, I rush through the screen door to answer like a woman on fire. "Hello?" I say breathlessly as I pick up.

"Hey!" It's Syd. "I have great news!"

"What's that?"

"I just came from your house and the remodel is done, done, done! And it's *so* gorgeous, Jess! You're going to love it!"

The remodel. A thing that used to seem so important, a thing I wanted so much. I—again—kind of forgot it was happening. "Wow, that's great!" I say anyway. "So you really like it?"

"Absolutely! It's amazing! The kitchen of your dreams. And more importantly, your house is no longer a construction zone. I arrived just as the workers were packing up their stuff. So that means you can pack up, too, and come home!"

My breath catches at the words. Sydney sounds so excited about the prospect. And I should be excited, too. This is what I've been waiting for, after all. The comforts of my big beautiful half mansion. The luxury of my brand-new fabulous kitchen. The convenience of pizza delivery and being able to grab milk and bread in a two-minute drive. And the internet. *The internet!* All the time, right at my fingertips. I've almost forgotten what that feels like.

I should be jumping up and down for joy. I should be champing at the bit to get off the phone, throw my clothes in a suitcase, and go speeding up Lost Valley Lane, never to look back. I should be feeling the relief drop over me like a heavy blanket.

Instead, though . . . I'm suddenly not so eager to go home yet. I mean, the snapdragons need me. I like to think maybe Grace needs me, too—or at least likes having me around. I'm expecting Matt tonight and still have some chocolate pie left that I'd hate to go to waste.

"Why are you so quiet?" Sydney finally asks.

"I'm just . . . not sure I'm ready to rush home."

"Wow. Color me surprised."

"Me too," I tell her. "But I'm kind of into taking care of Mabel's flowers now, and of course all the lost-and-found stuff . . ."

"And the police chief," she adds when I trail off.

I'm glad she's not here to see my cheeks flush even as I insist, "I do not take care of the police chief. He's a friend, a buddy, a neighbor."

Syd just laughs.

"Anyway," I proceed, "I guess I'll just do my time as planned. If you don't mind keeping an eye on the house a little longer."

"Not at all."

After a short pause, I admit, "I'm surprised you're not, you know, fighting me on this. Reminding me that I literally have no cell service and am super hard to keep in touch with, or how badly I wanted to come home after I first got here."

She seems to think that over before telling me, "Well, I miss you, of course. But you seem . . . content lately. More content than . . . maybe ever, the whole time I've known you."

This throws me, and I argue. "I was happy before, too. Before the big C."

"Happy, yes. But 'happy' and 'content' can mean two different things. You just seem . . . calmer the last couple of weeks. More peaceful. Except," she goes on, "for when I accuse you of being attracted to the police guy. Then you get a little riled up." She laughs again.

But I ignore the last part—seriously, why is everyone so interested in me and Matt as a couple?—and tell her, "I guess maybe I am. I mean, once I got over my outrage about the lack of internet . . . well, it would be hard *not* to feel at peace here."

"Then it's good for you. And Kevin made the right call thinking a summer getaway would help you do some more healing."

Though I've had the same thought myself, I kind of hate giving Kev credit for that, since we all know he was really just trying to shield me from the bigwigs making me feel like crap. But perhaps that in itself is enough that he *should* get credit. "Maybe he did."

"So you'll stay down there another month or so, and then you'll come home and get back to normal?"

"Yes," I agree.

I'm almost tempted to invite her and Jayden down for a weekend. I could relocate the lost and found from the spare bedroom, I could take them to the winery, we could eat at the Last Chance, and I could show them what might be the world's oldest working jukebox while they indulge in Melva's homemade pie. But . . .

The truth is . . . I'm not sure they'd see the charm. It took *me* a while, after all. And I'm not sure Sydney would understand how delicious I find Melva's chicken salad, or why I think Jo's long silver hair and hippie sunglasses make her so cool, or why I consider Grace's backyard a genuine work of art. Some kinds of beauty just take a little longer to see than a weekend.

So I listen happily as she tells me all the fun stuff the two of them have been doing, and how they met Kevin and Patrick at a rooftop bar in Over-the-Rhine the other night, and I realize that a month ago I would have felt a little left out, but now I'm just . . . glad for her. Glad for all of them. Glad my friends are happy and well loved.

CHAPTER 22

"Can I ask you somethin' personal?"

I cast Matt an annoyed sideways glance on the back porch. We're pairing wine with chocolate pie. "Why stop now?"

He chuckles, grins—but then goes surprisingly serious. "It might be none of my business."

"Again," I say, "why would you quit prying into my private life at this point in our friendship?"

He looks amused, cute. When I was younger, I couldn't have dreamed a man in his forties could still ever look cute, but Police Chief Cordray seems to pull it off with regularity. Once more, however, his expression turns somber. "Guess I was wonderin' about . . . cancer."

"Can you be more specific?"

"You told me it's completely gone now, right? I mean, guess I don't understand how that stuff works exactly."

His concern tugs at my heart when I least expect it. Sometimes I forget that people don't know these things, and that they care. So I take a sip of wine and say, "I think it all works differently for different kinds of cancer, and for each individual person actually. But they tell me there's a ninety percent chance mine will never recur, so I'm truly in good shape."

A visible relief washes over him that I'm not wholly ready for. "That's great, Jessie. I'm really happy to hear that."

"Thanks," I tell him, not quite meeting his eyes, even now still not quite ready for his care, or the fact that it might be affecting me emotionally.

"Can I ask you somethin' else?" he asks.

"Could I stop you if I tried?"

Another soft laugh from him that reaches my solar plexus. Yet then . . . "I know the last time we talked about this, you seemed uncomfortable, and I'm not tryin' to be nosy, but we know each other better now, and . . . I just still wonder what was it like for you? To go through it."

Yes, I was uncomfortable back then, worried about things like pity. But even now that those issues have fallen away, it's hard to answer—because he can't know what a big question he's asking. The truth is, if you've gone through the big C, you understand, and if you haven't, you can *never* understand.

When I don't reply right away, he says, "You don't have to answer if you don't want to."

But I quickly tell him, "It's okay." And it is. "I talked about it a lot on my social media, because I wanted to demystify it and wanted people to know it's not always a death sentence. And I wanted women to be proactive in detecting breast cancer since, if you catch it early, they can usually treat it. But what it's like is . . . well, that's different for every person, too. And for me, it was . . . hard." My voice has gone softer than intended.

He responds gently as well. "I bet you wished you had your mom and dad around."

I hold in my gasp but feel it in my chest. I've never told anyone that. I've never said those words. And no one ever said it to me, either—until now. But the truth is . . . "The whole time. I wished every day that I could just call my mom and have her come take care of me. Like moms do, you know?"

He nods. "Yeah."

"You know what they say about cancer," I go on. "If the disease doesn't kill you, the treatment will. In my case, the chemo was rough.

And I'm grateful that both my brain and body seem to have bounced back for the most part. It leaves some people in a fog for a long time. For me, things got better once the chemo ended, but I still don't always remember things as well as I used to." Yikes, did I just say that? Out loud? To him? I've thought it before, been aware of it, but I haven't voiced it, even to myself really, because I don't want it to be true.

"Well, I'm glad it's over for you and that, like you said, you bounced back."

"The radiation was easier on me," I tell him. "Some people have a tough time with it, but I did well. I moisturized twice as much as they told me to. I exercised twice as much as they told me to. And that seems to have worked for me."

He's smiling softly. "I'm glad." Then he adds, "Thank you. For tellin' me this stuff. I thought you'd probably wanna slap me."

I tilt my head, give him another teasing look. "And yet you asked anyway."

"Glutton for punishment, I reckon." He swallows a sip from his wineglass, then leans back in his rocker. It's dark out, the air is cool and summer sweet, and fireflies blink on and off in the distance. "I think you like me more than you used to."

"It would be hard to like you less than I did at first," I retort.

He laughs and offers up, "Maybe I'm just an acquired taste."

"Perhaps so." I don't look at him, though. Because I'm wondering where this is going.

"Know what I like about *you*?"

I flit a glance his way, then back to the fireflies. The moon casts a ribbon of light on the lake in the background. "What's that?"

"That you're not as tough as you act."

"I'm *plenty* tough," I insist.

"I know you are," he appeases me. "But at the same time, you're not, and sometimes you even let me see it."

I'm completely honest when I say, "Something I'm suddenly regretting, Chief Cordray, now that you're feeling the need to shine a light on it."

He ignores that, however, and tells me, "I love that you quit wearin' a hat when it's just me and you. I like bein' able to see your face." His voice goes deeper. "Your eyes. Your neck. Your mouth."

Oh boy. I feel that in inconvenient places. But I quickly regroup. "If there's something you're getting at, or some point you're attempting to make, make it."

His laugh tells me I'm making *my* point—that I'm not *always* soft and it would be a mistake to think I am. "I guess what I'm tryin' to say," he replies, "is that if I like you and you like me, sometimes I wonder why we're just sittin' here drinkin' wine when we could be doin' other fun things."

Okay, I'm pretty sure he's talking about fun things that happen in a bed, and no matter what I might feel when he flirts with me, I wish the conversation hadn't gone in this direction. I thought he knew where we stood—I thought we were friends who drank wine and soaked up the summer nights and that was our thing and we were both cool with it.

"I'm in no place for an affair, Matt," I bluntly inform him.

He takes that in and finally says, "I'm not sure what that means. 'In no place.'"

Oh brother. I really have to clarify this? Well, fine then. "I'm recovering from cancer. I'm trying to start feeling normal again. I hope at some point I can begin to feel . . . a little bit *pretty* again. It's, frankly, a weird place to be." Crap, I've been far too open. Stupid wine. So I move on. "And sex just complicates things. I mean, I just started liking you—why would you want to mess that up now?"

The words pull a small grin from him. And a slow-in-coming reply. "Okay," he finally says. "I get it. We're just back porch drinkin' buddies."

He sounds like he actually understands. Which is a relief. "A wine-drinking buddy isn't a bad thing," I point out.

"You're right." I watch then as he drains his glass, sets it on the table, leans over to pat my knee with one hand, and says, "But this wine drinker's gonna toddle off to bed now." He pushes to his feet.

"Because I turned you down?" Maybe he *is* disappointed, pouting.

"Just tired," he replies. But he looks kind of sad, and I fear I've truly hurt his feelings.

"I hope you understand," I tell him as he steps down off the porch. When he came on to me after we first met, turning him down was a matter of common sense and not being into meaningless sex with a stranger. And now it's something . . . closer to self-preservation. But I don't quite care to confess that. "I'm really just not in the right . . ."

"Place," he finishes for me. "Yeah, I know. You said. It's okay, Jessie."

I want to say a million things. I want to tell him how broken I feel physically. How even though I walk around acting normal, I don't want a man to see me naked right now, skinny and covered with fresh scars, both outside and in. How even though I let him see me without a hat, I still don't feel attractive and that seems like a big part of sex to me. How I'm not good at truly letting go and surrendering completely to the experience because I have control issues, and the few times I've really done that, I've ended up hurt by putting trust in the wrong guys. And yet I can't tell him any of those things—I've told him far too much already. So I stay quiet, sorry that an otherwise nice night is ending this way.

He's halfway across the yard when he stops and looks back, shadowy in the light from the porch. "Just so ya know, you're plenty pretty, and I know you've been through somethin' hard, but I wish you could see yourself the way I do." With that, he turns to go again—but comes to a halt once more, spinning back to face me, even more of a shadow now. "And if we had sex—I know we're not gonna, but if we did—it wouldn't make you like me less. You'd definitely like me more. I'd make damn sure of that."

After which he really leaves—I hear his back door close a minute later. I sit with my final sips of wine, listening to crickets and tree frogs, digesting his words.

I wish you could see yourself the way I do.

If we had sex, you'd definitely like me more. I'd make damn sure of that.

I blow out a breath, toss back the last of the wine. Now I'm tired, too. Tired and trying not to feel those last words of his too much. Even so, they settle down inside me, in ways both troubling and comforting.

I carry in the wineglasses and empty plates, lowering them into the sink. Then, despite that it's nearly midnight, I take a shower in the pink-tile bathroom, perhaps needing to wash some parts of the evening away.

After drying off, I go to the mirror to apply my scar cream. It's the usual routine, done in front of the mirror because the port scar is pretty high and it's easier to find in the mirror than looking down. Though I still don't spend much time looking at *myself* in the mirror these days, at my face. But for some reason, just now, I do.

I wish you could see yourself the way I do.

I smile at myself. It's a fake smile, a practice smile, to see what it looks like. But it . . . helps fill out the thin face with no hair falling around it. I've not sure I've done that since losing my hair—smiled at myself in the mirror, allowed myself to see that my smile is still there, and it *is* still pretty.

I was blond as a child, and after my hair darkened in my teenage years, I started getting blond highlights, and eventually went all the way blond after college. Now it's as brown as can be. And it's getting a little longer, enough that the curls frame my head more. It's only a slightly bigger helmet than I had a month ago—but it's thicker, maybe even thick enough that my scalp wouldn't sunburn without a hat. Maybe.

I look at my eyes. Matt once told me they show up better without all that hair. No denying that they look much bigger—at first I felt like one of those tiny stuffed toys with the too-big sad eyes—but maybe it's okay. They're bright, wide, hazel—and my eyebrows are coming back in a little fuller.

I don't look the same as I did before, and maybe I never will—who can say? But maybe, just maybe, I'm starting to see what Matt sees, because right now, at midnight in the middle of nowhere, I don't mind very much. In this moment, I'm okay with being just the way I am.

part 3

love

CHAPTER 23

The next time I see Matt, he waves and smiles as he's getting in his truck to go to work, like nothing uncomfortable ever happened between us. Funny how much I care about that, how relieved I am. Ugh. I care.

And the next time he taps on my back door with a bottle of wine, a few nights later, I'm even more relieved, and happy to see him. I hold up one finger, then go about grabbing glasses and some lemon meringue pie I picked up at the Last Chance, kind of hoping to share it with my wine buddy.

We catch up. He tells me Samantha got to swim with dolphins and it seems to have been the highlight of her summer so far, which pleases him because "if the dolphins rank higher than boys, that gives me less to worry about." I tell him I've been deadheading snapdragons and think I'm seeing new buds! I also catch him up on the latest lost-and-found news, which is several more items claimed, although just as many haven't been—at least not yet.

He shrugs and says, "You can't expect a high success rate at this—the fact that you're findin' owners for *any* of it is downright amazin', if you ask me. Although . . ." He pauses and points his fork at me. "Afraid you're kinda in trouble at the post office."

I sit up a little straighter in my rocker, stunned. "What do you mean?"

"Somebody mailed us a new lost item. Came yesterday. Nothin' new had shown up for years, but guess all this recent hoopla is makin' people think we *want* their lost junk—when we already got more than we know what to do with."

I blow out a breath. "Yikes. What was it?"

"A necklace, I think. A locket with a picture inside and some engravin' on it."

I instantly slide into work mode and say, "I'll pick it up tomorrow and get it posted. It should be a lot easier to match with whoever lost it if we don't let years pass by first."

"Good point."

Neither of us mentions that I'll be leaving soon, and now perhaps even leaving the town with a bigger mess than they had when I arrived. It feels like too huge and messy a topic when I'm just enjoying his company and the pie and the wine and that things seem simpler between us again compared to the last time I saw him.

As the last vestiges of a purple sunset fade over the horizon, bringing darkness on in full, we're joined by a few fireflies. Less, though, than earlier in the summer.

"Did you know they only live a few weeks to a couple months? The lightnin' bugs?" Matt asks. He must be noticing there are fewer now, too.

I answer, "Like butterflies, I guess. Most of *them* don't live long, either."

"Seems a shame, so little time."

"I guess they have to pack a lot of living into every day," I suggest, but I'm annoyed at myself because it reminds me of what Grace said about life being short, and regrets, and I almost feel like I'm arguing against myself, even without Matt knowing it.

"Sometimes," he says, "I wonder if I'm wastin' *my* time, livin' here."

That surprises me so much my jaw drops. "Does it *feel* wasted?"

"No." He shakes his head. "Feels . . . right, mostly. Just not what I planned when I left. And not the choice I figure most people would make."

"Then I guess you're not wasting it."

I look over to see him in profile, staring out over the dark water in the lake below. The moon isn't especially bright tonight, just a crescent high in the sky, and the porch light's not on, so *everything's* darker. Still, I study the shadow of his cheek, his jawline, the dark stubble there. And I find myself asking the same question. Am I wasting *my* time? My summer?

I mean, sure, yes, in some ways I've filled my time wonderfully. But when it comes to Matt, I mean. Is it possible Grace is right? Possible Sydney's right? Is there supposed to be something more between us than I'm letting happen?

The man has succeeded in making me feel *almost* pretty at the time of my life when I've felt the *least* attractive. He's made me look forward to seeing him—with or without a hat. He's made me like him, no matter how hard I tried not to.

And yet, all the reasons I've pushed him away remain. I don't have a successful track record with men. I'm not good with feelings. And no matter what people say, sex comes with those. And sure, I'm good at putting up walls and wearing armor and all that, but . . . what if it were to fail me this time?

He turns to look at me—and appears surprised to find me already looking back. "You starin' at me?"

"No," I lie. "Just thought I saw something flying around in the dark over by your house."

"Probably just a bat."

I sit up straighter, letting out a small gasp. "A bat?" I've almost even forgotten I *made up* the flying thing.

He sighs. "Calm down. They're not gonna bother ya, and bats are everywhere, city and country both—you just don't know it 'cause you're not lookin' for 'em."

I have no idea what to believe on this topic, so I tilt my head and ask, "Really?"

He just shakes his head. "City girl."

We talk more about bats—it's mainly me interrogating him about being *sure* they're in the city, too, and wondering where they go during the day—until he finishes his pie and asks, "Got any more of this? I could go for another slice."

I nod. "Give me your plate."

A minute later, I'm back out the door, standing in front of his chair, handing him his pie—which is precisely when he rocks forward unexpectedly, the plate bumps his body, and the pie smushes into his chest.

This brings him standing up out of the chair—even though I'm already in that space—and I've trapped and caught most of the pie on the plate, but my other hand is trying to wipe yellow filling and fluffy, sticky meringue off his chest. Which is firm beneath my fingers through his T-shirt. And he smells good. As usual, I don't even know what it is he smells like, just . . . manly soap or something.

"Oh my God, I'm sorry," I'm mumbling.

And he's murmuring, "It's okay, it's okay."

"But it's your Dollywood shirt," I say rather dumbly. Because I know he likes it since it holds a memory. His shirts seem less silly to me all the time.

"It'll wash," he assures me as he takes the plate from my hand and lowers it to the table next to us. Then his free hand presses down on mine—the one busy wiping at his chest—until my palm is flat against his shirt, flat against the warmth of him, and I can feel his heartbeat. I could swear the spot between my legs is pulsing in time with it.

He uses his other hand to tilt my chin upward, forcing me to lock gazes with him.

I still haven't taken a step back.

I could.

I should.

But a heavy whoosh of want is pushing through my body, and I'm suddenly having trouble thinking straight.

"Jessie," he says. Ever so simply. Pragmatically. In one word, he's asking me: *What's it gonna be?*

Every ounce of my brain still thinks this is a terrible idea, one that will take a controlled, managed, pleasant situation and send it spiraling *out* of control. But that's the problem with sex. The brain so often gets overpowered by other insistent organs.

It's been a long time since I've been with a man.

And God help me, I want him.

And he's making this seem so easy, so right.

But the little bit of sanity still persisting inside me insists on putting *some* sort of safeguard in place. So I hear myself say, "Just to be clear, this is only sex. Like, between friends." Oh Lord, my voice came out hot and breathy. I sound ready to melt for him. I sound like a woman not nearly as in control as I like to think I am.

And then he has the nerve to say, "Friends don't have sex."

"Friends with benefits," I argue. Everyone knows about those.

"No such thing," he claims.

I blow out a breath. I still feel his heartbeat beneath my palm—and between my legs. Is he really going to make this difficult? "So you're saying . . . you can't take this casually?"

"I can take it however you want, Jessie, but we're more than just friends and have been for a while now, if ya ask me."

Oh boy. He's a much more complex man than I ever could have predicted the first time he flirted with me. *That* guy, in my mind, would have been *all about* casual sex. But this guy . . . this guy is . . . I really can't think anymore. I really just want to press myself against him, move our bodies together, get lost in it.

Finally I suggest, "Maybe we shouldn't . . . worry about labels." Mainly I'm thinking he's saying all the wrong things, things I don't want to hear, things that should be making me change my mind—but I don't *want* to change my mind.

"Agreed," he says. Thank God. "There are better things to worry about."

"Like what?" I ask, still as breathless as a schoolgirl in a back seat.

"Kissin' you. Gettin' your clothes off. That sorta thing."

Yes. I want those things, too. But then his words make me remember. So many things. I swallow nervously. "Matt, I have scars."

"Everybody has scars, Jessie."

"No—I mean from the cancer surgeries."

"I don't care."

Right answer. Without missing a beat. Still, this part is hard for me, and I can't let it go that easily. I feel the need to warn him, for both our sakes. "I'm . . . my body's not . . . perfect. Not even close."

"Neither is mine. Are you talkin' yourself outta this?"

I suck in my breath. "No."

"Then quit thinkin' so much and just kiss me."

My hands find his face; his close over my ass. He pulls my pelvis to his as our mouths crush together and it's . . . heaven. A strange sort of heaven—I've never been an "urgent sex" sort of gal, but this has been so long in coming that now it feels like a bursting dam.

It takes a second for our lips to start moving over each other's, but when they do . . . mmm, it's a really good kiss. Firm, hot, powerful. Down below, he's hard where I'm soft, pressing into me, and we're moving together and that's perfect, too. This is still almost surreal to me—I didn't come here for this. I never expected anyone to want me—or for me to want anyone back—so soon.

"Let's go inside," I say between kisses.

"Okay," he murmurs deeply, and I take his hand and lead him in the door, through the house.

I hate to stop the hot perfection of the summer night make-out session, but if I don't, part of me fears we'll end up doing it on the back porch, and that's just a bridge too far here. I need at least an ounce of decorum if I'm to come out of this sane and feeling like I have any control over the situation at all.

As we enter the cloud-covered bedroom, his eyes, for some reason, fall on the teddy bear on my bedside table. "Who's the guy?" he asks.

I try not to smile. "Meet Edgar J. Growlington the third."

Matt shrugs, looking playfully jealous. "Seems fancy."

"He is," I concur. He wears a tweed vest and burgundy ascot. Then I volunteer way more information than I need to. "He's been with me for over twenty years. My mother and I were in a gift shop one day after my father died, and Edgar caught my eye. She insisted on buying him for me even though I was well past what most people would consider teddy bear age. And he's been with me ever since." That's when I realize I've never told anyone that. Not even Sydney. Not even Kevin. It's been my secret. Because the idea of a grown woman loving a stuffed animal is so . . . not Jessica Fox, WRTB 11.

"Sounds like he's pretty special to ya," Matt observes.

"We've been through a lot together." A fact I understand only as I say it out loud.

"And he gets to sleep in your bedroom every night? Lucky guy."

I want to commend Matt for the perfect segue back to why we're here. I have no idea why I started blathering on about Edgar, but it's definitely time to shut up. Because my body is still pulsing like crazy in all the right places. Places which, again, I never expected to pulse like this so soon.

"Kiss me some more," I say—before this has a chance to get awkward, before I have a chance to remember reasons to feel weird.

Thankfully, like on the porch, the kisses consume me. I run my fingers through his hair while his hands explore my waist, back, bottom. We fall onto the bed and keep kissing and touching until, finally, he pulls back to start lifting my top.

I raise my arms, let him remove it. And my heart beats harder. Scars.

I realize I'm holding my breath, holding it until I actually can't breathe, so I blow it out and push up his Dollywood tee. He takes it off. His chest and stomach are nice. Not chiseled and perfect—he's not twenty-five. But he's fit and attractive, and I like what I see. I like what I'm touching. I like it enough that I stop thinking about scars.

There's a lamp on, so now I lean over away from him just long enough to turn it off.

"Don't want the bear to watch?" he asks.

I laugh, loving him a little bit in that moment—since he knows good and well why I turned it off. I reply, "Exactly," and adore him for making this part so easy.

More clothes are removed. My shorts, his jeans. My bra. All that's left is underwear. And whereas back on the porch I thought this might go lightning fast, now we've slowed down, and it's undeniable that, as I've always known, turning out the lights in this room doesn't really make it dark. Something in the whiteness of the clouds on the walls and ceilings illuminates the space no matter the hour. I see him, the planes and contours of his body, and I know he sees me, too.

I forget about that, though, when he begins kissing my breasts.

But I remember it again when he runs his fingers over the scar at the top of my right one, just below the dimpling left behind from removing the lump, and then he explores the port scar higher up on the other side. And I'm on the verge of telling him he's started doing a crappy job of letting me forget about my imperfections . . . when he begins to *kiss* the scar on my breast.

His mouth is gentle, reverent, almost worshipful in a way that makes me pull in my breath. I feel the kisses in the crux of my thighs. And then he kisses the other scar, too, in the same way—like it's some beautiful part of me that warrants his attention, and much to my surprise, something in this pleases and pleasures me all the more.

"Are there others?" he whispers, sounding as if he's discovering gold or lost treasures. Making them . . . normal. Maybe even better than normal.

"Under my right arm," I answer, suddenly not trying to hide them anymore. I even lift the arm and turn my body to offer it to him.

He finds it with his fingers, explores it gently with soft little strokes. I don't feel it much, because of severed nerves from lymph node removal in that area—and yet . . . I do.

"Can I show you somethin'?" he whispers deeply.

"Sure."

He raises off me and twists his torso, pointing to his own scar—on his side. It's a large, jagged slash. And I instantly like it—because it's just another part of him and finally something we have in common.

Reaching up, I run my fingertip over the length of the rough skin there. "Some altercation with a dangerous criminal back in Lexington?" I ask.

He grins down at me. "Fell on a garden hoe when I was ten."

I laugh—but then quickly say, "I'm sorry. That sounds horrible."

"It was." He's smiling. "But just wanted you to know you're not the only one with scars."

"Thank you," I whisper, and I get it now. I suddenly understand how little my scars matter to anyone but me. Okay, maybe on the air at WRTB in a dress cut the wrong way, they would raise eyebrows. Though they shouldn't. And here in Lost Valley, in the real world, they don't matter at all. Even so, I slant him a half grin and say, "But you know that's a little different."

He just shrugs. "Not really. Scar's a scar."

I think about that a minute. Maybe he's right. They're never fun to get. And like he said before, everyone has some.

That's when he adds, "You can kiss it if ya want."

I let out a soft laugh, and I do want, so I roll us over in bed until I'm on top. I kiss my way down his chest and then over to his side. I kiss his garden hoe scar and wonder what he was like as a little boy. Then I forget about little boys because he's definitely a man, a man whose body I want to kiss some more, until I'm done with kissing and, with a desperate prayer, ask, "Do you have . . . ?"

"Lord, please let me have my wallet on me," he murmurs more to God than to me, and I hate that he has to pull away even long enough to lean over the bed and rummage in his pants.

Fate smiles upon us and he has what we need, and soon enough I'm straddling him, easing my hungry, suddenly empty-feeling body down onto that hardest part of him, filled and fulfilled, moving together, feeling the wonder of having given in to myself, the wonder of: What if I'd really left this place without letting this happen? Because this is maybe one of the most unpredictably and unexpectedly perfect moments of my life.

I feel like . . . a woman again. Like a whole, desirable, vital, vibrant woman. Like his eyes are touching me. Like I'm dissolving into him, giving myself over to every sensation, letting myself be swallowed up by the moment, the sex, the intimacy. And like everything is suddenly right with the world.

CHAPTER 24

Afterward, I get up, go to the bathroom, close the door, and a few minutes later, find myself still hesitating there.

Now that it's over and I'm not in bed with him anymore, I turn . . . sheepish or something—about letting down my guard down so much, even about . . . how comfortable I got with my own body. He made me feel beautiful, but that was in the dark. The partial dark, at least. In the light of day, or even just in lamplight, how much more noticeable might my scars seem? The outside scars. Or maybe the inside ones, too. I suddenly *feel* my nakedness in the bathroom light.

"You comin' back?" Matt finally calls.

I purse my lips, try to formulate a reply. "I might take a shower."

"Want some company?" he offers. And when I don't answer right away, he catches on quick, adding, "Or . . . want me to leave?"

"That might be best," I say from the other side of the door. "Save us from feeling awkward in the morning."

"And just makes it awkward right now," he points out ever so bluntly.

I blow out a breath and try to be honest. "Afraid I'm not very good at the morning-after stuff."

"Don't take this the wrong way," he says from the bed, "but you're not great with the five-minutes-after stuff, either."

I grab a towel, wrap it around me, and holding it together in front, open the door. "Look," I tell him, "this is actually the nicest thing to happen to me in a while, but I'll be leaving soon, you know? So maybe it's easier not to make a big deal of it."

Our eyes meet in the dimness as he says, "Suppose I shoulda seen this comin'."

Honestly, I expected more of an argument and am surprised when he pushes the covers back, stands up, and reaches for his underwear on the opposite side of the bed. Unfortunately, his butt is undeniably attractive and I can't help noticing. I bite my lip, waiting silently as he pulls on his jeans and tee.

Afterward, he walks over to where I'm still standing in the towel. Catching sight of the stain on his chest, I say, "Sorry about your shirt."

"Totally worth it," he says, then cups my cheek in one warm hand, kissing the other. Despite myself, a fresh burst of desire blossoms inside me, that fast. From a cheek kiss.

But he's already walking across the room to the door. As he passes the bedside table, he tosses a glance at my teddy bear, now illuminated in the glow of the bathroom light, and gives a terse nod of acknowledgment. "Growlington."

As he walks away, I can't help but smile.

When I wake up the next morning to find only Edgar by my side, I'm relieved. I made the right call. It's nice to lie there not caring what I look like or how the early-morning light might change things or if I'm supposed to offer him breakfast.

Though as I eat a bowl of cereal with a toasted English muffin a few minutes later, I can't deny that as I gaze out the window, I'm wondering if he slept well, if I made him sad or mad or none of the above, if he's awake or still asleep, and if he thought the sex was as good as I did.

Well, that last part is mostly a lie—I know he did. The sex was great; we were totally in sync. I bite my lip, though, remembering how much I let myself go at certain moments. Honestly, that's the thing I hate about sex. For it to be any good, you have to really let yourself go, but the letting go leaves me embarrassed afterward.

I told Sydney that once and she said, "It didn't make you feel embarrassed—it made you feel vulnerable. Two different things."

I didn't argue the point and just said, "Well, whatever it is, I don't like it." Frankly, I don't even like the word "vulnerable." Some people act like it's a good thing—that it means you're all open and unafraid. To me, though, it's always had a more negative connotation: You're unprotected and therefore in danger. Young girls hitchhiking are vulnerable. Zebras on the Serengeti are vulnerable. People with low immune systems are vulnerable. Nope, to me, there's nothing good about vulnerability.

In the same conversation, Sydney said she thought my lack of vulnerability was the whole reason I never really end up in lasting relationships. But in my opinion, armor has served me well in life, and that's just who I am, a woman who takes care of herself. So well, in fact, that it took cancer and some bigoted station managers to finally get the best of me for a little while.

So I'm good with how things ended last night. And I hope Matt is, too. Whether or not we officially labeled it, it was exactly what I told him: casual, FWBs.

An hour later I'm out working in my snapdragons when the man himself strolls over in his police uniform. And an unsettling thing happens. Inside me. When I see him crossing the lawn in my direction, my impulse is to go to him, slide my arms around his neck, and pull him into a kiss.

Whoa. What the hell is *that* about?

I don't really have time for analysis, though. I only know I sent him away. Because I don't want to form any weird attachments. So I look up at him like we are indeed still just a couple of pals and say, "Hey."

His grin acknowledges *my* lack of acknowledgment that we had hot, grinding, steamy sex last night. "Hey." Then he asks, "How'd you sleep?"

"Well, thanks. And you?"

"Little lonely, actually. But I'll survive. Thank God Goldie's a good cuddler."

So I've been replaced by a Yorkie. But it's my own fault, so I don't go there. I just keep fiddling with the Martian heads on a clump of bright coral-colored flowers.

"Busy tonight?" he asks. "Or . . . is it too soon and you'd rather me keep my distance?"

I actually love that he's just upfront about it—and I'd be lying if I said I didn't also love that he already wants to see me again. I mean, at breakfast I was feeling cool and detached, but now I'm a little more caught off guard with the suddenly-wanting-to-kiss-him thing.

See, this is what happens, how simple relationships get complicated. You have sex with your neighbor and now you want to kiss him when you see him. And you have to wonder if he thinks you're gonna have sex with him all the time. And you have to decide what you want. I have *no idea* what I want. This is why I like deadheading snapdragons—it's such a simple task, no consequences other than new blooms.

So I'm just honest. "Unless someone suddenly brings the internet to Lost Valley today, under which circumstances I would have a whole lot of TV to catch up on, I'm probably free. What did you have in mind?"

"Steak," he says.

Which is different than sex. But maybe doesn't exclude sex. The answer feels cryptic. "Steak?"

"I have some rib eyes. I was thinkin' we could invite Grace over and grill out."

Despite myself, I think it sounds like a lovely evening. Even if it *is* maybe too soon. But the Grace buffer will help. "I suspect Grace would love that," I tell him. "I'll go over and invite her a little later."

He smiles. "Great."

"Anything else we should add?" I ask. "I need to run to Mr. Freeman's anyway."

He thinks a minute. "I've got some potatoes we can bake on the grill, and some corn on the cob. But he had a bin of nice-lookin' watermelons out yesterday."

I nod. "I'll pick one up. And I'll get some pie, too."

"Sounds good," he says, and our eyes meet. And . . . crap. I feel it between my legs. It's so much more than an eye meeting was just yesterday. I've gone from detached to let-me-get-us-some-dessert in a heartbeat. In fact, I barely recognize myself.

I try to quash it all down as I tell him, "Have a good day out catching all the big criminals of Lost and Found."

Though I've never seen Grace use a walker at her house, just like on the Fourth of July, she's planting one before her with every step as she makes her way to my back porch. Uneven ground, I guess. Matt escorts her, making sure she gets where she's going.

"Oh my," she says, pausing to peer out over the lake. A hawk glides low across the water. "I always forget what a nice view ya got here. I mean, I got my own view, but this is good, too."

"You should come over more often," I tell her, suddenly feeling shortsighted not to have invited her before now. She's just always struck me as a homebody and has even acknowledged as much. But maybe these days it's partly because she's reached a stage in life when it's not easy to go out. I know she still drives sometimes, but that Mr. Freeman brings her groceries out to her car. And now I notice the silent effort it takes for her to get up onto the porch.

Food sizzles on the grill—Chef Matt made me promise not to touch anything with the tongs while he was gone, so I resisted the urge—and it all smells delicious. In addition to making a tall pitcher of iced tea, I've cut slabs of watermelon and arranged them on a plate, and as we sit down to eat at the small back porch table a little while later, I can't deny it's a lovely summer night.

If I were back in Cincinnati, what would I be doing? Could be anything. After getting home from delivering the news, I might change into leggings and take a walk around the neighborhood, I might have something DoorDashed for dinner, or I could be out with Sydney at a patio restaurant a few blocks from home. But all things considered, this feels just as good as any of that—only in a different, more secluded way.

"You look nice," Matt says to me across the table. "Never seen ya in a dress before."

The frock to which he refers is extremely casual: a gauzy, beige tank dress with buttons up the front and a small belt at the waist. The truth is, I don't even know why I brought it, because life here hasn't called for dresses, and my whole barely-there-hair vibe feels like a better fit with the most casual of shorts and capris. But something made me open up another suitcase and put this on—maybe because a dinner party for three seems about as fancy as it's going to get around here. And maybe my slightly thickening hair makes me feel a little more . . . like it's okay to show a bit of interest in my appearance again, a hint of femininity. Or . . . maybe the sex did that—who can say? Regardless, I accept the compliment graciously, with a small smile. "Thank you." Then I add, "The corn's delicious."

"Sure is," Grace says. "Ya outdone yourself at the grill, Matt."

"Comin' from a lifelong cook," he tells her, "I'm flattered. How's the family?" It never occurred to me, but I guess with Matt's long history on Lost Valley Lane, he must know them.

"Doin' good," she answers, then talks about her granddaughter Leah's job a little, before turning to me. "And, honey, I meant to tell ya, my other grandgirl, Lydia, seen you on the news in Saint Louis the other night!"

"Saint Louis?" I feel my eyebrows shoot up. "Are you sure? Is *she* sure?" Maybe something was lost in translation.

Yet Grace is nodding emphatically. "That piece they showed on the Lexington news? Sounded the same. Was you talkin' about the lost and found. She heard our little town mentioned and started payin' attention. So ya didn't know about this?"

I shake my head as I cut my steak. "Not at all. But it must've gotten picked up by some other outlets. These days, human interest stories get passed around a lot as filler for slow days." I smile, pleased that attention to my endeavor here is continuing to expand. "That's great, though. It should draw more eyes to my social media, and to our lost items."

"Good in *some* ways," Matt says, appearing dubious as he forks a bite of potato into his mouth.

"Some ways?" I ask.

"Ran into Junior this afternoon on patrol and he said a couple more new lost things showed up today."

I blow out a breath. "Wow. One yesterday and two today. That could add up to a lot, fast."

"Yep." He wipes a napkin across his mouth.

I nibble my lower lip. "Would you rather I'd never started this since I'm not able to see it through?"

Our gazes meet across the table, and even though we're talking about the lost and found, I realize we're also talking about something else. His smoldering eyes make my skin tingle.

"No," he finally says. "I'm happy for . . . whatever good comes from it while you're here." And darn it, it's hard not to like him. He's so utterly reasonable all the time. Then he reverts back to talking solely about the items at the post office. "Might have to go back to usin' Mabel's garage for storage, though, since Junior won't be givin' up his new office without a fight." He grins, teasing further. "See what you've gone and done."

I can't resist giving him a smile. Teasing makes him more handsome.

"I'm going to the library tomorrow," I inform him, "to share about the new necklace I picked up today from Jeannie at the post office. I'll stop by again on my way. And I'll post something to try to stem the tide of new items." I blow out a breath. "A person could make a full-time job out of this."

Matt chuckles. "Shitty pay, though."

"You can say that again. Lucky for Mabel that she found the one sentimental bone in my body."

I'm aware that, while eating, Grace has been switching her gaze back and forth between us as we've talked, and now she says, "Hogwash and hooey."

I focus widened eyes on her. "Pardon me?"

"You care about things way more than ya like to let on, honey—I see it ever' day. Ya talk a good game, but you're all caught up in my Walter's art, and the pictures on my walls, and the stories I tell, and good Lord, you even like my noisy cat. And those are only the things you're sentimental about with *me*. You care about ever' dang one o' them lost things ya try to find homes for. Ya care about your job and your friends and your hair and . . . for heaven's sake, I cain't think of much we've talked about that you *don't* get wrapped up in."

It's not often that I'm left speechless, but this blindsides me so thoroughly that I can't concoct one single solitary comeback or argument.

So it's Matt who chimes in, adding, "She's right, you know. It's like I keep tellin' ya—you're not nearly as tough as you like to think."

"Keep it up, and neither one of you will get any pie," I threaten. "And it's Melva's chocolate cream. That tough enough for ya?" I even toss my napkin on the table for good measure.

They both just laugh, though, and Grace challenges me with, "You ain't got it in ya to keep pie from an old lady."

I think that over for a minute and finally answer, "Okay, maybe not. But this one . . ." I point in Matt's direction. "You I'm perfectly willing to withhold things from." Double entendre intended.

The look on his face seems to say: *We'll see about that since you liked it, too.*

I'm trying to decide just where I'm going next with this when the pager at Matt's belt begins to buzz.

He's never without that pager, but in all the time I've spent with him, I've never heard it make a peep—until now. He looks down at it, his demeanor going more serious as he asks, "Use your phone?"

"Of course."

He steps inside, and when he comes back out a minute later, he's in a rush. "Gotta take a rain check on the pie, ladies."

I sit up straighter, surprised. "There's an actual emergency?"

"Yep." Then he mutters under his breath, "Damn meth addicts."

"Meth addicts?" I echo.

"One just walked right into Scooter and Betty Keel's kitchen—gotta get over there as backup for my deputy."

With that, he's gone. And when I hear him actually activate a siren on his pickup truck, I'm almost amused given the lack of traffic here—but not quite.

I say to Grace, "I guess I've heard about drug problems in Eastern Kentucky, but since I got here, it never crossed my mind."

She's nodding in the chair next to me. "Lot better than it used to be," she informs me. "There for a while they was poppin' up right and left. For a time, I do believe it was only livin' across from Matt that kept Daniel from draggin' me over to Saint Louis."

"What do they . . . do?"

"Break into places, and sometimes just walk right in folks' houses, like Matt's dealin' with right now. Lookin' for drugs or money or somethin' to sell. Ain't got no fear—the drugs make 'em too desperate for fear. That's what's scary."

"Wow," I say, taken aback. "Lost and Found seems so peaceful."

"It is, honey, it is. But ever' place has somethin', I reckon. I imagine Matt'd tell ya drugs is about the only real problem we got here, and we're lucky it seems to crop up less lately. There for a while, we even lost a few of our own."

"Lost . . . how?"

"To the drugs," she says, making me feel pretty ignorant. "Carol Patterson's daughter got hooked on the Oxy after a back injury and finally overdosed. So did Bucky Grainger. In a lotta cases, like those, it's folks who got prescribed too many painkillers after an accident and couldn't get off 'em. That's how we lost Bobby Clark, Joy Lynn's husband, too."

I gasp. "Joy Lynn's husband?"

Grace nods. "Was a sad thing. Now, mind ya, he was never what you'd call a good egg, but she was just over the moon for him since they was teenagers. She put up with a lot, let me tell ya, more than I thought she should've for Toby's sake. That boy's seen a lotta hard things. And ended up losin' Bobby in the end anyway."

"I knew it," I say. "I just knew someone had broken her heart. But I had no idea it was . . . by dying."

"Look at you," Grace replies, shaking her head. "Gettin' all sentimental over a rough case like Joy Lynn Clark."

I lift my eyes to hers. Damn it, she's so right about me. "Point made."

Then she grins. "See ya took my advice."

I'm thrown by the abrupt change in subject. "About . . . ?"

"Matt, of course."

I let out a sigh. I mean, I could deny it, but Grace seems to have my number. I'm still stunned, though. "How could you tell?"

"How could I miss it would be the better question. You two sittin' there makin' moon eyes at each other all through dinner."

I have no idea what moon eyes are, but I object anyway. "I don't believe we were making any kind of eyes at each other."

"Then how did I know you done the deed? How was it anyway?"

Normally, I wouldn't feel comfortable discussing this with someone twice my age who I haven't known very long, but given how much I adore Grace, I just roll with it. "Nice."

She juts out her lower lip. "Just nice? That don't speak very highly of the event."

I bite my lip. Fair enough. "Okay, it was more than just nice. It was . . . really, really, really . . . hot," I confess.

A broad smile unfurls across her face. "That's more like it."

"But I'm actually thinking it might be good he was called away for work, because now it's complicated."

"Honey, it's only complicated if ya make it that way."

"I don't want to get attached," I remind her. "Since I'm leaving and all."

"Ya keep sayin' that," she points out.

"Well, it's a valid concern."

Her dismissive expression tells me she disagrees. "I'm just sayin' that if I was somewhere temporary and found a fella I had that good of a time with between the sheets, don't know as I'd worry so much about tomorrow as I would about today—and milkin' every bit o' fun from it I could."

CHAPTER 25

After pie and a pretty sunset, I walk Grace home, thinking it might have been more practical to do that while it was still light out, since it's slow going on the unsteady ground for her and her walker. I gently tuck one arm around hers in case she stumbles.

"This is why Daniel's always wantin' me to move away with him," she says. "Now that it ain't druggies, it's me gettin' old. But I do perty good for an old gal, I think."

When she reaches the road, her steps come easier and I no longer feel the need to hold on. I smile at her and agree. "I think so, too. And you know if you ever need anything, you can call me. Well, while I'm here, anyway."

After we get her up her front steps, she says, "This was a real nice evenin'. I'm sorry Matt had to miss out on some of it, but it was real nice indeed."

"Just nice?" I ask. "That doesn't speak very highly of the event."

At that, she lets out a loud, chortling laugh.

Once she's safely inside and much surer on her feet, I walk back across Lost Valley Lane in the dark, feeling so much less alone here with the sound of the crickets and the quiet house awaiting me than I could have imagined when I first arrived. Matt's truck still isn't home, but I don't feel worried because he's the most capable-seeming man I've ever met.

As I head inside, I'm wondering if everyone's right—including Matt himself—about me making things more complicated than they are. And an unsettling thought hits me. That someone who wears armor . . . *needs* armor. That maybe someone who wears armor and puts up walls to protect themselves isn't actually strong at all. That a strong person wouldn't require those things. Remembering how whipped about like a willow I felt upon coming here, I realize maybe the only difference between that and my usual life was that cancer had stripped all my armor away—and now I've put it back on.

My head feels like it's about to explode with this shocking revelation when the phone rings. A welcome distraction. I walk over to pick it up. "Hello?"

"Hello there, my lovely." Kevin. I smile.

"It's good to hear your voice."

"Likewise."

When I ask what he's been up to, he tells me he's been very busy with Patrick's Nana. Patrick twisted an ankle, putting him on crutches for two weeks . . . "And so I picked up the reins. Because those pariahs who call themselves his family obviously weren't going to do it, so I had to. I'm pretty exhausted—we've had doctor's appointments galore for her—but at the same time, I feel good about it."

"I guess fate stepped in and sort of forced you to step *up*," I suggest.

"It'll do that sometimes," he agrees cheerfully enough.

"How's Patrick's ankle *now*?"

"Mostly better, my poor baby."

"Give him a hug for me," I request. "And how's your, um, diet, dare I ask?"

"I'm sure it'll go really well whenever I get around to starting it," he replies smartly.

When I catch him up on the lost-and-found progress, he says, "I'm aware. You're all over the news circuit, lady. People are loving this story." He's aware of the Lexington piece and informs me it aired not only in

Saint Louis but in Louisville, Nashville, and Columbus, too. “And we’re airing it tomorrow ourselves.”

“Oh, so I suddenly make the cut?” I ask snidely.

“It’s only logical,” he tells me. “And this particular decision was mine, not anyone else’s. Though I’ll make sure the bosses are aware that you’re hot property, making a splash all over the Midwest, and could be lured away at any moment.”

I plop down into the easy chair beside the phone, a little flabbergasted. “You don’t really think that? That another station would pursue me based on the lost and found?”

“Who knows, mon ami?” Kevin only starts throwing French phrases around when he’s feeling especially chipper and optimistic. “And for my sake, I hope not—I’d be devastated. But stranger things have happened, and I want to reinforce for them that you’re still relevant, out there garnering attention and making things happen. Because you are. It’s impressive, Jess.”

“I haven’t really done anything,” I argue, leaning back into the cozy chair. “It’s a hobby to pass the time. The fact that it’s getting picked up by news outlets is a fluke.”

“There *are* no flukes, mon cherie.”

I just laugh. “Okay, whatever you say, monsieur. So . . . any Tiffany updates?”

“Yep, got a good one for ya.”

My adrenaline spikes a little just from that. “Lay it on me.”

“She mispronounced Vevay. Phonetically.” The Indiana town within our viewing area is actually said “Veevee,” with long *e*’s and in a short, clipped way.

“No!” I say, scandalized.

“Yes. And the emails did rain down from many a Vevayan offended that a Cincinnati anchorperson didn’t know how to say the name of their beloved hamlet.”

"She's . . . really unprofessional, isn't she?" I conclude. I'm actually sort of embarrassed for the station. "I mean, it's so easy to prep and *not* make those kinds of mistakes."

"I hear ya, girl. Maybe fate's stepping in for *you* in new ways, too, if you know what I mean."

The next day is a busy one. I swing by the post office to mail a claimed Bible and a claimed trophy, and also to pick up the two new lost items, a photo album with historic pictures and news clippings about a World War II pilot and an old-looking copy of *Wuthering Heights* with an inscription: *To my great lost love, the one who got away, the one who holds my affection forever. Timothy.* That one nearly stops my heart, and added to the antique locket I picked up yesterday, my work is cut out for me.

Outside the post office, I make a video—in my fedora—explaining that new items have arrived and urging people not to send more. I explain that the town is already overrun with many years' worth of lost things and that anyone can do what I'm doing, posting them online and asking people to share. "In fact," I say into the camera, "tag me in your post, and I'll be more than delighted to share it here on my page, too."

Once I reach the library in Brandywine, I post the new items, along with the video, and I check messages to discover I have two more claimed pieces—yay!—and a lot of what appear to be dead ends. But what Matt said is true—I can't expect a high success rate, so I don't let that get me down.

I buzz back to Lost and Found—by which I mean I drive a lot of twisting, curvy mountain roads, but at least I'm getting used to the route—and grab a quick egg salad sandwich from Joy Lynn, the whole time remembering what I learned from Grace last night about why she's so chronically unhappy. I mean, maybe there are other reasons, too, but when the love of your life overdoses after putting you and your kid through hell . . . well, if I felt sad for Joy Lynn before, now I feel much worse and as if I at least understand a little better why she can be so mean.

Part of me doesn't want to contribute to her heartbreak by continuing to feed into it, but the jukebox is all that stands between Joy Lynn beating me up and the relative peace we've established, so when I'm done, I walk up to it as usual. There are a few other customers, but that no longer even fazes me as I call over, "What number today, Joy Lynn?"

"D12," she says.

I drop in my money and punch the buttons, and Elvis begins to croon "Love Me Tender." My heart breaks a little more for her as I walk sadly out the door feeling like an enabler, like maybe she once was to her Bobby. Ugh. Maybe this is a habit I really need to break.

The skies have been overcast all day, and as I pull in the driveway, it begins to rain. It's fortunate timing, though, since I was planning an afternoon of digging through more lost-and-found stuff, deciding which to post next. Up to now, it's been a pretty random process, but I'm starting to feel the time constraints that come with my temporary stay, and the fact that no one is going to take this task over when I leave. Suddenly I'm trying to find the items that seem the most potentially treasured, the most valuable, the most cherished by someone long ago.

I ditch my hat and shoes, pull on a pair of comfy sweats, and plop down on the bed in the spare room with a storage container I've never opened before. Removing the lid, I spy lots of paper in this one. That already sounds time consuming and more complex, but I dig in anyway.

The first thing I pull out: what appears to be an unpublished novel! If I had Wi-Fi, I'd google around to verify the unpublished aspect, but since I can't, I read a little and decide it's not my cup of tea, yet surely someone who went to the trouble to write a novel—one that appears to have come from an actual typewriter in pre-computer days—wouldn't have tossed it out on purpose. What if this is the only copy? The author's name is on it, so that should be a big help when posting.

Next, I pull out a handful of . . . letters, I'm guessing, tied up in a blue grosgrain ribbon. They look old and I love them already. Someone kept them, meaning they were saved and valued. I almost want to leave them the way they are, undisturbed—there's something secret and romantic about the ribbon—but there's no way I can get them back to where they belong if I don't dig for clues.

On top, shoved under the ribbon, is a small note that says: *I found these in an old dresser I bought at a flea market in Santa Fe in 1988. They seem special. I've held on to them for years and don't know what to do with them.*

I open the first letter.

> *Dearest Millie,*
> *I hate how far away you are and wonder if ever I'll see your beautiful face again. How can I prove myself to your father when he hates everything about me from the color of my skin to my prospects for the future? We're doomed, my love, yet you have my heart and that will never change.*

Whoa. I have to stop, take a breath.

I also look at the envelope. Sent from A. Chen in New York City to Millie Anderson in San Francisco. The letter I'm reading isn't dated, but I can just barely make out the postmark: 1958.

My mind whirls in a hundred directions. Why did Millie's family move? How old were Millie and . . . A? I stop and look ahead—Andrew was his name. Did they ever get together? Did they get past her father's prejudice? And if not . . . where did they end up? And with whom? Did either of them ever find happiness with someone else?

My afternoon is lost in Andrew's words. I spend hours reading his every letter to Millie. I don't have her responses, of course, but the fact that these still exist means she loved him, too. The next time I'm able to, I'll google around to see if by some miracle I can find out anything about them. But right now, I'm drawn into the heartbreak of their love, the distance between them, and all the devotion Andrew spills onto the pages of his love letters.

This is why I keep up walls and wear armor. Heartbreak. It's all around. It's here for Millie and Andrew. It's at the Last Chance Café in Joy Lynn's haunted eyes. If I stop this thing with Matt now, I'll never have to know heartbreak. It'll just be a very pleasant memory of that police chief I lived next door to for a few months, who was so different from me, but who made me laugh, and made me feel pretty and normal when I started out just the opposite, and how we had that one amazing night together that made me feel . . . whole again.

He's made me feel whole again. That's being dramatic about it, admittedly, but . . . it's true.

So maybe I'm wrong about the stupid armor? Maybe I'm actually better off as a bendable, swaying little willow tree? Maybe it's better to risk complications and heartache and God knows what else than to . . . feel nothing, experience nothing, and walk through life standing tall and . . . a little bit empty inside?

The truth is, I don't know the answer to that question. There's a lot to be said for keeping oneself safe from harm.

As a result, I decide to eat ice cream for dinner and just see what tomorrow brings.

The next day is bright and hot and clear. I make a long-haul Walmart run to Hazard, and while I'm there, I buy a simple sundress in a calico print and a second flowy sleeveless dress that falls past my knees and feels sort of easy and breezy to me. Just for everyday wear when I'm in the mood. I've never been much of a casual dress wearer—for me, dresses have always been tailored and professional-looking for on-air presentation. But the one I wore the other night felt good on my body, and maybe I'm ready to change things up a little.

I also didn't wear my hat. Easier because I was going to Hazard, where no one knows me or would think: *Oh, hey, Jessica isn't wearing a hat.* The anonymity felt good, and no one blinked twice. I guess that means my little helmet of brown hair isn't *just* a helmet anymore—it's actual hair. Very short hair, but presentable hair just the same.

I put on the easy-breezy dress when I get home. It's a mellow but uplifting shade of blue that's almost periwinkle, and I feel like wearing it, even only to police the Martian heads, water the petunias, and read a book on the back porch. I've finished the JoAnn Ross novel and moved on to another on Mabel's shelves—one by Robyn Carr that sucked me in immediately.

When dinnertime comes, I cut up a Mr. Freeman tomato, then shred a carrot with a peeler and tear up a head of lettuce for a salad. Sometimes I still buy my salad in a bag, but I've learned that other times I actually like handling the fresh food myself, turning it from one thing into another. It has the same satisfying effect that deadheading the snapdragons does to create more flowers.

Speaking of which, I have so many new blooms! The deadheading is paying off big-time, and while I was in Hazard, where they have a decent internet connection, I posted a few pictures of my beloved blossoms online. Life isn't all about lost items—I still want to show people things I'm *finding* along the way, too.

When a light rap comes on my back window, I look up from where I'm washing dishes to see none other than the police chief next door against the backdrop of an electric-pink sunset. He's gripping a bottle of wine by the neck and casting me a hopeful look. My heart flutters unexpectedly.

I hold up a finger, turn off the water, wipe my hands on a dish towel.

"Hey," I say, stepping outside a minute later with two wineglasses.

"I like the dress," he tells me, starting to pour while I hold.

"I was in the mood for a change," I explain, "so I picked up a couple of things at Walmart."

He glances up at me, clearly amused. "You've never struck me as a woman who updates her wardrobe at Walmart."

Funny, because I've worn mostly simple summer tops and shorts for the entire time he's known me—not exactly haute couture. But maybe I give off a vibe that goes beyond that. Maybe it's the fedora. "I'm not," I confess. "But when in Rome . . ."

This makes him laugh.

"Want the pie you missed the other night?" I ask. "I still have some. Chocolate cream."

He pats his stomach through his T-shirt. "All these wine-and-dessert dates are startin' to add up on the scale. But it's worth it, so yeah, I'll have the pie."

Dates. Worth it. I take in all his word choices as I go inside and cut the last chunk of pie into two healthy slices. But then I try not to examine it all too much. Because who am I kidding? Of course they're dates. The Lost and Found version of dinner and a movie. Just simpler, slower, like everything is here.

"Did you get your meth addict under control that night?" I ask as I hand him the pie, careful not to spill it on him this time and happy when we're both in rocking chairs unscathed.

"Yeah, got the situation resolved," he answers, even if it comes out sounding discouraged. "Much as it can be. I mean, the girl's still an addict. And Scooter and Betty are never gonna feel quite as safe in their own home again. So it's awful. But it's the best we can do. And now that we're gettin' better laws in place about narcotics, we're finally creatin' less addicts, and at least in my jurisdiction we're seein' a big drop in incidents."

"I was surprised to discover that even Lost and Found has an ugly underbelly. I'd really started to think it was all blue skies and blackberries here."

"No words," he tells me, "for how much I hate drugs. Seein' what they do to people firsthand . . ." He stops, shakes his head.

"Well, I'm glad it's gotten better." I bite my lip. "But I . . . shouldn't be worried, should I? That someone's going to just walk into my house?" In the city, I lock the door anytime I'm going farther than my own yard, but here I haven't been as careful. Particularly when I walk to the winery.

Matt gives a quick shake of his head. "Not much deters an addict, but most folks around here know where the police chief lives, even the users. If I thought you were in any danger whatsoever, I'd be standin' guard at your door."

I take that in and, despite myself, like the protectiveness. I'm so accustomed to having to protect *myself.* And silly as it may seem, I proceed to eat my pie feeling a little bit safer in the world for having Matthew Cordray sitting next to me.

"How's your Dollywood shirt?" I ask. "Did it survive?"

"Haven't done the laundry yet," he tells me. "But either way, that was worth it, too."

I look away because his sexy grin is moving all through me, and it feels different now that we've had sex—more intense, slicing directly to my core.

He's wearing the ugliest T-shirt I've ever seen on him—white with the words "Great Smoky Mountains" in navy blue above an equally navy-blue bear in silhouette. Yet the main thing I notice is how well it fits him—not muscle-guy tight, but just right. It hugs his shoulders where it should; it fits his chest in a way that reminds me how much I liked kissing it. I consider defusing my own reaction by teasing him about the shirt, telling him maybe I should have crammed a piece of pie into *that* one. But I'm uneasy, torn, and decide maybe it's better not to bring up the whole pie-spilling incident, because that would also be bringing up the whole sex-having incident.

We talk for a while about random things. "I didn't realize Grace had trouble getting around until the other night." "Samantha's comin' home in a few weeks—can't wait to wrap her up in a big bear hug." "Did you see the snapdragons? I do believe I single-handedly saved the flower garden." "Sky's clear tonight—ton of stars out." And on and on the conversation goes until the pie is gone and the wine bottle's empty. Things have turned easier. Okay, I'm still aware of his body next to me, still remembering kissing it, and I'm still taking in the deep timbre of his voice and the stubble on his jaw in a whole new way—but it puts me at ease that we're not talking about it.

Setting my empty glass aside, I stand up and walk to the edge of the porch, lean against a wooden post, and take in the stars. "You're right," I say, gazing upward. "So many. I can't see the stars at all where I live."

"How come?" he asks.

"Light pollution. I'm directly across the river from downtown Cincinnati."

"Damn, I'd hate not being able to see stars."

I'm still peering up at them, taking in the vast numbers, as I blow out a sigh. "It's like anything else, I guess. You don't realize what you don't have." I glance over at him. "I'd almost forgotten. About the stars. That they could look like this, that the sky could seem so full of them. My dad and I used to sit in lawn chairs in the yard on summer nights and eat ice cream. He knew some of the constellations and could even point them out."

"Do you have that same skill?" Matt asks.

I'm still studying the star-studded cosmos, trying to figure that out myself. "I might see the Big Dipper," I tell him, squinting a little. Then, talking to myself as much as to him, I remember out loud, "And if I follow the dipper's handle, that should lead me to Cassiopeia, which is a big W in the sky." I tilt my head one way and then the other. "And I . . . maybe see it?"

Matt gets up, comes to stand behind me. "Show me."

I turn my head to find his face close to mine. Like the other night, I can smell the manliness of him. It makes me feel like an animal in the wild, suddenly responding to scent this way. But I look back to the starlit expanse above us and try to point it out.

Problem being, when there are a million stars in the sky, I'm not sure how to help him differentiate between them all, and I'm saying,

"It's a dipper, like a ladle of sorts." I'm pointing up to where I think it is, but the truth is that I'm not sure.

What I *am* sure of, though, is that even though we're not touching, I feel him there, *like* we're touching. An electric current sizzles in the bit of space between us. And it's getting hard to take.

"Not sure I see it," he says. "My dad used to study that stuff, too, but I wasn't good at seein' it then, either. Mostly I just think all those stars are awesome to look at."

I nod. "They are."

We stand there like that, silent, taking them in, the billions of pinpoint lights that remind us how mind-blowingly enormous the universe is.

"I'm tryin' to leave," he announces abruptly.

I swing my head around to look at him. He's still so, so close. I can practically taste him. "Huh?"

He lets out a big sigh, drops his gaze to mine, but then shifts it back to the sky. "It's clear to me you're not sure what you want—when it comes to you and me. So I'm tryin' not to be some pushy creep who keeps tryin' to get you into bed again. I came over here just . . . wantin' to see ya. And now I'm figurin' it's time I say goodnight. But . . ."

I pull in my breath. "But?"

"It's hard to make myself go."

"Why?"

"You *know* why. Because I want you."

Now I blow that breath out, my chest tight with lust and confusion. Maybe I wish he would persuade me a little, even if that's un-PC. Maybe I don't want to have to make the decision on my own. Since maybe the decision scares me. I don't recognize this person who's so . . . willowy, bending first one way and then the other. Usually I know what I want. When it's about sex and romance, sometimes it's the wrong choice, but I don't normally hesitate to take control of the situation—until now.

Though I have to, I suppose. Because he's being a gentleman, doing the right thing.

So I guess all I can do is . . . follow what my body . . . and my heart . . . are telling me.

I lower both hands to my sides, then reach back to find his, pulling them up around my waist until he's hugging me from behind.

We stay that way a moment, and I have to bite my lip when I feel the hardness of him pressing into me.

"Does this mean," he whispers in my ear, his breath warm on my neck, "that you like standin' here lookin' at the stars with me . . . or that you want me, too?"

"Both," I whisper back.

CHAPTER 26

"That's, um, good news," he murmurs in my ear.

And then he's kissing my neck—little velvet kisses that send electric shock waves through my veins. I let out heated, audible sighs as my body melts into pleasure.

I try really hard not to think too much. And for better or worse, something about Matthew Cordray makes that easier than usual—particularly, it seems, when there's kissing and bodily contact involved. For a moment, I'm trying to fight how good it feels, trying to examine: *Is* this what I want? *Should* I let it happen again? Is going with the flow making a measured decision, or is it just . . . letting go?

But all the questions fall away the longer he kisses my neck, the more I feel how hard he is behind me. They fall away and I simply . . . surrender.

When one of his hands glides up my torso, coming to cup the underside of my breast, I rasp, "Would you like to go inside?"

And he says, "Not especially." Which shocks me to death until he adds suggestively, "It's nice out *here*."

Oh. I see now. I bite my lip as his hands continue to roam and graze, and surrender or not, I hear myself tossing out a perhaps unnecessary tidbit of honesty. "I've never had sex outside."

"In your whole life?"

Is that odd? I wonder but don't ask. I guess it comes back to the fact that sex, for me, has never been the hot, urgent thing it seems to be for many people. Until right now maybe. I'm struggling to think. "I've lived in the city since I was twenty, so yes, not in my whole life."

"We need to change that." His fingertips are skimming their way down my outer thigh now, toward the hem of my dress, as he bunches the fabric in his hand.

Somehow I manage to inquire, "Wh-what's so great about it?"

"Tell me that breeze doesn't feel good on your skin, on your legs."

"It does," I admit. But it's not just the breeze that feels good. It's his fingertips, grazing upward now, under my dress.

"Tell me those stars aren't takin' your breath away."

"They are." But it's certainly something more than the stars making my breath catch.

Though I see what he means—in that moment, the night air and the millions of stars shining down on us enhance every sensation, every touch, every beat of my heart, as we both go quiet and I give myself over completely to what's happening. The outdoor air on my flesh feels like an extra way he's touching me as his hand finds its way between my legs. He doesn't hesitate to slip his fingertips inside the elastic of my panties, and I gasp as he reaches the sweet spot.

Part of me wonders if I should be doing something more than all this sighing and gasping. Usually I . . . take part, maybe even take a little too *much* control. The other night with him, I got on top; I made myself responsible for my own orgasm, as feminist chicks have been taught to do since the sexual revolution of the last century. And yet, just now I'm not sure I *need* to take control or responsibility—Matt seems to be doing pretty good at this on his own.

Soon enough, he's lowering my panties, and I'm wriggling free of them, aware of the breeze touching places that are usually covered. And then his pants are open and I'm using my hands to brace myself against the post as he pushes into me from behind.

Apparently there are stages to surrender, because I thought I was surrendering a few minutes ago, but the deeper we get into this and the more he moves inside me, the more surrender comes. The rhythm of his fingers sends me toppling into oblivion just before he reaches that point himself. My legs give out, but he holds me up—yet we still collapse slowly to our knees.

It feels animalistic again as he slumps a big hug around me. The moon shines down on us and it's a moment of brutal, honest realness. A moment when I would perhaps usually slink off to the bathroom to avoid all that—but I can't figure out how to do that right now. I'm on the verge of feeling awkward when he says low in my ear, "That was nice."

I suffer the impulse to make a joke he won't get: *Just nice doesn't speak very highly of the event.* But I know by "nice" he means *really, really* good. And hot. And sweet. And spectacular. And maybe that doesn't have to be awkward. So I just say, "Yeah, it was."

I get another kiss on the neck in response.

When we're standing up again, pulling our clothes back into place, Matt says with a half smile, "I know you want me to go, but can I at least get a kiss goodnight this time?"

I think everything over quickly and go with the easiest response at this moment: more surrender. "You can stay if you want."

He laughs a little. "Does that mean . . . hang out here on the porch, or can I come in?"

The answer leaves me in barely more than a whisper. "You can come in."

As we enter the shadowy bedroom, he nods shortly toward the bedside table and says in a low, acknowledging voice, "Growlington."

It makes me laugh.

"I hope he knows there's a new sheriff in town."

"He doesn't mind," I say. "It's not like that between us."

"Good to hear. I wouldn't wanna get mauled."

And with that, we turn back the fluffy white covers and crawl into bed, curling up together on a cloud.

He falls asleep quickly and I envy how comfortable he is. Always, it seems, no matter what's happening. What I love, and what I hate, at the very same time, is how different this feels than any other connection I've had with a man before. Maybe it's just where I am right now, both geographically and in my life. Everything about the past year has stripped me bare, forced me to see how much I'm not in control of the things that happen to me. And most of that has been pretty awful. But some of the parts here, some of the parts with Matt, have been the opposite.

Still the central issue remains. I'm leaving in a month. And even if I wasn't, what do Police Chief Matthew Cordray and I really have in common? Some unexpected chemistry. Some unexpected ease. Some unexpected mutual appreciation. And scars. But we live in two different worlds.

Maybe it's a mistake to let him stay. A mistake to let myself *get* that comfortable, the way *he* is.

And yet, when he snuggles a little closer, I lean into it. Because it feels good. *He* feels good. Not just his body, all of him.

Stop thinking. Stop thinking and sleep. Let it be like Mabel's clouds—just float and don't let anything else matter but the floating, but the comfort of the now.

August rolls into the Kentucky mountains like a breezy dream. Sunny days that are long and hot but not oppressive feel like summer perfection to me. I am assured by Matt that this lack of humidity isn't normal for August, and everyone from Grace to the crowd at the Last Chance can't stop talking about what a nice stretch of weather it is.

Those weeks bring more cookouts with Matt and Grace, more watermelons and fruit salads, and I even make another strawberry poke cake, just without the flag design this time. They bring sweet morning walks around the lake and glasses of wine with Jo while we watch Socks play in the field, where the giant mimosa still holds on to a last few wispy pink blooms. They bring nights in Matt's arms that stay as hot and sweet as the first times.

They bring phone calls from Sydney where "When are you coming home?" turns into "Don't rush it," after I tell her I'm sleeping with the police chief. She says, "I miss you, but you need good sex more than I need a manicure buddy." She and Jayden are still going strong, and she promises we'll all get together when I do come home—she wants me to get to know him, and it's getting serious. "And I've informed him that once you're back, I'll need some major Jessica time to make up for missing the whole summer."

They bring more snapdragons and sunshine, more sunsets and moonlight, more tomatoes from Mr. Freeman, and more pie from the Last Chance Café.

They are actually days more busy than lazy, though—those hours I used to struggle to fill continue to be gobbled up by work on the lost and found. A few more new items arrive at the post office, but not many. Instead, as I requested, people tag me in their own posts about things they've found and I share them. In even better news, a great-grandchild of the WWII pilot came forward to claim the album of clippings and pictures, and the owner of the newly arrived locket was located—it was lost on vacation, and the woman who owned it was thrilled to get it back as it was a gift from her late mother.

My social media pages are blowing up with astronomical new numbers due to the news exposure throughout the Midwest. And by mid-August an even more immense change results from all those news outlets sharing the story about the Lost and Found lost and found: tourists! Jo and Conrad begin seeing their weekend visitors increase substantially, and they even get a few day-trippers out looking for an off-the-beaten-path place to do some wine tasting on weekdays.

Weekend business is on the rise at the Last Chance, too. When I stop in for a ham and cheese one day on the way back from Brandywine, Melva comes out from the kitchen to tell me about it. I've never seen her smile so wide. "I'll need another waitress on weekends if this keeps up," she says.

That's when Joy Lynn delivers my lunch and even *she's* smiling—a rare sight indeed. "Best tips I ever got," she announces. "Actually gonna be able to pay the bills this month."

"Yep, things around here might just be lookin' up," Melva remarks as she makes her way back to the kitchen.

Even as I sit there eating, a young couple comes in for lunch, and I overhear them in the booth behind me telling Joy Lynn that they've just visited the winery. "Cute little town," the girl says. "We heard about it on the news."

"But where's the lost and found?" the guy asks. And I realize he thinks it's a place—that you can go see the Lost and Found lost and found.

I turn and introduce myself as the person in charge of it, explaining, "Sorry, it's actually just a bunch of stuff in boxes at my house."

Even though they seem disappointed, when I'm ready to leave, the whole mood of the café still feels somehow lighter than ever before. As I walk to the jukebox, I simply glance over at Joy Lynn behind the counter. I don't even have to ask anymore—she smiles over at me and says, "L8."

I punch it in, watch an old record drop into place, and hear Frank Sinatra begin to sing "High Hopes."

Jo's been telling me for weeks about the big harvest late in the month, how the timing is based on Conrad constantly checking the grapes' acidity and sugar levels until they're just right, how people in the community volunteer to come help, and that they make a party of it.

When that day finally comes, I put on my special hiking pants and gym shoes, along with a high-necked T-shirt to protect my radiation area, and Matt, Grace, and I load into my car and drive over to the winery. Mr. Freeman, Junior Barnett, and other friends and neighbors

I've met are all there as well. A young guy from the *Chronicle* brought a camera to take pictures for the paper.

Grace stays with Jo at the tasting room, where she'll be setting up for lunch, but Conrad gives the rest of us a short lesson on how to snip off the bunches of grapes with the gardening clippers he's handing out along with large wicker baskets. For some of us it's brand new, while for others who've helped out before, it's a refresher course.

The work in the grapevines is hard but satisfying, and soon my basket begins to fill. I think of all the good wine Conrad is going to create as I stop to take a few pictures. I breathe in the warm summer air as the sun inches upward in the sky, feeling grateful my hair is thick enough that I no longer need my floppy hat. Though, remembering Matt's sunburn earlier in the summer, I was careful to apply thick sunscreen to the backs of both our necks.

When my basket is full, I find Matt one row over and ask him to help me haul it to the end of the vines, where Conrad will come by with a tractor and wagon to load them up and carry them to the winemaking room in the barn. Matt kisses me when we lower the basket to the ground, and I decide that's another nice thing about no floppy hat, and no silly cowboy hat—no brims to bump when kissing.

The crowd is large enough that the grapes are harvested by noon, after which we're rewarded with a lunch of mini-croissant sandwiches, fruit salad, potato salad, deviled eggs, snack chips, pink lemonade, iced tea, and an array of desserts. As we sit around the stone patio snacking and relaxing, a twentysomething couple who helped with the harvest pull out a mandolin and a fiddle, then proceed to play and sing bluegrass music.

I've never really paid much attention to bluegrass, just regarding it as old-fashioned mountain music, but it's actually amazing. I think I could sit forever in the shade of the big tent Conrad has put up, listening to the distinctive sound with these people I've come to care for. The longer I sit there, the more I feel the soul of this little community that seemed so dead to me when I first arrived. Now I realize I just couldn't see it because it wasn't on display—it was tucked away between the mountains and under the trees, but it was there all the time.

When people finally begin to leave, Mr. Freeman drives Grace home so that Matt and I can stay and help clean up. We end up having dinner with Conrad and Jo—Conrad grills pork chops and corn on the cob, and we drink wine and talk until well after dark.

By the time we depart, I'm exhausted and sorely in need of a shower, but I'm still sorry to see the day end. I feel, in a way, like I lived a whole life today. Some days are like that, long and filled with . . . little pieces of everything. Today was people and grapes and sunshine, music and food and butterflies, sweat and bees and clouds, blue skies and wine and laughter, stories and nature and work, aching muscles and dirty hands and smiles. I hope I remember every bit of it for a long time to come.

Later this week I have two doctor's appointments in Cincinnati—cancer checkups. They've been on the calendar since before I even arrived in Lost and Found, but I forgot about them until my phone buzzed with a reminder text during a social media check at the Piggly Wiggly this morning.

Given the three-hour-plus commute, it makes sense to spend the night at my house in the city and drive back the next day.

The weird thing is . . . how odd that suddenly sounds to me.

I should be eager to see my remodeled kitchen. I should be thinking very seriously about just leaving Lost and Found altogether at this point. Summer's almost over, after all. I guess I've been waiting for some . . . Bat-Signal from Kevin, some indication that Tiffany's out and I'm back in. But I also guess I've gotten very patient about that because I've become so unexpectedly busy here.

The mild weather of early August has given way to a more typical level of heat now that it's later in the month, so it's already hot as I walk to the winery just before lunchtime. I have the strong urge to talk to Jo.

As a transplant here, she's told me many times about a homesickness that waxes and wanes, and I wonder if she might be able to help me make sense of how odd I feel as the end of summer approaches.

Socks greets me as I ascend the lane toward the tasting room and I lean down to pet him. "Hey there, buddy." He trots alongside me the rest of the way, and when I open the door to step inside, he goes in first and I follow.

"Good morning and welcome to Lost Valley Vineyards."

I pull up short, blinking at a woman I don't know, a middle-aged, heavyset blonde wearing a Lost Valley Vineyards golf shirt like the ones Conrad often works in. Who is she and why is she welcoming me to a place I'm at several days a week?

"Um . . . is Jo here?"

"No, I'm sorry, she's not. But I can help you with anything you need."

I doubt that. I don't mean to be snide, but . . . *I harvested grapes here just a few days ago,* I want to tell her. *I belong.* Instead I simply explain, "I'm a friend of hers."

She leans her head back in understanding. "Ah. Then maybe you want to talk to Conrad? He's in the winemaking room. If you give me your name, I can let him know you're here."

"Or I can just go on back," I tell her.

She almost seems inclined to stop me as I stride past her toward the winemaking area but thinks better of it.

I push through the door to find Conrad surrounded by the baskets and bins of grapes we picked over the weekend, which he appears to be busily sorting. Looking up, he gives me a smile. "Jessica—hi."

"Hey," I say. Then I hike a thumb over my shoulder. "Who's the chick? And where's Jo?"

He blows out a long sigh. "That's Angela—we had to hire someone with no notice. I'm just grateful we had a few résumés on file from back when we first opened and thought we might need more staff—since we suddenly do."

"Because of the way business has picked up?" I squint as I ask, though, suspecting there's more to it.

"That's part of it. I actually need to interview for some weekend help, too. But the urgency is because Jo's in California—I'm not sure for how long."

I flinch. "California? What for?" This seems sudden. She was just here.

"Her sister is dying."

My shock deflates into sadness. And still a little surprise. "I didn't even know she *had* a sister."

"They were never close," he explains. "But when Jo's nephew called, she went."

I nod. "Of course. I'm just . . . taken aback." I'm shaking my head, at a loss.

"That makes two of us," he says. "That's why I needed someone out front. I'd handle the tasting room myself, but I've got wine to make."

I sigh, seeing that he's been left in the lurch by the bad timing of fate and harvest and death. Had this happened earlier in the summer, I might have offered my help, but somehow I've ended up with my own responsibilities here.

I feel bad for Conrad, and for Jo, and almost strangely sorry I've managed to increase their business since it's suddenly the worst possible time. We talk a bit longer, during which I tell him to give Jo my love. And I want to offer more: *Let me know if you need anything while she's gone.* Or *Is there any way I can help?* Because I've learned that's what people do in Lost and Found—they let you know they're here for you. But I'm about to leave for a couple of days myself, and soon for good, so I resist the urge . . . since what's the point?

And as I walk back down the lane a few minutes later, sun blasting down, I realize it's very possible—maybe even likely—that I'll never see Jo again. Of course, perhaps that's overly dramatic—I know where the winery is and I can always come for visits, or I could even invite her to Cincinnati.

And yet . . . will any of that happen? I mean, she didn't even say goodbye.

That's horribly selfish, I know. She had a million things to throw together and think through, not to mention stress and grief and worry. Of course saying goodbye to me wasn't at the top of her priority list.

But it still hurts me that she's gone.

And once I get back to my regular life, who knows if I'll ever truly carve out the time for a day trip to Lost Valley. And what do Jo and I really have in common anyway? We're in entirely different generations, we have different pasts—and different presents, too, once I head home. I guess we were just . . . summer friends, acquaintances passing on the road of life. Even if it felt like more.

CHAPTER 27

I'm sulky as a teenager who just got dumped by her BFF. Only it's stupid to be sulky—Jo is off on a life-changing mission of helping a loved one die. It's ridiculous that I have the nerve to feel . . . forgotten. Or abandoned.

Though I'm slightly appeased when I tell Matt later that afternoon and he's just as stunned. "I'll stop by tomorrow and ask Conrad if there's anything I can do," he says.

It makes me realize that maybe, in ways, I like him better than I like myself. He's good people. That's what my mother would have said. And it's what my mother would have done, too. Her first thought would be to ask how she could help. Mine was to say to myself: *I'd help but I'm too busy with my own things*. I scrunch up my nose at the thought as we sit on the back porch drinking Conrad's wine.

As we chat, Matt mentions his daughter. "She got home the day before school started."

I blink. "School already started?"

"Earlier every year, seems like. Anyway, she's comin' down for Labor Day weekend."

I smile softly. I've never been a parent, but sometimes I can practically feel how much he misses her just dripping off him. "I bet you can't wait."

"You have no idea," he tells me. "If you're still here then, you can meet her."

Why does this throw me a little? "She . . . knows about me?"

He tosses me a sideways glance. "Well, just that you're stayin' next door and I've been seein' you. Is that okay?"

Honestly, it gives me pause. Because I never thought about . . . being part of his life, like in a way that would make him tell the people he's closest to. And for more insecure reasons, too. "Sure," I say anyway, perhaps halfheartedly. "Except . . . won't she think I'm some weird, lonely lady with bad taste in hairstyles?"

This makes him let out a laugh. "For your information, she follows you on social media, and she loves what you're doin'—for the lost items, and for Lost and Found."

I balk slightly. "Really?"

"Anyone with over a hundred and fifty thousand followers is awesome in her book. She's dyin' to meet you."

Although I'm not sure when I started caring what teenage girls think of me, this reaffirms my faith in our youth and reminds me I actually *am* pretty cool, even with very short hair. And if Matt wants to introduce me to his daughter, well . . . I *am* living next door to him and we *do* spend a lot of time together these days, so it's no big deal.

Maybe the bigger deal is when I say, "Well, if I'm still here then, it'll be nice to finally meet her." *If I'm still here then.* I have no idea where I'll be in less than two weeks. That seems strange.

I choose not to think about it and change the subject to some of the more interesting lost items I've recently unearthed: an autographed Donny Osmond record album made out to someone named Terri, a Ziploc baggie of baby teeth labeled *Adam Jeffrey b. 4/3/92*, and a small painted portrait of a young girl standing in a field holding daisies, with *My Miranda, 1988, by Mary Parelli*, in the lower right corner. I'm beginning to realize that no matter how deeply I dig into the boxes and bins, there will always be more lost things in this town.

So the next morning I head out early to Brandywine. I have a lot of work to do, especially since I'll be taking a couple of days away later in the week. As has become the norm, there are a ton of messages to read and reply to—many being false leads, and when it comes to items of monetary value, like the diamond engagement ring I posted a few days ago, you get people on fishing expeditions. After that, I comb through new comments on all the "open cases" posts, making notes in my logbook, and then I finally get around to posting new items.

I work until noon and then take a break, walking down the street for a sandwich, and I finish up the workday's tasks around two. I still feel sad about Jo and realize I've probably thrown myself into the lost and found as a distraction, but that's okay—I got a lot done.

The only negative aspect to the day is that I have upward of twenty lost items currently unclaimed and today brought no new "founds"—a good "found" would have cheered me up, and reminded me I'm doing something worthwhile.

I'm about to close my laptop and hit the road back to Lost Valley when a new message pops up in my inbox. And since a person without internet doesn't have the luxury of thinking, *I'll answer it later*, I click to open it.

I find a very long message from someone named Benita Kelly. She lives in Biloxi, and Thomas Bennett Hartfell is her great-great-grandfather! A former slave, he was the first Black attorney in Jackson, Mississippi, passing the bar in 1880. She goes on to tell me how the line descends to her—she's an attorney herself and an avid genealogist. *The portrait would mean so much to me—I'd be honored to hang it in the entryway at my practice. I'm so grateful someone cared enough to save it all these years!*

Normally, I would fact-check some of this—but a click on her name quickly shows me she's who she says she is, and I can tell she's a smart, savvy, reliable woman. I can't believe it—I have a message from the great-great-granddaughter of Grace's distinguished gentleman!

I'm so heartened that I fight back tears of joy. All this time, not one single clue or lead has arisen from my post about Mr. Hartfell—and now *this*! A home for an important piece of history, a way of getting it back where it should have ended up in the first place. I can't help thinking that sometimes fate does have a way of putting things to right.

I tap out a quick reply to Ms. Kelly, expressing my elation and telling her how thrilled Grace will be to hear the news. I say I'll be in touch about shipping the portrait, and I ask her permission to share her photo online when I report that this particular lost item is now found. Then I slap my laptop shut, slide it into its case, and leave the library with a skip in my step, so excited to get home to Grace that I can barely stand it.

CHAPTER 28

I drive faster than I should, taking curves at a dangerous clip, and I have to struggle to calm myself down.

When I get home, I practically screech my car into its spot, slam the door, and nearly jog across the road and up Grace's front steps. The front door is standing wide open, so rather than knock, I grab the screen door handle, yelling, "Grace? Grace, where are you? I've got great news!" I step inside. "I've found out where your picture belongs—your distinguished gentleman!"

That's when a man I don't know with silvery hair—but who I recognize immediately as Grace's son, Daniel—walks through the doorway from the dining room. "Hello?" he says. "Can I help you?"

Okay, this being-greeted-by-someone-I'm-not-expecting thing is getting to be an unpleasant habit. "I was looking for Grace," I explain, then point over my shoulder. "I'm her neighbor across the road."

"Jessica," he greets me with a small smile.

I nod, pleased that she's mentioned me. "You must be Daniel."

"One and the same," he confirms.

"Is she here? I have some exciting news for her."

"I'm afraid she's . . . not."

My back goes ramrod straight. I can tell already that something isn't right here, that she's not just on an outing to town. "What's going on?"

"We're moving her to my home in Saint Louis."

I simply stand there, dumbfounded, crestfallen. "Just like that?"

He nods. "It happened fast. She and one of my daughters are on the road home right now. I stayed behind to pack up another carload of her things, and we'll come back to deal with the rest bit by bit."

"She left . . . for good? Without any warning?" I ask. I'm confused, remembering how many times she's told me she doesn't want to go to Saint Louis or leave her home or Walter's magical backyard. "She didn't even . . . say goodbye."

"That's my fault," he tells me. "I didn't give her much time. You see, she took a fall. Yesterday. So we came straightaway. It's just too dangerous for her to be alone now. I know it's hard for her to leave her house, but it's time."

I stand there with my mouth hanging open, trying to take all this in. "When did she fall? Why didn't she call me? Or Matt?"

"She couldn't get to the phone."

Of course. I feel like an idiot for even asking.

"Over the course of an hour or two, she managed to drag herself over to the couch and eventually pulled herself up onto it. That's when she called me. She knew. She knew what I would insist on doing. She knew it was best, too, or she would have never let me know."

I nod some, now nibbling my lip. To think at some point yesterday Grace was lying here, needing help, and I had no idea. I feel sick to my stomach thinking how alone she must have felt. And she didn't call Matt or me afterward, either—she called Daniel. He must be right—she must have finally been ready to go, even if she didn't really want to.

And somehow, today, when I left the house for four or five hours, her family came and packed her up and took her away, that quickly. I can't believe I wasn't here to see it happening, wasn't here to hug her and tell her how much she's meant to me these past few months.

I want to crumble into pieces, but instead I hold myself together enough to say, "Tell her I'll miss her. We were . . . friends."

"Wait right here." He holds up one finger, then disappears into the dining room to return a moment later. "She asked me to give you this." He's carrying the framed photo of Grace standing in front of her house.

I tilt my head, staring at it, then lift my surely perplexed gaze back to her son. "She doesn't want it?"

"She thought you'd value it more than she does," he explains.

I could argue the point but decide to just take the gift at face value. "Please tell her I'll cherish it," I say, taking it from his hands. "What will happen to the house?"

"To be determined. We might keep it, for getaways, and ask Matt to keep mowing for us." Same as he mows Mabel's, he's mowed Grace's yard all summer as well. "Or we might sell it. If we can get anyone to take that mess out back." He points vaguely in the direction of the backyard.

To that, I suggest with a soft smile, "Or you might find someone who thinks it's as beautiful as she does."

But Daniel looks tired, and like a man who has no time for my wishful whimsy. "I also need to do something with that cat of hers," he laments on a sigh. "Matt has agreed to feed it for now, but if you know anybody who'd want it—"

"She didn't take Ophelia?" I interrupt, horrified. And as if on cue, the pretty black-and-white kitty comes gliding smoothly around the corner, none the wiser that she's just lost the person who loves her. She lets out one of her loud meows.

"My wife's allergic," Daniel explains.

"But . . . how did your mother feel about that?"

He just shakes his head. "Not happy. But it wasn't really a choice."

My heart is breaking as I look down at sweet Ophelia, and I hear myself say, entirely unplanned, "Tell Grace I'll take her home with me, and I'll take care of her until I find a good place for her. Tell her I promise she'll be cared for."

"That's . . . awfully nice of you."

"I just don't want Grace to stress over it. It's hard enough to lose someone you love without having to worry about their well-being." Though I don't mean to imply that Daniel's the big bad wolf here—I know he's in a tough position.

That's when he says, "It's only a cat."

Okay, I liked Daniel well enough up to now, but he's pushing his luck with that one.

"Ophelia was her pet—she loves her," I remind him. As if to back me up, Ophelia lets out another hearty meow. "It matters."

"You're right," he replies then, shaking his head. "Just a lot to deal with right now unexpectedly."

And I feel like a heel. "I'm sorry—I didn't mean to be rude."

"No, don't apologize. I'm glad Mom has nice people who care about her."

I'm not sure what else to say. I do care. And I'm heartbroken. Devastated, actually. But it seems like the conversation is winding down, because he has a lot to do in little time.

Meanwhile, I'm still trying to wrap my head around the fact that Grace is gone. And even much more than with Jo, I'm almost certain I'll never see her again. Ever. How did that happen?

"Can . . . you give her a message from me?"

"Sure."

"Tell her I found a home for the portrait of the distinguished gentleman who was hanging on her wall. I found his great-great-granddaughter."

For the first time, something in Daniel appears to soften. "The bearded man? In the suit with the old-fashioned tie?"

I nod enthusiastically, somehow having forgotten that Grace had the photo his whole life.

"That picture has hung in our dining room since the day I was born. I noticed it was gone and wondered where it could be." He's smiling a little now. "So you really found a relative of his?"

I'm smiling, too, as I nod some more. "He was the first Black lawyer in Jackson, Mississippi. And his great-great-granddaughter is an attorney as well."

"Well, how about that—ya don't say. I can't wait to tell her."

I smile, happy and sad at the same time. "I felt the same way."

Five minutes later, I'm crossing the road back home with a photo of Grace tucked under one arm and a meowing cat dangling from the other. The cat doesn't seem to meow out of distress—I feel like she just enjoys hearing herself talk, and I wish I could understand what she's saying.

Matt crosses the yard toward me, barefoot—apparently this strange and alarming sight left no time for shoes. Goldie trots merrily alongside him. "What's goin' on here?"

"I seem to be adopting a cat," I inform him. "Temporarily anyway." I meet his gaze. "I can't believe Grace is gone. Just like that."

He nods. "I know. It's gonna be strange without her. She's been in that house my whole life." He blows out a long breath.

I feel like I'm about to drop something, and I still have to go back for the litter box and other cat supplies. "Can you hold this?" I ask, motioning to Ophelia.

He takes the cat awkwardly from my arm as she lets out another mew. "Do you, um, *want* a cat?" he asks. "Even temporarily? You don't strike me as a cat person."

"Not especially," I admit. "And I'm not, really. But I refuse to let her be left alone."

"I'd take her myself," he says, "but I already have *one* left-behind pet."

"And a killer at that," I add, casting a judgmental glance down at the guilty party.

Matt looks down at her, too, then defends her honor. "I don't think she'd mess with a cat."

"Tell that to Darnell Henry's chickens."

He shrugs. "Good point."

"If you want to help me out, you can take her inside and then go grab the litter box and cat food."

"I'm on it."

The last time I had a cat, I was ten. I did not provide the cat care—only the cat petting and the harassment of attempting to force it to wear doll clothes and drive a Barbie convertible. Neither endeavor worked out well for me.

So that night Matt instructs me in Cat 101, teaching me how to deal with the litter box, how often the cat should be fed, and informing me I should expect cat hair everywhere. Great.

But at least it's Mabel's furniture, not mine. It's started to *feel* like mine, but it's not.

Ophelia makes herself at home and continues blaring out random meows. I wonder if she's missing Grace, realizing she's gone.

Matt and I eat a sad sort of dinner consisting of hot dogs and French fries from a bag in the freezer that don't taste much better baked than they probably would have if we'd left them frozen. But neither of us has the energy for more. The hot day has led to a drizzly, overcast evening and the weather matches our moods.

Sitting at Mabel's kitchen table, I say, "I can't believe I'll never get to eat Grace's brown beans again."

Matt just slants me a glance. "You're leavin' soon—you probably wouldn't have had 'em again anyway."

The words slam into me like a punch to the chest. But I can't argue them. "I guess you're right."

And as we continue to eat, I wonder if I should be talking to him about things like . . . the future. Should I be asking if . . . he would ever want to come to Cincinnati to see me? Should I be wondering out loud what happens when I go?

But the very notion just feels like too much right now, too heavy—it's already been a rough day. And now I'm somehow stuck with this cat to care for, because for some insane reason I insisted upon that.

After dishes, we lie on the couch in a loose, cozy embrace while Ophelia perches in a windowsill across the room, looking calm enough—yet I sense she's out of sorts. She's somewhere strange. I sympathize with her, knowing how that feels, and I share that with Matt as she lets out a quieter-than-usual meow.

"Don't worry," he says, "cats are resilient. She'll adjust to wherever she is." And I find myself thinking maybe my spirit animal is a cat—*I'm* pretty resilient, and I seem to adjust to wherever I am, even if I'm not always happy about it.

I lift my head from his shoulder to ask, "How do you know so much about cats anyway?"

"Are you kiddin'? I grew up with cats. And dogs. And a variety of other animals. That's life in the country." A moment later, he eases out from under me. "I'm gonna head home, let you get some rest. And get to know your foster cat. I'll see ya tomorrow night, okay?"

As I nod and he leans down to kiss me, I'm liking how coolly he handled that. Without ever alluding to the fact that we're both too sad about Grace to want to fool around tonight, he made an utterly graceful exit and gave us both the space we might be needing right now. To think that not long ago I worried about things being awkward with him.

When he's gone, I get up and pet the cat. She seems stiff about it, though, so I grab the ball of yarn tucked in with the rest of her things and lure her into playing for a few minutes, which comes complete with some mrows and mews. After that, she acts much more comfortable when I lift her into my lap and stroke her fur. "I realize we don't know each other very well," I say, "but you're safe here."

So much has been going on since I got home that I've nearly forgotten Grace's lovely gift to me, so when I spot it on the mantel across the room, where I propped it earlier, I walk over and take it down, studying it closer. I can't believe she didn't want it. I love that she wanted me to have it.

I flip it over to see what kind of hanger it has—and then I gasp. Grace has written me a note on the back. Even as rushed and busy and emotional as she must have been this morning, suddenly getting ready to leave her home of so many years, she took the time to write this to me.

> *Dear Jessica,*
> *Someday when you're gone, somebody will find this and think it's lost, not knowing that it just outlasted both the giver and the receiver. Maybe not everything we find was lost. Maybe some of it was just loved and left behind as a testament to that love.*
> *Grace*

I press my palm to my chest, overcome with emotion. It's true—someday no one will know what this photo represents, who Grace was, why it mattered. And maybe the vast majority of the things in the lost and found will never . . . be found. Because things just outlast their meaning, outlast the people who cared for them.

That idea's a lot less sad than the alternative one I've been working with all this time, so I turn the picture back over and smile at the only piece of Grace I have left—well, other than the cat.

But if it's not all lost, what do we do with it?

I think back to the young couple I met at the Last Chance, people who came here hoping to *see* the lost and found. It seemed a preposterous notion to me at the time, but . . . I wonder if some of the more interesting items could be put on display somehow. Main Street has more than its fair share of empty storefronts. So maybe someone should do that. Maybe I'll tell Matt about the idea before I go home for good. Or Junior Barnett.

As I place the picture back on the mantel, I find myself thinking about change. Change, change, change—the only constant is change. Even in Lost and Found, a place that once seemed to me like it probably *never* changed, Jo is gone, Grace is gone, and I have a foster cat. All since yesterday.

◆ ◆ ◆

When I'm awakened the next morning by a strange sensation, I open my eyes to find a cat walking across my stomach, and the sight makes me smile. "Good morning," I say, childishly pleased that she likes me enough to walk around on me.

"Meow," she replies.

After getting up, I make breakfast—eggs and toast for me, dry cat food with a splash of milk for her—and I think about my day as I eat. My doctor's appointments are tomorrow afternoon, so today I need to pack an overnight bag, confirm plans to see my friends while I'm in town, and remind Matt to come over and feed the cat.

I look down at her, eating at her bowl nearby. "I feel bad leaving you so soon," I say, "but it can't be helped."

She seems much more concerned with her Meow Mix than with me, quiet for once, but I don't mind. An independent pet who doesn't need constant attention, yet who's at least interested enough in companionship to wake me up in the morning, seems like . . . me in ways.

But when I recall why I suddenly *have* a cat, I let out a sad sigh, get up, and walk to the front door. Stepping out onto the front porch, I peer across the road at Grace's little house. Light rain last night left behind a layer of misty mountain fog that floats like a ghost around her yard and makes the place look as lonely as it suddenly is.

"Mornin'."

I turn to see Matt in his uniform, heading to his truck, and lift my hand in a wave.

"I'll start tryin' to find the cat a home today," he calls as he rounds the fender.

Something in my stomach tightens, and against my better judgment I say, "You don't have to."

He stops, looks up at me. "Why not?"

I bite my lip, still hesitant—but at the same time certain. "I think I'll keep her. I think she needs me."

He tilts his head, a small smile playing about his mouth. "I thought you didn't want a cat."

"I don't. But that feels secondary right now."

"And what about when you . . . ya know, go back up north? Not just today, but for good."

"I'll take her with me," I answer, simple as that. I've given this zero thought, but it doesn't matter.

"She'll shed on your swanky furniture," he warns me.

I narrow my gaze on him. "How do you know I have swanky furniture?"

He just shrugs. "Don't you?"

I nod. "Of course. But that's okay. She's already been abandoned once—I won't make it twice."

Several hours later, I make a trip to the Piggly Wiggly so I can reach back out to Benita Kelly, and while I'm there, I text Kevin and Sydney about our plans over the next two days. I'm looking forward to seeing them—a nice by-product of the doctor visits and . . . well, the general upheaval of being home and having to start thinking again about practical questions. Like when I'm coming back and what the status of my job is and whether I'm going to miss being here in the mountains or enjoy getting back to my real life once and for all.

I see that Benita has given me permission to share her story, so while I've got a signal, I create a post about finding the rightful place for Mr. Hartfell. I'm still sad thinking of Grace, and how much I wanted to tell her about Benita myself, but I try to push it aside.

The truth is, though, she's staying on my mind in everything I do today. I still can't believe she's gone. Out of my life. And even out of her own life, in a way—out of the life she knows. I just hope she'll be happy living with Daniel. My heart feels heavy as I get back in the car.

A glance at my lost-and-found binder in the passenger seat reminds me that this project has gotten so big that some days I think converting it all onto my laptop would make more sense—but I still don't want to. I like flipping around in the pages, and I love watching the section I created at the back for "closed cases" get thicker. There's just something about making notes and circles and check marks with a pen that's more satisfying than it could ever be on a computer—old-school, tactile organizational delight.

Having already packed for tomorrow, I decide to have a late lunch at the Last Chance, and I even have enough time to take my binder in with me, spread out in a booth, and do a little work. Maybe updating the binder will be a distraction from mourning Grace's departure.

Easing my car into one of the marked spots lining Main Street, I grab up my purse and logbook, then step out into another hot day. Sun has long since burned away this morning's fog.

As I walk past the narrow alley between the Last Chance and the storefront next to it, a dark shadow blocking the sunlight catches my eye and I turn to look. I spy two people hugging. Which is weird enough given that I've never seen anyone in that alley all summer, but . . . is that Matt? Hugging someone?

My heart seizing, I take a step back to shield myself with the building, like *I'm* the one being caught at something—and then I peek around the corner to try to figure out what I'm seeing.

Oh God—it *is* Matt.

In a long, full embrace with another woman.

And I don't know why it takes me a minute to discern who, because it makes perfect sense when I realize that, of course, it's Joy Lynn.

CHAPTER 29

I feel like someone just plunged a dagger into my heart.

No, not just someone. Police Chief Matthew Cordray.

Maybe I'm seeing this wrong? So I keep looking, watching.

But no, it's an intense embrace in the shadowy alley, the kind of embrace *I* often share with him these days—and Joy Lynn's clinging to him in a desperate way that makes my chest ache even more.

He pulls back slightly then, his hands at her waist, before bending forward until their foreheads are touching. He whispers something to her.

Part of me wants to keep watching, in that mode of self-torture when you can't look away from the thing that's killing you, but a bigger part of me can't stand another second of it. Unable to catch my breath, I rush back to my car, get inside, toss the book aside, and slam the door.

And then I attempt to catch my breath. Because maybe there's some logical explanation for why he would be touching her this way, whispering to her this way.

But I can't think of one.

I try not to squeal my tires as I pull away from the curb, but I want to be far, far away. Far away from that alley, far away from everything. It already pains me that I have nowhere to go but home, and that home is right next door to him, which is going to make it hard to feel very far away from this. So I just drive, trying not to react, trying not to think.

I don't do a very good job at either. My mind whirls.

I can't believe that apparently I was right about him and Joy Lynn in the first place but forgot about it somewhere along the way when they quit seeming likely to me as a couple. I came to think he was so much more evolved than her. And knowing of her past, her husband's overdose, just makes this somehow seem even more . . . ugh. Is he taking advantage of her sorrow? Is she needy because of it? Did they get cozy in the course of her husband's drug problems and him being a cop?

And what the heck has been happening between Matt and me anyway? Have I misread it all? Which one of us is the sidepiece here, and does it even matter?

Of course he and I have never talked about our relationship because I've always insisted it's casual, which means he's not even doing anything wrong. Right? And yet it *feels* very, very wrong to me. I keep trying to tell myself maybe there's some non-heinous reason for what I just saw, but each time, a defensive part of me instantly rebels, not wanting to be naive or foolish.

Does Joy Lynn even know he and I are a thing? No—because if she did, she'd come closer to murdering me in my sleep than asking me to play "High Hopes" on the jukebox. The irony of the song hits me since I suddenly don't feel very optimistic about *anything*. I thought I'd become so happy here, but it all suddenly seems fake, grounded in pretenses. Is happiness real if it's based on something false?

The worst part of this, though, isn't even his behavior (since casual or not, this seems horribly deceptive to me)—the worst part is how awful it felt to see. Apparently something downright catastrophic has happened: I care about him. In a possessive way. And apparently I thought he cared about me, too. Even though we never said it. It just seemed that way. It just seemed so . . . good. And now I feel so silly, in so many ways.

Arriving home, I stomp into the house, resolving to ignore any attempts he makes to see me. We see each other pretty much every night now. When on earth is he finding time to hook up with Joy Lynn?

Well, it's obvious: during the day, when he's supposed to be working. Yuck.

Of course, she works during the day, too, but clearly they're squeezing it in *sometime*.

I thought I knew him. I really thought I knew him.

And even if, by some miracle, there *is* some logical explanation for what I saw, I still feel . . . obliterated by this new realization that I'm crazy about him, and that I've let myself get so ridiculously attached to him.

I punch some couch cushions to expel some anger—and that's when Ophelia goes darting across the room, clearly wondering what kind of lunatic she's been forced to cohabitate with. But I can't care about that right now. In fact, I'm *tired* of all this caring. I cared about Matt. I cared about Grace. I cared about Jo. I even cared a little about Joy Lynn. And where has it all gotten me? I'm alone and punching couch cushions.

Remembering I never ate, I go grab an apple I got from Mr. Freeman and chomp into it like it's the enemy. I eat it angrily. I guzzle a bottle of water because I'm tempted to guzzle a bottle of wine instead, and I refuse to do that because now wine and Matt go together in my mind. I'm standing at the kitchen counter, still wanting to punch something, but there's nothing soft enough not to hurt myself, so I go plop down on the couch and just stare blankly ahead, feeling more alone than I have . . . since I first got to Lost and Found.

When something brushes against my ankle, I see that the cat has come to look up at me, probably still trying to decipher why I'm acting like a nut. I reach down, pick her up, and pet her. She purrs, and I feel a little less alone.

But I'm still pissed. And hurt. And confused.

And then it hits me that I'm exhausted, so I lie down, my head on one of the pillows I beat up, and I'm out like a light—the sleep of the emotionally spent.

When I wake hours later, a blazing neon sunset shines through the back windows—but it brings me no joy, only blinding me instead.

That's when I realize someone is rapping on the back door—and it's Matt.

Without a plan, I thrust myself up off the couch, walk over, and yank it open.

"Hey, I got home late. Have you eaten? I was thinkin' of firin' up the grill—could you eat a burger?"

It's only then that he sees on my face the maniacal glare of the unhinged.

"What's wrong?" he asks. I instantly despise how concerned he looks. Like he cares about me or something.

"What's wrong?" I spew back at him. *"What's wrong?"*

This is the moment he begins to understand he's in the presence of a madwoman—his eyes widen and his jaw goes slack.

"What's wrong," I say, "is that you're a creep."

His eyebrows shoot up. "I am?" He's clearly astonished.

Well, let me just end his confusion. "I saw you, Matt."

"Saw me what?"

"And I know we're not exclusive or anything. I know I've made a huge deal out of keeping this thing between us casual. But still . . ."

His brow is knit now. "Still what? What are you so upset about, Jessie?"

"You and Joy Lynn," I say, my voice thick with disgust. "I mean, I always wondered if there was something between you, but I eventually decided I was wrong. Only it turns out I was right. And even if you haven't *technically* done anything wrong, did you really think what we have is *so* casual that it's all right to be hooking up with somebody else who I see all the time? Who sees *me* all the time? Is that the kind of man you are? The kind who thinks it's okay to be spending your nights with one woman and making out with another in an alley during the day?"

When I finally finish, his expression is all twisted up and even more confused looking. "Wait a minute," he says. "Are you sayin' . . . ? You think . . . ?" He stops, gives me a look. "I don't know what you think you saw, darlin', but are you accusin' me of makin' out with my own sister?"

He has a sister? "No!" What is he talking about? "Didn't you hear me? I saw you with Joy Lynn."

"*Who is my sister.* You know that, right?"

Now I'm the one slack-jawed. "Huh?"

"Joy Lynn is my sister." He keeps saying that, as if it makes sense, when it doesn't.

I blink, possibly as confused now as he is. "What? Wait. Are you sure?"

"Am I sure?" He sounds incredulous, which I get, yet I'm just so stunned. "Yes, I'm sure."

"But . . . how is that even possible? I mean, why would you never have mentioned that?"

He's blinking now, too, still trying to catch up to the gargantuan misunderstanding. "I guess I thought I did. Did I not? Did you really not know?"

I'm shaking my head, which feels like it might explode at any second. "No. No, you most certainly *never* mentioned that. *Ever.* You once claimed she liked you. And then she once indicated to me that she did not. But no one *ever* said anything about the two of you being *related.*"

"We have a stormy relationship."

I blow out an audible breath. "That part I knew. The part about being siblings, though . . ." I'm shaking my head some more, still trying to wrap my brain around this. There *is* a logical explanation. I'm not a silly fool. He's still into me. Okay, wait—maybe I *am* a silly fool, just in a different way. "You . . . never talk about her. All the hours we've sat on this porch together, and you never talk about her."

He lets out a sigh. "Guess she's not my favorite topic."

"Oh." I suppose I can understand that. She seems like such a handful, and now I'm learning she's a handful he can't just walk away from.

He holds his hands out, palms up. "She's part of why I can't bring myself to leave Lost and Found. Her and Toby got nobody. Nobody but me."

"Grace told me about her husband dying."

He nods. "Another reason I hate drugs so damn much. But the fact is, he was never a great guy and she's made a lotta poor choices. And sometimes she still does, so I don't bend over backward makin' things easy for her—she still needs to grow up some even though she's pushin' forty." He runs a hand back through his hair. "Regardless, though, without Mom and Dad here, I feel some responsibility for her. I'm her big brother."

"I get it," I murmur, still taking it in.

Now he's the one shaking his head. "I still can't believe you thought . . ."

And I'm still taking other things in, too. Like how phenomenally relieved I am. And how incredibly much I've come to care for this man. And how fragile and nutty it's apparently made me. "I'm an idiot," I declare for more reasons than one.

He tilts his head, flashes a sexy sort of grin. "Well, it's nice to know ya care. Never thought you'd be the jealous type. I like it."

I sigh, not crazy about having let that cat out of the bag. "Don't let it go to your head, Chief Cordray."

The man understands me enough, and respects my sensibilities enough, to just—that easily—move on, simply asking me with raised eyebrows, "You wanna burger or not?"

Okay, I do and I don't. The normalcy of spending some time with him after all this appeals. A lot. But it almost seems like a bad idea—I don't enjoy the level of emotion I've suffered for him today.

I'm hungry, though, and that wins out, so I say, "On one condition."

"What's that?"

"That we never speak of this again. I'll go chop up a tomato and get some cheese." And with that, I walk away, needing to escape my embarrassment—and some other feelings, too.

I still can't believe Joy Lynn is his sister.

I still can't believe the other part, either. The part I don't want to put a label on.

But I know what the label is anyway. I'm pretty sure I've fallen in love with the cowboy next door.

"You're quiet," Matt observes as we dine on burgers and baked beans across from each other at the little back porch table.

"I know." I've been sitting here feeling distant, withdrawn, embarrassed. Lots of things. More than I can even name. "Sorry. It's been a weird couple of days."

"I get it," he says. "And I'm sorry if I made it worse by . . ." He gives his head a short shake. "I really thought it had come up somewhere along the way that Joy Lynn is my sister, for God's sake. And like I said . . . she's not my favorite person. I just love her anyway."

"That must be frustrating." Suddenly, I don't mind being an only child—I guess siblings can be a crapshoot, even when you're raised by the same parents. Then I ask, reluctantly, "What was happening today anyway, in the alley, when you were hugging her?" Reluctant because there's a part of me, which I can't control, that's trying to pull back and doesn't want to dig deeper, get closer. Ironically, I know it's me trying to *take* control of the situation. The situation where I think I'm in love and that's terrifying. But I ask anyway.

"Trouble with Toby," he replies on a sigh. "He ran away last night."

"Oh wow," I reply, realizing these are problems I've never had to deal with.

"She found him—at a friend's," he adds quickly. "But there's a lotta trouble there, and frankly, I don't blame the kid—he hasn't had a great life so far. I probably need to get more involved, do more than just occasionally take him fishin'." He drops his gaze, clearly feeling guilty.

But I think he's noble. He doesn't *have* to do *anything*—but he wants to, because he's a good guy. Crap. Maybe it would have been better in the long run—for me—if he wasn't, if he really *had* let me down. If I saw him letting *other* people down. It would make leaving so much easier.

"Anyway," he says, "I don't go around huggin' my sister too often—our relationship is pretty much that she loves me until she hates me until she needs me, and today she needed me, so I was there."

I only nod. Instead of telling him what a good guy he is. Because I don't want to keep reminding myself.

Yesterday and today have just been . . . too much. Suddenly, a couple of days away sounds like a much-needed vacation. And . . . maybe it should be a permanent one. Maybe all the emotion these last two days is the universe sending me a message—maybe it's time to say goodbye to Lost and Found and go home where I belong.

"Will you feed the cat while I'm gone?" I ask.

He takes the last bite of his burger. "Sure."

"Maybe visit with her a little?" I add. "She strikes me as independent, but like she still values some company."

"When will you be back?"

The question hangs in the air and I can barely look at him. His eyes feel like they're touching me again. But this time seeing through me. Understanding me too much. Maybe they're seeing me pull away, even as I attempt to carry on a totally normal conversation with him. "Day after tomorrow. Probably in the evening."

"So you have two doctor's appointments?"

"Mm-hmm," I say between sips of iced tea. "Just checkups, though. Nothing bad."

"What else is on the agenda?"

"Seeing Kevin and Sydney. And just generally checking in on my . . . life."

I instantly feel weird having said it. Like this, here, *isn't* my life. Like it doesn't count. But the last few days have reminded me that . . . well, this softer, gentler chick I've let myself turn into here . . . that softness comes with pitfalls. The ones I've known all along. The reasons I toughened up in the first place. Life is easier when you don't let yourself get all wrapped up in people . . . and feelings . . . and romance.

So I decide it's a good time to say, "Speaking of which, I have an early morning, so . . ."

He almost hides his surprise, but not quite—I see it in his eyes. Despite the upset of the day, he thought we'd be together tonight. Especially since I implied as much *last* night. And since I'll be gone for a couple of days.

"No problem," he says anyway. "I understand."

As we carry dirty dishes inside, I wonder just exactly how much he *does* understand. How transparent I've become.

As he goes to leave a moment later, he grabs my hand, kisses it, and then leans in to kiss my forehead. "'Night, Jessie."

"Goodnight," I murmur. Despite having just eaten, my stomach feels hollow.

I wait near the kitchen counter as he opens the back door and steps out into the darkness.

But he stops before closing it and peers back at me. "Summer's almost over," he says. "And I know you wouldn't stay if I asked ya to, so I'll save myself the embarrassment. But I'll be sorry to see you go."

He doesn't wait for my reply—just gives me one last look, shuts the door, and heads home.

Despite myself, I walk over to the window and gaze out into the dark. There are no more fireflies blinking in the backyard. He's right—summer's almost over.

CHAPTER 30

The next morning, Ophelia wakes me by walking on me again—and of course bellowing a loud meow or two. Not shy, this cat. It's five minutes before my alarm, so I kind of feel like we're in sync, she and I. I also feel bad knowing I won't be here tomorrow for her to walk on. "I hope you don't feel abandoned when I don't come home tonight. I promise I'll be back." When I reach out and pet her, she begins to purr. When it comes to the cat, maybe Grace's loss is actually my gain.

I put on my periwinkle dress, and before leaving, I make sure Ophelia has plenty of Meow Mix and water, along with fresh litter in her box, and I turn on a few lights. I toss my overnight bag in the back seat, my fedora in the front. That's more from habit than really expecting to wear it, though. I've gotten comfortable with my brown curls and even how much more prominent my features are with the short hair. It's just a new, revised version of myself.

As I go about the business of getting ready to revisit my real life, I feel something inside me begin to harden. A necessary thing. It's not a new feeling—in fact, it's something old, familiar, almost comfortable. Armor. The first time I ever felt it was after my mother died. When I was, at the age of twenty, made an orphan. I'd lost my parents too close together, too unexpectedly, too early in my life. I had to toughen myself up—it was the only way to keep facing each day, keep moving forward. It's become a part of me, this toughness, which I've let go of so very much—and just as unexpectedly—since I came to Lost and

Found. But it's wrapping around me again right now, creeping back inside, reminding me: Taking control of situations is how we protect ourselves in this world.

And though I had planned to leave quietly, without a peep, instead I follow the sudden compulsion to walk over to Matt's house and knock on his front door. His truck is there, so I know he's home.

He answers in a wrinkled tee and pajama pants, hair mussed, jaw stubbled—but he looks pleased to see me. "Mornin'. Come to say goodbye?"

He thinks the pulling back of last night has passed or I wouldn't be here. He's misunderstanding entirely, and that makes me feel worse about what I've come to do. But the part of me wearing the armor can't care about anyone's feelings; that's how this works. I don't smile—there's nothing to smile about here. I get down to business. "Matt, I wanted to let you know that I'll probably be leaving in a week or two, for good. So I've been thinking . . ." I don't make eye contact. I can't.

"Yeah?" He sounds wary, like a man who's starting to catch on.

"When I come back, it probably makes sense that we . . . not see each other anymore."

He sways backward, like I've hit him and he's trying to regain his balance. "Whoa." He blows out a breath. "Didn't see that comin', Jessie."

I want to ask him not to call me that right now, or anymore period, but I hold my tongue—it's easier to just move forward and get this unpleasantness concluded. "Well, we both knew all along that this was temporary . . . and casual." Of course it's not casual and hasn't been for a while now, but I have to tell the lie anyway.

I feel him looking at me, squinting slightly, trying to make sense of this, but I still don't meet his gaze. "I guess," he says, sounding unconvinced. "But damn, girl, could ya be a little colder about it? Or more . . . abrupt?"

I didn't think he'd call me on it. He's perhaps the most easygoing person I've ever known, and I thought, even if he was wounded, that he'd just let it be, let me walk away like it was nothing. So now I feel like a jerk, but so be it. “Isn’t it *always* abrupt when people part ways? I mean, I don’t know how else to do it than just . . . do it.”

He appears tense, jaw clenched tight. And my chest aches. I don’t like hurting him. But I don’t like me hurting, either. And I have to walk away before the leaving hurts even worse.

“Well, is there anything else?”

Ah. He’s dismissing me. Good. I guess.

I press my lips tight together, my heart pounding. This is harder than I expected. Harder than it’s ever been before. Because I love him. I forgot to factor that part in when I got the bright idea to march over here and break up. Finally, though, I just say, “No.”

But when he starts to close the door, I ask, “Will you still feed the cat?”

He rolls his eyes like it’s an idiotic question. “Of course. Have a good time goin’ back to your *real life*.”

Then he does shut the door, almost slamming it, leaving me breathless and feeling a little ill. Like I’ve done something stupid, made a mistake. But then I take a deep breath, blow it back out, get hold of myself. This is for the best. A long, drawn-out parting with him stretching over the next couple of weeks would ultimately be torture; it would slowly rip my heart out.

Apparently, I’ve decided that ripping it out really quickly is easier.

I guess there’s no easy way to walk away from someone you’re in love with. So I’ve done the best I can here. Now the Band-Aid has been yanked off, it’s done, and we can both start dealing with it.

I happen to be fortunate enough to have a whole lot of distractions lying dead ahead. Maybe that’s why I did it *now*. Going back to the city today is the beginning of *really* going back. I can’t let myself feel stuck in two places, caught in between. It’s time to move on.

And as I walk back across the yard and get in my car, I feel . . . stronger, tougher, more like Jessica Fox, WRTB 11.

The drive feels strange, almost like crossing into another dimension. Particularly as I encounter traffic on the expressway, something I've almost forgotten exists. The closer to the city I get, the heavier it becomes, and my reflexes aren't as quick as they used to be when I have to keep accelerating and then putting back on the brakes. Were there always this many people trying to get places? I'm sure there were, but they all seem to be in such a hurry.

Matt stays on my mind the whole time. I miss him already. But it's okay and that'll pass. As I get farther and farther away, it's easier for everything about Lost and Found, Matt included, to start feeling a little like . . . a dream. A very nice one at times, but a dream.

As I go past the exit that leads to my house and cross the Brent Spence Bridge into Cincinnati, the city feels a bit like an old friend I haven't seen in a while. But as I traverse Fort Washington Way, a short, hectic corridor that cuts through the heart of downtown near the riverfront, it feels . . . awkward, like meetings with old friends sometimes do. Like maybe we don't connect as much as we used to. The buildings that rise into the sky suddenly feel too tall, the crisscrossing lanes and ramps too complicated. I've clearly been away too long.

As my car glides into the Lytle Tunnel, I'm unexpectedly relieved to get away from the busyness of downtown, and Lost and Found feels a world away. I never expected to experience such mixed emotions, about leaving there, coming here, any of it. Part of it is Matt; part of it is *everything*. I guess, despite myself, I've just come to appreciate a slower pace, a simpler life.

But as I told Matt a few hours ago, I knew all along that my life in Lost and Found was temporary, and wasn't the idea to get away from it all and relax? Doesn't this just mean I actually accomplished that? Any weirdness I'm feeling right now is simply a matter of getting back in the groove.

When I envision that—me back in the anchor chair, back in the habits of dinner out with friends, the theater scene at the Aronoff, drinks with Sydney in Over-the-Rhine, and even playing euchre with

Kevin, Patrick, and Nana—it all feels more normal and less awkward. I'll feel better about leaving Lost and Found for good once I really have my life back. That'll make it easier to . . . stop caring so deeply about people I don't have much in common with, places I have no link to, and lost items that have nothing to do with me.

I reach the medical center with time to spare, and I enjoy the luxury of texting Sydney to let her know I've arrived safely. See? It's nice to be back! It's nice to text a friend on the fly!

When I walk into my surgeon's office and say hello to the receptionist, Debbie, she remarks, "Look at you! You look wonderful, and your hair is super cute."

"Thanks," I say with a smile, truly valuing the compliment.

Even before she winks and adds, "And just so you know, I don't say that to everybody. The short look really suits you!"

Of course I can't help but think of Matt, who has assured me of that for months now.

The visit goes well and as expected: Dr. Ramsey thinks my post-surgery breast looks great. He asks about discomfort and I tell him I only have a little nerve pain under my arm, where the lymph nodes were removed, which he says is normal and I already knew. He concludes, "You've healed very nicely."

After he walks out, I pull back the exam gown and look down at my breast, at the scar and dimpling that have bothered me since the surgery. But bothered me much less thanks to Matt acting like there's nothing unusual about my breast at all. I can't stop a rush of gratitude for the way that unanticipated connection restored my feminine confidence when I didn't expect to see it again for a very long time.

One building and a very long corridor away is my oncologist visit and next exam, and all goes well. She's happy to hear I'm full of energy and seems especially pleased to hear I've been away for the summer at a quiet cottage on a lake. "More people should do something like that after going through treatment," she says with a smile.

I neglect to say I was forced and hated it at first, and just agree, "Yeah, they probably should."

But if they do, they should guard their hearts because you never know when people and places are suddenly going to start mattering to you when you least expect it.

Still, the doctors' visits leave me once again grateful to be alive and healthy. I've spent too much time feeling sorry for myself and not enough remembering that not all cancer patients get the privilege of rebuilding their lives and regrowing their hair. As I exit the parking garage back out into the hot late-August sun, I resolve not to lose sight of that again.

And yet, I also leave feeling . . . weirdly impatient, all the more eager to know where I stand, to grab on to my future and move into it, right now.

Now, I'm not so thickheaded that I don't understand what I'm doing: I'm still distracting myself from Matt and the town of Lost and Found by trying to throw myself back into my Cincinnati life. But it continues to seem like a wise move. Get back to what's comfortable, what feels safe and normal. And really, Matt's the only thing I'll miss in Lost and Found anyway. There's no more Jo. No more Grace. Next week August turns to September. The summer is truly gone.

So even though the next part of my plan was to head home for a few hours, I don't. I'm having dinner with Kevin and Patrick later, but on a lark, I decide to stop by the station anyway before crossing the bridge back to Riverside Drive. I thought I'd be more excited about seeing my kitchen—but this feels more pressing, like I can't wait another hour, another minute, before I get my job situation squared away and back under my control.

As I put the car in park outside WRTB, I glance toward the fedora in my passenger seat. Despite myself, I find myself reaching over, putting it on.

Armor? Maybe. Or could be I'm still just embarrassed about the reasons I was sent away from WRTB in the first place.

But when I enter through the employee entrance, the hallway is empty—there's no one to be embarrassed in front of. As I approach Kevin's office, I hear him on the phone—half his job seems to be talking on the phone—so I wait outside to let him finish.

"Mm-hmm, I understand," he's saying, "but I think it's a terrible mistake." It's a pretty typical work conversation for him, and a moment later, he hangs up.

I give him a few seconds to regroup, then lean my head around through the doorway and raise my eyebrows. "Good afternoon, Mr. Callahan," I greet him cheerfully.

He flinches, caught off guard. "Jess! What are you doing here?"

I widen my eyes. "Hello to you, too."

He takes a breath, lets out a laugh. "Sorry. Hi—come in." Then he gives me a once-over. "You look great!" he says, motioning to my dress. "All . . . flowy." He uses his hands to make flowy motions.

I shrug, smile. "Yeah, I've been getting into more . . . fluid clothing lately. Letting myself be a little feminine."

"It becomes you," he reassures me as I settle into the chair across from his desk. He knows feeling feminine has been a challenge for me since treatment. "Are we still on for dinner?"

"Absolutely," I tell him, "and I can't wait to catch up."

He plants his elbows on the desk, steeples his fingers. "Then . . . what's up? Is this a social call or . . . ?"

I purse my lips, realizing I've come in without a plan. But it doesn't matter—I'll just be honest. "I'm ready to come back," I say. "Again. But this time I'm well rested and recovered and I even have some hair." I stop and tip my hat to him like I'm in an old-time movie. "I don't look like a cancer patient anymore, so that should please the guys upstairs, right?"

I'm smiling, trying to joke even though it's a dark topic—but Kevin isn't. He pushes out a long, tired breath and says bluntly, "Jess, I just hung up with them, and I don't know how to tell you this, so I'll just say it. They've decided to keep Tiffany as evening anchor."

Somehow this shocks me as much as it did the last time I was sitting in this chair. Only for different reasons now. I explode, "Even though she can't say 'goetta' or 'Vevay'? Even though I've become a social media darling this summer? Even though Rob has to repeatedly correct her and clearly doesn't like her?" Kevin told me on the phone once that the longer they work together, the clearer it becomes that Rob isn't a fan.

"Even though," Kevin confirms gently. "I fought and I argued. I told them Rob is asking about your return—he's come to me twice about it in the last week." He shakes his head. "But they won't budge."

I take a deep breath, trying to wrap my head around this. I feel like I've spent the last year of my life constantly wrapping my head around things. Angry thoughts and emotions barrel through me in the form of threats. *What if I sue them? Or at least start a social media campaign announcing that they ousted me when I got cancer?* And plain, old-fashioned hurt. *They don't want me anymore. They think I'm old and uninteresting. They never valued me for anything but my looks.* And judgment. *How incredibly awful to fire someone who's trying to get their life back after cancer.* Finally, though, I just ask, "Are they offering to buy out my contract or what?"

"Actually," he begins, hesitating, "they want you in the morning spot."

I take another deep breath, push it back out. Somehow this adds insult to injury. They want me to take Tiffany's old job, a downward move. "You mean the spot that starts at four thirty a.m.?" I inquire dryly.

But good old Kev tries to put a positive spin on it. "It's early, I agree. But you know this business—it ebbs and flows and you gotta roll with the punches. And it's a fun group in the morning—people love the Cockadoodle Crew." He goes on, singing the praises of the wacky Cockadoodle guys and all their shenanigans as if that's going to win me over, as if I'm a shenanigan-loving gal.

The longer he talks, the more I can tell he's assuming I'll *take* this job, since it's the one being offered me, and since I do indeed need to pay the bills. I sit there feeling like the arrow on one of those spinning-wheel carnival games. First I'm spun one way, then another. I keep trying to get back some control of my life, but it continues feeling further from my grasp.

And as strongly as I felt the need to push my way into Kevin's office, truly believing he'd be able to call up the muckety-mucks upstairs and confirm my imminent return, now I feel an equally strong need to escape. So I finally tell him, "I'll be back for a checkup with my radiologist in two weeks, so I'll give you my decision then."

I don't even know what I'm thinking, mind you. I thought I'd be *home* in two weeks. And as everyone knows, I can come home anytime now. Anytime at all. I've spent all day telling myself I need to get back to my life—but so much of that is tied to my work, in *who I am* at work, in *how I'm seen*. I have no idea what I want right now. Again, I am an arrow on a spinning wheel. Back to being that willow whipped about by the winds of my existence.

"Really?" he asks, sounding defeated, and a little like a whipped-around willow himself.

"Really," I say firmly.

He sighs, beginning to accept the fact that I'm actually going to think about this and not just let myself be shoved into the nearest available slot. "All right, Jess. I get it. I really do."

I stand up. "And I think I'll take a rain check on dinner tonight."

He pushes to his feet now, too. "Jess—no. Come on. You can't do that." You can't mush together the friendship and the work relationship, he means. It's a rule we've long tried our best to adhere to.

But I shake my head. "It's not you—you know that. I just think I'd be lousy company now. I need to go lick my wounds. Surely you can understand."

His eyes tell me he does, even if he's not happy about it. "Call me if you change your mind."

"I won't," I say, then walk out the door.

I make the drive to Riverside Drive despondently. This is so not what I expected. And like so many other times in the last few months, I feel stupid to have thought I understood a situation—only to feel blindsided all over again, for, like, the fiftieth time this summer.

I arrive at my house around five and find myself sneaking furtively inside, scampering like a mouse, because I just don't feel like talking to Nancy or Bob right now. I let myself in the back door and meet my new kitchen—and it's . . . beautiful.

So beautiful. Modern and light, and the granite and light fixtures I picked look fantastic.

I wish I were as excited about it as I should be. Especially given that it cost a small fortune.

It's not long before I realize there's no food in the place—because I was supposed to have dinner with Kevin and Patrick, and breakfast with Sydney tomorrow, so I told Syd not to bother when she kindly offered. I plop down on my swanky couch—it *is* swanky; Matt was right—and try to decide what to do with myself now that I don't have dinner plans. Or a job. As in, nothing to look forward to, tonight or ever.

And then I remember, *I have internet!* And while I would have bet good money that a night back at home would have me walking around the neighborhood and taking in the city skyline, followed by Netflixing my little heart out, turns out I'm more in the mood to work on the lost and found.

Having expected a whirlwind of social engagements, I didn't bring my binder, but there are plenty of messages and comments to catch up on. I even get a hit—a family Bible claimed by someone so diligent as to link me to their Ancestry.com page to show me they're legit. The ones who save me from asking all the questions and trying to research it myself are my kinda people.

When a glance out the front window shows me Nancy and Bob climbing in the 'Vette out front, I take the opportunity to order a pizza. Now *that's* something I've missed—pizza delivery. I even order two—one to take back to Lost and Found to be reheated.

As day slowly turns to night, I get a lot done—but I find myself easily distracted by every little noise outside. And irritated by seeing so many people out on the brick sidewalk that lines the riverbank, even though the historic neighborhood has always drawn a lot of visitors.

When fireworks explode over Great American Ball Park directly across the Ohio, indicating the Reds hit a home run, I flinch at the loud annoyance. I used to love that—it always seemed so festive—but now it's suddenly more of a nuisance.

Ugh, how do I not love my home right now?

I've *always* loved my home.

This makes no sense.

Coming back here was supposed to make everything feel better, not worse.

And when I finally close my laptop, caught up on lost-and-found business and having eaten my fill of pizza, I have no choice but to quit distracting myself and deal with all the cold, hard truths smacking me in the face right now.

I open the door and step outside into brightly lit night. Walking across the street, I sit on a wooden bench next to a statue also seated there, of James Bradley, an abolitionist who bought himself out of slavery and went on to study with Harriet Beecher Stowe's father in Cincinnati. The statue is life size, and I lean my head over on his shoulder as I gaze at the city lit up across the river from me.

Can I take the job being offered to me? And if I don't, what else will I do? Try to get an anchor job in another city? If that sounded exciting to me, I'd think: yeah, maybe. But the truth is that, instead, it just sounds . . . exhausting. And I'm tired enough already.

I weigh the pros and cons.

Here, I'm a public persona, a local celeb, and I enjoy some fanfare. But I'm also truly passionate about the work—I enjoy delivering the news, connecting with the public, interacting with my coworkers. I've always loved the exciting environment, and the fact that I'm quick on my feet, good at addressing problems as they arise. And the truth is, even as awful as the hours are, Kevin's right—the Cockadoodle Crew guys are very popular and get a similar level of fanfare—they just have awful hours and fall lower in the hierarchy.

Would I miss that fanfare? Would I miss being someone people see as accomplished? Would I miss the challenges?

And what if, ultimately, the answer to those questions is no? What if I decided that the easy pace, the kind people, the simpler fulfillment I've discovered as part of a quieter existence this summer are actually things I want more of? What then?

I sit with Mr. Bradley awhile. Part of me wants to just curl up in a ball someplace where the wind can't whip me around anymore. But a stronger part of me, a part that suddenly isn't about armor so much as—to my surprise—about . . . hope, considers what I know about James Bradley, how he took a situation over that he had no control of and found a way out of it. How he then helped others figure out how to take control of their lives, too. Sometimes in life we just need a push that points us in the right direction.

"Thanks, Mr. B.," I whisper in his statue ear before I get up and walk calmly back across the street to my half mansion that, while just as grand as ever, doesn't feel so idyllic to me anymore.

The next morning I wake up not from a cat walking on me, but in response to a randomly honking horn somewhere down the street. And with that awakening comes a fresh sense of clarity.

I reach for my phone and text Sydney. I'm so sorry—don't kill me, but I have to cancel.

What's going on?

I'll call you later.

Are you okay?

I quickly reply, Yes. Better. Better than I thought I was.

What are you talking about? You're worrying me.

I'm sorry—I promise to explain. But all is well. Like I said, better than I even knew. I'm starting to get some much-needed clarity about lots of things.

What things?

Myself. My life. What I want. Who I want to be.

So basically, nothing important.

I laugh at that one and promise again to call her in a couple of hours.

Then I get dressed—in my Walmart sundress—and drive back to WRTB. I don't bother with the hat today. I think I'm tired of bothering with things when it comes to this TV station. I walk in, all business, and head straight into Kevin's office.

His eyebrows shoot up, understandably, at yet another unannounced visit. It's probably getting annoying, but I don't let that deter me from my mission. "I'd like to buy your grandma's cottage."

His jaw goes slack. "You *what*?"

"I'd like to buy it. I want to move to Lost and Found. Which is to say, I'm turning down the Cockadoodle Crew. I don't want to go backward, Kev. And to my great surprise, Lost and Found suddenly feels like moving forward—just in unexpected ways."

He looks utterly confused—by all this. But I watch him pull himself together, and rather than reply to everything I've just said, he instead announces, "I have good news. I was literally just about to call you. Tiffany resigned—she just accepted a job offer in Portland. They want you back at evening anchor."

part 4

found

CHAPTER 31

I sit staring at Kevin for a very long time. What is he telling me? That my long personal nightmare is over? That I have my job back? My life back? The life I've worked for and loved and thought had been taken away from me? That now it's suddenly mine again, just like before, just like I wanted?

It's instantly easy to see the future from this vantage point—the clouds have parted and the skies are clear. I know what my life holds. A predictable sort of fulfillment, no more big surprises. It sounds . . . so comfortable, like a cozy chair or a grilled cheese or a comfy sweater on the first day of winter.

I've been more than a little mad at Tiffany, especially since last night—but maybe she's moving on because she doesn't want to be a part of ousting me. Maybe she's not so bad, after all. And now I can have back everything I loved and valued before this all started. I'll still be pissed at the higher-ups, but I can get over that and get back to normal. I can remind them all how well I do my job. I can use my public platform to educate people about cancer and treatment, and use it to help other women. I can still have that bit of fanfare that lifts my ego and makes me feel accomplished and important in the world.

Or . . . I can let it all go.

I can feel relevant because I help people find lost things, and through that bring new business to an old town. I can feel important by making *other* people feel important, one on one—something the kind people of Lost and Found have taught me to do. I can find fulfillment in building a new, quieter sort of life. In fireflies and the chirp of crickets. In a glass of wine with a man I care for. I can find out what the view behind the cottage looks like when autumn turns the leaves gold and orange. And then what it becomes under snowfall—maybe the lake freezes, maybe Matt and I can ice-skate. And then in spring, when the dogwoods and crab apples bloom. I can plant tulips and hyacinths in the fall and have flowers come March or April.

I came here . . . resolved. And more than that, happy. I came here knowing what I wanted. Why should Tiffany's decision change that?

In fact, it suddenly seems so simple. Here, I was at times coddled for having had cancer and then, conversely, shunned. In Lost and Found, I quit wearing my hat a while ago and people treat me kindly, with or without very much hair. The man next door even treats me like I'm beautiful, and because of him, I see a different, stronger, more honest version of myself in the mirror. The simple people there, living simpler lives, treat me with simple acceptance.

And when I think of Matt . . . oh, who am I kidding? The idea of leaving him was so horrible that it turned me downright mean and heartless. He's everything I never thought I wanted—but I do. He's my opposite in so many ways, but it turns out they're ways that balance me. And maybe I balance him, too, at least a little. He's a pretty balanced guy already, a man who knows what he's about, and I admire that. I want to be that way myself.

So I look at Kevin and finally tell him, "I'd still like to buy your grandma's cottage."

He sits there appearing perplexed. Uncertain. I've thrown him for a loop repeatedly lately, but I know this one takes the cake. He narrows his gaze and asks, "What are you saying, Jess?"

"I know," I answer. "I'm surprised, too. Here you are, telling me I can have my entire world back, just the way I wanted, and suddenly, after all this, I don't want it anymore. I want *that* world. The one in Lost and Found."

He lets out a heavy breath. "Jess, I'm not sure you're thinking clearly. This is a lot to give up. You have a whole life here."

I tilt my head. "Do I? Because it doesn't really seem that way anymore. I have a couple of amazing friends here, but that might be the only thing I'll miss. I think I have a life *there* now. A life I've fallen in love with, in fact."

He leans forward across the desk. "Falling in love is . . . chemistry. It doesn't always last—you know what I'm saying? You might be romanticizing it."

I get and even appreciate his concern. He's my dear friend, trying to look out for my best interests. "Maybe," I say, "but I don't think so. I feel . . . valued there. In a different way. Valued just . . . for me. For the things I do. For the way I am, with or without a fabulous wardrobe or pretty hair."

"Jess, I know this thing with Tiffany sucked—you didn't deserve that. But are you sure you want to give up a career you've worked so hard for?"

I take a moment and think that over. I give it its due diligence. But I conclude, "It feels . . . like less to me now, like less than it was even a week ago. Because it's all so fleeting, based on someone else's whims. I think I want a life where I get to make my own decisions."

When Kevin's cell phone rings just then, he looks down at it and presses a stressed palm to his forehead. I'm probably responsible for at least some of that, but I still ask, "What is it? Something wrong?"

He says, "I'm so sorry, Jess, but do you mind if I take this? It's life-changingly important."

My eyes fly open wider. Life-changing things are something I'm well in tune with these days. "Absolutely—take it."

He picks up and says, lovingly, "Hey, honey." Patrick. And a long moment later he tells him, "I meant it. I'm sure, I'm so, so sure. I promise. There's nothing I want more."

I have no idea what they're talking about—are they getting married? Having a baby? But as I wait, it hits me: Kevin hasn't called *me* honey in a while—and that seems like a good thing, like he's realized I don't need to be babied anymore.

When he hangs up, appearing at least partially relieved and smiling in a way that makes him look much younger, he fills me in. "I told Patrick I want his Nana to come live with us."

I sit up straighter in my chair. "What? Kev, that's . . . huge. Beyond huge."

"I know. But . . ." He stops, shakes his head. "In another way, it's not. Because it's not even a sacrifice, you know? I love him. And I even love her. And I'm realizing that . . . you think people are always gonna be there, but then they're suddenly not. Like *my* grandma." I nod, loving Kevin more in this moment than I already did. Then he adds sadly, "And now . . . you." Apparently at some point in his conversation with Patrick, he realized I'm serious. He realized I'm moving away—not just for the summer. "How am I gonna stand this place without you, Jess?"

I give him a bittersweet smile, glad he's beginning to understand and accept the decision that suddenly seems crystal clear to me. "You'll be fine," I tell him.

"I'm not sure," he argues. "It's always been me and you, together, through the good times and bad."

True. This is the end of an era in more ways than one.

And that's when I know I have to come clean with Kevin about a few things. Those things we never talk about. "I love you, Kevin," I tell him. "So, so much. You're an amazing friend to me, and I can't imagine the last twenty years without you."

He looks gobsmacked. Because of how we don't ever do this. But a few seconds later, he manages, softly, "Same here, Jess. Same here."

We talk a little more, about real stuff. I confess I've struggled with feeling like a burden to him, and he assures me I never was and never could be. I tell him how mad I was at him early in the summer, but how now I'm just incredibly grateful. He claims his work life is going to be miserable without me around.

"Maybe you'll finally start coming down to Lost and Found more," I suggest. "I'll paint the spare bedroom and find someplace else to store the lost stuff."

"My God, Jess, of course I'm coming down. I'm coming down so much you'll get sick of me."

"So I can buy the house? You think your parents will agree?"

He sighs. "How could they not? I think you love it a lot more than we do. I'll call them tonight and we'll work it out. Only, Jess, how will you live? Financially, I mean."

I thought this over last night. "I'm guessing property values are a lot lower in Lost and Found than on Riverside Drive. I should be able to live on the money from selling my house for a long time, which is basically the money from my parents, and I think it would make them happy to know they're allowing me to follow my bliss. And beyond that, I'll figure it out."

"But your house, Jess. Your big, beautiful Riverside Drive house. And your new kitchen! You can really leave that behind?"

This is another thing I thought through long and hard last night, and I'm surprised at the true level of contentment filling me as I say, "That house was my dream come true, and I got to enjoy it for a long time. Now I'm ready to let someone else experience that particular dream while I put updated porches on my *new* dream." I lean forward slightly. "You don't mind, do you? If I renovate a little. Replacing the porches would really improve the vibe."

He laughs. "Of course you can do whatever you want, make it your own." Then he glances at a clock and says, "I know it's early, but you wanna stay for lunch? I feel like we have a lot to talk about."

"You're right, we do," I tell him. "Only . . . I really feel like I need to get back to Lost and Found. I have a cat now and—"

"A cat?" he practically screeches. "What?"

"Long story," I tell him. "And a boyfriend."

Shock and confusion reshape his face. "Wha . . . ? What haven't you told me?"

I keep it simple. "I've been sleeping with Matt for weeks and I'm in love with him."

His jaw drops. Then he blinks several times. I see his mind racing. He wants to yell at me for keeping secrets, but instead he jumps to something that seems more important. "Matt's a great guy, Jess. But if this move is because of him, surely—"

I hold up a hand. "Stop. I know everything you're going to say. What if it doesn't work out? What if he breaks my heart? What if the new wears off and we suddenly get tired of each other? But you know what? I never take chances. Because I'm always too afraid of the consequences. I need to take this chance, Kev. I need to let myself care about someone, no matter how it might turn out in the end. I need to be brave, and strong—not a willow."

He squints. "A willow?"

"Never mind," I say, shaking my head. "The point is, I'm sure about this. I'm not sure about the future or what it holds, regarding Matt or anything else. In fact, I broke up with him in a mean way right before I left, so he might hate me now."

"Eek," he interjects.

I ignore that and keep going. "Still, I know I need to make this change. I know I need to follow my heart. Anything less will be a cop-out and always leave me playing the what-if game. I've built an actual life in Lost and Found, and now I want to go live it and see what happens next."

On the drive out of the city, I call Sydney and tell her everything. Including the same long-overdue things I said to Kevin—that I love her and she's my best friend and she means the world to me.

She cries.

I get it. I even get a little weepy, too. The one thing I have, perhaps, not really factored into all this is the reality of leaving my friends. I don't have many close ones, but the ones I do have are like family to me—I love them and will miss them. I'd even almost started looking forward to euchre with Nana.

The thing neither of us says, though, is something we both surely know—that things are changing. She and Jayden spend most of their time together now. She talks about his dog like she's co-parenting it. So even if I were there, things would be different. Things change. Life changes. And as much as I have lamented that at times, maybe it's *meant* to change. Maybe, no matter how content we might be in one set of conditions, we're ultimately meant to go out and experience others. Maybe that's what life is about—soaking up all the experiences, the good and the bad and everything in between, and looking back in the end knowing you really *lived.*

Syd and I make all the promises, about visiting and phone calls, and I think we'll keep them—even though I know it won't be the same. But we both try to believe it will. Love can adapt.

I conclude the call by saying, "I'm so sorry I didn't see you—I'm a terrible friend. But it's been a really emotional twenty-four hours, and getting back home suddenly feels . . . urgent."

"You're already calling it home," she observes softly.

I hold in the tiny gasp I feel in my chest. "I guess I am."

"I suppose it speaks volumes," she says, "when your whole idea of home becomes something new."

By the time we hang up, the interstate is starting to wind its way into the lush, green mountains, and a part of me still can't believe I want to give up my Riverside Drive mansion for Mabel's cottage. And yet a *bigger* part can't believe it took me so long to see everything so beautiful about this hidden gem of a place I've found. And maybe . . . *every place* holds its own beauty if you just take the time to find it, open your eyes to seeing it.

As I leave I-75 and twist my way around and through the mountains to get home, it hits me anew how far away Lost and Found feels from everything familiar to me. And also how much I've quit minding that.

The closer I get to Lost Valley Lane, the more it feels like coming back to a safe place—and yet there are still a million questions. How *will* I make a living? Yes, I'm in good shape financially, but I don't want to burn through my assets and be left with nothing. And will my fresh love of this little town sustain? Or will the winters feel too long? And will the lack of entertainment and pizza delivery finally wear me down? And . . . what about Matt?

Yes, he said he wouldn't be sorry if I stayed. But it's a pretty vague statement in a way. It could have meant: *Stay for* a while*; don't rush back to your other life while we're in the throes of passion; let's enjoy each other a little longer and* then *you can leave.* Or it could have meant: *Buy the house next door—but remember, if we ever break up, it will be incredibly painful and awkward for both of us twenty-four seven.*

Plus I *did* actually break up with him yesterday. In a really jerky way. What if he's had enough of me and my flightiness, my meanness, the fact that I seem like someone who doesn't know what she wants and isn't very nice sometimes? In fact, why did he ever like me at all?

When I turn onto Lost Valley Lane, my chest is stretched tight as a rubber band. What if he can't forgive me? What if he *does* forgive me but doesn't want something long term? I've raced back here to tell my lover we can continue being together, but how will Matt take it when I announce I've quit my job and am buying Mabel's house? In fact, dropping that bombshell the very day after I unceremoniously told him we were through might harken back to some of my more maniacal-seeming behavior from earlier in the summer. He might start wondering exactly what he's gotten himself into and decide it would be wise to run screaming in the other direction.

As I drive past his house, I see that his truck is home—and then I spot him sitting on his front porch in the shade, bare feet crossed at the ankles and propped up on the porch rail near the one-eyed chicken.

When I get out and start toward the cottage with two pizza boxes in my hands, I hope he'll come over. That's always how it's been between us; even when I've been distant or pushed him away, he's come over.

But this time he stays put. He doesn't even glance my way.

I don't blame him a bit. But it makes my chest ache still worse.

I know what I have to do.

Instead of going inside, I walk toward him. Like yesterday, I have no plan. But at least good intentions this time. I only hope they don't blow up in my face.

On my approach, I see he's wearing jeans and his Dollywood shirt, which looks to have survived the pie incident from a while back just fine. And I can't deny how happy I am to see him, that even while he's ignoring me, the very sight of him turns me all melty inside.

"Hi," I say hopefully, trying for a smile.

He glances over absently, like I'm an irritating buzzing fly, but says nothing.

Though it's getting hard to breathe, I try to forge ahead. "How's my cat?"

He looks straight back ahead of him. "Well fed and still meowin'."

"Good." I nod. "I kind of missed her and her meows." *And I kind of missed you, too. And not just kind of—a lot.* But I, of course, keep that to myself.

Then he motions to the pizza boxes. "What's this?"

"One and a half of my favorite pizzas from a place near my house. Should be enough for two or three microwaved meals at least."

"Well, enjoy," he tells me, then once again turns his eyes back toward the road.

"I was thinking we could, um, share it." I'm almost astonished all over again at how much I'm dying to do something as simple as share a pizza with Matthew Cordray. But I'm still getting used to such feelings, and to actually letting myself have them.

He tosses me a sideways glance, appearing skeptical and understandably confused. After which he finally crushes my every hope with, "Probably best we don't. Like you said, probably best we don't see each other anymore."

My knees nearly give out. That's it. I've blown it. To smithereens. I've ruined everything. With my stupid armor. My stupid need to protect myself and never take a risk with my emotions. Which I'm pretty sure backfired anyway, because my emotions are already involved here and they're making me want to crumble into pieces.

"Okay," I whisper sullenly. There's a lot more I could say, of course, but I'm not sure it makes any sense to. An apology would sound almost . . . hollow, all things considered. What reason does he have to accept, or to believe in me at all? I've treated him abysmally at times, most recently yesterday, and he's probably good and tired of it, and who can blame him?

I'm turning to go, pizza boxes in hand, tail tucked between my legs, when he asks, "So what's the verdict? When ya leavin'?"

I stop and turn back toward him, meeting his gaze because he's finally looking at me. I love his eyes. And I wish I could know what he wants the answer to be, how he really feels, if there's any chance of redeeming myself—but I've certainly never encouraged him to share his feelings with me, and in fact spent quite a bit of effort doing the opposite. At last I tell him, "I'm . . . not, actually."

He pulls back slightly. "Ever?"

Moment of truth. *Just spit it out.* "I quit my job and told Kevin I want to buy the cottage. And part of the reason is that I've fallen in love with this little town, and the lost and found, and the lake, and the sunsets—all of it. And part of the reason is that I've fallen in love with . . ."

That's when I stop. Because holy crap, I've veered recklessly into dangerous territory here.

He says nothing, though, doesn't bail me out in any way. He just holds my gaze, one eyebrow arched, daring me to finish the sentence.

I take the dare. "You." Because isn't that how you risk? Isn't that how you take a chance and follow your heart and all that stuff I told Kevin I wanted to do?

Of course, I'm sweating now, profusely, and feeling like I might throw up. I've never been so honest with someone whose response has the ability to make or break me.

I can see I've caught him entirely off guard with this news. Which makes sense—I'm still pretty caught off guard, too.

I love you, too, Jessie. I'm waiting for him to say that. Praying for it. *Please, please, please end the suspense and give me that thing I've never had because I've always run from it—real love.*

Instead he says, "Wow. Didn't see that comin', either—any more than the stuff you said before you left." He runs a hand through his hair. And I want to throttle him. Because it's just hanging out there, my ultimate confession, with no response. I'm sure I deserve it, but ugh.

And I still can't quite read his eyes, so I have to bite the bullet and ask, "Is it . . . a good wow? Or a that's-kind-of-overwhelming wow? Or a you're-too-mean, go-away wow? You can be honest—I can take it."

"It's a good wow, Jessie," he says, voice low, in a way that radiates through my solar plexus. It's not *I love you, too,* but it's a step in the right direction, thank goodness.

And so, on reflex, I decide to try to turn this back into something light. That's my MO, after all—my safety net. "I'm glad," I tell him, taking a few steps back in his direction. "Because I'm thinking this turn of events will be beneficial for your sex life."

At which point he stands up, walks to where I'm standing, and extracts the pizza boxes from my grasp, lowering them to the chair he just vacated. Then he takes my hands in his to say, "More than just my sex life. My life, Jessie. You're good for my life." He squeezes my hands in his.

"I'm so sorry about yesterday," I tell him. "I was afraid. I don't get close to many people. I mean, I have two close friends—that's it, in my whole adulthood. What does that tell you? I'm crappy with relationships."

His eyes have softened now. He's back to being the Matt I know. "Maybe I can help you do better."

I feel that in my chest, in a good way—in my heart. "I think you already have. I just still need to work on it."

"Did you mean what you said? About bein' in love with me?"

The question steals my breath. Such scary words. I've never felt more vulnerable. But I have to keep being brave. "Yes. I tried not to be, but I just am."

He leans forward, touching his forehead to mine. "That's the best news I've heard in a long time, darlin'."

"Yeah?" I ask.

"Yeah. 'Cause I'm in love with you, too. Tried not to be," he adds with a little grin. "But I just am."

And just like that, I can breathe again. I'm revived, a woman who's been brought back to life. I look at him, and he looks at me, and I feel . . . found.

And in an effort to be more open and communicate more clearly, I say, "Police Chief Cordray, would you kiss me already?"

"That'll be my extreme pleasure, ma'am." With that, he cups my cheek in his palm and gives me maybe the best kiss of my life.

All Matt's kisses are delicious, but perhaps this is the first one I'm so very ready for, so eager to surrender to. I came here convinced this would be the great lost summer, yet it's turned out to be the summer I found . . . everything. Beauty in nature, beauty in people, beauty in the old and forgotten, beauty in . . . myself. I found recovery and renewal. I found blackberries and snapdragons and mimosa trees. I found the courage to take off my armor and to . . . feel. And when I least expected it, I found . . . love. And maybe most of all, I found . . . me.

EPILOGUE

One year later

They say jump and the net will appear. It's scary advice to give to anyone, and scary advice to take, but I suppose that's where I put my faith when I made the decision to give up my life in Cincinnati and move to Lost and Found.

So much has happened since last September when the Callahan family agreed to sell me Mabel's cottage at a very fair price, grateful that a trusted friend was happy to give the place the love it deserves.

Since then, I've painted most of the rooms and all the wooden cabinets, keeping a warm modern-cottage vibe, and I've had the exterior repainted the same soft yellow but changed the trim to gray to match the gray composite decking I updated the porches with. The shed and garage were painted to match, though I still—to my shame—don't go in the shed, and won't until the day Matt assures me it's somehow magically become snake-proof.

Now the place holds the charm I expected when I first pulled up—complete with snapdragons of every color—and the only thing I'll never update or replace are Mabel's clouds. They're whimsical almost to the point of seeming silly at times, but they still lull me to sleep like nobody's business, and remind me of the woman I try to honor every day working with the lost and found.

Last fall I followed through on putting the lost and found on display. Turns out that in addition to the Last Chance Café, Melva owns several of the empty buildings on Main Street, and when I came to her with my idea, she told me to pick one and do whatever I wanted to it, rent-free, as her thanks for reviving interest in the town.

And so, with a little stripping of original hardwood floors, painting of original tin ceilings, and the moving in of some display cases, by Christmas the Lost and Found Lost and Found was born. In it, I showcase the best of the best—the oldest items that may not ever find homes, like Sarah Hawkins's tiny Bible and other historical treasures. People love looking at these pieces of simple, everyday history, even when they're under glass for protection, with photos and text added to the display where beneficial. I also put on display the more interesting modern items—however much I can fit in at any given time. Visitors like seeing the things I've posted on social media and enjoy thinking that if they look long and hard enough, maybe they'll discover something that once belonged to someone they know.

Entry is free but we heartily encourage donations to help us defray costs since, seriously, despite how it might seem sometimes, I'm really *not* made of money. And it was earlier this spring when I really began to be concerned about that—how long I can subsist this way without going bankrupt—but that's when the net appeared.

That's when enough short pieces about the lost and found had circulated around the country that a major network approached me with a proposal, offering me a generous paycheck for a weekly piece featuring a lost item of my choice, to be run on their national evening news, and their morning show as well. And then . . . well, even more magic happened.

Now that the world has discovered Lost and Found, many people are happy to make the trek. We get day-trippers by the dozens, and road-trippers work us into their routes. In addition to the Last Chance, which does a healthy business every day and is packed on weekends, Main Street now boasts a bakery, a sandwich shop, and—my favorite—a pizza parlor, which even delivers within a five-mile radius, which means Matt and I have started having Pizza Fridays. And not only that, but the pizza even comes with a movie! Because . . . more magic.

When people discovered how much I've hungered for the movies and TV most of them can stream, they started sending me DVDs of their favorites! Matt bought me a DVD player and, voilà, I've come flying back into the early days of the twenty-first century!

But back to the changes in town. Mr. Freeman's store has so much business that he's hired part-time help, and Melva's taken on additional cooks and waitresses. Word is that we might even get an ice cream parlor next spring!

There's a farmers market in the Piggly Wiggly lot every Saturday May through October, too. Saturday visitors can bounce from the Lost Valley Vineyards to the lost and found to the farmers market to one or more of the eateries in town, and in addition to finding it a quirky way to pass the afternoon, they've learned they can actually survive the day without internet and post their pictures when they get home.

Speaking of the winery, Jo got back last October after the passing of her sister and was happily surprised to find me still here. We continue to be good friends and my daily walk still leads to the tasting room most days—no matter how busy I've become.

Now I'm suddenly a woman who runs a local attraction with a part-time staff of three, keeps the lost and found moving online (with an office and storage behind the display room now, thank goodness), and records five minutes of high-quality video to send to the folks in New York every Friday morning.

One of the most exciting parts for me: I'm back on the air, doing what I love—what I've *always* loved—just in a new and more meaningful-to-me way! Whatever I feared I might be giving up by walking away from WRTB has come back to me tenfold, maybe even a hundredfold. The network is kind enough to allow me to keep a string of my videos running on a TV in one corner of the lost and found with a few chairs for those interested enough to sit and watch.

Are there moments I get frustrated with running to Brandywine or the Piggly Wiggly to do the technical parts of the job? Sure. Do I now sometimes feel like I have *too* many tasks on my plate and find myself wondering what happened to my quiet, lost summer from last year? Absolutely.

But I love my work, I love what I've been building here, I love that the whole town and its residents are benefiting so much, and I wouldn't have it any other way. Predictably, people do keep sending us lost items, but I've quit discouraging that online—that which we originally didn't want is now our bread and butter. If Wi-Fi ever comes to Lost and Found, well, that might make life, and my job, a lot more convenient. Or . . . it might just make things feel a little too busy.

My house on Riverside Drive sold quickly, and Nancy and Bob were heartbroken to see me go. They even made a day trip to the lost and found and bought a case of wine from Conrad. Nancy says she loves telling everyone that she knows the lost-and-found woman on the news. She also couldn't stop raving about my hair.

Which is to say that—so far anyway—I've kept it relatively short. It's cute, and cool in the summer. And though people tell me it makes me look younger, the odd part is how little I suddenly care. Age is something I've quit noticing about others, too—it matters less and less every day.

Today is Saturday and the museum is hopping. In between ruminating about how much has changed since this time last year, I'm busy greeting guests and having photos taken with people excited to meet me—and I'm in the middle of answering an old man's questions about the Hawkins Bible when Matt steps up to tap me gently on the arm. "There's someone here who wants to say hello." He's smiling and I'm pretty sure I already know who it is, but despite that, when I glance over to see Grace, being pushed in a wheelchair by Daniel, my heart leaps in my chest.

I rush over, bend down, take her hand in both of mine. "Grace! I'm so happy you're here."

"Just look at you, honey. It's good to see your face. And look at all that pretty hair you got now." Then she glances around the room, taking it all in. "I'm so proud o' ya for all you've done for our little town. I barely recognize the place. Ain't been this busy since the seventies!"

"It's not the same without you, Grace," I tell her. "And Ophelia misses you."

She squeezes my hand. "God bless ya for takin' her in. That done my heart good."

"I love her and can't imagine life without her now." And since Daniel has drifted away to talk to Matt, I can ask her, frankly, "How are you, Grace? How do you like life in Saint Louis?"

The way she pats my hand tells me she remembers our conversations about not wanting to go, but now she assures me, "It ain't half bad, to tell ya the truth. Do ya know that if we run outta milk, my daughter-in-law can drive right up the street, at any hour of the day or night, and get some? And people bring pizza and other food right to our door! So there's somethin' to be said for city life, I guess."

I smile, having also seen both sides of that particular coin.

"Overall," she goes on, "I'm content enough. Woulda liked to stay in my little house forever, but things change. They just do. Ya cain't stop it, much as ya might try."

"*You're* telling *me*," I say, having learned that lesson myself.

Grace's house is a rental now. And for not being online, it gets a surprising amount of business. Sure, sometimes it's Kevin and Patrick, like when Sydney and Jayden are already in my guest room, or vice versa. And Grace's family is staying there themselves for a few days, claiming they'll come more often now that there's more to do here. But flyers at the winery, the Last Chance, and the lost and found keep Matt's phone ringing—he and I manage the place for Daniel together, and Joy Lynn gets paid to clean it between visitors.

Speaking of Joy Lynn, she seems happier than she used to—likely because, between tips at the Last Chance and the cleaning job, she has a lot more income. Some people are happy with simpler existences and

I admire that she's happy with hers. She doesn't request as many sad songs on the jukebox these days.

When the front door opens behind Grace, I look up to see Samantha come in with a friend. She's a fun, sweet girl who thinks I'm the best thing since boy bands, and she, Matt, and I even took a beach vacation in June.

And as for me and Matt, well . . . though the days are sometimes busy, the nights are still filled with wine and fireflies and kisses and . . . more than kisses. It's the longest, best relationship of my life. Sometimes he hints that he wants to get married. Sometimes I think that sounds like a nice idea. But I'm not in a rush, and I appreciate that he's an easygoing man who makes me happier than I've ever been.

Just then a young twentysomething guy taps me on the shoulder. "Excuse me, but . . ." He's pointing down at the display case near the front door that holds the love letters of Andrew Chen and Millie Anderson. "I can't believe this—I mean, my girlfriend kinda dragged me here and I didn't even know this place existed before today—but these are my grandparents."

My jaw drops. It's all I can do to keep myself from grabbing him by the shoulders and shaking him. His girlfriend stands behind him, beaming, while he looks stunned. "Are you telling me," I ask, "that Andrew and Millie got together in the end? After being separated by a whole continent and a father who didn't think he was good enough for her?"

The guy blows out a breath. "Yeah. But I mean, I never even knew they were apart. They've always just . . . been my grandma and grandpa, you know?"

"Do you have any pictures of them?" I ask excitedly. "I'd love to see them."

He whips out his phone and shows me an elderly couple—the man Asian, the woman white. They look utterly sweet, and I'm awed and a little breathless.

"You have no idea how happy this makes me. I cried over those letters. I didn't think they had a chance. I've been heartbroken for them for over a year now."

The guy smiles. "Well, now you don't have to be. And I can't wait to give my grandmother these letters and get the whole story from her. You don't think about that kinda thing, you know? Like where your family came from or how people got together, or that maybe they had actual . . . problems and stuff."

His youthful innocence amuses me, but I know what he means. The lost and found reminds me every day that every life has always been filled with . . . emotions, and that most of it all links back to love, of one kind or another.

Meeting this young man, who turns out to be Andrew Chen III, is a reminder to me that miracles happen all the time. Things that seem unlikely happen anyway. People defy the odds. And life usually works out the way it's supposed to.

I never could have dreamed I was supposed to end up making a new life for myself in this tiny little town in the middle of nowhere. But look at me now. I came here lost. And I stayed here when I found out what I really wanted, what filled my soul. Sometimes we need new starts and don't know it. Sometimes we can serve the world better in a role we didn't even realize existed. I've learned that the road to anywhere begins with opening your heart. Thank goodness I opened mine when I did.

After a ceremonial handoff of the letters to Andrew with much fanfare and photo taking—and a promise from him to send me pictures of his grandparents looking at the letters—Matt's eye catches mine from across the room. We know each other pretty well now and I suspect we're both thinking the same thing.

We're looking forward to the big dinner tonight at the Last Chance welcoming Grace home. But we'll also be happy to head home afterward ourselves—maybe drink a little wine, look up at a few stars, and fall asleep in each other's arms.

Life, it turns out, is all about balance. Sometimes you're lost, sometimes you're found, and sometimes you're in that space in between, just floating in the clouds, trying to find your way. And over time, I've learned the in-between space isn't actually as scary as it might seem. As Mabel once whispered in my ear, it's the journey.

Author's Note and Acknowledgments

In 2016, I went through treatment for breast cancer. One spring day, when a friend who happens to work in the book industry was "babysitting" me after chemo, I was feeling very weak and useless, and I bemoaned, "I guess this will just be the great lost summer of my life."

She instantly replied, "*Lost Summer*. That's a book title."

I agreed, and decided I would write it, just based on that little nugget of inspiration, once cancer was behind me. And in the months that followed, a story began to form in my head. I wanted to explore ageism and beautyism in our society and, of course, on a deeper level, healing.

As you've already figured out, the book title changed during production, something that's pretty common in the publishing industry—but without that initial conversation, and the words "lost summer," this story never would have come into being.

It took a lot longer than I expected to get around to writing the book—partly due to other projects and professional obligations, and partly due to learning, like Jessica, that healing in the soul sometimes takes longer than in the body. But just letting this story percolate inside me during that time was, in itself, an act of healing. Writing books is what I do, and putting a new story together, even just in my mind, helped me begin to feel like myself again. And so, for obvious reasons, this book is very near and dear to my heart, perhaps more than any I've ever written.

Besides the cancer experience, I drew many other tidbits in this story from my real life, so many that I couldn't begin to name them all. But the Hawkins pocket Bible is completely real—a tiny treasure I found in my father's things after he died, which I suspect was a flea market find. And Teresa Medeiros, that Donny Osmond album is all for you—a small nod to thank you for early encouragement when we first met thirty years ago. You said to me, "You have the magic," and it meant more to me than you could possibly know.

Although I fear this is not an exhaustive list, I'll do my best to thank those who helped bring this story to life in one way or another.

To Lindsey Faber: Thank you for the inspiration and for suggesting the perfect town name, which became a jumping-off point to the lost-and-found aspect of the story.

To Jacqueline Daher: Thank you for feedback and editorial suggestions that made this book what it ultimately became. I couldn't ask for a more supportive, uplifting cheerleader for my work!

To Deb Haas: Thank you for answering my questions about TV newsrooms. Any errors are completely my own.

To my friends at Brianza Gardens and Winery in Crittenden, Kentucky: Thank you for the setting that inspired Lost Valley Vineyards.

To my agent, Laura Blake Peterson: Thank you for believing in me and my books! I'm so grateful we connected!

To Lauren Plude and Sasha Knight at Montlake: Thank you for your amazing praise and enthusiasm for this story. It's a true gift to work with such kind and wonderful people, and I send my gratitude to the rest of the editorial team as well!

And though this isn't a thank-you, to anyone currently on that cancer journey: Please know that I'm sending you strength, love, hope, and healing.

About the Author

Toni Blake is a *USA Today* bestselling author of more than forty contemporary romance novels published by Montlake, Avon Books, Harlequin, Penguin Books, and more. Her books have received the National Readers' Choice Award and Booksellers' Best Award, and her work has been excerpted in *Cosmo*. She is a two-time nominee for the prestigious RITA Award and a two-time recipient of the Kentucky Women Writers Fellowship. Toni lives with her husband in northern Kentucky and enjoys traveling, crafts, and spending time outdoors. For more information, visit www.toniblake.com.